PASSION'S EMBRACE

"I said, let me up!"

"You know you don't mean that darlin'," Cameron slurred thickly in what was clearly an American accent.

Cassie's heart thumped wildly with fear and it took a moment before she managed to bring the emotion under control. "Sir," she countered in what she hoped was a stiff, no-nonsense manner, "I most certainly do mean it."

"In a minute you'll be begging me to stay," he promised as his mouth came down to cover her own.

Cassie could only gasp in outrage. How dare he? She struggled beneath his weight, using all of her strength in an effort to release herself from his hold. "Please, listen to me. You are burning with fever. You don't know what you are doing."

"Don't I?" he asked with a short laugh as his hands came to frame her face, holding her helpless against his next move. "Perhaps this will show you that I do," he continued, his lips moving against hers in a passionate assault.

Cassie tried to calm herself, but her heart skipped a beat. If nothing else, this man certainly knew how to kiss, she thought, and all of a sudden she knew that she was not going to make him stop. . . .

ROMANCE REIGNS
WITH ZEBRA BOOKS!

SILVER ROSE (2275, $3.95)
by Penelope Neri

Fleeing her lecherous boss, Silver Dupres disguised herself as a boy and joined an expedition to chart the wild Colorado River. But with one glance at Jesse Wilder, the explorers' rugged, towering scout, Silver knew she'd have to abandon her protective masquerade or else be consumed by her raging unfulfilled desire!

STARLIT ECSTASY (2134, $3.95)
by Phoebe Conn

Cold-hearted heiress Alicia Caldwell swore that Rafael Ramirez, San Francisco's most successful attorney, would never win her money . . . or her love. But before she could refuse him, she was shamelessly clasped against Rafael's muscular chest and hungrily matching his relentless ardor!

LOVING LIES (2034, $3.95)
by Penelope Neri

When she agreed to wed Joel McCaleb, Seraphina wanted nothing more than to gain her best friend's inheritance. But then she saw the virile stranger . . . and the green-eyed beauty knew she'd never be able to escape the rapture of his kiss and the sweet agony of his caress.

EMERALD FIRE (1963, $3.95)
by Phoebe Conn

When his brother died for loving gorgeous Bianca Antonelli, Evan Sinclair swore to find the killer by seducing the tempress who lured him to his death. But once the blond witch willingly surrendered all he sought, Evan's lust for revenge gave way to the desire for unrestrained rapture.

SEA JEWEL (1888, $3.95)
by Penelope Neri

Hot-tempered Alaric had long planned the humiliation of Freya, the daughter of the most hated foe. He'd make the wench from across the ocean his lowly bedchamber slave — but he never suspected she would become the mistress of his heart, his treasured SEA JEWEL.

Available wherever paperbacks are sold, or order direct from the Publisher. Send cover price plus 50¢ per copy for mailing and handling to Zebra Books, Dept. 2427, 475 Park Avenue South, New York, N.Y. 10016. Residents of New York, New Jersey and Pennsylvania must include sales tax. DO NOT SEND CASH.

DECEPTIONS OF THE HEART
PATRICIA PELLICANE

ZEBRA BOOKS
KENSINGTON PUBLISHING CORP.

To Robin Kaigh, for believing. Thank you.

ZEBRA BOOKS

are published by

Kensington Publishing Corp.
475 Park Avenue South
New York, NY 10016

First printing: August, 1988

Printed in the United States of America

Chapter One

Cassie snapped the reins over the horse's back as a shiver ran down the length of her spine. It was chilly, and the light mist that had fallen all day had turned into a cold, steady downpour. Her hands and feet were almost numb and she could not wait to get home and warm herself before a good roaring fire.

She should have known better than to leave the house with only her cloak, but the early morning call had been an emergency and she hadn't had time to think about donning the proper outerwear. She had rushed, only just awakened from her bed, to the accident and worked from upon her arrival till past dusk without a thought but to see to the injured.

The train's derailing had caused untold agony, and although she had long administered to the ailing, she had never before witnessed such horror.

At first glance, the shock of it had nearly caused her to turn her buggy around and head home. Bodies, in every degree of mutilation imaginable, lay strewn about the lush green, English countryside, and she doubted her ability to withstand the sight of such suffering.

Now, after the long day of caring for the injured, doing what she could to soothe the pain of the tormented, she was exhausted. Cassie promised herself she'd sleep late tomorrow. Annie could look after the babies. Still, the comforting thought did little to wash away the horrors she had seen this day.

So engrossed was she in her thoughts that it took a moment before the sound of a low moan penetrated her consciousness. At first, she thought it was her imagination. Had she heard so many in their suffering today that the sounds lingered and were following her, to her doorstep? She pulled the buggy to a stop and strained to hear over the sound of falling rain. Nay, she heard it again. 'Twas not her imagination, but a real call for help.

She listened, and again came that low, anguished groan. It was coming from the trees to her right, and without a thought as to the wisest plan of action, she jumped from the buggy and moved toward the voice.

Cassie walked carefully between the trees and through the underbrush. 'Twould cause only further injury should she stumble upon her intended patient. Thick branches, heavy with the accumulation of the day's downpour, slapped mercilessly at her, drenching her already damp figure as she pushed farther into the dense foliage.

She could see nothing. Amid the trees, the night was as black as Satan's soul, and a prickle of fear ran down her spine as the moans suddenly ceased.

The prickle of fear suddenly turned to cold, breathless terror, as she realized her precarious position. Was this a ruse? Had someone been playing her false?

6

Cassie called out, "Hello! Is someone there?" Then she silently cursed herself for her foolhardiness. What if someone were lying in wait for her? She had just given them her position as clearly as if she had lit a candle.

Involuntarily, Cassie took a step back. Her heart pounded with fear, and her only thought was to rush back to her buggy, when a low, muffled sound brought her to a stop. She could not be mistaken. There was an injured man nearby. After all her years of tending to the sick, she knew well enough the sounds of suffering.

Carefully, she moved on. The sound was growing louder. Suddenly, her foot struck an object that gave beneath the pressure of her boot. She had found him.

On her knees, Cassie checked her would-be patient. Her gentle, exploring hands moved over a prone figure, for she could see nothing. She was not wrong. It was an extremely large man. His face was slightly sticky, but she knew not the cause of his distress, for in the rain she could not distinguish what she suspected to be blood from water.

She spoke in a low, comforting tone. "I have come to help you. Can you hear me?"

"Sarah?" came a slurred reply.

"If I lend you my strength, do you think you could walk?"

When nothing more than another moan was forthcoming, Cassie tried to haul him to his feet. Quickly, she found herself shaking from the difficulty of the task.

"Listen to me," she said, once again on her knees, leaning close so that her voice might penetrate his consciousness. "You have been injured. There is no one but myself to see to your care. I cannot leave you

7

here. You must help me. Do you understand?"

Cassie had almost given up hope when she heard his weakly replied, "Aye."

"Good," she returned, with more than a little relief. "Now, put your arm around my neck and I will pull you into a sitting position."

As the man followed her bidding, his arm knocked her hood from her head, and water seeped down her exposed neck in cold rivulets.

A low-hanging branch snarled in her hair, and by the time she had gotten him to a sitting position against a tree, her long dark tresses had lost their restricting pins and clung wetly to her face and neck.

Cassie shivered as the force of the driving rain seemed to increase. She was freezing, and had no doubt that the injured man was as cold or colder. Had he his wits about him, he'd no doubt be complaining of that fact right now.

Again, Cassie knelt upon the ground. This time, her knees sank into oozing mud from the sodden leaves which had been disturbed by moving him. Her dress, already blood-stained and reeking with the stench of the dying, was now completely ruined.

"Can you hear me?" she asked again. Not able to see the condition of the man, she reached out and found his head lying limply upon his chest.

He did not answer, but his breathing was steady, if a bit faint.

Cassie gave a silent curse, mingled crazily with a prayer, that she would find the strength to get this man to safety.

"Please," she begged as she shook him slightly. "Please, can you not hear me?"

Cassie had to lock her jaws to stop her teeth from chattering. She couldn't remember when she had been so cold. She shook him again. If he didn't soon respond, she'd have no alternative but to leave him and go for help. With a heavy sigh, Cassie came to her feet. She knew that should he lapse into unconsciousness, there wasn't a chance of finding him again, for his moans would not lead her back. But what alternative had she? They'd both soon die if she remained.

"I'm going for help."

"Nay, Sarah," he groaned, clutching her soaked, mud-splattered skirt to his face, "do not leave me."

Cassie tried to open his clenched fingers, but they seemed made of steel rather than flesh and blood.

"Please," she gently coaxed the delirious man. "You must release my skirt. I must get help."

"Stay," he pleaded.

"Will you get up?"

She felt movement against the material of her dress and imagined him nodding. "Aye, anything. I'll do anything."

"Put your arm around my shoulders. I'm going to try to lift you, but you must help."

Cassie tugged with all her strength, and just when she thought it hopeless, she felt him begin to slide up the trunk of the tree. Cassie pushed him back to rest against the tree, pressing her body tightly to his lest he fall again as she gasped for air and tried to still the weak trembling in her limbs.

"Walk," she ordered sharply, no longer having the strength to plead and cajole. "You must walk, or I will leave you here."

Slowly, and without releasing her pressure against

9

him, she turned and again slid his arm over her shoulder. Gripping him tightly about his waist, and holding onto tree trunks for support, she led him back toward her buggy. Like two children, who had discovered the cooking sherry and finished it in one sitting, they stumbled and staggered until they reached the dirt road. There, all his strength seemed suddenly to dissipate. She couldn't hold him by herself. He was so big, so heavy.

Cassie felt her stiff, aching knees begin to buckle. The buggy was some yards away and she knew she hadn't a chance of reaching it. Suddenly, and with a small, startled cry, she fell under his weight directly into a large puddle of muddy water.

If she thought she was cold before, Cassie soon learned the true meaning of the word. She almost screamed as the icy water seeped through her heavy clothes and chilled her to the bone.

"Get off," she sputtered, acutely conscious through her shaking chill that he was lying full length upon her. She hadn't the strength to move him another inch, and wild fantasies ran through her mind of being found dead in the morning beneath this stranger, in what was clearly a lover's position.

Oh God, why on earth had she stopped? Why had she answered his call for help? She should have marked the place with a branch, something, and sent Joseph back to find the cause of the groaning.

"Let me up this instant," she ordered, having suddenly had enough of this man to last her a lifetime.

A flash of white teeth should have warned her of his changing mood, but Cassie was too annoyed and cold to notice his suddenly grinning face. Slowly, his hips

10

began to slide suggestively over hers.

"I said, let me up!"

Cassie's assumption that he meant nothing by the movement soon proved to be erroneous. His soft chuckle instantly brought her to startling awareness. "You know you don't mean that, darlin'," he slurred thickly in what was clearly an American accent.

Her heart thumped wildly with fear, and it took a moment before Cassie managed to bring the emotion under control. "Sir," she countered in what she hoped was a stiff no-nonsense manner, "I most certainly do mean it."

"In a minute you'll be begging me to stay," he promised as his mouth came down to cover her own.

Cassie could only gasp in outrage. How dare he? What in God's name did he think he was doing?

She struggled beneath his weight, using all her strength in an effort to release herself from his hold. Had her earlier fears been correct? Was his injury merely a ruse, an act to catch her unprotected?

Immediately, she knew the thought to be false. He was burning up with fever. She had never known lips to hold such heat. No one, no matter his expertise, could fake a raging fever.

"Please," she begged as he released her mouth to nuzzle his blazing lips against the skin of her throat. "Listen to me. You are ill. You don't know what you are doing."

"Don't I?" he asked with a short laugh as his hands came to frame her face, holding her helpless against his next move. "Perhaps this will show you that I do." His mouth moved against hers in a passionate assault, forcing her lips to part. Instantly, his tongue slid into

11

her mouth, probing sensuously.

Cassie continued to push against his weight, but pinned as she was, she might as well have tried to move a mountain. She could do nothing except pray he would soon come to his senses, or pass out.

She lay there quietly, almost calmly, waiting for his urgent, fevered kisses to cease. And then, something inexplicable happened. A slight flutter began in her breast, kindling a liquid warmth that soon spread to her stomach. Her heart skipped a beat. If nothing else, the man certainly knew how to kiss, she thought as she slowly, very slowly, began to enjoy the touch of his mouth. Idly, she wondered if she would be sorry to have him stop. And then berated herself for acting such a fool. Of course, she wouldn't be sorry. She was simply allowing him to kiss her because she had no alternative, and the poor man didn't know what he was doing.

Her lips tingled as he expertly ran his tongue along the sensitive flesh just inside, and her heart skipped yet another beat, seconds before it began to pound furiously. That was good, she mused clinically, believing her reasoning powers to be operating as usual. She'd have to remember this technique—if she ever found the opportunity to kiss someone she really wanted to. . . . And then, she moaned involuntarily as his hand released her face and slid down, stopping only when he covered her breast, bringing her body the most intense pleasure.

From somewhere not far off came a familiar yet troubling sound. Cassie frowned as the noise grew louder. What was that sound? she wondered, and then gasped with sudden awareness. It was the wheels of an approaching carriage! And they were going to be killed if she didn't do something immediately! Cassie pushed against the man with a strength born of pure desperation. She felt him move, and then he was off her. But Cassie still couldn't rise. The weight of the mud and the water held her fast, and the carriage was closing down on them.

Helpless, she screamed, "Stop! I'm in the road. Stop!"

A sharp curse cut through the night air, and the sounds of the carriage being brought to a halt filled Cassie with relief.

"Thank God," she whispered softly.

"Who goes there?" a deep voice rang out, still a safe distance away. "Who are you?"

"Cassandra Talbot. I've had a bit of a mishap. Could you lend me a hand?"

Cassie fought to control hysterical laughter as she recognized the voice of Benson, the Montforts' driver. Jane Montfort was her dearest friend, and Benson knew Cassie well from the many times he had driven both young ladies. Thank God, she was safe at last. Benson would help her, and in a few minutes she'd be home, sitting before a crackling fire, warm and dry.

She heard him jump to the ground, and gasped as she remembered the disheveled condition of her dress. As fast as her stiff fingers allowed, Cassie smoothed her skirt more modestly about herself.

"Good God!" came Benson's deep gravely voice as the lantern he held lit up the immediate area. "What happened?" And then, nodding toward the now silent man at her side, he asked, "Did you do him in?"

"Oh no, Benson," she assured him, giggling softly as

she realized how the situation must look. Apparently, Benson thought the man was her attacker and his still position clear evidence of how she had handled the assault.

"Thank God you came in time," she added as he reached for her hand and pulled her out of the mire. Silently, she denied the double meaning of her thanks, for Cassie would never admit, even to herself, that anything untoward had occurred between her and the stranger. "I was driving by and heard this man moaning. It appears he has sustained an injury. When I attempted to help him into my buggy, we both fell and I couldn't get up."

Cassie staggered beneath the weight of her sodden cloak as Benson released her hand. Determinedly, she gritted her teeth, ordering herself not to fall again.

Noting her difficulty, Benson instantly untied the soaking garment and let it fall heavily to the ground, replacing it with his bulky driver's coat. Then, effortlessly, he lifted her trembling body and placed her safely inside Jane's warm, dry carriage.

"Nay, Benson," she protested between chattering teeth, "now you will be chilled." Her stiff fingers fumbled as she sought to unfasten his coat and return it.

"Do not concern yourself. I shall have you home momentarily." And then, almost as an afterthought, he nodded toward the man in the road. "What shall I do with him?"

"We cannot leave him," she reasoned, her voice shaking as uncontrollably as her body.

Benson nodded, then left her only to return a moment later with the delirious stranger in tow. Propping the man up on the carriage step, he quickly discarded his muddy shoes and jacket. Obviously, his trousers would have to stay in place since a lady was present.

With a grunt and a mighty shove, Benson flung the man inside, onto the floor, and if he was a bit careless as to how his burden landed, Cassie soothed herself with the knowledge that the man was horribly heavy and Benson had done his best.

The door slammed, and a moment later she could hear her horse and buggy being led to the side of the road. She'd have to send Joseph back for it later.

Benson then gained the driver's seat and the carriage leaped forward, its force rocking the man onto Cassie's feet. She reached down to push him aside, meanwhile searching the darkened coach for a lap rug to use as a cover.

Instantly, she was lying full length upon him, her wrists locked in a bone-crushing hold. The scream that rose in her throat was swiftly cut off as his free hand was clamped over her mouth and her nose. "Not a sound," he warned, his voice suddenly strong and tight with tension.

He was dragging her back to the seat, holding her in a viselike grip to his side. "Where the hell are we?" he asked as he shot a glance out the carriage window.

Cassie could hardly breathe, much less answer him. She struggled to free herself but her feeble movements only caused his hold to tighten, so forcefully that blackness seeped around the edges of her mind, and she felt herself going under. Her eyes closed, and she slumped against him. So this is what it is like to die, she thought, her mind amazingly calm.

What made him relax his deathlike grip on her Cassie was never to know. But when the blackness finally lifted, the two of them were wrapped snugly in the voluminous folds of Benson's coat. She was nestled close to his feverish body, enveloped safely in powerful arms that had lost all desire to harm her.

As her shivering began to subside, she was overtaken by a sleepiness such as she had never before known. The last thing she remembered was the smell of his hair as he nuzzled her neck, murmuring huskily, "So cold."

Chapter Two

"Sarah, damn you to hell," came a low growl in Cassie's ear as the carriage rolled to a jarring stop before her home, sending the two sleeping people flying to the floor.

Once again, she landed atop the stranger, who instantly gripped her tightly to him.

Would this man's mind never clear? How much longer would he believe her to be Sarah?

Her arms were useless, pinned tightly between their bodies, and she kicked out wildly in an effort to free herself, groaning in mortification as the door was flung open and Benson peered in. Her skirt was twisted up around her knees, and Benson was no doubt getting an eyeful.

"Might I be of some assistance?" he asked, a note of amusement in his voice.

Frustrated and embarrassed, Cassie almost shrieked, "Benson, for God's sake help me up! This fool believes me to be someone else and will not release me."

The truth of those words was only too apparent as

Benson tried, to no avail, to free the lady from the man's hold.

"I'm afraid I cannot," Benson grunted as he tried yet again to pull the man's arms from her.

"This is ridiculous. He is naught but a man. How much strength can he possess?"

"I've heard stories of great strength among those who are ill, particularly the insane."

"Good God, do you suppose?" Cassie asked, a sudden shiver running down her spine.

Benson shrugged. "I know not, but 'tis obvious help is needed."

"Get Joseph," Cassie directed.

"I'm afraid to leave . . ."

"Hurry and get him," Cassie interrupted. "I'll be all right. Hurry."

Cassie looked down at the man who held her. His eyes were open, his expression one of determination. "You will not leave me," he said fiercely.

Cassie felt her fear disintegrate. He wasn't going to hurt her. Not while he thought her to be Sarah. Managing at last to work one hand free, she inched it up to caress his burning cheek, as she would any other patient, denying a sudden, surprising rush of tenderness. "I shall not leave you. I promise."

The man closed his eyes and gave a long sigh of relief.

"Come into the house with me," Cassie dared to suggest. And remembering the man's obssession with Sarah, and hoping he'd care for the lady's well being, she added, "I am cold."

The man beneath her grinned and Cassie felt an

amazing thumping in her heart. "Shall I warm you?" he asked.

Cassie's face colored at the implication. Apparently, he knew this Sarah all too well. Then, another thought occurred to her. Perhaps the lady was his wife.

A gentle smile touched the corners of her mouth and she whispered in what she prayed was a wifely fashion, "Shall we go inside first?"

Cassie almost cried with relief as his arms loosened from around her back. A moment later she had managed to pull herself up to a kneeling position and offered her hand to him. "Can you get up?"

"Aye," he returned as he lifted himself on his elbows. Then, a low moan came from his throat and he toppled back to the floor. Even in the near dark of the coach, Cassie could see the pasty gray hue of his skin. It was obvious he was unable to move on his own.

"Wait," Cassie soothed, pressing him down as he strained to raise himself again. She covered his trembling form with the heavy coat. "Help is coming."

He grasped her hand and held fast as if his very life depended on keeping contact, and perhaps it did. Cassie had seen others in the grip of delirium and knew how important it was for them to have something to hold on to.

In truth, Cassie had little to say in the matter, for he would not release her hand. Even when Benson returned with Joseph directly behind him, he refused to relinquish his hold, and Cassie was forced to stay at his side as the two men lifted him and brought him into the house.

"Good God!" Diana exclaimed upon seeing Cassie's

19

disheveled condition. She jumped up from her reclining position on the sofa. "What happened to you?"

Cassie could imagine the sight she presented — her face and long hair caked with mud, her dress soaked and stained with everything from grass to blood.

"I found him along the side of the road," she explained, her hand still clasped in his as Joseph and Benson carried the man to the spare bedroom. "I had a bit of a time getting him home."

"A bit of a time! The two of you look like you were rolling in mud."

"I'll explain later," Cassie called out. "Have Annie heat water for a bath."

He was sleeping again, and Cassie was finally able to free her hand. "Would you make him as comfortable as you can, Joseph?" she asked, keeping her voice low, lest he awaken again and cause further disturbance. "I'll be back as soon as I change."

As she reached the door, she turned and added, "Benson, would you show Joseph where my buggy is as soon as you are able? I don't want to leave it overnight, but warm your insides with a cup of tea before you leave."

Cameron Chandler groaned with the pain that racked his body. Jesus! What the hell had happened to him? The last he remembered he was on a train, enroute to Kensington, and his niece. Where was he, and why the blasted hell did his whole body ache?

Slowly, he opened his eyes to find himself in a strange bed in a small room he did not recognize.

20

Where was he? He couldn't remember a thing after the crash. That was it! The train had been in an accident. He could remember now being thrown across his compartment. His head had smashed into the window. He lifted his hand and brought it slowly to his head. His hair was caked with dirt and perhaps blood. Had he been thrown clear of the wreckage? Had someone found him and administered aid?

Ridiculous question. Of course someone had found him. He had not bandaged his own head or crawled into this bed under his own power. But whose bed was it? Where the hell was everybody?

Cassie paced the sitting room floor with nervous energy. She should have been exhausted from this day, but the news that Joseph had brought back had instantly restored her strength.

What was she to do? She had known Chandler was coming, but had somehow pushed the thought from her mind, ignoring the inevitable consequences. Oh God, she had to think! She had to do something.

Her first thoughts had been to leave, but she had instantly reconsidered. Running was not the answer. The twins' uncle was a man of considerable power and wealth. It would not take him long to find her. And then what? Panic suffused her being. He'd take the children away. Back to America, no doubt. It would be the end of her. She couldn't allow it. She wouldn't allow it.

"Cassie, you are causing a draft with that infernal pacing. Will you please sit?"

21

Cassie gave a sheepish smile as she eyed Diana from across the small room. How did the woman remain so calm? Did she not realize their world was crashing about them? But of course she didn't. Diana was no more than a companion, someone Cassie had taken in in her hour of need. She couldn't understand the fear that plagued Cassie.

Cassie waved Cameron Chandler's identification papers toward Diana. "It appears the twins' uncle has made good his promise to come. I confess I know not what to do. According to his last letter, he believes Catherine still alive. When he finds out otherwise, he will take the children."

Diana rose from her chair and came toward the younger woman. "Cassie, you need not worry so. You've as much right to the children as he. You are their aunt."

"Aye, but I have not the wealth behind me to fight him should he choose to oppose me. What court, even in England, would favor a woman — particularly one who can barely make ends meet — against a man such as he?" Cassie couldn't stop the tears that glistened in her dark blue eyes. Her voice was filled with utter despair as she whispered, "I have not a chance."

She sat in one of the sitting room's small chairs and lowered her face into her hands as huge sobs tore at her throat.

Diana dark eyes watched her for a moment, not at all perturbed that Cassie was suffering. Meanwhile, her mind raced to find a solution to the dilemma. A plan was beginning to take shape and she strained to clarify it. A dark scowl came over her beautiful face as

22

she tried to think above the annoying sound of Cassie's crying.

"Cassie, for pity's sake stop that crying. What will tears accomplish? We must think. If we are bright enough, I believe we will benefit by this."

Cassie gave a tearful snort. "Benefit by losing my children?"

Diana hid her annoyance. "Cassie, they are not your children any more than they are his, but . . ." She grinned as her thoughts grew more definite in form. "Perhaps Mr. Chandler could be persuaded to reimburse you for your loss."

"Diana, I'd not believe you think me capable of selling the twins."

"Of course not, dear," Diana countered smoothly. " 'Twas simply a thought that since the man is so well off and we are constantly struggling to make ends meet, he might consider . . ."

"Out of the question! I'd not take a farthing from him."

Stupid bitch! Diana groaned in silent frustration. Then, gaining some control over her emotions, she spoke aloud in a more tender, pleading tone. "Cassie, be reasonable. For God's sake, why should he benefit by your efforts? You are the one who saw them through the worst of it. You walked the floors late into the night during every illness. You struggled and pinched pennies for a yard of cloth so they would not have to wear rags. Will you let him take them now, while accepting naught but a thank-you-kindly for all your trouble?"

"They were no trouble," Cassie insisted. "I love

23

them."

"Well, if you truly loved them, you'd want the best for them, correct?"

Cassie nodded.

"Would you not agree Mr. Chandler can give them the best?"

"Oh God, Diana, stop it."

Diana frowned. All right, she'd stop, but she wouldn't give up. Considering his injury, the man in the next room was going to be with them for some time. A hint of a smile curved her lips. If she couldn't get this little fool to listen, perhaps . . . just perhaps he would.

Cassie came to her feet with a sudden thought. "The children will be needing a nurse! Perhaps he would consider . . ."

"I doubt it," Diana snapped. "The man can afford the best. Why should he choose you?"

Diana gave a disgusted sigh as Cassie began to pace the floor. Just how she had ever gotten herself mixed up with this paragon of virtue was beyond her, but she knew she had had enough. It was time to move on. Mr. Brighton had been making overtures toward her of late. The man was disgusting, to be sure, but if she were smart, he might prove a steppingstone out of this tiny village and back to London. Damn, she could hardly wait to see the sights again. It had been so long.

"I've got it!" Cassie almost shouted as she came to a sudden halt. "The letter was addressed to Catherine. He doesn't know of her death."

Diana gave her a sour look. "A fact of which we are aware."

Cassie laughed aloud and fairly danced about the small room. "Aye, but what you are not aware of is that Catherine has just made a miraculous return from the grave."

"What in God's name are you about?"

Cassie giggled happily. "Mr. Chandler has never seen his niece. Catherine and I are but a few years apart in age. Why should he suspect anything amiss?"

Diana gazed at Cassie for a long moment as dawning respect entered her dark eyes. She hadn't thought Miss Almighty Perfect had it in her to be devious. Damn, but it was beautiful! Foolproof. All they had to do was keep him in the house until he recovered. Once in America, they'd never be found out. Diana didn't even think to ask. She was going. She was getting the hell out of here.

Cassie sat alone in her room, overwhelmed by guilt. Her hair was still damp from the evening's bath, and as she released the thick tresses from the pins that held them to the nape of her neck, they fell in soft, moist ringlets about her face and down her back. She stared into the small mirror over her dressing table. "This is the worst thing you've ever done in your life, Cassie," she whispered aloud. "No doubt you will burn in hell for the lie, but that eventuality is not going to stop you. You are going to do it anyway." Sighing heavily, she lowered her face to her hands, no longer able to face the self-loathing in her eyes. It went against the grain, this act of deceit, but no matter, she'd do anything short of murder to keep the children. She could not let him take them away.

An evil voice crept into her consciousness. *If you hadn't stopped your carriage, he would have died. He would no longer be a threat. Even now, should you creep into his room.* No! Oh God, she couldn't allow herself to think like that. She had no need to wish him dead as long as she held to her plan. He would never know she was not his niece. She would not lose the babies.

His letter told of taking Catherine back to America. It might not be so very terrible. She would miss England, but she had no one holding her here. No reason to stay. She would do it and the consequences be damned.

She rose then, slipped a fresh nightdress over her naked body and was just about to slide into the bed, when she heard soft moanings from the next room.

Quickly, she left her room to see what had disturbed him. She had sat with him for hours tonight, bathing his forehead with cool compresses as she tried to ease the fever. When she had left, he was sleeping soundly. She prayed he wouldn't start thrashing about again, for the noise would surely awaken the children.

Cassie quietly opened the door to his room and entered. There was no movement from the bed. A candle burned upon the fireplace mantel, lending a soft light to the small room.

"Who are you?" came a low voice from the bed.

Cassie gave a silent groan. Was he again in the throes of delirium? Oh please, she couldn't go through that again. Cassie knew her only chance to keep him calm was to pretend to be Sarah, for he had made it clear Sarah's presence was what he wanted.

26

Cassie prayed her voice sounded natural and calm as she answered. "It's Sarah, dear."

Cameron's dark brown eyes squinted as he watched the beautiful young woman walk toward him. He had seen her before, but where? God, she was a sight in that thin nightdress, with her hair hanging free, falling about her shoulders and down her back. She must have come running at the first sound he'd made, for she had forgotten her robe and the glimpse of flesh he saw beneath her nightdress made his body ache with need. He had been weeks without a woman, but if luck was with him, tonight would see the end of his enforced celibacy. His body stiffened as her words registered. What game was she playing? How could she have known about Sarah? Had he called out? Had he said her name? Damn, he must have been completely out of his head, for he hadn't even thought of the bitch in years.

Silently, he watched as this vision moved toward him. Cameron felt his pulse begin to race at the sight of her naked curves, outlined now by the light of the candle behind her.

She reached down and touched a cool hand to his forehead. Her smooth brow creased into a frown. "You seem cooler," she said. Her fingers felt for the pulse at his throat and she almost jumped at its rapid rate. Her eyes widened with shock. He was breathing so hard, so erratically.

"Are you in pain?"

"Aye," he returned, almost laughing as he caught her hand in his. "I suffer every time you are not near."

Cassie groaned inwardly. Her playacting had

worked, but to what end? He seemed even more excited. "Hush," she said, trying to calm him. "Go back to sleep."

Cameron almost grinned. If he played this right, he'd soon have her in his bed. "Sarah, stay with me." And when he saw her hesitate, he raised his voice a fraction, "I need you."

"Hush," she whispered again. "The house sleeps. You'll waken the children."

Cameron felt a twinge of guilt at her words. Had she a family? Was he playing a game with a lady of honor, a lady who had no cause to be treated so shabbily? But then, she bent to brush away the hair that fell over his forehead. As her low cut neckline gaped open, exposing her gleaming breasts, all thought of confessing vanished from Cameron's mind.

"Oh God!" he groaned.

Cassie jumped, her voice strained with fright. "Have you a problem breathing?"

"Nay. All is well." And as he watched her eyes fill with relief, he knew she was about to leave again. Cameron forced his voice to take on a breathlessly weak note—which was not at all difficult, when he called to mind what lay beneath the nightdress. "Stay with me for a moment," he begged.

Cassie sighed, reluctant to remain. She had no idea what might happen next. And since all were asleep, it would take some time for anyone to come to her assistance. Finally, she gave in to the pleading in his eyes and allowed him to pull her down so that she sat at his side. "I will stay."

She tried to ignore the quickening of her pulse as his

28

long, bronzed fingers caressed the inside of her palm. She wriggled her hand, but could do nothing to release his iron hold. Her palm grew moist, her body alert, ready to spring into action at the slightest untoward movement. Would he never fall back to sleep?

"Do you have any water?"

Cassie, lost in thought, jumped at the sound of his voice, then smiled sheepishly. "Of course."

Her hands shook as she poured the liquid into a glass and handed it to him.

"I'm afraid I cannot . . ." he said weakly.

"I'm sorry," she returned, suddenly realizing that he couldn't drink it himself. What could she have been thinking? The man was ill and could not fend for himself.

Cassie tried to pull him into a sitting position, but she might as well have tried to lift the house. Giving up, she moved to the head of the bed and reached behind his head and shoulders.

Was the man filled with stone? She could barely budge him. It took a moment of harsh grunts and pure determination, but she finally got him into a sitting position. Having no alternative, she wedged her body between his back and the headboard. He lay heavily upon her, his head nestled upon the softness of her breast, as if on a pillow, while Cassie desperately tried to ignore the strange sensations that flooded her.

Cameron had to bite his lip to keep from laughing aloud. He had never imagined that being injured could be quite so enjoyable. Hopefully, the low groan that escaped his throat would be mistaken for a gasp of pain. In truth, his body was aching but not in the way she imagined.

Cassie reached a trembling hand to the bedside table and retrieved the glass.

Cameron nearly finished it in one swallow, Cassie soothed softly, "Easy. You mustn't drink too fast."

Cameron nodded as she replaced the glass, but when she tried to move from behind him, she found herself pinned in place.

"Do you think you could lift up a bit?" she asked.

Cameron grinned. "I'll try."

Even later, Cassie couldn't quite figure out how it happened, but suddenly, and with a soft squeal, she found herself lying at his side, his arms holding onto her as if he'd never let go.

Before she could utter a single cry of protest, his mouth closed over hers, while she struggled to free herself of his unwanted embrace. This couldn't be happening again! A shiver of apprehension ran down her spine. Had Benson's mention of possible insanity been proven correct? Was she harboring a man who was sicker than she supposed? Could he truly be insane?

Nay, she reasoned silently, while praying her supposition correct. Chandler had been injured. Obviously, he had been on the train that had been derailed, and the blow he had taken to his head was causing him a tolerable amount of confusion. 'Twas as simple as that and certainly no cause to panic. She had naught to fear, after all, for she now knew who he was. Cassie's fear subsided with the comforting thought that were she in any real danger, she need only call out and someone would eventually hear her. Although she continued to try and free herself from his grasp, she had to admit it was becoming increasingly difficult to ignore the pleasurable sensations his mouth caused.

Oh, how the man could kiss! Had he studied the art? She had never known so much could be accomplished by the simple coming together of mouths. She hadn't realized a man's touch could make her heart thunder, or that his scent could bring a dreamy quality to her usually alert mind. Before this night she had not known her body could ache with such longing simply because his tongue caressed the roof of her mouth and his warm hand slid down the curve of her hip.

But she could not allow herself to indulge in these pleasures, could not afford any lapses in rational thought. Nay, he was, as of this night, her uncle, and she'd do well to keep that thought in mind.

Still, what harm could a simple kiss bring? Surely he was too weak and lacking in stamina to indulge in anything more . . . and this felt so good.

Cassie tried to banish these errant thoughts from her mind. It wouldn't due to linger overlong with such temptation, not when the fate of her babies was at stake. She had to get away from him, no matter how delightful this encounter.

The mistake she made was in struggling. She should have remained calm and still. No doubt he would have eventually realized she was not responding. But what she did was raise her arms to push against his chest, and the shock of touching his bare flesh did her in.

Her mind screamed for her to stop, but she couldn't. With a will of their own, her fingers moved through the rough, curling hair that covered his chest,

31

and a delicious, liquid warmth raced through her to places she had not before been aware of.

His low, animal growl did little to bring her back to the danger at hand. In truth, the sound of his pleasure brought her a sense of power she had never known, encouraging her to continue her exploration of his naked skin.

His mouth slashed violently across hers, the hunger in the kiss all but robbing her of her senses. She couldn't think of anything but to have more. Her lips parted beneath the pressure of his mouth, and it was her turn to groan as his tongue filled her with his taste and scent.

Cassie forgot her plan. Her mind, usually so clear and bright, lost its capacity for rational thinking. The blood raced through her body, and her pounding pulse deafened her to the world outside the bedroom door as his arms pulled her closer, ever closer.

Now, his hand was beneath her gown, sliding up her long leg and over her bare hip. His fingers spanned her narrow waist, spreading fire as they traveled upward from midriff to the soft underside of her breast.

Cassie couldn't stop the sudden jerking of her body as his fingers slid over her rounded breast to linger at her shoulders, where he began to massage away the last of her resistance.

She felt her body begin to soften under the expert manipulation of his fingers, and she had relaxed almost to the point of sleepiness before she realized his hand had moved lower.

All the languid sensation his massage had sought to impart evaporated the instant his fingers closed on the sensitive fullness of her breast. The pad of his thumb rotated the darkened tip, bringing it to a hard bud. He didn't stop, his fingers moving, kneading, pressing, until she thought she'd go mad from the tingling sensations that filled her being.

He rolled her to her back and parted her legs as he slid his burning body over hers. Her nightdress was pushed above her breasts, her naked body exposed to his hungry gaze. His breath was hot and moist as his mouth brushed enticingly against the soft flesh that beckoned. "God," he groaned, "you are so beautiful. Who are you?"

Cassie, adrift in a world of sensation, barely heard the murmured words. As his mouth moved to discover the taste of her, she arched her hips to meet him, ignoring the annoying voice that demanded sanity.

"Tell me your name." Cameron grinned down at Cassie's dazed expression. It took a long moment before she managed a mind-clearing blink and asked, "What?"

"Shall I call you 'darling'? Would you rather I never know your name?" Cameron had known women before who thought it safer to never disclose their identity. Perhaps she was married. She had mentioned children. Too bad, he mused as his hands moved over her smooth skin. He would have enjoyed a bit of dalliance with one so lovely and so willing, but not if she had a husband lurking somewhere in the background. Cameron considered himself a man of the world, but he drew the line at certain things. Taking a married woman to his bed was one of them. Still, there was always the exception to the rule, and this woman was,

33

after all, already in his bed. What harm could it bring to sample her charms?

"My name?" she gasped as reality came crashing through the flood of desire that had left her weak and helpless. She was filled with horror and self-loathing at her shameful lack of will power. How had she ever allowed this man to overcome her common sense? To fill her with a need that had known naught but the discovery of still more pleasure?

What had she been about to permit? Who was she trying to fool? She wasn't permitting a thing; she was begging for it. Mortification made her cheeks flame, and for the first time in her life, Cassie could not find the courage to look into the eyes of a man. At this moment, she doubted she would ever be able to face this particular man again.

"My name?" she repeated dumbly.

Cameron chuckled at her confusion. "Do you not have one?"

Annoyance flashed in her dark blue eyes, and Cameron groaned inwardly at the lovely sight she made. Her dark hair, gleaming with red highlights, was spread in riotous disarray over the white pillow. Her lips were moist and swollen from his kisses, and desire had flushed her skin with a golden apricot glow. God, but he had stumbled upon a rare beauty. He'd be sorry to see this night end.

"Catherine," Cassie finally replied, with almost vicious glee. She had a need she couldn't control to see this man brought down a peg. "Catherine Chandler Devon," she added, waiting to see the effect of her words, eagerly looking forward to his expression of shock and horror. For a moment, Cassie thought herself doomed to disappointment, for his mind was on other matters and did not immediately relate the name to his niece.

"Pretty name," he murmured as he gave into the need to take her mouth once more.

Suddenly, his body jerked as her words penetrated the fog of desire that held him in thrall. His mouth left hers with a sharp gasp. His eyes opened wide as he prayed that the name was only a coincidence. It couldn't be! God, please, she couldn't be his own niece!

Chapter Three

Cassandra's cheeks flamed at the lie. She couldn't bring her gaze to his as she sat now on a chair beside the bed. She hoped fervently that Chandler would believe her flush to be from embarrassment, rather than guilt arising from a lie. She was, at heart, no liar, and the strain she suddenly found herself under gave her a moment's pause. Perhaps she should simply tell him the truth. Maybe he wouldn't feel it his responsibility to care for the children. Maybe, knowing of her involvement since their birth, he would quietly leave them in peace.

Cassandra gave the slightest shake of her head. She couldn't chance it. If Chandler insisted on taking them to America with him, how was she to fight him? She knew she'd never be able to stop it. No, this was the only way, and if it went against the grain to live a lie, keeping the children was surely worth it.

"I can't believe you're Catherine."

Cassandra shot him a frightened look, suddenly sure he had seen through her story. "Why?"

Cameron shrugged, conditioned by years of difficult situations to keep his emotions hidden behind a calm façade. She never knew the torment and horror that had filled him upon learning her identity, nor the shameful longing that remained. How the hell could this desirable woman to be his own flesh and blood niece? Emily's letters had kept him reasonably well informed of Catherine's progress into womanhood, but he had never imagined to find someone like this! "The women in our family are not known to attain such beauty. I never would have guessed you to be my niece."

Cassie smiled at the compliment. "It's late. I think you should rest now. You've taken a nasty blow to your head."

Cameron had almost forgotten. He reached up now and touched the bandage wrapped around his head. As she started to rise, he asked, "You mentioned children before. Whose children?"

"Mine," Cassandra lied again, her heart sinking, for she knew it was never going to end. One lie only led to another.

Cameron gasped. "You have children?"

"I see my mother hadn't time to write you of their birth before she died." Her hesitation was barely perceptible as she continued. "I have two babies, twins. Their father died the night they were born."

Cameron lay awake a long time after Cassie left the room. He didn't know it then, but it was only the first of many similar nights to come.

"Madam, my request is not to be denied. In order to appear polite, I have, so far, refrained from issuing a command, but you will not stay here, living on the edge of poverty. I have no heir. It is only reasonable that it should be you."

This was too much. Cassie couldn't bear it a moment longer. He thought her to be his niece and was telling her his holdings would be hers upon his death. She couldn't go on with this deception.

But before she could speak, Diana's voice rang out from across the room. "He is right, Catherine," she quickly injected, afraid the stupid bitch admit to everything. Pretending total absorption in her needlepoint as she sat before the fire, Diana had been listening intently to every word that had passed between Cameron Chandler and Cassie. Damn, but she wasn't going to allow Cassie's conscience to ruin what would most certainly be an extremely profitable arrangement. Diana's gaze never wavered from her sewing as she continued with a nonchalant air, "Think of the children."

She cursed to herself. It wouldn't do to appear too eager. She had put a bit too much emphasis on the word "think." She breathed a quick sigh of relief when neither Cassie nor Cameron seemed to notice. "Mr. Chandler is their uncle, after all," she went on. "Why should they be left without?"

Cassie pressed her eyes shut. Aye, Cameron Chandler was their uncle, but she was their aunt! Why didn't she have at least as much say in the matter? But she didn't dwell on the question. She already knew the answer.

38

Diana almost gave a shout of glee as Cassie, with her eyes lowered and fingers nervously twisting in her lap, asked, "When would you expect us to be ready?"

Cassie paced the deck of Cameron's ship, the American merchantman, *Baltimore Lady*. Her teeth worried the soft flesh of her bottom lip, while her hands twisted the skirt of her dark blue traveling dress into a thousand wrinkles. Soon after depositing his new found dependents on board ship, Cameron had rushed off to visit his solicitor. Cassie had almost fainted with horror to learn of his appointment with the elderly Whitehall, but she could not detain him, no matter how distressed she was. He had left her in the care of his captain, promising to return within the hour.

For the fortnight it had taken him to recuperate from his injury, she had succeeded in keeping him secluded from anyone who might impart the truth in idle conversation. Cassie sighed. Now it appeared that all her efforts were for naught. She had not a doubt that the game would be up once he saw Mr. Whitehall, who would most certainly mention the death of Chandler's niece. She knew the old gentleman well enough to be sure that he would offer his condolences to the bereaved uncle, and, that would be that.

Cassie would not be surprised to see the constable accompanying Chandler back to the docks. Chandler would, of course, believe her to have impersonated Catherine for the sake of the money involved. It was too late. No one would ever suppose her love for the children had driven her to it. *That's what comes of deceit,* she told herself. *You knew it was wrong, but you did it anyway.*

"Are you feeling better?"

Cassie swung around with a gasp of surprise. How had he managed to come aboard without her noticing? Her gaze had barely left the docks for more than instant in the last hour.

During his short absence, she had readied herself for a scathing censure, a most horrifying condemnation, before being carted off to prison, a fitting end for her crime. Her heart pounded with fear at the sound of his voice, and her cheeks flushed bright crimson.

When she finally realized the expected accusation was naught but a gentle inquiry after her health, she looked up at him in wide-eyed confusion. She had completely forgotten her claim of illness, the feeble excuse she had given him to keep him at her side.

Cameron smiled at her look of surprise, then cursed the explosive surge of desire that suddenly suffused his being. He had been in her company every day for more than two weeks, and his yearning for her had not subsided. At first, he had believed that learning her true identity would see an end to this desire, but it had not. In truth, the longing had grown in strength as each day passed.

He had to find a means of satisfying the needs she aroused in him—before he committed an unpardonable act. In the close confines of his ship they were bound to come in intimate contact a dozen times a day. He prayed there was at least one lady among the passengers who might be agreeable in assisting him to overcome this sinful urge.

Cassie could not stand his silence a moment longer. She was so filled with guilt that she noticed neither the softening of his smile nor the hunger of his gaze. Had she been more attentive, she might have realized the reason for the sudden lapse in conversation.

She steeled herself for the coming blow. "What did you find out?"

"Excuse me?"

"I mean," she stammered, blushing profusely at her own audacity, "I mean, did your meeting go well?"

Cameron shrugged. "Mr. Whitehall was a bit under the weather. I won't be seeing him this trip."

"He wasn't there?"

Cameron gazed down at what appeared to be a joyful expression in her blue eyes. He was mistaken of course. There was no reason for the girl to be gladdened at the news of Mr. Whitehall's illness. "No, I had to conduct all my business with his partner."

Cassie burst into laughter as relief flooded her entire being. She felt herself slump against him and only vaguely saw his astounded expression. "Oh, I'm so sorry." She bit her lip, but try as she might, she couldn't stop the laughter from bubbling forth. "I hope he'll soon be well."

Cameron could see his niece was growing hysterical. Perhaps the strain of leaving her home had been too much for her. "Are you all right?" he asked, concerned.

"I really don't know," Cassie replied, taking the opportunity offered to plead illness. "Perhaps I should rest a bit," she suggested, still having trouble controlling her laughter.

"Let me help you below."

Despite her usual insistence on propriety, Cassie offered no objection as he swung her into his arms. She ignored the startled glances and raised eyebrows of

41

the crew and passengers. At that moment she cared not what anyone thought, for she doubted she had the power to stand, never mind walk, so extreme was her relief.

Momentarily sated, Cameron sighed as he rolled off the lovely lady who shared his bed. The shame of it wasn't his careless use of this woman to combat his real desire, for she was an equal partner in this casual act. The real shame was the wasted effort. Neither his lack of sobriety nor the lady herself had made the slightest difference. God help him, he wanted only Catherine.

Never had a woman tantalized him so, and he knew in his gut it was completely unconscious on her part. She treated him with the respect due an uncle. Why couldn't he forget the sight of her naked beneath him? Her touch, the taste of her mouth? He prayed nightly for an ease to this ache, knowing he was damning his soul to hell with his evil thoughts. As yet, his prayers had gone unanswered.

Cameron pretended sleep, ignoring the lusty lady's hand as it moved between his legs. Her intent was obvious, but he'd had enough. It didn't matter the lady's skill. It didn't matter the times they had used each other. It was clear that the time they spent together did naught but cause him to long for a softer, sweeter, and infinitely more delectable lady.

Damn, but it wasn't as if he hadn't tried to ignore Catherine's presence. He barely looked at her anymore and never visited the children lest he by chance encounter their mother. Why the hell did this have to happen to him? Why did she plague his mind till no other satisfied?

Cameron's heart constricted as he realized the extent of his future suffering. How was he to bear her constant presence in his home? Would he be forced to vacate his own property lest he succumb to these sinful urges? Or would be eventually overcome this incestuous desire when faced with her daily presence? His spirits rose slightly. Would it begin to fade in time? God, he prayed it to be so.

A sudden thought occurred. Perhaps he had been going about this all wrong. Perhaps in trying to avoid her, he had only caused himself to exaggerate her charms. Mayhap he needed to know her better, so her intrigue and allure might grow faint with familiarity.

Convincing himself of the logic in this line of reasoning, Cameron sighed with some relief. Of course. To know her would ensure the loss of her fascination. Why had he allowed her supposed magnetism to grow to such lengths in his mind? What was he afraid of? It took two to participate in this act. Surely she felt none of the desire that had haunted him these last weeks.

He would allow his feelings for her to die a natural death, rather than try to wrest control of them. It stood to reason that they would dissipate from lack of indulgence. Cameron smiled into the darkened room, feeling the first moment of relief in more than a month.

The lady at his side was breathing more evenly. He imagined her to be asleep. He smiled as his hands moved to caress her lush, smooth form beneath the light coverlet. He would take her again, but this time there was a lightness to his soul, a joy in his actions, for he was no longer using her as a substitute. Nay, he'd enjoy this woman as she should be enjoyed, and never give another thought to the lady who had tormented his every thought since their first meeting.

Chapter Four

Cassie laughed as she watched Christina investigate her brother's eyes with a dangerously probing finger. "No darling," she gently admonished as she separated the curious, crawling twins. "I know his eyes are intriguing, but I think it best to allow Christian the use of them for the next fifty or sixty years."

Cassie laughed again as she watched her tiny niece's mouth grow into a deliberate pout. "It will do no good to work your wiles on me, missy. I know the workings of the female mind." She reached down to tickle Christina's bare, rounded belly and growled affectionately as she covered her tiny face with a dozen kisses. "You'll have to find someone of the male persuasion if you expect to win favor."

"What does the poor child want that you will not give her?" came a voice, deep in tenor and rich with humor, from the doorway.

Cassie had no need to look up. She would recognize that voice in a crowded room. Instantly, her heart

45

began to pound with dread. Because of her continued lies, she could not, no matter how she tried, ever relax in this man's company.

He had kept his distance since coming aboard, and for that Cassie had been grateful. The less she saw of him, the better, for her mind refused to allow her to forget the intimate moments they had shared.

Cassie smiled stiffly, her eyes demurely lowered as if she were shy. Actually, she was anything but. To all others, she was outgoing and friendly, but guilt has a way of influencing even the strongest of personalities. "Nothing too drastic," she replied to his question, "only her brother's eyes."

"And you won't let her have them?" He smiled as he made himself comfortable on the floor and picked up the little girl. "Poor little thing," he murmured, nuzzling Christina's sweetly scented tiny neck. "To have such a heartless mother."

Stifling a groan, Cassie finally allowed her gaze to move in his direction. Cameron Chandler could only be described as pure, magnificent male. She had never seen a man so breathtakingly handsome. He was sitting in the direct light of the porthole and the sun was shining on his almost blue-black hair, creating a halo effect around his head and body. Cassie found she had to force her hands to her side lest she suddenly reach out and touch him.

She seemed always to forget, or perhaps denied, just how striking he was, and constantly found herself surprised whenever she saw him. As his gaze caressed the child in his arms, Cassie took the opportunity to study him closely. To say he was handsome was a laughable understatement. His skin was bronzed from hours spent in the sun. Laugh lines crinkled at the corners of his eyes as he played with Christina. White teeth flashed as the baby cooed in response to his attentions. Even the scar that ran from his cheek to his jaw took nothing from his looks and only seemed to emphasize his manliness. On another man, such a scar might have caused revulsion. On Cameron, it somehow added a certain dangerous appeal.

Cassie longed to reach out and soothe the pain such a scar must have caused, but she dared not. She doubted they'd ever grow close enough for her to even ask him about it

Her heart melted with tender emotion as she watched this huge man fuss over the tiny child. Laughing softly, she said, "It is amazing how the female so easily entices the male into her web of intrigue. It begins even now."

"Mayhap they learn this art from their mothers?"

Cassie glanced up, her cheeks coloring prettily. She had no trouble reading the suppressed desire in his dark eyes. "I've enticed no one."

"Not deliberately perhaps, but a woman such as you tempts by merely breathing."

Cassie nervously took Christian up on her lap. Her eyes refused to meet those of the man sitting across from her. Anger and longing mingled within her. Her soft mouth narrowed to a thin line. She refused to take the blame for the carnal lust of others. "Well, since I must go on breathing, I'm afraid it cannot be helped."

Cameron grinned. "Catherine," he said quietly.

Cassie glanced up.

"It's obvious we've begun this relationship on the wrong foot. I'd not see us remain stilted and uncomfortable in each other's company. You are my niece. You will be living in my house." He sighed and then went on, "No matter my obvious attraction to you, I swear you need not fear my presence."

Cassie lowered her gaze again, her fingers nervously smoothing the silky hair of her nephew.

"Can you not forget what has passed between us?" he persisted. "Can we not start again?"

Forget? Forget how it felt to be held against him? Forget the taste and scent of him? Forget the knowledge that they were not related as she'd led him to believe? God, if only she could forget.

Cameron's heart thudded in his chest as he watched the beautiful woman opposite him. He didn't know whether to laugh or cry at the silent nod of her head. He felt none of the expected relief this new understanding should have brought. Nay, all he felt was the constant ache that he prayed would soon depart.

"You've barely walked outside this room since coming aboard." He smiled as she looked at him over the baby's head. "I'd hoped to persuade you to come on deck this afternoon."

Cassie smiled. "I cannot leave the babies. No doubt Christina will have her way the moment I turn my back."

"I've asked Marshall to come and sit with them for a time." He hesitated a moment and found he had to force out the next words, "Would you take a walk with your uncle?"

Cassie laughed bitterly to herself. It was impossible

48

to think of this man as her uncle, yet if she did not, she risked losing everything she held dear.

"Of course, I will walk with you. Do you prefer me to address you as 'uncle'?"

"I do," Cameron sighed, reasoning that perhaps the constant reminder would eventually persuade his body to accept what his mind knew—they were blood relations.

Cameron was laughing as he closed the door to the cabin and followed Cassie into the ship's narrow companionway. She had reminded the seaman, Marshall, again and yet again, to watch out for Christina's wily tricks. "Apparently," Cameron remarked, "you don't trust the child. She is but nine months old. Surely she is not as smart as you make her out?"

Cassie grinned as she turned back to look at him. "She's smart enough. I'd not leave her with a man without due warning."

"Does she take after her father or her . . ." he began, when the ship lurched suddenly and Cassie was flung the few feet to the opposite wall. Just as Cameron reached for her, the ship righted itself and she came staggering back into his open arms. ". . . mother," he finished with a gasp, his body rigid with controlled desire, his eyes closing with pleasure as her body came up hard against his.

"Her mother, I think—" Cassie's voice broke, and her words were stilted and disjointed as she breathed in the intoxicating scent of his warm breath. For an instant, her body seemed to melt against his hard frame. "Women are usually more devious than men. Aren't they?"

"Are you?"

"What?"

"Devious."

"At times, I suppose." But she barely knew what she was saying. Her eyes were drawn to his mouth. Her lips tingled with the knowledge that he had but to lower his head an inch to touch her. Her heart thudded against her ribs and she felt her body grow even more yielding against his. The blood pounded in her ears, and her breathing grew shallow and labored. More than anything, she wanted him to kiss her. She needed to feel his mouth again. She needed to taste once more what was now just a memory. But she knew she could not allow it. She had to stop this, and she had to stop it before she weakened and chanced disaster.

"You can let me go, Uncle." She tried to smile. "The ship has righted itself."

Instantly, Cameron's arm dropped to his side. Unable to speak because of his intense passion, he simply nodded and watched as she turned away and began to climb the steps to the upper deck. He took a long, steadying breath, cursing his lack of control. He had failed the very first test. Damn it, if keeping away from her wasn't possible, he'd have to acquire some self-control. How many times were they to come in contact in the years ahead? He couldn't go through this every time. If he was going to live with her, he would have to learn to master his emotions.

* * *

"His niece, my arse. We should all 'ave a niece like that one."

Cameron spun around at the sound of the four laughing crewmen. Without a second's thought, his fist struck out and contacted with the closest available mouth. Cameron never realized he'd hit the seaman until he saw him sprawled at his feet.

"I trust that settles the question of Mrs. Devon's relationship to me."

"Aye, sir," murmured one of the men. Cameron glared at them, then gave a small smile of satisfaction as the three who were left standing looked down at their boots. A moment later, they helped their fallen comrade to his feet and all four slunk wordlessly away.

Cameron's hand throbbed and he cursed the discomfort. Apparently, he had hit the man's teeth, for there was a deep gash across his knuckles. He only hoped the bastard's mouth hurt as much.

The sight of Diana Colt coming toward him deepened his scowl. Since recovering from an initial bout of seasickness, the woman was forever seeking him out. It wasn't like Cameron to dread a woman's company, especially a beautiful woman, but for some reason, he could not tolerate Diana.

He watched as she puffed out her chest. Christ, if she wore her gown any lower, she needn't bother at all.

Diana moved so close, her nearly exposed breasts actually brushed against his chest. Her heavy perfume almost turned his stomach.

The woman never gave up. How many times was he to decline her advances, before she understood he was not interested? Had she been someone other than

51

Catherine's companion, he might have considered taking her, despite his growing disgust with her cheap, blatant ways. She was undeniably beautiful but the more he grew to know her, the uneasier he became in her presence. He couldn't quite put his finger on it, but something about her didn't ring true. Perhaps it was simply her type of woman. He had never cared for the obvious. The cheaper and more openly available they appeared, the less his desire.

Diana hadn't missed the punch Cameron had landed. The sight of his hitting another man had sent a thrill of sexual excitement coursing through her. God, what she wouldn't do to feel such power for herself. She could just imagine how rough he could be, and the thought brought tingling sensations to every part of her body, leaving her slightly breathless. She watched avidly as he flexed his hand, then cried in sugary sweet tones, "Oh, you're bleeding. You must let me take care of that for you."

Cameron shook his head. "I'll have the doctor look at it later."

But Diana insisted, taking his arm and steering him inside. For a small woman, she had amazing strength and Cameron almost laughed as a crazy picture of her, holding a man in her bed through sheer physical force, flashed through his mind.

Cameron's mouth curved into a sneer as he sat in a chair, while Diana knelt at his feet. Apparently she had positioned herself so he might have a better view of her barely concealed breasts. She could have just as easily taken care of his scrape seated in the chair beside him.

Amazingly, he had received none of her sympathetic ministrations while lying injured from the train wreck. During the more than two weeks it had taken to recover, it was Catherine who had seen to his care.

Cameron wondered if Catherine had any inkling of her friend's improprieties. He doubted it. Although women were usually the first to notice this type of behavior in other women, he imagined Diana kept a tight rein on her wayward sexual impulses in Catherine's presence. The two could not be more different and he wondered how they had ever managed to remain friends.

Leaning forward as if to examine her artfully placed bandage, Diana's hand came to rest with seeming inattention high upon his thigh. As Cameron determinedly, and not too gently, removed her hand, she raised her eyes to his and smiled knowingly. "I could make it better for you if it aches."

Cameron hadn't a doubt it was aches of another kind she had in mind, for her eyes were fixed on his crotch. His mouth thinned to a straight white line. God, but he longed to tell this bitch where she could peddle her wares.

Suddenly, his eyes widened with surprise as he realized why she seemed so unappealing. She reminded him of his wife! She didn't look like Sarah, and perhaps that was why it had taken him so long to understand and reason out his feelings. Where Sarah was tall, this woman was short. His wife had been blonde and Diana was dark, but they were the same lying, conniving bitches beneath their sweet façades. He knew a whore when he saw one. Too bad he hadn't been as knowing in his youth. God, what suffering he would have avoided.

Cameron's disgust turned suddenly to anger. His hands balled into fists and he knew he had to get away from her before he lost control and smashed her simpering face. For, in his mind's eye, the features of his wife had blended suddenly with Diana's and all the pain he had once known came to bombard his senses.

True, he hadn't loved Sarah for a very long time. She had managed quite skillfully to kill any feelings he had once had. He had been so damn young when she destroyed all his illusions. He suddenly felt bereaved for the poor innocent he had once been.

Cameron had helplessly watched her flirt with a score of men. And Sarah had somehow convinced him the problem lay within himself. Though he had fought to control his violent jealousy, he could not. There had been countless fights. He had accused her of taking lovers. But she had always laughed at his suspicions, and, like a fool, he chose to believe her artful denials. Among other things, she was an expert liar; he had to give her that.

It wasn't hurt he felt at finding another man in his bed. It wasn't even shock, for he had instinctively known something was wrong the moment he had entered the house. It was rage. The same kind of rage that threatened now to destroy his rationality.

Cameron came suddenly to his feet, glaring down at Diana with abhorrence. Leaving her in open-mouthed astonishment, he moved swiftly to the door. Just before he left, he turned to her and said very firmly, "Thank you, I have no need of your ministrations."

Chapter Five

The room was dark, so dark, she couldn't see her hand before her face. Cassie muttered a sharp curse as her toe suddenly hit the wooden bunk and blinding pain surged up her foot and leg. Her lips thinned with fear. Her knuckles whitened with the effort to hold herself steady as the ship bucked, reared, and then plunged again into the deep valley between two towering walls of black, raging water. Groaning from its bowels to its mast, the ship fought to ride the next crest. Once again, it shuddered and growled with disappointment as the menacing seas grew, black and forbidding, a hundred feet above the bobbing craft. Again and again, the gigantic waves smashed with a thundering roar upon the deck, washing away any who stood in their path.

Cassie reached a trembling hand toward the babies, who miraculously slept on, oblivious to nature's ferocious display. She couldn't remember ever being so afraid. Her heart hammered wildly as she prayed that this night they would not all be swept into the voracious mouth of a sea gone wild with power.

Cassie spun about stifling a scream as the door to her room suddenly opened and smashed against the wall. The pounding in her throat threatened to strangle her as she strained to make out who had entered. All fires had been extinguished at the beginning of the storm; even the small light of a candle was forbidden. She could see nothing and her imagination ran riot as an ominous silence filled the room. "Who's there?" she asked in quavering tones.

"Don't be afraid," came Cameron's deep, reassuring voice.

Cassie almost slumped to the floor with relief. "Why did you wait so long to speak?" she demanded.

Suddenly, he was there, holding her in his arms. "I'm sorry I frightened you, but I couldn't see a thing."

"I'm not afraid," she breathed as she pressed her body closer to his. "Not now."

Unmindful of the havoc she wrought, Cassie's soft arms clung to his neck, delighting in the security of his embrace after endless hours of terror. Her hold tightened as she hungrily absorbed his calming strength.

Cameron tried to pull away. He had come to assure himself of her safety. He hadn't meant to take her in his arms, but the sound of her obvious terror had unconsciously brought him to her side. Cameron stifled a groan as the warm scent and feel of her lightly clad body threatened to rob him of his hard fought resolve. He knew she wore only a nightshift, and he clearly remembered what he had once found beneath this same type of garment. He had to get out of there. "Are the babies all right?" he asked as he deliberately

57

put her from him.

Cassie nodded, then realizing Cameron could not see the movement, she said aloud. "I don't know how, but they're sleeping."

Cameron chuckled. "The storm has nearly spent itself. You should be able to sleep soon."

Cassie sensed him moving away. He was leaving her alone again and she suddenly couldn't bear the thought. "Don't leave me. Please! I know I'm an awful coward, but I can't help it." She pressed herself against him again. He was cold, he was wet, but he was the only sanctuary she had in this nightmare of a storm.

"Catherine, oh God, I have to go," he groaned as his arms, with a mind of their own, moved around her.

Cassie heard the pain in his voice. "I'm sorry," she murmured. "That wasn't fair." She tried to move away, only now it was he who refused to let her go.

She shivered as his mouth came to rest upon her hair. He was murmuring soothing words of comfort, as a father might offer his child. But the breathless tone of his voice negated his innocent intent. Instead, the low, sweet murmurings made Cassie hungry for closer contact. She felt the chill leave her body and pressed closer, searching for still another kind of heat. His warm breath bathed her face in sweetness, and Cassie found herself unable to resist the urge to lift her lips toward his. His mouth was hot, burning hot, as his lips moved over her closed eyes, down her cheek, in an unerring search for her warmth. His hands cupped her face and his voice trembled with a yearning he couldn't deny. "Once," he groaned. "Just once."

Cassie sighed at the sweet sensation that filled her being. Despite the cold, despite the dampness, she was

58

warm; she was where she belonged.

His lips grazed her mouth, feather-light, moving away only to return again. Her lips parted and tingled at the sensuous touch of his mouth, and the tingling went on until it reached every part of her body.

He prayed for her to stop him, to give him the slightest sign of resistance, but Cassie was beyond rational thought and only tightened her hold, pulling his face closer. His mouth hovered above hers, as if resisting forbidden pleasures that would surely bring damnation. In the end, the temptation of her willing arms proved too much. With a muffled cry of pain and despair, he gave into his need and took her mouth with all the hunger and torment he had known these past weeks.

Cassie moaned with joy as his mouth slashed hungrily over hers, forcing her warm, eager lips further apart, sucking at her breath, filling her with his taste, his scent. She clung to him weak-kneed, moaning again as their tongues met enticingly, tasting, savoring.

He probed deep into her mouth, running his tongue over her teeth, the roof of her mouth, luxuriating in the honeyed sweetness, determined to take all he could in this one stolen moment. He signed with growing pleasure as she moved closer. His mind reeled with excitement as he realized his attempts to use others as a substitute were for naught. No other could compare with this delicious woman. Greedily, he drank from her, taking everything he could, knowing this moment would never come again, praying it would be enough to last a lifetime.

Abruptly, he pulled away and Cassie nearly fell

against the bunk. He was gasping for breath. His voice was shaking and heavy with pain when he spoke. "Help me, Catherine. This must never happen again."

She would tell him now. She would tell him and the consequences be damned. She knew he felt more for her than an uncle felt for his niece, and she didn't want him to go. She couldn't bear to let him go.

Cassie reached out a hand, but found only emptiness where he should have been. She moved through the blackness, until she felt the door. It was closed once again. Her soft call was lost in the howling wind. He was gone.

The deck was strewn with seaweed, jagged pieces of torn sail, and a maze of rigging. Huge chunks of railing were ominously missing. The merchantman's two top masts and sails were gone, but the "Lady," as all on board called her, sliced like the wind over the smooth glasslike surface beneath her.

Cassie stood at the bow, as was her habit every morning, and breathed lustily of the sweet clean air. She savored these few moments each day, for the confines of her cabin made the journey particularly difficult and more than a little monotonous. Her only relief was found in the occasional moments when Mr. Marshall, free of his usual chores, would come and sit with the babies.

She smiled as the ship suddenly lurched forward, catching a stiff breeze, hastening them over a blue-green sea now grown as calm as bathwater.

Cassie's heart was filled with the joy of simply being alive. She had lain awake all night, silently reveling in her plan to tell Cameron the truth and imagining the wondrous results. She laughed as her skirt billowed out in front of her, and her hair, suddenly relieved of several pins, did likewise.

With a guilty start, Cassie left her place at the bow and hurried below. Poor Diana. From the first, this voyage had not been easy for her, and Cassie wondered now how badly her friend had suffered during the endless, stormy night. Cassie felt a deep sense of shame that she had been so involved with her own cares and had entirely forgotten Diana's welfare.

When she knocked and opened Diana's door, Cassie knew even more reason to feel contrite. Diana lay upon her bunk, moaning even though the ship's movements were now smooth. "Oh, Diana," Cassie cried softly as she moved forward, "I'm so sorry."

"For what?" came the weak reply.

"For leaving you alone so long." Cassie opened the tiny porthole and began to straighten Diana's light coverlet. "Would you like something to eat?"

"Oh God, no!"

"Lean forward and I'll fluff your pillows."

"Please, just leave me. I need to sleep."

Cassie nodded with sympathetic understanding, even though she herself had never suffered this malady. "I need to talk to you," she said as she left. "When you feel better, come to my cabin."

Cassie smiled as Diana leaned against her doorjamb a few hours later. "You look decidedly better, dear. I hope we make it to port without another storm."

"Oh please, don't even talk about it," Diana

groaned. "What was it you wanted to talk to me about?"

Cassie wanted to cry out she was madly, passionately in love, but such a confession, coming from a grown woman, somehow seemed silly. So, instead of telling her friend her true feelings, she only hinted at them. "Well, I was wondering what you thought of Mr. Chandler. I know it's a bit late to be talking about it, but we are going to live with the man and we know virtually nothing about him."

Diana shrugged. "What can I tell you?"

"Nothing, in all probability. I just wondered what you thought of him."

"Well, I suppose he's all right. He does like his good times, though," Diana sneered, remembering how often he had rebuffed her advances in preference to one or another of the women on board. "I imagine him quite a jolly fellow."

"Cameron?" Cassie flushed with embarrassment at having inadvertently used his given name. "I mean, Mr. Chandler."

Diana shot her a look of surprise. *So it's Cameron, is it? Well, we'll soon put an end to that!* "He has taken a particular liking to one or more of the ladies on board. Rumor has it that Mrs. Sheridan has shared his bed on more than one occasion. And . . ." Diana wrung her hands in a purposeful, nervous gesture.

"And?"

"I don't think I should tell you. You might be upset."

Cassie's heart pounded with dread. "Tell me," she pressed.

Diana shrugged again, as if she had no choice but to tell the truth. "He made advances toward me."

Cassie's eyes widened with astonishment.

"You needn't worry. I put him in his place. Apparently, he's no better than most."

No better than most! Cassie shivered. Good God, she had almost confessed the truth to him! He was nothing but a womanizer, and what she thought special between them was obviously no more than another conquest to him. God, how could he dare to entice his niece to his bed?

Cassie ignored the fact that she was not his niece. He thought she was, and that was enough to fuel her anger.

Chapter Six

Cameron stood on deck and watched the green shoreline come slowly into view as the early morning sun began to burn off the drifting clouds of fog. They would be docking in a few hours and he was no closer to coming to grips with his feelings than he was at the beginning of this voyage. He knew the size of his plantation would ensure fewer encounters, but would that matter? Just knowing she was there was enough to guarantee his continued pain.

Cameron was a man possessed. He couldn't keep away from her, even though he realized every moment spent in her company increased his torture. He sighed, knowing he was forever doomed to suffer this pain, knowing, too, that there was no one who could ease him of those sinful urges. Since the night of the storm, he had taken no one to his bed. In all probability, he would continue his voluntary celibacy. Taking other woman as substitutes for Cassie was a useless pursuit. These unidentifiable faces brought no joy, no satisfaction.

He sighed again. He should have allowed Catherine

and the babies to stay on in England. He could have made arrangements with the family solicitor to see to their care. He need not have taken it upon himself to bring her to his home. He need not have caused himself this suffering.

But he hadn't known then what effect she would have on him. Granted, he had, since the first, felt a measure of attraction, but he hadn't imagined it would grow to such mammoth proportions. Mayhap he would suggest a return trip. He doubted Catherine would argue overmuch, for he suspected she suffered as he.

Perhaps it was best that they part, but Cameron's chest filled with pain at the mere thought. He could only imagine what he would suffer if he put his thoughts into action.

"Damn," he muttered softly. There was no answer. He couldn't keep her with him and he couldn't bear to see her go.

"Is there a problem?"

Cameron stiffened at the unexpected sound of her voice. He turned to face her and almost moaned at the exquisite sight she made. She was wearing her traveling dress again, and the dark blue fabric perfectly matched her eyes. Though pale from having spent so much of the voyage below, she still looked magnificent, especially now with the sun turning her auburn hair to a flaming mass of lusciously tempting curls.

He almost reached out to touch her and had to force his arms to his side lest he unconsciously do do. He couldn't remember a time when a woman had so affected him. Even as a very young man, when anything in skirts aroused him sexually, he had never had such an overpowering desire for any woman. What had he ever done that God should see fit to inflict this torture?

Cameron forced a smile. "Nay, nothing is wrong," he told her.

Since the night of the storm, Cassie had come to the conclusion that Cameron had merely given in to a weak, impulsive moment. No doubt, his erotic feelings had been aroused by the frenzy of the storm. Indeed, her own feelings had run high that night. In truth, she had to bear part of the blame, having so eagerly responded to him. She found herself unable to fault him overmuch. Since that night, he had treated her with the utmost respect, and her anger and disappointment had gradually dissipated. Also, she had come to realize that if the man enjoyed a casual dalliance, she had no right to judge. What he did with his life was his affair, and she'd do well to mind her own business. "How long before we dock?" she asked.

"We're waiting for the tide. Probably in an hour or two." He smiled again. "Are you anxious to see your new home?"

Cassie smiled. "Is it truly as big as you've hinted?"

"Bigger."

"And I can have my own horse?"

"More than one, if you like."

"Then, I'm most anxious indeed."

Cameron laughed at the devilish gleam in her eyes. Cassie had rarely shown him a glimmer of her lively personality. For too long, they had each suffered under unbelievable stress. Only now, after many weeks, was she finally able to relax in his company.

66

"I take it you ride?"

Cassie gave a low laugh, her blue eyes alight with merriment. Cameron couldn't know she had once been considered superior in sitting a horse.

"I've tried it once or twice."

A smile hovered about his lips. "Once or twice? Why do I get the feeling it's been considerably more than that?"

Cassie laughed. "I'm sure I have no idea."

Cassie's eyes grew huge with astonishment as she watched the hub of activity below. Never had she imagined such confusion, such noise. No one seemed able to remain in one spot for more than a moment. Under the hot sun, teams of black men, stripped to the waist, were unloading cargo from a dozen or more tall-masted ships. The rhythmic sound of their deep voices lent an exotic flavor to the setting as they sang out in a language foreign to her ears. More than one tired, bedraggled traveler was obviously having a hard time restraining his annoyance while hunting down his individual possessions.

Peddlers were shouting out the excellent quality of their wares, while beruffled and parasoled ladies, sitting in fine carriages, sent servants to fetch one particular item or another.

When an occasion fist fight broke out, no one tried to stop the battered participants from inflicting further damage on each other. Instead, the onlookers urged them on with encouraging shouts.

Cassie smiled as Cameron, standing nearly a head over most of the crowd, elbowed his way through the mob and back to the ship. One or two men who seemed to take offense at his passing, instantly stifled any protest when they spied the murderous look in his eyes.

The *Baltimore Lady* had docked almost an hour earlier and they were more than anxious to leave the ship. After waiting some time, Cameron had gone in search of his carriage. His annoyance was clear as he moved up the gangplank. Apparently, it had never arrived.

"I've sent word to Hill Crest. Someone should be along shortly."

Cassie nodded and turned back to watch the bustling activity below.

Her eyes widened with interest as she noticed one woman who was talking to a seaman. She had seen only one woman nearly as beautiful, and that was from the carriage window on her trip through London to the ship. From this distance, the woman looked uniquely colorful. Her rosy cheeks and lips were clear evidence of excellent health, while the dramatic cut of her dress emphasized her lush figure. Topped off by the reddest hair Cassie had ever seen, she gave an overall picture of an unusually bright, lively character.

"What do you find so interesting?" Cameron asked as his dark gaze followed hers.

"That lady. Who is she?"

"Which lady?"

"The one with the red hair, talking with the seaman."

Cameron laughed as he finally realized to whom she referred. "I'm sure I don't know."

"What's so funny?"

"My dear Catherine. Surely you're not as innocent as all that. Have you never seen a lady of the night before?"

Cassie wasn't totally ignorant in the ways of the world. She knew well enough the expression and its meaning. She had simply never seen such a sight before. Having lived most of her life in the country, she had found little opportunity to come across this type of woman.

Cheeks flaming, she strove to retain her composure, shooting Cameron a look of annoyance, which did little to stop his merriment. Trying to cover up her display of ignorance, she said, "That wasn't the one I spoke of."

"Which one, then?"

"She's gone now."

It was apparent he didn't believe her. "I assure you, you'd not find half so much interest upon closer inspection."

Cassie's irritated look suddenly dissolved into bubbling laughter. "Don't you have something to do?"

"Actually, I should speak with the captain before we leave." Cameron smiled down at her affectionately, and Cassie suddenly preferred being laughed at to this tender expression. "You don't mind if I leave you alone for a few moments, do you?" he asked.

"Please, don't give it a moment's thought."

Cassie sighed with relief as Cameron moved away. Again, she turned her attention to the activity on the dock. A few men were creating a raised platform with a dozen or so planks placed on several small barrels. It looked very shaky indeed and she wondered if anyone was going to be brave enough to walk upon it.

Apparently, they had done this task before, for they were finished in a matter of moments. A crowd of men began to form before the platform and Cassie gave it her full attention, wondering what was about to happen.

Suddenly, she gasped. Her eyes widened with horror as she realized she was about to witness a slave auction. A young girl, somewhere in her late teens, bound at the wrists, was pulled upon the platform. A long rope was tied around her neck, and with this, a man forced her forward until she stood center stage.

Cassie was mortified. The girl stood before these laughing, licentious men without a stitch of clothing. Cassie allowed her gaze to wander over the docks again. The pretty ladies had disappeared. The hawkers had stopped their shouting as all potential customers were obviously otherwise engaged. It was suddenly ominously quiet, the only sound an occasional screeching seagull and the constant gentle lapping of waves against the ship's hull. A small group of men gathered around the auction block, murmuring comments about the girl. Cassie's pulse thudded. Would not one of them stop this? Did not one among them pity this poor girl?

Cassie turned fiery red as she watched the auctioneer move closer to the crowd and begin to speak. With a businesslike air, he went about pointing out the girl's qualities. "Look at the width of those hips, mates," he advised as he ran his hand over the girl's quivering flanks. "A prime candidate for breeding. I'd say she's worth double the asking price." He gave an evil chuckle and said, "And if any of you fine gents are a wonderin', she's a virgin all right."

"Can you guarantee that, Charlie?" one of the men from the crowd called out.

Charlie grinned as he listened to the foul snickering. "You ain't going to test her out, if that's what you're hintin' at, Boggs. You'll have to buy her if you wanna be the first."

Amid the crowd's raucous cheers, the man called Boggs jumped upon the platform and began to poke at the terrified girl. First, he forced her jaws apart and looked into her mouth. Egged on by the others, he ran his hands over her full breasts and tiny waist. But when his fingers stopped to probe between her legs, Cassie almost screamed her indignation. She'd had enough!

Her cloak was before her, lying over the ship's railing. Without another thought, she grabbed the garment and ran down the gangplank.

Cassie was a tiny woman, but her outrage at what she had witnessed gave her the strength of a small tornado and she easily pushed her way into the crowd. She never hesitated, but jumped to the platform and raced toward the obnoxious man, shoving him until, with a startled cry, he fell from the rickety stage. She was a blur of speed as she snapped the rope from the girl's neck and flung it at the auctioneer, grunting with satisfaction as she hit him squarely in the face. An instant later, she placed her cloak around the shivering girl's shoulders and glared into the crowd.

Nearly beside herself with rage, she never noticed the men actually take a step back from this raging whirlwind. She wasn't aware of their sudden silence, nor the shocked looks of disapproval she received. Her blue eyes were blazing and her lips were twisted into a

71

sneer of disgust as she approached the auctioneer. "You need not begin your bidding. I will pay whatever you ask."

The auctioneer actually felt himself cowering before this woman's righteous wrath. In all the years he'd performed this duty for his captain, he had never witnessed such a phenomenon. True, you sometimes found a woman present at a slave auction, but they always kept at a discreet distance and had someone else bid in their behalf.

This lady's audacity clearly gave him a moment's pause. But his confusion soon changed to anger as the onlookers began to chuckle, calling out words of encouragement to Cassie, while others jeered at his obvious lack of control. Charlie Hendrix was nobody's fool and this little piece of fluff wasn't going to bamboozle him. He had to get rid of her before she caused more of a ruckus and maybe cost him his job.

"This ain't no place for a lady, miss. You'd best find your man and have him bid on the girl, if'n you still want her."

Not knowing the auctioneer's surname, Cassie nevertheless addressed him in her most refined, ladylike manner, "Mr. Charlie, the matter is settled. I only await your price."

Charlie groaned. What was this world coming to? Whatever happened to sweet little ladies who did as they were told? Charlie didn't come by this job by chance. His boss had chosen him because he had a way of controlling a crowd. He wasn't the kind to allow a woman to take control of any situation, not even one with her looks and high and mighty attitude. His mouth twisted into a sneer, and had Cassie not been so enraged at what she had witnessed, she would have surely felt a measure of fear. As it was, she ignored the man's obviously rising temper and held her ground.

Charlie spit out between clenched teeth, "I told you, lady, this ain't no fittin' place for you."

Cassie raised her chin a notch, and even though she was smaller than the man she addressed, she somehow appeared to be looking down at him. "Sir, if you refuse to name a price, I can only assume you have none. In that case, I will take her with me." Cassie began to guide the girl toward the edge of the platform.

For an instant, Charlie was completely dumbfounded. Then, amid the wild cheers of the crowd, he realized he was watching his captain's profit, and maybe his own job, walk away and he wasn't doing a damn thing to stop it. Charlie lunged for Cassie, flung the black girl away and held Cassie's arms behind her.

A lone voice was suddenly heard among the laughing crowd. "I'll pay four times your price if you throw that one in, Charlie. And I don't care if she's a virgin or not."

This brought a thunderous reaction, and the men went wild, calling out one outrageous price after another, some of them adding graphic descriptions of what they would do with the two women.

Cassie was was so stunned by what was suddenly happening she never thought to struggle to free herself. When the crowd noticed what they presume was her apparent willingness to be auctioned off, the bidding went wild. Men began to lick their lips in hungry anticipation as they took in her fiery windblown hair, flushed cheeks, and lush curves. "Hey, Charlie," called one man, "we can't see what we're buying. Ain't you

73

gonna do somethin' about that?"

Charlie Hendrix grinned as dollar signs danced before his eyes. He didn't know who this bitch belonged to. He didn't know who she was, but she deserved no better than she got for interfering in his business. His hand reached around her shoulders and held her in a tight grasp. "How much do I hear for this little hellcat?" he shouted to the growing crowd.

Cassie screamed and began to fight him with all of her strength. Suddenly, all went silent, for the men seemed to understand at last that this was not the type of woman they had first imagined.

Cameron had been talking to the captain of his ship when he noticed a blue blur race past his peripheral vision. At first, he thought little of the sight, but when a sudden, hushed silence fell upon the docks, followed almost immediately by wild cheers, he knew something was amiss.

"Jesus Christ!" Cameron muttered in astonishment as he moved to the railing and took in the sight below. What the hell did she think she was doing? Without another thought, Cameron charged down the gangplank and into the crowd, shoving people with stunning blows, until he stood almost directly before Cassie. His dark gaze glittered with a murderous rage as the auctioneer held her tightly in his arms. His fingers itched with the need to bash the man's face in.

His voice was deadly calm. "You will release the lady, sir."

Cassie almost cried with relief as she heard Cameron's voice, then winced in pain as Charlie tightened his hold.

"The bitch tried to steal my property," he snarled.

"Release the lady, sir."

Charlie should have realized the menace in Cameron's softly spoken words, but he was too wound up with the cries of the crowd to notice. Instead, he repeated the last bid.

Cameron moved fast. Instantly, he was on the platform. Cassie was flung aside, and the auctioneer was lying at Cameron's feet, moaning and holding the side of his face.

Cameron picked her up and flipped her over his shoulder.

Shocked into silence, Cassie listened to the crowd scream their approval. Cameron lingered just long enough to order Charlie to bring the slave girl, unharmed, to Hill Crest where he would be paid for her purchase. Then, he jumped down and walked calmly through the group of laughing men.

Cassie was dumped, quite unceremoniously, into a closed carriage, where a moment later a somewhat out of breath Cameron joined her. As the door slammed shut, the driver called out, a whip snapped in the air, and the carriage moved off.

Overcome with shame and fury, Cassie's anger knew no bounds. She took out her blinding rage on the first available person. "Gutless swine," she snarled at Cameron. "Wretched beast!" In an instant, she was off her seat, lunging at him. Her hands balled into fists and she landed two clean shots before he managed to still her. Though her hands were now secured behind her, that did not stop her verbal assault. "You clod!" She shrieked. "Half-witted bore! I'm going to kill you for that."

Cameron's dark gaze danced with delight. "For saving you?"

"It's not the fact of saving, but the means," she shot back hotly, struggling to free herself. "How dare you fling me over your shoulder? Scurvy bastard!"

Cameron chuckled. "It appears that the sea voyage has done much to increase your vocabulary."

"Let me go this instant, or I swear I'll . . . "

"You'll what?" Cameron's words were low and husky as his gaze was drawn to her heaving breasts.

Cassie was dangerously close to tears, but she'd be damned if she'd allow this beggar to see her cry. "Let me go," she repeated in a now quavering voice.

Cameron dismissed the thought of pulling her onto his lap and allowing himself the luxury of soothing her wild emotions. He couldn't chance prolonged contact. He hadn't planned on riding with her to his plantation. She, Diana, and the babies were to have been driven there accompanied by Jessie, one of his servants.

"Why did you do it, Catherine?" he asked quietly.

Her blue eyes glistened as she answered him. "I did what any human being would have done to save another."

"Catherine, you'll have to understand our ways if you mean to stay."

"You're not condoning slavery!"

Cameron shrugged, unable to tell her his true feelings on the subject. "A necessary evil," was all he said.

She stared at him in disbelief. "Don't tell me you own people!" she spat out contemptuously.

"Slaves, Catherine."

"Dammit! Aren't slaves people?"

76

Cameron shrugged. "In a manner of speaking, I suppose."

"How very kind of you to suppose," she sneered with heavy sarcasm. "I'm not staying here. I refuse to stay in a country that permits such barbaric actions. And most particularly I refuse to live with a man who believes there is nothing wrong with slavery."

Cameron knew she was giving him the perfect opportunity to solve his painful dilemma. He had been mulling over the prospect of sending her back to England, but now that she herself had declared her wish to leave, he was loathe to allow it. He couldn't let her go, no matter the pain of keeping her. And he couldn't tell her of his secret work. The less she knew about that, the safer she'd be. "Do you expect me to pay for yet another crossing?"

"I expect nothing from you. I'll pay my own way, thank you."

Chapter Seven

Without knocking, Cassie stormed into the library. Her hair was in wild disarray and she was spoiling for a fight. "How much?" she demanded.

Knowing very well to what she referred, and not at all pleased with her nasty attitude, Cameron glared at her from behind his desk. "Why?"

"I pay my own bills, Mr. Chandler."

Cameron's mouth hardened. "She's yours. What difference does it make how much she cost?"

"I beg to differ with you, Mr. Chandler." Her voice dripped disdain. "She's not mine. Anyone with an ounce of moral fiber knows you cannot own another."

"Meaning, of course, that in your opinion I am totally unprincipled?"

"I've no right to judge you, sir."

"Perhaps, but you are certainly doing so."

Cassie ignored his taunt. She'd gain little by making an enemy of this man. "How much did you pay?" she asked again.

"Two hundred dollars."

"What?" she gasped, her eyes wide with astonishment.

"I take it you didn't know the price could range quite so high." Cameron shrugged. "Don't worry about it."

Cassie dug into her skirt pocket and blushed beetred as her hand came up with naught but a few coins. She didn't have enough for a return voyage, let alone the exorbitant price asked for one slave's freedom. "I don't . . ."

Cameron leaned back in his chair and studied the beautiful lady across the desk. Apparently, she was suffering some degree of embarassment. No doubt she had not realized the price of the girl when she had interfered with the auction. "I told you not to worry about it."

Cassie bristled at his overbearing attitude. Her spine stiffened with determination. "I'm afraid I must, Mr. Chandler. No one has paid my bills since I was a child. I can take care of myself."

Cameron grinned. "Not even your husband? My, my, you must have been quite an extraordinary wife."

"Who?" she asked, her anger momentarily causing her to forget her fabricated tale.

"Your husband. You know, the father of your children."

"Mr. Chandler, I feel no need to discuss my husband, or our life together." She glared at his grin. "I insist on paying for the girl."

"With that?" He gave a low chuckle as he eyed the few coins in her hand. "Why, there must be all of two pounds . . ."

"Two pounds, six shillings," she interrupted, placing the whole of it before him. "If I might borrow some writing materials, I will send for the rest."

Cameron shrugged. He came to his feet and waved her toward his chair. "Be my guest."

Cameron watched as Cassie sat and began to compose her letter. He knew she was writing her solicitor in London, but he had no intention of allowing this message to be sent. Besides the money for the slave girl, she was undoubtedly requesting enough for passage back to England. Though knowing they'd both be better off if separated, Cameron was not about to let that happen. No, he said to himself with an ironic laugh as he waited for her to finish. He couldn't let her leave because, obviously, he still needed to suffer.

Cameron smiled with satisfaction as he stared at the envelope. Once Cassie had left it on the sideboard, it had been easy enough to extract from the other letters lying there. Briefly, he considered opening it, then decided that what he was doing was bad enough. He wouldn't add to the crime by invading her privacy. With a confident grin, he walked to the library and the waiting fire.

It would be some time before Cameron was to learn how much suffering could have been avoided had he given in to his first impulse.

This wasn't going to be easy. Cassie sighed again as she tried to make the young girl in the tub understand that she no longer had anything to fear. The girl cowered away from Cassie. God, what she must have suffered at the hands of those brutes!

Cassie moved the cloth, rich with sweetly scented soap, over the poor thing's quivering shoulders. "What is your name?"

No response.

"I wish you could understand me." Cassie sighed. "If you can't tell me your name, I'll just have to give you a new one." Cassie smiled. "Now, what shall I call you?"

Cassie's eyes widened as the young girl, soothed by the heat of the bath and the gentle ministrations of her mistress, suddenly smiled in return.

Cassie laughed. "With a smile like that, I couldn't call you anything but "Sunshine." Welcome to your new home, Sunshine. I hope you will be very happy here."

Sunshine immediately echoed her mistress's laughter and Cassie relaxed. With some patience and time, she and Sunshine would become the best of friends. And why shouldn't they? Weren't they both torn from their roots? Taken without choice away from all they knew and loved? Brought, although under different circumstances, to live in this house? "Well, it won't be for long, Sunshine," she said to the bewildered girl. "We'll be on the first ship home, the moment Mr. Whitehall answers my letter."

Cassie smiled as she cantered Midnight along the outskirts of a huge field. Even though Cameron was a despicable slave owner, she had to admit that the blacks seemed content enough. Right now, the field workers were eating a substantial midday meal prepared earlier that morning by the women, then transported in huge wagons out to the fields. Afterward, the men were permitted a rest period before resuming work until sundown.

Cassie could see the slaves were well cared for. They were housed in clean, if plain quarters and apparently given plenty to eat. Cameron treated them more like paid workers than slaves.

Still, the idea of slavery rankled. England had prohibited the owning of slaves in its colonies the year before, and Cassie had actually forgotten the practice still existed in this country, forgotten that is, until she had watched the auction from the ship's deck.

It had been six weeks since she had come here, and, in truth, she couldn't find fault in Cameron's method of operation. Except for the fact that slavery did exist—no matter the apparent satisfaction on all sides—she would have been content.

As Cameron watched Cassie head her mount toward the wooded area of his lands, he turned to one of his trusted overseers. "Take over for me, Joshua," he instructed, giving the man his pocket watch. "See that they get back to work in fifteen minutes."

Cameron swung himself into his saddle, his eyes on Cassie's small figure cantering almost out of sight. "I'll be back later. If I don't make it, stop them at the usual time."

Cameron's huge black stallion flung giant clumps of soft, moist earth high into the air as he responded to his master's directions. Cameron urged Black Magic faster, unable to resist the lady's silent, unconscious allure. There was rarely a time when he saw her that he didn't contrive some means to keep her in his company.

Cassie heard the pounding of hooves behind her and reined Midnight to an abrupt stop. A moment later Cameron pulled up at her side. "Is something wrong?" she asked, immediately thinking of the babies.

Cameron smiled. "Everything is fine. Why?"

Cassie shrugged. "You were riding so fast, I thought there might be a problem."

"I saw you riding and thought you might not be averse to company."

Cassie smiled, happy to have him at her side. No matter what efforts she made to remain indifferent to this man, she was helpless in the face of his overwhelming magnetism. Again, and for the hundredth time, she wondered what he would do if she told him the truth of their relationship. If only she could trust his reaction. If only she could be sure.

Cameron sighed as he leaned back against a boulder and gazed at the narrow stream of swiftly flowing water beside which he and Cassie sat. "It's been more than six weeks since you've come here. Are you still planning to leave?"

Cassie shrugged, unable to face the possibility right now. She had never felt so content, she realized with a start. She was really happy here. Happier than she'd been in a very long time. Just not having to worry about the children's daily care was a delight. Oddly enough, she seemed to appreciate them all the more when she didn't have to be constantly in their presence. And the fact that all her money problems were no more gave her spirits an added boost. For years, she had worried daily over the most trivial, mundane matters. The returns on her modest investments never seemed to be enough, and she constantly found herself in dire straits.

"In truth, I love your home, Cameron. I'd like nothing more to stay. But . . ."

"But?"

"Can you not do something about this slavery business?"

Cameron shrugged. "What would you have me do? Free them all? Where would they go? What would they do?"

"They could stay here, couldn't they? They'd have to work somewhere, why not here?"

"It would bankrupt me in a year to pay them a salary, Catherine," he lied.

"Nonsense! I'm sure it costs more to keep them as you do."

"Do you think they'd be better off free?"

"Probably not. No doubt many would suffer, but at least they would live like men and do what they wished with their lives."

Cameron chuckled. "Do you hold freedom above all else?"

"Do you not? Did your country not fight two wars with mine over that very principle? How would you fare being another's property?"

Cameron gave a silent groan. She didn't know just

how close to the mark she had come, for he was more her property than his own man with every passing day. He went to sleep thinking of her. She was first in his thoughts upon awakening. And it was a rare moment, indeed, when she left his mind during each long day.

"Things will change in time, Catherine. You must have patience."

"I'm afraid it is not I who must exercise that saintly attribute, but the poor souls who are held captive by this hated practice."

Cassie almost choked on her laughter as she sipped at the ruby red port. "You beast." Her eyes glittered with delight as she tried to glare at him from across the small table.

Cameron chuckled. "Is that how a niece addresses her uncle?"

"Only if the uncle is you. You lulled me into thinking I had you, and then you sprang your trap."

Cameron smiled as he leaned back in his chair. "It's called strategy, Catherine. The point to chess is to try to figure out your opponent's next move."

Cassie sighed. "Would that I could. I have never met a man quite so baffling."

"Indeed?" Smiling, he lifted a quizzical brow.

Spying the teasing light in his eyes, she asked, "We are talking about chess, aren't we?"

"Are we?"

A small shiver raced through her body as Cassie watched his eyes grow warm and glowing. Deliberately she set aside her answering need, ignored her suddenly hammering pulse, and took a deep breath. "You know you need not spend every evening at home on my account. No doubt there are many who await your company."

"Are you asking me to leave my own home?"

Cassie grinned. "I've no objection to spending an occasional evening alone."

"Not to worry, Catherine. There is no other I'd rather be with."

"But . . ." She hesitated and flushed.

"But what?"

"What of your lady friends? Will they not grow annoyed at being ignored?"

"Mayhap I see them during the day."

"Do you?" she asked and then gasped at her audacity. Unwittingly, she gave a low groan of embarrassment. Would she never learn to watch her tongue in this man's company? What right did she have to question him about his personal life?

Cameron laughed. "No. As a matter of fact, I have no lady friends."

"But I thought . . ."

"What did you think?"

Cassie worried her bottom lip. "I'm sorry. I have no right."

"Tell me."

"It's not important." Cassie placed her half-empty glass on the table and rose to her feet. "It's late. I should be going up now."

"Just a minute," he remarked as he stood and took her arm as she tried to pass. "You're not going to leave me wondering about that comment all night. What did you think?"

Cassie grimaced as she remembered the rumors aboard ship. She couldn't meet his gaze, but kept her eyes upon the buttons of his shirt. "Well, you are far from homely and obviously a most eligible bachelor. It is unlikely that you would suffer too much loneliness."

"How far?" he grinned.

"What?"

"How far am I from being homely?"

Cassie laughed, her gaze lifting to his. "Are you fishing for a compliment?"

Cameron laughed. "Madam, if compliments were food, I'd have died of starvation by now."

"I doubt that. I think there are many who are all too eager to bestow a crumb or two."

Cameron smiled and shook his head, his eyes gently caressing her face.

"Not a one?" she inquired, suddenly breathless as he moved almost imperceptibly closer.

"No one important."

"But there should be, Cameron. Your wife has been dead five years. A man shouldn't live his life alone."

"I'm not alone. I have you and the children. It is enough." Almost enough, he corrected silently.

Cassie knew she should move away, but she couldn't seem to get her feet to obey her mind's insistent commands. He smelled so good, a delicious blend of soap, tobacco, leather — and man. Cassie shivered. Gooseflesh broke out along her arms and raced down her back as his warm breath teased her cheek.

"It's late," she whispered with a regretful sigh.

"I know."

87

"I should go up now," she said again, and her voice trembled.

Cameron nodded, his heart pounding with the need to pull her into his arms. "Go to bed, Catherine. Go now, before it's too late."

Cameron leaned against the railing of the wide balcony and looked out over the large darkened gardens. He had gone to bed hours before, only to toss and turn, his body tortured with need. Was it never going to pass? Would he never again know peace? How much longer would he be able to hold out against her silent call? How much more could he take before he lost all control?

He threw his cheroot into the garden with a sigh of disgust. It had to stop. As of this night, he would refuse to think of her except as his niece. It was over. Finished. He wanted no more of the pain she brought. He would send her home.

The decision brought him a measure of relief. It wouldn't be easy, but it had to be done. If he ever expected to sleep again, he had to get her out of his house.

Still, his mind was troubled, returning again and again to the delicious memories of her. He walked toward the stairs at the end of the balcony. Perhaps a brisk walk would clear his churning mind, provide some distraction from this endless aching in his heart and loins. If he did not find a way to stop thinking of her, he would go mad.

A white curtain fluttered from Cassie's open window. And, as he approached her room, he could see the dim light of perhaps a single candle. A frown puckered his brow. What on earth was she doing? Why was she still awake? Perhaps she wasn't awake. Perhaps she had merely forgotten to extinguish the light.

Cameron moved to her doorway and glanced inside. His breath caught in his throat and he almost choked at what greeted his eyes. He couldn't move. He tried, but he couldn't walk away. His heart thundered so, he was sure she could hear it. He watched, mesmerized by the sight of her sitting in a tub, dreamily soaping her enticing breasts. Her movements were so slow, so sensuous, he wondered if she didn't realize she was being watched.

Cassie had tossed and turned for hours. She had read, counted sheep, and tried to will her body to relax, all to no avail. The house had been quiet for hours and still she couldn't sleep. Finally, she left her bed and, on silent feet, went to the kitchen for several buckets of hot water, hoping a bath would soothe her into sleep.

Cassie sat in the tub, waiting for her body to relax, until her skin began to pucker. Leaning with her head against the tub's high rim, her plan to leave the plantation came again to mind. She signed heavily. She'd be sorry to go, but it was probably best to get out of here while she still could. Tonight, she had once again been tempted to tell him of her deception. She'd never imagined anyone capable of instilling such desire in her. Desire that grew in strength as each day passed. She had no false notion of modesty. She knew a lady didn't think about such things. She didn't care. She only knew that she wanted him and had wanted him from the first. How much longer was she to bear this constant, nagging need and do nothing about it? Why didn't she tell him the truth? She knew him well enough. The man was not an ogre, after all. But a voice at the back of her mind warned: What if you tell him? What if you dare? What do you expect after that? Even if learning the truth doesn't cause him to order you out, do you honestly believe he'll want to marry you? Are you ready to face the fact that he very well might want you only for his bed?

Cassie was torn, too afraid of the consequences to make a decision. She sighed again and stood. At last, her body felt relaxed enough for sleep. Now, if she could only turn off her mind, she might actually be able to close her eyes.

Cassie stepped from the hip bath and was about to reach for her towel when a strangled cry caused her to glance up. Sunshine had forgotten to close her draperies again and a man was standing in the darkened doorway of the balcony. The scream that rose in her throat was cut off only when she realized it was Cameron. Shocked, she stepped swiftly backward, colliding with the tub, losing her balance and almost toppling back into the water.

She straightened up, breathing hard. Looking at him with round eyes and parted lips, she didn't have to ask why he was there. She knew. Even without being able to see him clearly, she knew. She tried to speak, to say something, anything to break the tension between them, but no words would form.

Barefoot, Cameron moved silently out of the

shadows, heart racing wildly, a thin film of sweat coating his lightly clad body. Never had he imagined anything so lovely. He grew lightheaded at the sight of her naked beauty, and the excitement she aroused in him made him wonder if he was going to live past this moment.

In the candlelight, her satiny apricot skin shimmered like gold, and her long auburn hair tumbled down her back in damp, gypsy curls. Droplets of water rolled to her breasts gathering provocatively at the tips where he longed to lick them away.

He stood staring at her, unable to take his eyes from her breathtaking contours—the tiny waist, the gently flaring hips, the long, slender legs. Helpless before the power of such beauty, he moved forward, eyes glazed with the desire that had tormented him since their first meeting. The scent of the jasmine she'd used in her bath mingled with her own intoxicating fragrance, invading his senses until he ached with every breath he drew.

Cassie closed her eyes, moaning at the raw need she read in his gaze. He wanted her—even thinking her to be his niece, even knowing the consequences of that desire. He wanted her, and God help her, she no longer had the strength to fight this pull.

She opened her eyes and let her gaze wander over his tall, lean figure—the expanse of bronzed skin revealed by his open shirt, the dark wavy hair, mussed and tumbling over his forehead as if he'd just come from his bed. And the picture of this man abed filled her with a shiver of excitement. She could feel his gaze traveling down the length of her, searing her body. She could feel it just as surely as if he actually touched her. Her body swayed, weak with the heady sensations that swept through her.

She had to talk to him. Now—before this went any further. She had to tell him the truth. Her hand trembled as she reached for her robe.

"No," he said, moving nearer to her. He couldn't bear the thought of being denied this pleasure. He had to look at her, had to touch her. God help him, he had to love her.

Cassie's mind screamed. Enough! Please God, she had suffered enough. She was going to tell him and the future be damned. "Cameron, we have to . . ."

"Yes, Catherine, we have to," he interrupted as he reached her at last and took the robe from her fingers, tossing it to the floor. "It doesn't matter any longer who you are. I only know I want you. I can't control this desire. I've finished with trying." He reached out for her and slowly brought her to him. Jesus, he was drowning in her eyes. He couldn't himself. There wasn't a power on earth that could stop this. "If my soul is damned to hell for this," he murmured, "so be it." And then his mouth closed on hers.

Everything that Cassie was going to tell him vanished with his kiss. All she could think of was the exciting male scent of him. All she knew was the strength of his body as she leaned into him. All she wanted was the feel of his warm chest against her breasts, his arms holding her close, and the taste of his mouth.

Her moan of pleasure was swallowed in his hungry growl as his tongue parted her eager lips and delved deep into the sweet, moist recesses of her mouth. His head swam, he was giddy with the scent and taste of her. "I want you," he said, pulling away briefly. "I want . . ." And then, his mouth ravished her lips again, sucking in the delectable warmth, taking everything.

She pressed close to him, eagerly caressing his powerful chest, his shoulders, his neck. As one hand traveled up to move through his crisp black hair, her other hand dared at last to travel the scar along his cheek.

"I've wanted to touch you here for so long," she whispered as his mouth left her lips to nibble at her shoulder and neck.

"It's ugly. Don't," he murmured against her heated flesh as his hand came up to cover hers.

But her fingers lingered on the scar, and she lifted his head so her lips and tongue could continue the caress. Her voice was low and husky as she said, "There is nothing ugly about you. Don't you know how beautiful you are?"

Cameron smiled, his eyes shining with love. "No. Why don't you tell me?"

Cassie's heart pounded as she gave him a teasing smile. "Perhaps I'll show you instead."

Cameron grinned, enchanted by her daring.

"You should smile more," Cassie said. "You don't look half so frightening when you do."

"Do I frighten you?"

"Sometimes," she sighed as her hands moved once again over his chest.

"Are you afraid now?"

"Only of myself," she groaned, her eyes glowing with pleasure in the dim light. While she threaded through the thick hair of his chest, she pressed her lips to his neck. As her tongue sought out and savored the salty taste of his skin, she murmured boldly, "Right now, I'm afraid I'll never get enough of you."

Feeling him stiffen, Cassie was amazed at her own daring behavior. She had never been with a man before and barely knew the whole of it. Still, she displayed not a glimmer of maidenly shyness. She felt as if she had always loved him, felt as if she belonged in his arms. Without hesitation, she continued her deliberate seduction.

Cameron groaned as the heat of her mouth seared his flesh. He was growing harder, his desire thickening, throbbing ready to burst. He fought for control as she moved lower, trailing moist, fiery kisses over his skin, spurred on by his obvious pleasure.

"No more." He shuddered as she ignored his gasping plea and continued the delicious journey over the rough prickly hairs of his chest toward his waist. Determinedly, he brought her to stand before him. He was gasping for breath, his whole body trembling, his mouth against her hair, breathing in her warm scent. His hips moved against her belly and his mouth came down again on hers.

Then, in one fluid motion, he swept her up and carried her to the bed. Unable to let go of her, his mouth devoured hers as he stripped away his pants and shirt.

Simultaneous groans sounded as heated flesh slid thrillingly over heated flesh. He was desperate to possess her. He wouldn't wait. He couldn't wait. He couldn't stop. She felt so delicious, so wonderful, so warm, so smooth. God, he had never known such delight, such pleasure.

His heart thudded in his ears. It was pounding . . . pounding. Suddenly, he realized that the sound he heard was not just the beating of his heart. It was coming from down the hall. Someone was banging on his door.

Chapter Eight

"Mr. Chandler, sir! Mr. Chandler." The pounding continued.

"What the hell is the problem, Stevens?" Cameron muttered angrily as he jerked open the door to his room at last and faced his overwrought houseman.

In his excitement, Stevens forgot his studied manner of speech. "Joshua's went and got his head smashed. One of the horses got spooked. He went to see what was the trouble. He's hurt bad. Real bad."

"Jesus!" Cameron pulled on his boots over his bare feet and ran down the long hallway toward the stairs, shouting over his shoulder, "Send someone for Doc Reilly. Do it fast! And get out to the barn. I'm going to need help getting him in the house."

Cassie overheard the shouting voices. Someone was in serious trouble. Someone would be needing her help. Not taking the time to put on her underthings, she quickly slid her cotton dress over her shoulders and smoothed it into place. Moving swiftly, she pushed her feet into soft kid slippers and pinned her hair behind her head. She grabbed her small black bag, then ran from her room and up the stairs to the servants' quarters.

"Jessie!" she called out as she knocked on the housekeeper's door. "Jessie, wake up!"

By the time the sleepy woman answered the insistent knocking, Cassie had nearly pounded the door in.

"Lord almighty! What's troublin' you, missy?"

"Joshua's been hurt. Go downstairs immediately. I'll need whiskey, needles, thread, and plenty of clean sheets. Hurry!"

Cassie was flying down the steps as the front door opened to admit Cameron and Stevens, who were carrying the severely injured Joshua. Blood was gushing from the man's head.

"The dining room. Quick!" Cassie ordered.

The two men instantly obeyed, following Cassie as she flung chairs out of their path. With a single sweep of her arm, the candlesticks and crystal punch bowl that stood upon the polished wooden table went crashing to the floor. No one seemed to notice or care about the splintered glass or the destruction of a priceless antique.

"Jessie! Dammit, hurry up!" Cassie called out as she moved to the unconscious man on the table.

The housekeeper ran into the room, breathless with haste. Cassie grabbed a sheet from her hand and with Cameron's help placed it beneath Joshua's head. From her bag, she took a pair of tweezers and began the long, slow process of removing white splinters of bone from the damaged area. There was a hole in the man's head about the size of a gold sovereign. From the look of it, Joshua didn't have a chance, but she couldn't just sit by and watch him die. She had to do something.

She had to at least try.

"Jessie, get blankets. Lots of them." Then, without looking up, she asked, "Cameron, do you think you could help me here?"

Cameron blanched. It wasn't the sight of blood that made him queasy, but the gray matter swelling from the wound in Joshua's head. What the hell did she expect him to do?

"How?"

"While I clean out what I can, would you shave away some of his hair? It will be in my way when I sew him up."

Cassie worked a few minutes more. Suddenly, she shook her head. "No, this isn't going to work. I can't just close the wound. It will be a miracle if he lives through this. I wouldn't want to see it all go to waste the first time something touches his head."

Think, Cassie, think! she said to herself. As her hands worked automatically, her mind sought out a means of prolonging the man's life. "Where the hell is the doctor?" she muttered against the impossible feat she faced. Maybe he could suggest something. Maybe he had a miracle or two.

"Jessie! Get me some water and clean rags. There's blood everywhere. I can hardly see what I'm doing."

Cameron blotted up the blood as Cassie continued to gently remove the bone fragments. She had to be careful, extremely careful, lest she inflict further damage to what was probably an already damaged brain.

"Jesus, the hole's as big as a silver dollar!" Cameron commented as he leaned over her shoulder and noticed for the first time the actual size of the injury.

"That's it!" Cassie cried out with a sudden smile.

"Get a silver dollar and hammer it flat. Hurry, do it now!"

Without question, Cameron moved to do her bidding. It didn't matter that her orders made little sense to him. Cameron knew she was well versed in the art of healing, and if she didn't sport the title of doctor, it wasn't from lack of knowledge.

"Jessie, get over here and wipe this blood."

"I . . . I don't think I can."

"Get the hell over here and do it. I don't give a damn if you think you can or not. This man is going to die if we don't hurry."

Jessie, whimpering with fear and shaking from head to toe, did as she was told. Cassie ignored the housekeeper's moans of disgust and continued working. She was still at it when Cameron returned with a flattened silver dollar.

Cassie glanced at the object in his hand and nodded her approval. "Drop it in a glass of whiskey, and pour more over your hands," she ordered, then turned to the terrified housekeeper. "Stop that whining," she snapped, "and get me more light!"

A badly shaken Stevens returned from answering the door. "Doc Reilly," he stammered, "he—he's over at the—the Morgan place. The missus is—is in trouble. This is her—her seven—seventh time and the baby don't want to come."

Cassie nodded, never looking up, unconsciously muttering curses of frustration as she worked to save the man's life.

With Cameron at her side holding a lamp, she worked for almost an hour, carefully removing every splinter of bone she could see until the wound was free

99

of all but seemingly undamaged gray matter. Finally satisfied with her labors, she called for more clean rags soaked in whiskey.

Instantly, the rags were produced. As she used them to cleanse the wound of any unseen foreign matter, she ordered again, "Jessie, get me the needle and thread."

After dipping her hands, with the needle and thread, into a bowl of whiskey, Cassie carefully placed the flattened coin over the opening in the man's skull. Then, she began to sew his skin over it.

The sun was coming up, and the chirping of birds could be heard as they welcomed the new day.

Cassie sighed with exhaustion as she finished wrapping the final bandage around Joshua's head.

"Can we move him?" Cameron asked.

Cassie nodded. "Just be very careful."

Cassie was sitting in the small day room, too weary to make the trip upstairs. Her eyes were closed as she leaned back and rested her head.

"Here, take this," Cameron offered.

Cassie smiled as she opened her eyes to a half-filled snifter of brandy. "Do you suppose I'm capable of downing this much at one sitting?"

"I'd say that anyone who can curse like a man can drink like one."

Cassie swirled the amber liquid and glanced toward Cameron, who was kneeling at her side. "What are you talking about? I don't curse."

Cameron laughed. "Don't you?" His hand reached out to gently cup her chin. "I'm afraid you'll never convince Jessie of that."

"Did I curse at her?" Cassie asked, shocked.

Cameron grinned. "Well, let's just say that when you order someone to do something, you're most emphatic about it."

Cassie's cheeks colored with embarrassment. "Oh dear! I'll have to apologize. I didn't realize."

Cameron pulled her to her feet and held her against him in a warm, comforting embrace. "Finish your brandy and I'll take you upstairs."

Cassie put the glass on a nearby table. "I don't need it. I'm tired enough."

"Do you realize how wonderful you were tonight? If Joshua makes it, it's because of you."

"If Joshua makes it, it will be a miracle, plain and simple."

"You'll never convince me, lady. I saw you work."

Cassie smiled and lifted her face to him. "Cameron, there is something I have to tell you. Something very important." She could see the expectant look on his face, but a great wave of exhaustion suddenly swept over her. "But not now," she said, slumped in his arms. "It's going to take some explaining and I'm too tired."

"Tomorrow, darling," he murmured, just before his mouth took hers in a long, sweet kiss.

"Yes, tomorrow," she whispered as he lifted her in his arms. She was asleep before he took the first step.

"What was all the ruckus about last night?" Diana asked as she watched Cassie tie her hair with a bright green ribbon.

"Joshua was kicked by a horse. He was very badly hurt."

"Oh, really? Is he all right now?" Diana asked, not in the least concerned. What she really wanted was an excuse to talk to Cassie about her dress allowance. Damn, but she couldn't attract a street urchin in the rags she was forced to wear. She had to get her hands on some money.

"I hope so. I checked on him this morning. He's still sleeping."

"Cassie, I've been meaning to talk to you about some new clothes. The gowns we brought from England are really most unsuitable, unbearably hot for this climate."

Cassie nodded. "I know. Maybe Jessie has some material we could use. I'll ask her later."

"Cassie, the twins' uncle is a wealthy man. He believes you to be their mother. Surely he has mentioned an allowance."

"Actually, the subject has never come up."

"Well, could you bring it up?" Damn, but this woman had to be the stupidest bitch she had ever come across.

"Oh Diana, I couldn't." Seeing her friend's clear look of disappointment, she continued, "Don't worry, dear. Mr. Whitehall will be sending me a bank draft shortly. We'll both get a few new things when it arrives."

I only hope I'll be young enough to put them to use, Diana thought snidely to herself.

Cameron, on his way downstairs, was drawn to the sound of laughter coming from the nursery. Pausing at the open doorway, he took in the lovely sight of Cassie sprawled upon the floor, her skirt hiked up above her knees as the two babies climbed over her stomach. Each twin pushed at the other as they tried to share their cookie with Cassie.

All three faces were smeared with melted cookie. But one in particular enticed, and Cameron found himself fighting the urge to lick the sweet traces from her mouth. Being dressed for a day of business and heading for his Baltimore offices didn't deter Cameron from giving in to at least one impulse and joining in the fun. A few minutes later, his masculine laughter rang out along with Cassie's and the twins'.

"Do you have to go into the office today?" Cassie asked as she held out her arms to Christian.

"I wasn't planning on it, but as it turns out, I must."

"You'd better go before the twins cover you with cookie crumbs."

Cameron smiled as he sat on the floor opposite her. "You know, I don't think I've crawled on my hands and knees in more than thirty years."

Cassie laughed. "You make yourself sound ancient."

"I was, until you came."

Cassie's soft laughter gradually diminished as she recognized the look in his eyes and watched him move closer. "It's getting later. Don't you think you should go?"

"I thought we might find a moment to talk before I left."

Christina was clearly telling them she wanted to continue the fun as she climbed over Cassie's shoulder and fell, with a delighted childish shriek, upon her brother. With a laugh, Cassie said, "It would probably be better if we waited till later."

Cameron nodded, but showed no inclination to

leave. Instead, he leaned closer. He no longer worried about damnation if he should touch her; now he worried about losing his mind if he didn't. He was rarely in her company when he wasn't aroused. Damned already for his thoughts, he'd given up any hope of salvation in return for the pleasure of her every softly spoken word, her gentle laughter, her sweet kisses. All were like balm to his tortured soul. Their eyes held as the two squirming children vied for their attention. Neither adult seemed to notice the presence of the little ones. Cassie was suddenly breathless, and her lips parted eagerly, awaiting the taste and touch of his mouth.

Suddenly, a small, chubby hand came up to smack loudly against Cameron's slowly descending mouth. Cassie's laughter filled the air as Christina made it quite clear she didn't like the idea of being squeezed between the two of them.

"Do you suppose she did that on purpose?" Cameron asked as he took his handkerchief and wiped melted cookie from his mouth.

Cassie shrugged. "Knowing Christina as I do, I wouldn't doubt it." Her cheeks blazed as she added, "I can't say I blame her."

Cameron's heart leaped at the inference and he waited for her to go on. When she did not, he coaxed, "Don't you? I wonder why?"

"I wouldn't want to watch you kiss another."

"Why?"

She shrugged again and smiled. "I wouldn't, that's all."

"Well, I'm going to kiss you, regardless of Christina's objections." Determinedly, he put the babies from them.

Cassie smiled teasingly. "I wonder why?"

Cameron gave her a lazy grin, his dark eyes alight with pleasure as his mouth hovered above her own. "I am, that's all."

Chapter Nine

"Sonofabitch!" Cameron crumped the letter and threw it across the room. His fist slammed hard against the desk top, but his mind was too filled with rage for the pain to register. It had happened again. Once more, he'd been taken in by a pretty face, an alluring smile, and gentle ways. Would he never learn? Would he forever play the fool to the swish of an enticing skirt?

First his wife, and now Catherine. He laughed bitterly—but she wasn't Catherine, was she? No, the lying bitch wasn't his niece. Catherine was dead.

She was smart, whoever she was. He had to give her that. Jesus, when he thought of how he had suffered, how he had tried to resist her allure. Principles he hadn't suspected he possessed, had brought him indescribable torment until her irresistible appeal had left him powerless. It no longer mattered that incest had never been an issue. He had *thought* he was committing a most grievous sin, and she had allowed him to believe it! That in itself made her beneath contempt.

Christ, the experience with Sarah had almost killed

him. How many times had she cuckolded him? One would think that after the years of torture with her, he would never again be taken in by a pretty smile. Didn't he ever learn?

His mouth thinned to a hard line. How the bitch must have laughed. But it was the last laugh that counted. She didn't know it, but there was a huge debt to be paid — and he was anxiously awaiting the first installment.

Cameron stood at the window and watched as Cassie dismounted in a cloud of dust. In the hour he had waited for her, his temper had grown from wild irrationality to calm deliberation. He knew what he wanted. He knew what he was going to demand of her. His mouth twisted into a grimace as he watched her smile and say a few words to the stable boy. He doubted she'd smile so readily after today.

He paced the floor, waiting for her to enter the house. When he heard Stevens tell her he was waiting to see her in the library, he moved behind the desk and sat.

Finally, she knocked and entered the room. "Did you want to see me?"

Cameron looked up from the letter which he'd retrieved and placed once again on his desk. Looking at her flushed cheeks and windblown hair, his chest twisted with the longing he had for so long despised. Nodding briefly, he directed her to sit. His voice was low and strained when he finally broke the silence between them. "You seem healthy today, Catherine."

Cassie's fine brows rose with surprise. Her hand

moved as she sought to bring some semblance of order to her gypsy locks. She knew it was most unseemly for a lady to look anything but pale and delicate, but she wasn't about to apologize for her robust, healthy appearance. "Had you presumed me ill, Cameron?"

Cameron shrugged as a cruel smile twisted his lips. "According to this letter, I'd expect at least some degree of decomposition, since you're thirteen months dead."

Cassie gasped and shot to her feet, her eyes huge, her rosy cheeks paling to a sickly gray hue. "I . . . I . . ." she stammered, desperately seeking something to say.

Cameron chuckled humorlessly. He stood, walked around the desk and leaned his hip against the edge. Arms crossed over his broad chest, he looked down at her with an approving nod. "That's better," he said, "now you're beginning to look more the part. No self-respecting corpse would be seen looking so damned appealing, so long after her demise."

Cassie stepped back, gasping for breath as the room swayed around her. He knew! Good God, he knew, and he was in a towering rage. It wasn't supposed to happen like this.

"I . . . I was going to tell you . . . " she began in a quavering voice.

Cameron lifted a sardonic brow, and he smiled at her without a trace of tenderness. "Of course you were, my dear Catherine, but one does wonder when." His mouth hardened. "Excuse me, but what *is* your name?"

Cassie wet her dry lips with the tip of her tongue.

108

She longed to deny the truth, but knew, of course, the uselessness of continuing her masquerade. All was lost. God, why had she waited so long? Why hadn't she told him? With a hopeless slump of her slender shoulders, she replied softly, "Cassandra Devon."

Cameron nodded. "Catherine's half sister."

Cassie's head hung despondently. Her world was coming to an end. Surely after her deceit, he'd ask her to leave his home. The children would be lost to her forever. How was she to bear it?

She had tried to tell him. God, why hadn't she insisted? She opened her mouth to explain, but no words would come. What could she possibly say to erase the cold hatred in his eyes? What difference would it make now?

The room was totally silent but for the steady ticking of the mantel clock. Cassie waited, her heart pounding with dread. When would he speak? When would he begin his tirade? God, but she couldn't stand the tension much longer. She longed to run, like a coward, but forced herself to remain. Running would bring no answers. This was something she had to face.

Cameron watched her for a long moment before he moved. Slowly, he slid his arms out of his coat and hung it over the back of a chair. He was unbuttoning his shirt as he walked to the library door.

The sound of the door being locked crashed upon her ears and vibrated through every trembling fiber of her body.

He was moving toward her now, and the look in his eyes left Cassie little doubt as to his intentions.

She backed up as he approached. She hadn't expected this. "Don't do this, Cameron!" she pleaded.

Cameron stopped halfway across the room and smiled, "No?" He laughed. "Why not?"

"There's more between us than this."

Cameron chuckled cruelly. "Oh, indeed there is. There's lies, there's deceit, and we mustn't forget the forbidden pleasures of incest, must we?"

Cassie put out her hand as if to halt the advance. He couldn't take her, not in rage! God, she couldn't bear that. "Cameron, please," she choked as her eyes grew wide with alarm. "Stop!"

"That's good. That's very good, my dear." His expression was grim as he continued to move toward her. "A word that has haunted my thoughts for many a night. *Stop* tormenting yourself. Nothing can come of it. She is your niece. *Stop* tossing at night with wanting her. *Stop* watching her every movement. *Stop* listening for her laughter. *Stop* waiting for her to enter a room so your eyes might feast upon her loveliness."

His hand reached out. A rough knuckle caressed the smoothness of her cheek. "No!" she cried as she bolted and tried to run. But he was too quick for her, catching her arm and pulling her hard against him.

"Yes," he insisted as his hand reached into the thickness of her hair, yanking roughly until her face was raised to his.

She gasped for breath as with just one arm he pinned her fast to his unyielding body. "Don't do this, Cameron. Let me explain."

He laughed harshly. "More lies? I think not. No, the

110

time for talking is long past." His hand left her hair and lingered for just an instant at the bodice of her silk blouse. Then, his fingers hooked inside the material and ripped it to her waist.

Cassie paled. Both chemise and blouse hung in tatters, exposing her nakedness to the blazing hunger in his dark eyes. "No!" she cried, and her hand slapped hard against his cheek. But he was not deterred; he noticed nothing except the lush beauty of her naked breasts. His eyes were glazed with lust as desire for her took complete control of his senses. He was crazy with need, possessed of but one objective. He had to have her. He had suffered enough.

Cassie shruggled fiercely, but he was too strong for her. And her twisting, squirming movements against his fevered body only served to further inflame him. She panted, out of breath from her efforts to free herself, and the heaving of her flushed breasts drove him wild.

Lifting her higher against him, he fastened his mouth to one coral tip. Cassie stiffened and gasped with shock. She couldn't believe this was happening to her. She couldn't believe this man capable of hurting her. She'd never have imagined this to be the payment for her lies. Banishment, yes, but not ravishment. But, of course, she had not taken into consideration the hunger he had kept at bay these last months, nor the crushing disappointment in discovering that she was no better than all the rest.

Cameron's mouth left her breast, his eyes black with anger as he shook her roughly. "You want this as much as I. Stop lying. For once, tell me the truth."

His mouth closed over hers then in a brutal kiss that caused only pain. Cassie kept her lips tightly closed. If he meant to take her, she would not make it easy.

His mouth forced her lips apart and his tongue probed determinedly against her teeth, but she steadily refused him entrance. His hand reached for her hair again, pulling at the heavy mass until tears glistened in her eyes. And still she refused.

He yanked at her hair relentlessly until she cried out in pain, her mouth opening helplessly to receive his punishment. And then, quite suddenly, it was no longer punishment that was being inflicted. His kiss gentled, his hand soothed the injury to her scalp, and his arm softened around her waist.

"Cassie, Cassie," he murmured against her mouth, and she felt that familiar heat burst instantly to life. She was lost now, had no control. She couldn't stop her hands from moving beneath the fabric of his open shirt, grazing the warmth of his chest. Her fingers threaded through the curling black hair there, lingered at his nipples, then moved slowly downward, until his trousers prevented further exploration. She had wanted this for so long; she ached with the need to touch him, to have him touch her. She couldn't remember why she had fought him, why she had tried to stop this.

He felt her sudden response and groaned at the uninhibited eagerness of it. His senses swam with her touch, her scent, her gentle caresses. But she couldn't fool him. He knew what she was. She wanted it as

112

much as he. And if she wanted it gentle, it made her no less a whore.

He drew her down to the rug, his mouth never leaving hers as he stripped away the rest of her clothes. He raised his head then and smiled, truly smiled for the first time in hours as his gaze devoured her from head to toe. His mouth came down to her lips again, leaving her awash in sweet sensation. Her mind swam, she was floating beyond reality, knowing only the need building within her.

Her body moved against him, urging him on, pleading with him to give her more as she whispered his name again and again. His mouth moved to her neck, over her shoulder, nibbling, kissing, searing her flesh, until chills ran down her spine and she arched to meet him.

Cameron captured her hips and cradled her close to him, moving against her, rubbing and grinding, exciting her satiny flesh with the roughness of his clothing until she screamed out with her need for him. He pushed her to her back then, and allowed his mouth to run the length of her, smiling as she groaned and shivered beneath his lips.

She was lost in a world of pure sensation. She'd never known anything could be this wonderful and she ached for more. His mouth was at her breast, making every nerve tingle, and she thrust herself forward, offering herself up to him. His mouth moved downward, over her rounded belly, licking at her smooth flesh, taking the taste of her into him, coming finally to linger at the junction of her thighs. Cassie stiffened at the caress. He couldn't mean to touch her there! He couldn't mean to kiss her in so private a place! "No," she murmured, her words sounding slurred as if she were drugged. "Cameron, don't."

Cameron chuckled. She was good. There was just enough hesitation in her touch, just enough innocence in her manner. If he didn't know better, he'd think . . .

But he did know better, and he didn't want to think. Not now. Not with her lying so lusciously giving beneath him.

His tongue flicked out and tasted her moist, musk-scented softness, and his mind spun, trapped in the seductive delicacy. He buried his face in the velvety sweetness and heard her gasp with the shock of it. How long had he yearned for this? God, but he couldn't remember a time when he hadn't wanted to touch her, to breathe her, to taste her.

Cassie tugged at his hair, until he captured her hands and held them to her side. She tried to squirm away, but his weight kept her hips from all but the slightest movement. "Cameron, please," she moaned. "It's not right. Stop!"

But Cameron ignored her urgent plea. He'd have her, and on his own terms. She could play her coy little games, but he knew her for the lying cheat she was. She could plead her innocence forever, but he knew better. He wanted to weep with the pain of knowing better. *No, don't think,* he told himself. *Don't let her get to you again. Enjoy the pleasure of her body. Enjoy it until you die of the ecstasy.*

He tried to rationalize away the thrill of her touch.

114

She's no different than any other, he swore. If he imagined greater pleasure with this woman, it was only because he'd had to wait so long to take her.

She heard him groan with delight as her hips rose eagerly now to meet the wild caresses of his mouth. She couldn't stop the delicious torment, no longer wanted to. She whimpered with the exquisite sensations. She knew it was wrong. She shouldn't be allowing it, but, oh God, it felt so good! She wanted more. Oh please, more! Her stomach was tightening to an almost painful ache. She stiffened — and then, the blinding wonder of release came at last, washing over her in wave after wave of ecstasy. "Yes!" she cried out as her head twisted back and forth. "Yes, yes, yes."

She lay still then, utterly spent, her heart thudding. She couldn't move. She had never felt such utter exhaustion, such perfect bliss. Her eyes were closed, and a tiny smile touched her lips. She felt him move. He was sliding up the length of her. "I love you," she whispered softly. He released her hands, and her fingers slid into his dark hair. "Oh God," she said again, "I love you."

Cameron's chest constricted at her lying words. Oh God, if only, if only . . . He laughed harshly, bitterly, and she opened her eyes to see his dark gaze filled with pain and hate. "Sure you do, honey," he said. "As much as I love you."

"No, wait," she begged. "Let me explain." She watched as he stripped off his clothes.

"Later." He grinned maliciously. "Explain later."

"Cameron, please, listen to me." She tried to rise,

but he pushed her back to the floor and instantly straddled her body.

"Shut up," he growled angrily. He didn't want to hear anything she had to say, couldn't bear to listen to any more lies. Brutally, he entered her body, then gasped as he discovered her innocence. He stopped all movement. For a long moment, he looked down at her, bewildered. My God, she was a virgin. He could have sworn . . .

Tears glistened in her eyes. She didn't want him to take her in hate. "Please," she murmured softly.

It didn't matter, he told himself. What was done was done. It didn't change a thing. She was still a liar.

"Cameron," she whimpered.

He ignored her plea and began to move within her. His heart pounded, his breath became harsh and rasping. It was going to happen too fast. He had waited so long, he couldn't wait any longer. But it didn't matter, she was with him. He could hear her soft moans of pleasure; she was almost there. A minute more! He only had to wait a minute more.

Suddenly, he grew afraid. Afraid of the power she had over him. He was possessed with the need to hurt her, to make her suffer the way he had. He had to fight this, had to break free of her spell. But it was too late . . . Much too late. He quickened his movements, his heart filled with torment. She was evil. A liar, a cheat, and God knew what else—and still he wanted her. He felt the first tremors of her release and he wanted to curse her. He wanted to strike out, to see her suffer. And then—his body stiffened in wondrous agony, and

116

all he wanted was to take her into him and never let her go. God help him, he'd never be free. "Bitch, whoring bitch," he groaned, knowing the words a lie but saying them anyway.

Cassie's heart contracted at the cruel words, but she was too far gone to stop her body's instinctive response to the diabolical pleasure he was giving her. She wanted to kick, to bite, to hurt him as his words hurt her, but she couldn't stop this wonderful, terrible wave of pleasure mounting inside her. "I hate you," she gasped, even as her body was suffused with a sensation she had never before known, an exquisite all consuming assault on her senses that was building . . . building . . . she pressed his hips to bring him closer, deeper. Now!" she cried, her head thrown back, her body arched to take all he could give her. She clutched at him savagely, her nails raking his flesh. "Oh God, now!"

He heard her low, agonized cries, felt her body shudder and convulse beneath him. He grimaced, as if in pain. Nothing mattered now, but to take her in the way he wished to, and then to have her again and again — despite his hatred, or perhaps because of it. For an instant, he thought to push her away, to torture her as he'd been tortured. But it was too late; she was taking his heart, his soul, just as she would take his seed. He drove into her, harder, faster, thrusting deeply, forcing her to take all of him. Suddenly, his body stiffened, then was racked by a powerful shudder — and they cried out together as release came for both in sweet, almost unendurable rapture.

117

He lay slumped upon her, helpless, unable to do more than draw in shallow, gasping breaths. And with each breath, he seemed to draw in more of her haunting essence, a powerful drug that delighted his very soul and left him helpless, unable to do anything but drink more deeply of the delicious opiate. For a long moment only the sounds of their ragged breathing filled the room. Cameron rolled off her at last, and lay staring sightlessly at the intricate designs of the ceiling. He still couldn't quite catch his breath. Nothing like this had ever happened to him before, and he feared for his very life should it happen again.

What was he to do? He was totally under the spell of a woman who lied as expertly as she made love. He couldn't bear the agony again. He'd kill this one. There'd be no more duels of honor. He touched his finger to the scarred cheek. No, this time she'd be the one to die.

Cassie came slowly to her feet and silently dressed, thanking God for every moment that he did not speak. She wouldn't look at him, couldn't look at him without crying. How could he have done that? How could he have turned something so beautiful into something so degrading? It was lust, not love. Cassie shivered with disgust and self-loathing, thinking of how eagerly she had yielded to him. There was only one thing for her to do. Money or not, she was somehow going home. Before this man drove her out of her mind, she was getting out of here.

Holding her torn blouse together with shaking fingers, she was almost at the door before she finally

118

spoke. "I'm leaving this house today."

Cameron's guts twisted at her words, but he forced his voice to remain calm. "I can't stop you. Actually, I don't care where you go, or what you do."

Cassie felt tears sting her eyes, but willed them away. She had opened the library door when he spoke again. "The children will, of course, be staying."

"No!" She spun about and faced him, her eyes wide with fear.

"No?" his mouth turned up in a malicious smile.

"You can't do that. I have just as much right."

He shrugged as he dressed, unconcernedly buttoning his pants as if she weren't present, his casual movements belying the tumultuous experience they had just shared. His smile was hard, cruel, as he finally turned and took in her stricken expression. "You may be right. You are their aunt. I am their uncle. Why don't we go to court and see who has the most right to them?"

Cassie knew, as well as he, she didn't stand a chance against him. There wasn't a court, in either England or America, that would give the babies to a nearly destitute young woman. "Cameron, please. Don't do this," she pleaded, forgetting the need to keep the tattered edges of her blouse together. Her fingers twisted nervously. "I can't leave without them. I've cared for them since they were born." Oh God, it was just as she'd feared. He was taking them from her. She couldn't stay here, couldn't live under the same roof with him. But how could she go? How could she leave her babies?

Cameron forced his gaze from her open blouse and willed himself to control his emotions. He knew she had no choice but to stay. She had no money, no home to return to. He hated her, he felt nothing but disgust, but he couldn't help himself; he wanted her no matter what she was. And no matter the pain it caused him to keep her, he wasn't about to let her go. The knowledge that she had to stay, willing or not, caused him to groan silently. At the moment, he wasn't sure if what he felt was joy or horror. Shrugging with elaborate indifference, he said, "Then stay."

Chapter Ten

As he addressed her, Cassie's face turned scarlet, and she felt every inch the whore he had accused her of being. She could feel his gaze on her and knew it was filled, as was his voice, with cold hatred. Her eyes held to her plate, refusing to look at the man at the head of the dining table. Her back stiffened with anger and pride. She wouldn't take a goddamned penny from this man. It was enough she was forced to live here and eat his food. She'd die before she'd let him dress her as well.

Where in heaven's name was the money she'd sent for? She had written months ago, and then, fearing the loss of that letter, had penned another. And still she heard nothing. She vowed to write again, this very night.

Diana smiled at him sweetly, unaware of the battle that raged between the two. "Oh dear me, you're much too generous," she gushed, batting her eyelashes at Cameron.

He shook his head, beaming at her, openly flirting. "Not at all. It only stands to reason that since I've taken you from your home, I should see to all your needs. With my standing in the community, I couldn't allow my *niece* — " Cassie cringed at the inflection of distaste he gave to the word — "and her companion to dress shabbily. Not that you look anything but lovely," he added quickly, and for Diana's benefit alone.

Cassie made a halfhearted effort to eat, but succeeded only in pushing her food around her plate. She couldn't eat. The lump in her throat wouldn't allow her to even swallow water. He was deliberately trying to degrade her. His cruel, cutting remarks were obviously not enough. Why did the man hate her so? Yes, she had lied, but judging by the way he treated her, you'd think she had murdered someone. She steadfastly refused to look at him. Not that he seemed to notice. Since the episode in the library, nearly a week ago, Cameron had spent almost every available moment either away from the house, or with Diana. On the rare occasion when Cassie was unlucky enough to find herself in his company, he was, to put it mildly, downright nasty.

When she could take no more of the abuse, she gave as good as she got — and there were times when she would have sworn he was enjoying himself. Still, she couldn't stop the hurt which never seemed to lessen in degree. Since the time that they had lain together, his opinion of her had clearly worsened. The very sight of her seemed to disgust him. Cassie wondered how he would act when he had taken Diana as well. She sighed softly and bit at her lower lip, instantly contrite. That was cruel. Just because Cameron jumped from bed to bed, there was no reason to assume that Diana would be as weak as she herself had been.

She had no one to blame but herself. She should have told him from the beginning. She should have stayed in England. Now, it appeared, he wanted her to dress as well as his other women. Well, he could take his money and choke on it. And she sincerely hoped he would.

"Excuse me." Cassie came to her feet and threw her napkin on her plate. "I think I hear the children."

"Wait!" he commanded.

Cassie stopped in midstep and turned to see him coming around the table. "I've a need to talk to you. Sunshine will see to the babies. Step into the library, if you would."

Cassie shivered at the cold hard look in his eyes, but determinedly stood her ground. And when it looked as if she might refuse his invitation, he took her arm and led her out of the room. "You will excuse us, Diana?" he asked over his shoulder. "I've business to discuss with my niece."

If I would? Cassie repeated silently as he almost dragged her along. What option did she have?

The door slammed behind them, and as he abruptly released her arm, Cassie was almost flung into the center of the room. Cameron moved nonchalantly toward a table holding an array of bottles and glasses. He poured himself a drink without asking if she might like one. She bristled at his rudeness. Why, she wondered, did she allow herself to be bothered so by this beast's every action.

She stood silent, breathing heavily, trying to maintain a cool indifference. But then, her eyes, with a will of their own, darted to the carpet, and all the shameful memories flooded back. Her cheeks grew crimson. She had to get out of here. She could not stand this room, or the man in it, and she wasn't about to suffer any more than she had to.

"How lovely you blush," he remarked, praying his voice would not betray the rush of emotion that never failed to overwhelm him in her presence. He strolled toward her. His heart raced, and he found himself quite breathless just looking at her. He tensed, and fought away the urge to reach out and touch her. Still, he couldn't control the need to move closer. What power did this woman have? Why was it always so hard to keep away from her? Even knowing what she was didn't lessen his longing for her. "If one didn't know better, one might almost believe you a complete innocent."

Cassie's head snapped up. Her voice was shaking as angry tears welled in her eyes. "Well, one could never make that mistake with you, could they?"

He laughed, amused by the way she'd come back at him. "At least I'm honest about it. Can you say the same?"

Cassie sighed. "Why do you find it necessary to constantly insult me? You've had what you wanted. Why can't you leave me alone now? Why did you drag me in here?"

He laughed again. Had what he wanted? Did she think one crumb would suffice when a banquet was forever beckoning?

"I got the impression that you were throwing my generosity back in my face."

"Did you?" she retorted snidely. "I wonder why."

Cameron shrugged. "Perhaps because you neglected to thank me."

Thank him! Thank him for making her feel like a whore? "Perhaps because you neglected to offer the use of the account as an uncle would to his niece."

"Didn't I?" He grinned. "How did I offer it, then?"

"Is there a need to explain?" She mimicked his words: " 'I feel I owe you for all you've done.' Just what have I done to entitle myself to an unlimited clothing allowance?"

"What do you think you've done?" He gave a low, nasty chuckle. "You've made this house a home with your presence."

"I think your attitude is disgusting," Cassie shot back.

His smile was taunting. "Diana didn't seem to think it disgusting. She jumped at the opportunity to spend my money."

"Perhaps Diana doesn't know you as well as I. If she did, I doubt she would have been so sugary in her thanks." Cassie bit her lip, immediately contrite. "That was unkind." Her eyes flashed. "It's you who are deserving of my wrath."

Cameron shrugged, obviously indifferent to her anger. "The account was meant for you."

"I don't need it."

"You can't intend wearing those heavy wools and satins now? You must be suffocating in this heat."

"I'm just fine, thank you."

"Are you?"

"I said I was."

"You will use the account, Cassie. I'll not have others speak of my miserly ways." And when her jaw tightened with determination and she refused to reply, refused even to look at him, he continued nastily,

"Let's say it's payment due."

Cassie gasped. Her hand flew out without thinking, connecting smartly with his cheek. "You bastard!"

She moved back a step, suddenly aware of what she had done. He moved to close the distance between them. She wanted to stand fast and not show her fear, but as he continued to stalk her, she began to panic. His eyes were narrowed and dark with anger, and his mouth was twisted in a malicious sneer. "That's what you wanted, wasn't it? That's why you played your masquerade. What's the matter now? Isn't it enough?" He laughed cruelly. "Well, you can't blame me if I want to see more before I up the offer."

Cassie gave a silent curse. She had gone too far. She had aroused his anger, and anger was only a hairs-breadth from passion. Her heart thudded wildly as her eyes darted around the room, seeking a means of escape. It was clear what he had in mind, and she wasn't about to succumb to another bout of lust. "I don't want anything from you," she said, stalling for time.

He continued to stalk her with an evil gleam in his eye. "Don't you?" he asked insinuatingly.

"If you touch me, I'll scream," she warned as she moved back yet another step. Her voice shook, and she cursed the fact that he knew she was afraid.

"Will you?" He laughed again. "And who will stop what I've in mind?"

"I'm not one of your slaves, to do with as you will." She stepped back farther, almost at the door now.

"No, you're not. They wouldn't dare hit their master."

The door was pressed against her back. She tried to

move to her right, but his hand came out and prevented escape. "You're not my master."

She moved to her left and his free hand halted further movement. "Aren't I?"

As his mouth came close to hers, Cassie grew dizzy with his clean male scent. She tried to fight it. She closed her eyes and held her breath lest that intoxicating scent weaken her resolve. She had to get control of her emotions. He wanted her, but it was only her body he wanted. That knowledge alone should have been enough to disgust her. But it wasn't. Suddenly, she just didn't care, for she knew she wanted him easily as much. "I hate you," she gasped, suddenly breathless with desire.

"Good," he breathed, his mouth inches from hers. "You hate me, but you want me, don't you?" She didn't answer, but gasped and shivered as his hands moved from the door to cup her breasts. "Don't you?" he insisted.

Why was it so hard to breathe? He was hateful, he was cruel. She should despise him, but when he touched her, when he looked at her like this. Oh God, when he looked at her like this . . .

"Yes," she murmured weakly, eyes closed, head thrown back against the door. She cursed her weakness, unable to deny the truth, unable to resist his temptation any longer. "Yes, I want you," she cried as she flung herself shamelessly into his arms.

Hungrily, greedily, she sought out the taste of him, her soft sob lost in his deep animal growl. The sounds of their mingled gasps and low groans filled the silent room. She clutched at him, pressing against him, holding to him as if she'd never let go.

Cameron swayed, almost staggered with the impact of mind-shattering desire. She was in his arms at last. There hadn't been a moment in the last week when he hadn't longed to touch her again. Now he wondered if he'd ever have the strength to let her go. Her feet were off the floor, her arms around his neck, her lips fastened wondrously to his. His heart pounded wildly, threatening to burst. He couldn't believe the sheer joy that filled his being. Why had be avoided her this last week? Why hadn't he taken her again and again?

Gradually, their hunger for each other gentled to a slow-burning savoring of remembered scents and textures, a thrilling rediscovery of secret pleasures as tongues met and caressed, sliding, stroking, probing. He held her tightly, deepening the kiss while his fingers threaded through the thick red silk of her hair.

"Cassie, Cassie," he groaned, his voice breaking with the pain of wanting her. Tearing his mouth from hers, he grazed her sweet smelling hair, her eyes, her cheeks, swiftly returning to the luscious taste of her lips.

She moaned under his passionate assault. It was easy, so easy to want him. No matter how he might treat her, she wanted him.

He pressed her firmly between the door and his lower body. His mouth never left hers as he worked feverishly to undo the fastenings of her bodice, desperate to touch her naked flesh once more. His hands, hot and callused, found and covered her lush young breasts, kneading and lifting them as he brushed his thumbs over her darkened nipples. A low, guttural sound of pleasure came from deep within her throat.

She, too, was wild in her need to touch. She pushed aside his coat, and when her shaking fingers couldn't work the buttons of his shirt, she pulled the material free of his pants and slid her hands against the warmth of his flesh.

Burning for each other, their cheeks were flushed, eyes glazed, hair and clothing in wild disarray when a knock sounded at the door.

"Mr. Chandler, sir. Mr. Billings is here to see you."

They broke apart as fast as they had come together. Shocked at the intrusion, Cassie staggered and would have fallen except for Cameron's steadying arm. She gasped for breath, her head reeling as Cameron gently began rebuttoning her dress. His knuckles glided over her soft skin, touching the enticing flesh more than was necessary, until the closing of the bodice became as erotic as the opening had been. His eyes never left her as he called out, "Tell Mr. Billings I'll be with him shortly."

"Use the other door," he said, nodding toward it, unable as yet to take his hands from her. "I'll stall him."

He released her, and she began to move away. Suddenly, he grabbed her arm and pulled her back to face him. His mouth had regained its harsh lines, and his eyes showed none of the tenderness that had just passed between them. "You will use the account!" he ordered.

Cassie glared back at him. Wrenching her arm from his grasp, she marched toward the library door. Just before she opened it, she glanced over her shoulder. "Go to hell!" she said venomously.

Cameron grinned as he watched the door slam behind her. Jesus, but she was something.

* * *

Cassie had put down her book and was just about to snuff out the candle beside her bed when she heard the clatter of carriage wheels coming up the brick drive. It was late. She had heard Mr. Billings leave hours ago, and soon after Cameron had come upstairs.

Cassie sighed and came to her feet, sure that someone was in need of her services. She had been administering to Cameron's people — she couldn't bear to call them slaves — and her reputation for healing was slowly spreading throughout the neighboring plantations. Since Dr. Reilly was frequently incapable of helping his patients, due to his more than occasional overindulgence in spirits, the chore had quickly fallen to her.

Cassie pulled her dress on, smoothing the full skirt around her hips as she hurriedly slid her feet into soft kid slippers. She was hurrying down the stairs when the loud voices below caused her a moment's hesitation.

Cameron was speaking with a woman and their voices were tight with anger. "I'm sorry, Mr. Chandler, but I find I must insist! The child is willful, disobedient and unrepentant when punished. She causes more trouble than ten of the others. Why, the influence on my young ladies will soon be . . ."

Cassie moved quietly to the open doors of the library and peered inside. Cameron was standing with his back to her, towering over a woman of undistinguished countenance. She was older than Cassie had first imagined from the sound of her voice, and unusually thin, almost emaciated. Her blue eyes shone with distaste and her mouth was pursed in unattractive severity.

"Woman!" Cameron shouted, interrupting her, "I advise you to stop right there." He took a deep breath, obviously straining for control, then continued more calmly, "There are many schools such as yours. I have no doubt I can find the right one for Meghan." He gave her a short, dismissive nod, "Good night."

Without another word, the woman squared her shoulders, walked stiffly past a wide-eyed Cassie, down the hall, and out the front door.

Cassie was just about to turn toward the stairs again, knowing this was none of her concern, when she heard Cameron speak again. "This is the third school in as many years, Meghan. Do you suppose all but you were at fault?"

Curiosity got the better of Cassie. She hadn't seen anyone else in the room. Who was it he spoke to? Cassie moved into the room, craning her neck as she tried to see around Cameron's tall figure. Still, she saw no one else.

"Come in, Cassie," Cameron snapped, clearly annoyed. "If you must know what's going on, ask. Don't skulk around corners like some cowardly milksop."

Cassie jumped, and flushed guiltily. An instant later, her lips thinned in anger, for his nasty words, instead of causing her a moment's pause at her intrusion, only brought a rise of her temper. "I was not skulking about, Mr. Chandler, as you so unjustifiably put it. I simply thought I heard you speaking to someone."

"That I was." Cameron sighed almost sadly as he moved to sit behind his desk. "This is Miss Chandler.

131

Meghan, Miss Devon."

Cassie's gaze dropped to about hip level. No wonder she hadn't seen anyone. He had been speaking to a child. Cassie's eyes widened with amazement. Miss Chandler? Cameron's child? Cassie was confused. Why had he never mentioned her before? And why had she been sent off to school? The girl couldn't have been more than eight. Surely, she was too young to leave her father.

Cassie's face broke into a smile as she took in the sight of the waiflike child, standing alone before his desk. But for the blond curls framing a petite-featured face, she was the image of her father, with huge dark eyes exactly the same color as Cameron's. Cassie knew that, grown to womanhood, this girl would break many a heart.

"She's lovely, Cameron."

"I'm happy you think so," Cameron responded, his tone almost bored as his eyes moved to the papers on his desk. "Now, if one could say the same of her temperament . . ." He sighed with something like disgust and left the sentence unfinished.

"Take her upstairs, will you? Ask Jessie to put her to bed."

"No need to bother Jessie. I'll put her to bed."

As Cassie helped Meghan ready herself for bed, she remembered the overheard conversation. Could the snarling woman have been referring to this lovely creature? Surely not. Why Meghan was hardly more than a baby. How could she be the cause of any trouble?

"How long have you been at school?"

"Three years, all told."

"How old are you?"

"Eight and a half."

Why was it children always measured age in half years? Cassie, restrained the urge to smile, for Meghan's eyes were solemn and her demeanor sad. Cassie did not want the child to think that she was laughing at her.

"My name is Cassie, Meghan," Cassie remarked as she settled the child beneath the coverlet and smoothed the bed free of wrinkles. "I hope we can become friends."

"I don't think so."

"Why?" Cassie asked, surprised and more than a little intrigued with this strangely dispassionate child.

"I won't be staying that long." She sighed softly. "Father always sends me away. He doesn't like me."

"Good God, what nonsense," Cassie gasped. "Of course he likes you. Why, any father would love a little girl like you."

"Not him," Meghan said softly, appearing not the least upset.

"You seem so sure of it, Meghan. And yet the notion doesn't bother you."

For a brief moment, Meghan's dark eyes filled with incredible hurt. And then, just as suddenly, the pain vanished and was replaced with her previous cool reserve. Her eyes grew hard with denial. "It did once," she shrugged, and then continued with a wisdom that belied her tender years, "but I've grown accustomed to the idea.

"Miss Handley says, 'You can't help loving or not loving. It's just the way things are sometimes.'"

"How very kind of your Miss Handley to relate that

133

piece of information," Cassie remarked, her sarcasm directed toward the unknown woman who'd been stupid enough to inflict such hurt upon a helpless child. She hoped for both their sakes, she'd not soon lay eyes on the fool.

Still, regardless of other people's cruel remarks, what child could believe such a thing of her parent? — unless that parent had indeed displayed a lack of concern. Cassie felt her chest constrict with pain. This had to be the case. Damn that man to hell. Was he insane to turn this child away? Cassie knew well enough his hatred of her, despite his momentary passionate lapses, but to hate an innocent child? What could Meghan have done to incur his wrath? What was wrong with the man?

Cassie meant to find out, and she meant to do it now. She'd never be able to sleep with the knowledge of his cruelty.

A moment later, she stormed into the library and slammed the door behind her. Her lips were thinned in anger, her eyes filled with hostility. "I've a need to speak with you."

Cameron sighed without looking up from his papers. "If you mean to berate me for my careless words, I apologize in advance."

"Mr. Chandler, it matters not how you fling your insults at me. I'm a grown woman. My shoulders are broad enough." Cassie moved farther into the room and placed her hands on her hips. "What irks is the cruelty Meghan has been subjected to."

Cameron's head snapped up. "What the hell are you talking about? When have I been cruel? The girl attends the best of schools. She is denied nothing that is in my power to give."

"With the possible exception of your love."

Cameron laughed mirthlessly. "I see, it didn't take her long to find a champion. She is much like her mother, I think."

"Do you? Well, I'm sorry to disappoint you, but the fact is she is much like her father."

"I wouldn't know."

Cassie gave him a look that clearly bespoke her confusion.

"She is not mine, Cassie," Cameron sighed, his expression devoid of all emotion. "Her mother informed me of that lovely fact—much to her satisfaction, I might add—not long before she ran off."

Cassie laughed.

Cameron frowned. "I'm happy to see you find this amusing."

"It's only laughable because you believed her. Cameron, I've no knowledge of your relationship with your wife, but I can tell you this. Meghan is your child. If you looked at her but once, you'd see it for yourself."

He looked up at her in sharp surprise, then fell silent, considering her words. Astonishment quickly became confusion, confusion turned to pain, and pain to fury as he stared at the lady before him. "Are you telling me . . . ?"

"I am. I take it you're not blind as well as a fool. Look at her, if you harbor any doubts."

Cameron came quickly to his feet, his intent obvious.

"But before you do," Cassie added, "I wish to say a word. I hold you in the lowest regard, for in my mind, it doesn't matter whether she is yours or not. She was an innocent whom you sought to use as an instrument of revenge. I'll not soon forget the monster in you." She turned on her heel then, and left him. Her anger at him was so overwhelming, she dared not remain.

Two days later, Cassie walked into the drawing room to find Meghan and her father engaged in gentle, loving conversation. As Jessie led the child off to luncheon, Cameron looked up with a sheepish smile.

"Might I have a moment of your time?" Cassie inquired.

Cameron sighed. "Cassie, I fear I've not the strength for another assault on my character."

Cassie's cheeks burned with embarrassment. "I do apologize for my unforgivable outburst, sir."

"You need not. You were quite correct in your assumptions."

"Perhaps, but it wasn't my place to interfere."

"Sit down, Cassie." He nodded toward a chair that faced him. "It's time, I think, to explain." He waited until she settled herself before him. "I offer no excuses, merely my reasons—be they valid or not—for treating the child so.

"To say her mother and I had not the most perfect of marriages, is to put it mildly. I could hardly stand the sight of her, while she, in turn, felt much the same. Be that as it may—" he shook his head—"Meghan, from the moment of her birth, was the love of my life. I kept her with me every minute I could. Never had I felt closer to another human being.

"I hesitate to tell you of my wife and our overwhelming problems." Cameron stroked the scar on his cheek in an unconscious gesture. "To put it charitably, I had every reason to believe her when she told me Meghan's father was another."

Cassie felt her heart twist with pity. She could only imagine the pain he must have suffered. Emotionally estranged from his wife, he had then lost the only living creature he had loved.

Cameron shrugged. "I can only say the shock was devastating. My whole world fell apart. I found myself unable to look upon the child without disgust. I know I blamed an innocent for her mother's sin, but no matter how I tried, I was unable to help myself. Her presence was a constant reminder of my wife's treachery."

"And an insult to your manly ego," Cassie added, and then gasped at her daring.

Cameron smiled sadly. "I suppose. Although I didn't see it as such at the time.

"Needless to say, I have realized my error. I have much to thank you for and hope you can forgive . . ."

"Mr. Chandler, it's not I from whom you must seek forgiveness, but Meghan."

"I have."

Cassie smiled her relief and was about to speak further on the subject when Diana came into the room in a whirl of vivid color. Cassie bit her lower lip as she came to her feet. She felt as colorless as a washed out rag next to her friend. Diana fluttered her pink silk fan coquettishly. "How do you like it? she asked, turning a complete circle and curtsying prettily, all for Cameron's benefit.

"Lovely," he remarked as his gaze moved to Cassie.

"Why aren't you wearing your new things?"

"Because she didn't buy anything." Diana laughed. "Isn't that the silliest thing you've ever heard? Why, I don't know of any woman who wouldn't turn green with envy, except for her."

"Why didn't she?" Cameron asked as he studied Cassie, his eyes delving deep into hers, probing, searching for an answer.

"She says she has enough, but I don't know any woman who ever has enough."

"Would the two of you mind not discussing me as though I weren't here? I can answer for myself, thank you, Diana."

Diana shrugged. She had never met a woman so stupid. But, if the simpleton wanted to look like an old brown hen, that was all right with her. Every day she seemed to be making more progress with Chandler, and with these new clothes — she licked her lips with anticipation — he wouldn't stand a chance against her. When she became the new Mrs. Cameron Chandler, the first thing she'd do would be to marry the bitch off. They didn't need her around.

Cameron's dark gaze narrowed as he calmly allowed it to run the length of Cassie's figure, from her head to her toes, and back up again. "I told you to use the account."

"And I told you . . ." She blushed, remembering exactly what she had told him and not daring to the use the words again. Particularly not in Diana's hearing.

Cameron chuckled, knowing what she had been about to say. "What?" he pressed tauntingly.

"I told you I don't need anything."

138

His eyes danced with humor, and while Diana seemed occupied with examining the intricacies of her ruffled skirt, he mouthed the word, "coward."

Cassie could not stop her smile, nor her sharp intake of breath at his change of expression. How could he look at her like that? Didn't he care if Diana saw him? She squirmed uncomfortably as his dark gaze moved over her. She tried to close her eyes, tried to will away her answering need, but she might as well have tried to stop the wind. He was touching her. Cassie could feel it as surely as if he had reached out and used his hands. And she could not stop her matching response from bubbling to the surface. Her cheeks were flushed, her breathing shallow, and still he continued to caress her with his eyes.

"Well," Diana announced, unaware of the byplay between the two, "I've been invited to tea and I really must hurry along. Cameron dear, you don't mind if I borrow your carriage, do you? The Billings are a bit too far to walk."

Cassie bit her lip, unable to stop the flush of annoyance. Why did Diana call him "dear?" Was there something more between them than she supposed? Did he look at Diana as he did her?

Cameron seemed to remember at last that they weren't alone. His attention snapped toward Diana. "You're having tea with the Billingses?"

"Just Mrs. Billings. I met her at the dress shop today. She says she wants me to meet her sons, but they were not available this afternoon."

Cameron's lips tightened with displeasure. He'd have to warn Tom Billings before Diana had a chance to sink her fangs into him. Jesus, he wouldn't want to

139

see his worst enemy settled with this money hungry bitch.

"You don't mind, do you?"

Cameron shot her a puzzled look.

"About the carriage, I mean."

"No, of course not. Tell Stevens, and he'll take care of it."

"You did mind. Why?" Cassie asked after Diana left.

"What?"

"Why didn't you want her to go?" Cassie couldn't stop the question. "Are you jealous?" She asked, then colored at her audacity. When was she going to learn to keep her mouth shut?

Cameron chuckled. "Would it bother you if I were?"

"Of course not! Why should it?"

He shrugged. "I'm sorry to disappoint you, but I was thinking of something else. If I appeared jealous, it was not my intent." He came to his feet. "You will excuse me, won't you? There is something I have to do."

Cassie did not reply. What did she care? He could do as he wished without asking her permission. Feeling oddly angry at his abrupt dismissal, she stomped out of the room.

She was halfway up the stairs before she realized she was being followed. At the landing, she glanced over her shoulder to see a determined Cameron close behind. What was he doing? His room was in the other direction.

She said nothing, but walked on to her room, conscious of the fact that he was still following her. At her door, she turned and faced him. "What do you

140

want? I thought you said you had something to do?"

Without a word, he moved past her and into the room.

Cassie stood at the doorway, dumbfounded. She watched him walk toward her armoire. Her eyes widened with astonishment as he opened it, took out one of her few dresses, ripped the material to shreds and threw it to the floor.

Cassie ran across the room. "Are you insane? What are you doing?"

Cameron ignored her and reached for still another dress. Again, he tore the fabric and threw it at his feet.

"Stop!" Cassie shouted as she tried to wrench another dress from him, almost crying as it tore between them. "Why are you doing this? Stop it!" She was beating at his arms and chest with her fists, and when that had no effect, she threw an arm around his neck and tried to straddle him, kicking and screaming curses. But her efforts were in vain. Cameron was not to be deterred. Again, he reached inside.

Cassie fell to the floor, raging as she watched him methodically destroy every piece of clothing she owned. "All right," she growled as she came to her feet. "If that's the way you want to play."

In an instant, she was gone. She dashed down the hall and almost fell into Cameron's room. Her eyes darted wildly about until she spied her objective. By the time he thought to follow her, she had pulled his clothes from their hangers and was strewing them wildly about the room. Having less strength then Cameron, she was able to tear only a few things, but she grunted with satisfaction as she ground her heels into those that wouldn't rip. She was stomping on one

141

leg of a pair of trousers when Cameron walked up to her. "Need any help?"

"Pull this." She handed him a leg.

He did as he was told, and the trousers split at the crotch. He laughed. "This is fun."

"I'm glad you think so." She reached again into his closet.

"But this is more fun." Suddenly, he spun her around and started yanking at the clothes she wore. Cassie was momentarily paralyzed by shock as he tore her dress from neck to hem. But when he started on her sleeves, she gritted her teeth and went at him with equal zeal. By the time they were done, the two of them looked as if they'd been attacked by a madman wielding giant scissors.

Cassie turned away from Cameron's mirth-filled eyes. She knew she might laugh if she looked at him, and she didn't want to laugh. She didn't think it was at all funny. She was furious. Who did he think he was to destroy her clothes? The arrogance of the man was not to be borne. But even as she fumed, a smile was beginning to form at the corner of her lips. And then—as she chanced a look in his direction and saw his shoulders shaking—she, too, dissolved into gales of helpless laughter. She laughed so hard it began to hurt, and she found herself clutching her stomach while tears ran down her cheeks. "You are a beast."

"And you are a brat." He gathered her in his arms and held her close, satisfied for the moment to simply hold her near, feel her warmth and breathe in her scent. "You could have saved yourself a passel of trouble if you'd listened to me."

"Now, even if I wanted to go shopping, I couldn't go

into town. I've nothing to wear."

"The proprietress will come to you."

"And bring the entire store?"

"Why? Do you want to buy the entire store?" His eyes clouded with doubt. Had he been right from the beginning? Was she after his money? She had sworn she wanted nothing from him. But was it true? Or was she simply holding out for more?

Cassie shot him a withering glance. "How am I supposed to choose if I don't know what she has?"

"She'll bring the entire store."

Chapter Eleven

Cassie tied the wide, spotless apron around Meghan's waist and smiled at the little girl who mimicked her every movement.

Cameron had made it clear that Meghan would remain at home. In lieu of yet another school, a tutor was being sought, and Meghan fairly beamed with the joy of rediscovering her father's love. Indeed, the change in the child had been astounding. Meghan was no longer the shy, withdrawn, sad little girl who had returned home two weeks past, but a bright and bubbling eight-year-old, who sailed eagerly into each new day with delightful childish exuberance.

She adored Cassie and rarely left her side. In Meghan's eyes, Cassie was endowed with all the qualities of a miracle worker. Hadn't her father grown loving and gentle since Cassie's arrival? Wasn't there laughter in her home? This was something Meghan could never remember before. And best of all, hadn't her father promised never to send her away again? With a child's special insight, Meghan attributed all these wonderful changes to Cassie's influence. And naturally enough, she tried to emulate her in every way possible, imitating Cassie's speech and even her light, quick movements.

She also delighted in helping with Cassie's daily chores—especially those at the infirmary where she and Cassie began work each morning at nine sharp.

Here, to Meghan's immense pride, she was treated as a true helpmate. She took no offense that they believed her too young to visit when there was a case of fever. She didn't care that the door to the men's ward was barred to her. After all, she had more than enough to do. It was she they sent for bandages and salves when dressings had to be changed, she who sometimes joined Cassie and the midwife, Annabel, in feeding those too weakened by injury or childbirth to feed themselves. She didn't mind the menial jobs of sweeping and gathering soiled linens. Meghan, who had so longed for acceptance, was content simply to be needed.

Looking in on Joshua, Cassie returned his cheerful grin. It was a miracle that he had survived at all, more astonishing still that he would not be a permanent invalid. He was growing stronger each day. How it had come about, she would never know, but the hand of God was in clear evidence here.

Keeping a watchful eye out for Meghan, Cassie looked out in the hall where the child was sweeping the floor. Suddenly, Meghan stopped dead in her tracks, her face completely blank. Cassie sighed and nodded her head. This kind of seizure occurred several times each day, although Meghan never seemed to remember its happening.

Cassie had seen these symptoms years before, when

she'd been apprenticed to her grandmother, who had treated two children with this ailment which the French called petit mal, the little sickness. She remembered her grandmother assuring the worried parents that the frightening symptoms would disappear by the time the children were twenty years of age. Cassie was sure that this is what would happen in Meghan's case. In all likelihood, this was the root of her problem in school. Cassie had seen no sign of willful disobedience. No doubt the child just hadn't heard the schoolmistress's instructions.

Cassie vowed to speak to Cameron of his daughter's suspected ailment the first chance she got. To her dismay, it was to be sooner than she expected.

"What the hell is she doing here?" his voice suddenly boomed out. "Why isn't she out playing?"

Groaning inwardly, Cassie turned to face the object of her thoughts. His body was stiff with shock, his face almost purple with rage as he stalked into the small room. She'd never seen a man looking quite so incensed. Still, Cassie felt not the least intimidated, for she held no fear of this man. "Why do you suppose," she calmly responded, "you usually enter a room with a roar of disapproval, rather than a polite good day?"

Cameron bit back further comment, apparently realizing it was unseemly to upbraid Cassie in front of the other people in the infirmary. His dark eyes glared at her accusingly. "I'd see you outside, Miss Devon. Immediately!"

At the rear of the building, after listening to all she could of his sputtering anger, Cassie asked, "What would you have the child do?"

"Do? How the hell should I know? What does any

little girl do?"

"Most children of Meghan's age have governesses to watch over them."

"Why can't you watch over her?"

"In case you haven't noticed, I'm doing just that."

"In there?" Cameron nodded his head toward the whitewashed building that housed his sick and injured workers.

"In there," Cassie agreed, and at his sarcastic sneer, she continued, "Cameron, there's no need for you to bully me. Meghan is happy. She feels needed. Indeed, she helps . . ."

"I don't give a goddamn how she feels. It's too dangerous. Suppose she catches something? Jesus Christ, she's only eight years old!"

"Give me a little credit, Mr. Chandler," Cassie snapped, her anger rising. How could he suppose her to be so stupid? "There are no cases of fever at present, and Meghan knows she wouldn't be permitted in the building should any develop. There is no danger involved in her simple chores."

"Cassie, I couldn't bear it if . . ." Anguished, he found himself unable to finish the sentence.

"Cameron," Cassie soothed, instantly contrite now that she realized how frightened he was. She touched his sleeve in a comforting gesture. "She does little more than play with the babies." And at his continued look of terror, she went on, "I swear to you, should a case of fever be brought in, Meghan will not be allowed in the building. Does that satisfy?"

At Cameron's somewhat reluctant nod of agreement, Cassie took him by the arm and began walking toward a grove of trees where she could relate her suspicions about Meghan's illness in some privacy.

"Good God!" Cameron gasped when he heard what she had to tell him. His knees seemed unable to support his weight, and he found himself leaning weakly against a tree.

"Cameron, I've seen this before and I assure you, it's nothing to be so upset about. It explains, I believe, her moments of confusion and her reportedly difficult behavior at school."

"Will it grow worse? Will I find her writhing upon the floor in the throes of a fit?"

"As far as I know, it grows no worse. The symptoms usually disappear completely upon reaching adulthood. You might have her checked by a reliable physician. It will settle your mind, I think."

A tender smile brightened Cassie's face as Meghan dashed out of the women's ward and called out her name. Spying her father, she ran with unrestrained youthful excitement into his welcoming arms. "Annabel says it's a boy!" she announced with obvious delight.

Cassie stood in wide-eyed amazement. For every one dress she had ordered, which came to a total of five, including the one she had bought on the spot, six had been delivered. "There's been a mistake. I didn't order these," she insisted as box after box of frilly garments was placed on the floor of her room.

"Wait!" she shouted, shutting the door on the seemingly endless procession. "Mrs. Hays, would you mind telling me what is going on here?"

The owner of the dress shop stopped her happy

chatter, her hands stilled as yet another dress fell onto the bed from the box she held. An expression that bordered on hurt filled her eyes. "What do you mean? Are they not to your liking?"

Cassie's gaze shifted briefly to the huge pile of colorful silks and chiffons on the bed, then back to the startled Mrs. Hays. "Of course I like them, but they're not mine. I didn't order all this."

Mrs. Hays breathed a long sigh of relief. "Oh that! I know you didn't, dear. Mr. Chandler insisted I multiply your order by six when he discovered you only bought five gowns. He also included all the under-things you'll need, plus shoes, wraps, and . . ."

Cassie's lips thinned with anger as she interrupted the dress shop owner. "He did, did he?" she blazed. "Well, you can just repack all but the five dresses I ordered."

"I can't."

"Why?"

"They're already paid for."

Without another word, Cassie stormed out of the room and into Cameron's library, slamming the door behind her. She didn't care if she was interrupting him.

Cameron raised his eyes from the papers he was working on. "Good morning, Cassie," he said good humoredly. And when she simply stood there staring, her hands placed belligerently on her hips, he smiled. So the finery had come. He'd wondered what her reaction would be when she found out.

Cassie stood for a long moment simply glaring at him, obviously so upset she was rendered temporarily speechless. Finally, Cameron innocently asked, "You wanted to see me about something?"

"You might say that," she replied, nearly choking as she strained to keep her voice calm.

Cameron's laughter only added fuel to her anger. "Please don't feel shy. If you've something to say, feel free."

Cassie ignored his teasing and got right to the point. "How dare you presume to order my underthings?" she fumed. Her face flamed with mortification at the very idea. She could only imagine the conclusions Mrs. Hays must have jumped to. Cassie closed her eyes and took a deep breath as she fought for control. "I came with five dresses," she snapped, "and I'm leaving with five. You can just tell Mrs. Hays to take all the other things back."

Cameron came to his feet and moved at a leisurely pace from behind his desk. His easy grin and cool, confident manner were straining her temper to the breaking point. Her fingers itched to slap the superior smile from his face. God, but she was tired of his always getting the upper hand. She couldn't take much more of this man's arrogance. And if he did one more thing to make her feel as if he were paying her off for what had happened between them, she would not be responsible for her actions.

"I take it the dresses have arrived."

"They have."

"You seem a bit upset."

"To put it mildly."

Cameron chuckled at her sarcastic tone.

"So you think it's funny, do you? We'll see just how much you laugh when . . ."

"Don't say it, Cassie," he warned. "I don't take kindly

150

to threats."

Cassie's face grew red with frustration. "You, sir," she retorted hotly, "have to be the most arrogant, pigheaded . . ."

"*Me?*" he interrupted loudly. "Take a good look in the mirror, lady."

"*Me?*" she shouted back.

"Yes, *you*. Who refused to take the clothes in the first place? Who would rather walk around here like some poor, orphaned child, rather than accept a kindly made offer of refurbishing her wardrobe?"

"First of all, we've already gone over what I think of your oh-so-kind offer." She raised a finger and poked it close to his face. "Second, it's been a while since I was a child, Mr. Chandler, and I'll thank you to mind your own business. And third, I ordered five dresses because that's all I can afford."

"What do you mean *you* can afford? I tore them; I'll replace them. Besides, you have no money."

"Have you forgotten the letters I've sent to my solicitor? I should have the money any day now to reimburse you."

"I don't want your goddamned money."

"Too bad. You will have it in any case. *I* will pay for the five *I* ordered. You may return the rest."

Cameron grabbed her by the shoulders and gave her a hard shake. "You thickheaded little fool. I don't want your money and you will keep all the things I bought you."

"I will not!"

"You will!"

Cameron glared into her stubborn face, watching as her blue eyes became chips of ice and her small chin

151

lifted defiantly. Realizing it was a useless battle, he gave a long sigh and released her. "You win," he muttered, but before she had a chance to gloat, he continued. "As long as we've gone this far, perhaps you'd like to settle all accounts. I'll have a detailed bill readied before the day is out."

Cassie's mouth dropped open.

"Don't worry," he remarked coolly, knowing he had hit the mark at last, "I'll include everything. Sunshine's freedom, food, rent, the cost of the voyage, and your friend's clothes. Does that suit you?"

Cassie blanched as she realized the total would amount to a fortune. She'd be in debt for the rest of her life, but she'd die before she'd let this arrogant beast win the day. Her blue eyes sparkled with determination. She'd pay him back, every penny. She'd do it if it killed her. She straightened her shoulders and looked squarely into his satisfied smirk.

"Perfectly," she replied through gritted teeth.

The stable boy obviously didn't know what to make of it, but Cameron couldn't keep from grinning, and Meghan's laughter could be heard throughout the barn as she ran from stall to stall.

So this was how Cassie had taken her revenge. Cameron chuckled. What a woman! Since the first moment he saw her, she had brought nothing but turmoil into his well-ordered, peaceful existence. Still, he couldn't imagine living without her. Though constantly aroused to anger by her stubbornly independent ways, he had to admit that he'd never been so happy. Now, it appeared, she'd applied her unique imagination to the barn.

He had already seen the slaves sporting their new clothes, obviously cut down from the extra dresses he had ordered her. It had angered him at first, but he'd bit his tongue rather than let her know she had scored a point. The clothes were hers, after all, to do with as she pleased. Apparently not satisfied, she had gone a step further. Well, it was time to put a stop to this foolishness. If the woman wanted a reaction, she'd get it. Cameron shuddered to think what would happen next if he were brave enough to ignore this last episode.

"Ah don' think it be a good idea to let the horses eat at the curtains, sah," the stable boy said solemnly.

Cameron glanced at his newly decorated stable, adorned everywhere with feminine frills and lace. Trying not to smile, he asked, "Do all the stalls look like this?"

"Most," Manuel replied.

"Well, I quite agree, Manuel. It does the horses no good to eat lace fabric. Do you by any chance know how it happened, or why old Jenny here is wearing a lady's hat and a ruffled petticoat around her middle?"

The stable boy could only shake his head in wonder.

"No matter, I'll look into it. Have someone help you with the windows. And take that stuff off Jenny."

"What should I do with it all, sah?"

"Burn it."

"You'll never guess what happened."

Cassie glanced up from pouring tea as Cameron entered the drawing room. She offered him a cup and smiled. "What?"

"Someone broke into the barn last night and put curtains on the windows."

"You don't say." Cassie's smile was so tantalizing that Cameron found himself hard pressed not to join her on the couch and take her in his arms.

"Indeed I do. The culprits also found the time to dress Jenny and Thunder in the most outrageous costumes."

"Thunder?" Cassie looked puzzled.

"And Jenny."

Cassie bit her lip lest the laughter that threatened burst forth.

Cameron placed his cup on the table before him and steepled his fingers beneath his chin. So she thought it funny, did she? Well, he'd just see how prone to laughter she was when he finished with her. "What I can't understand," he said aloud, 'is why someone would go to all that trouble to poison my horses."

"What?" Cassie sat up straight. The soft smile that had been hovering about her mouth instantly vanished and her face paled. She looked as if she were about to faint.

Cameron felt a twinge of remorse, but steeled himself against the tenderness that filled him. The little twit deserved this, and more. If he gave into his soft-hearted feelings, there was no telling what she might do next. "Poison my horses," he repeated, as if she really hadn't heard him. "If someone wanted to do that, why didn't they just put arsenic in their drinking water? It would have been much faster."

"Oh no!" Cassie's hand shook. Her cup rattled.

"What? Did you burn yourself?"

"What?

"Did you burn yourself?"

"No, I . . . I . . ."

"You sounded as if you were in pain."

"Oh, no, no." She shook her head. "Are they all dead?"

"Who?"

"The horses. You said someone poisoned them."

"They might well have died if Manuel hadn't called me in time. They were eating material with dye in it. If I ever catch the stupid . . ."

Cassie gave an audible moan of relief. "Thank God!"

"Why do you think someone would wish the poor animals harm?"

"Oh, I'm sure no one would have done that on purpose. Perhaps it was a prank."

Cameron shrugged and watched Cassie's face grow red with guilt. God, she was so easy to read. The woman couldn't lie to save her soul. *Couldn't she?* a voice from within asked. *She fooled you well enough once.* Cameron felt his heart grow cold at the thought. Why did he have to think of that now? He was enjoying this little tete-a-tete. Damn it, why did she have to appear so innocent, so different from all the others? *Could it be she is?* asked the voice again. *No,* Cameron responded. *She's a woman and all women are alike.*

"I'm sure it will never happen again," Cassie murmured, her mortification and suffering apparent.

"What makes you think so?"

"Well, by now, whoever is at fault has probably realized how dangerous a prank it was."

"I hope you're right. I'd hate to see . . ."

There was a knock at the door and Stevens popped

his head into the room. "Miss Rosemary is here, sir."

Cassie could have sworn she heard Cameron groan, but she dismissed the thought in the next instant, looking stunned as Rosemary Cabet entered the room in a whirl of taffeta and the strongest perfume Cassie had ever smelled. "There's no need to announce me, is there darlin'?" asked the tiny woman as she pushed past a startled Stevens and flung herself into Cameron's arms.

"Oh darlin'," she continued, "it's been so long. I'm so happy to be home." With that, she reached up on tiptoe and planted a well aimed kiss on his mouth. Her arms clung to his neck, giving him no recourse but to allow the intimate greeting.

Cassie wondered how he could stand the smell of her. Even from where she sat, the scent was overpowering. It was all she could do not to lunge for one of the windows for a breath of air.

Cassie could feel her cheeks coloring with embarrassment as the woman deepened the kiss. It was obvious this Rosemary had eyes only for Cameron and had not noticed her as yet.

"How was your trip?" Cameron asked as he took her hands from his neck.

"Paris was . . . well, what can I say? Paris is Paris, after all."

Cassie almost groaned at the inane remark. Surely a visitor to that beautiful city could have done better than that. Is this what Cameron liked in his women? Good God, it was a miracle he could stand the woman, never mind sustain a relationship. And that there was a relationship grew even more obvious as the lady continued to press her small form tightly to his.

"We were just about to have tea. You'll stay, of course."

"We?" Rosemary asked as she tore her gaze from her host and looked around the room. Cameron performed the introductions and when he spoke of Cassie as his niece, the woman's flicker of jealousy turned to sudden delight. "I'm so pleased to make your acquaintance, Miss Devon."

"And I yours, Miss Cabet." Cassie would soon regret those words, never knowing they would be the last she'd be able to speak for nigh on an hour.

Stevens brought another cup, and Cassie settled down to what she'd hoped would be a pleasant afternoon. What followed was, in fact, one of the most frustrating hours Cassie had ever had to suffer through. Rosemary Cabet monopolized the conversation, yet proved herself incapable of completing a simple sentence. No sooner would she begin one thought, when another would apparently take precedence, and she would ramble on to yet another bit of nonsense. In one expulsion of breath, the woman might brush upon four or more topics.

Within half an hour, Cassie's mind was reeling as she tried to keep up with her. A dull throbbing had begun in her head and she longed to do nothing more than lie quietly in her room.

In the next half hour Cassie's headache grew unbearably intense. How she had lasted that long she could not imagine. All she knew was she'd go crazy if she had to take another minute of the woman's endless, nonsensical chatter. Cassie came suddenly to her feet. Both Cameron and Rosemary looked up at her, and the woman suddenly stopped speaking. Cassie breathed a sigh of relief. For the first time in more than an hour the room was quiet. Cassie almost hated to break such delicious silence. "You will excuse me?" she asked. "I must see to the children."

"Children? Do you have . . . ? Oh yes, Cameron dear, guess who I saw in Paris?" And when Cameron made no effort to guess, she went on, "Of course, it's not unusual to see him there. After all, he's been living abroad for years, but you'd never believe it, he married that little . . . By the way, did you know . . . ?"

Cassie shook her head and glanced at Cameron, who appeared to be in a trance as Rosemary's monotonous voice droned on and on. Cassie grinned. Only a trance could explain the smile that hadn't shifted in the last hour. He was enjoying this even less than she, if that were possible. Only he had no means of escape.

"No, Cassie, don't." Cameron shot suddenly to his feet, seeing an unexpected way to leave. He started for the door. "Let me. I haven't seen the children all day."

Cassie shot him a knowing glance. He wasn't going to foist this woman off on her, not if she could help it. "Perhaps Rosemary would like to go with you."

"Of course, Cameron darlin', I'd love to meet the little . . . I've been meaning to ask, did you see . . . ?"

A few minutes later, Cassie stood before the long mirror in the drawing room, listening to the voices upstairs. Did the woman never stop? Even from here, she could hear her shrill voice and shriller laughter as she oohed and aahed over the babies. How in the world could Cameron have someone like her for a lady friend?

She was a beauty to be sure, but her silvery blond hair and huge blue eyes hardly made up for the fact that the woman hadn't a sensible bone in her body.

Cassie glanced at her own image and grinned. So what if she couldn't compare to the lady in looks? She'd take a smattering of brains any day to empty-headed beauty. Cassie's grin widened as she tried to imitate the lady's walk. Over and over, she sashayed before the mirror. "Good God, how does she do that?" she said aloud.

A low chuckle was heard from the doorway and Cassie spun around with a surprised gasp. "I've often wondered," Cameron said with a grin. "It seems to me she should have thrown her back out years ago."

Cassie giggled, her cheeks pink from being caught in the act. "Perhaps she's a contortionist. A traveling band of performers once stopped in our town. One of the men could do that most amazing things with his body."

"Could he?" Cameron asked, his dark eyes warming as he moved toward her. "Such as?"

"Cameron, you can't leave her alone with the babies. Have you no pity? She might do their poor ears permanent damage."

Cameron smiled. "That was quick thinking. I owe you one for siccing her on me."

Cassie laughed. "You tried it first, Cameron darlin'," she mimicked their guest. "Lucky for me the lady needed a larger audience."

"Now, what kind of punishment do you suppose is in order?"

Cassie laughed, not trusting the wicked gleam in his eye. "What kind have you in mind?"

"Perhaps I'll invite her to dinner." Cameron laughed when Cassie's eyes closed as if in pain. "Of course, I'll be called to my office and you alone will have the pleasure of her sweet company."

"You wouldn't!"

"I would if you can't come up with a more enticing form of punishment."

"I've known you were a beast from the first, sir, but I would never have expected, even of you, such heartless actions."

Cameron shrugged. "There's one sure way of thwarting my evil plans."

"That being?

"No more arguments over money, Cassie. I want you to admit you are part of this family and owe me nothing."

"And if I refuse?"

"You know the consequences," he warned.

With only the slightest hesitation, Cassie grinned. "You have my word on it."

Chapter Twelve

Cameron's mouth tightened with annoyance as Tom Billings's eyes widened with delight. "Where have you been keeping her?"

Cassie smiled as she offered her hand. You speak as though Mr. Chandler has been keeping me a prisoner."

Tom took her hand and brought it to his mouth, lingering a bit overlong for Cameron's liking. "I wouldn't blame him if he had."

"Would you care for some tea, Mr. Billings? We were just about to have some."

"I'd be delighted, Miss Devon. There really is nothing like a hot cup of tea in the late afternoon, is there?"

"I quite agree, Mr. Billings."

Cameron laughed to himself despite his annoyance. Tea! Tom Billings, who had drunk nothing but Kentucky bourbon almost from the moment he left his mother's breast, was drinking tea!

"Diana, my companion, took tea with your mother

just last week. They've become fast friends. As a matter of fact, they're due back any minute from shopping."

Cameron gave a silent groan. Shopping again? What the hell was there left to buy? Jesus, the woman spent every waking moment spending money. The thought irked. It wasn't as though he couldn't afford it; he was annoyed because she was taking advantage of his generosity.

"Mother does little but rave over the lady."

"With every reason, I expect."

"You and your friend must come and take tea on an afternoon when I'm at home."

Cassie smiled. "I'd be delighted, Mr. Billings. I'm told your home is lovely. I'm most anxious to see it."

Tom grinned. "They say it lacks only a beautiful woman as its mistress."

Cassie smiled. Cameron glared, and Tom sighed as he watched her pour the steaming tea into fragile china cups, cups that looked oddly out of place in the hands of these two big men. God, but she was a beauty, Tom thought. He couldn't remember seeing a woman half so lovely. What luck to live so near. Why, he could see her every day, now that he was back from Europe.

Tom's blue gaze warmed as he pictured her sitting in his drawing room, pouring tea for his guests. He squirmed uncomfortably as his imagination carried the scenario a step further. They were alone, and instead of tea, it was something infinitely more interesting they were having. He couldn't remember when a woman had affected him so.

Cameron fumed as he watched the play of emotions on his friend's face. He had known Tom since they were children, and without much effort, could imagine his thoughts. Damn, but he was about ready to throw the bastard out of his house. And if Tom didn't stop looking at her like that, he probably would. Cameron's gaze darkened.

If either Tom or Cassie had taken the time to notice his presence and perhaps glance in his direction, they would have felt a moment's pause at Cameron's ominous look. It was easy to see Tom was enthralled. That much was obvious, but Cameron had a nagging suspicion it went further than that. Damn it, Tom hadn't been in her company ten minutes and already he was under her spell. Jesus, he wouldn't be surprised to hear a proposal of marriage any minute.

Cameron was quiet for a time as his black thoughts raged on. Suddenly, he felt a jolt of surprise as an idea occurred. Of course, it was the perfect solution! Why hadn't he thought of it before? The more he thought of it, the more reasonable it seemed. A slow, lazy smile curved his lips as he leaned back and relaxed for the first time since Tom's arrival. He almost laughed. It was going to be a shock when she heard it. She would glare. Her eyes would spit fire. Her luscious lips would tighten. She might even use some of that language she professed not to know. He chuckled softly. Suddenly, he couldn't wait for her reaction.

"Cameron, you have my undying sympathy. I can't imagine what torture it must be to have such a beauty in residence and have her be a niece."

Cassie smiled and lowered her eyes at the compliment.

"Neither can I."

Both pairs of eyes shot toward the man who was now

gloating with secret satisfaction. "What do you mean?"

"What I mean, my dear friend, is Cassie is no more a relative of mine than yours. She was half sister to my deceased niece and has taken care of Catherine's children since their birth."

"But . . ."

"I know, I know." Cameron gave a careless wave of long tapered fingers. "The whole town thinks her to be my niece. I thought it best to leave the matter as is, until the wedding of course."

"What wedding?"

"Why, mine and Cassie's. Who else?"

Cassie gasped and jumped to her feet as her teacup tipped and spilled its entire contents into her lap. She stood there staring, not thinking to wipe her skirt, not caring that the sopping pink material was now dripping tea onto the carpet. Was he out of his mind? Did he truly think he could coerce her into submitting to this wild scheme by announcing it as a *fait accompli?* Well, they'd just see about that!

"Oh my," Tom was on his feet. "Have you burned yourself?"

Cameron saw the look of fierce determination enter her eyes. She had turned startlingly white upon hearing his declaration. Now, she was growing fiery red with anger. Cameron had to do something and fast. The little spitfire was going to spoil the whole thing. And she was going to do it right in front of Tom.

"Darling, don't worry about it," he soothed, as if to ease her embarrassment over the stained carpet. "Jessie will get out the stain." And before she could utter an objection, he gathered her into his arms and kissed her quite thoroughly on her lips.

Conscious that they were being watched, and unwilling to cause more of a scene than this beast had already created, Cassie didn't fight him. Instead, she firmly, and not too gently, pushed at his shoulders. His eyes glittered a warning as he released her mouth. She glared back angrily at him. She longed to give vent to her rage. She'd give anything to slap that smug grin from his mouth. But not now. No, she couldn't afford to have it out with him now. Her words were stiff and stilted when she finally spoke. "Cameron, what will Mr. Billings think? I promise you I'm all right."

She was going to kill him! If he thought for one minute . . . She almost groaned aloud her frustration. She was definitely going to murder him.

Cassie beat a hasty retreat with the obvious explanation that her dress needed seeing to. She could hardly speak, so filled with rage was she, but her eyes spoke volumes. She couldn't wait to get her hands on him. Her fingers fairly itched with the need to do him harm.

Tom watched the play of emotion that passed between them. Something was wrong here. He could sense the tension. There was passion, yes, but there was something more. Was he mistaken, or did she seemed shocked at Cameron's announcement? Could it be that Cameron's statement was as much of a surprise to her as to him? Dared he hoped she felt no tenderness toward the man? Indeed, the way her eyes flashed, one would believe her to hate him. Tom grinned. From everything he'd seen thus far, he wasn't about to give up. It would be very interesting to see what happened here, very interesting indeed.

* * *

"Have a pleasant ride, did you?"

Cassie shot him a scornful glance. "Very pleasant indeed."

"I'm sorry I couldn't have joined you. The afternoon passed slowly while sitting before my desk."

"A pity." Cassie had not as yet had a chance to confront Cameron, having seen almost nothing of him in the past week. Indeed, it almost seemed as if he were hiding from her.

Cameron grinned at her sarcasm. Jesus, but he wanted to kiss her, and if he couldn't manage to get her into the library fast, he was going to do it right here in the hall. "I'd like to speak to you for a moment."

"So speak," Cassie returned insolently. She heard Stevens gasp behind her and knew she'd gone too far in the butler's hearing.

Cameron chuckled as he guided her suddenly rigid form down the long hall and into the library. The door had barely closed before she was flat up against it and in his arms.

"Take your hands off me." Cassie shoved with all her might and watched with some amazement when he allowed her to push him aside.

"I doubt you put up such a fight with Tom. You've seen him every day for more than a week. Don't tell me he hasn't tried as much."

Cassie turned hate-filled eyes toward him. "Tom is a gentleman. Something you know nothing of."

Cameron shrugged. "If he is, it's only because he knows you belong to me."

"Damn your soul, Cameron. I belong to me. I'll never belong to you. Never!"

He looked at her for a long moment. Her chest heaved with her anger and Cameron could not avoid taking in the delicious movement. His fingers ached with the need to touch her. And that wasn't the only thing that ached. Night after night, he lay in bed, remembering her scent, the silk of her flesh, unable to sleep with wanting her. If he couldn't persuade her to have him, and soon, he wouldn't be responsible for what might happen.

Lately, he'd been forced to spill his seed alone in his bed, something he hadn't done since he was an inexperienced lad. Sadly, it had now become a nightly habit, since taking another woman in Cassie's stead was out of the question. A faint smile touched his lips. If the practice went on much longer, he was sure to need eyeglasses. Besides, the lonely ritual, so satisfying in his youth, now provided no pleasure, only physical release. His body and soul yearned for Cassie, and nothing and no one else would suffice. He sighed heavily. "Sit down, Cassie. We need to talk."

She eyed him suspiciously, and moved only after she saw him sit behind his desk. She sat down opposite him. "What do we need to talk about?"

"Our marriage."

Cassie laughed and came to her feet. "There's no need for any discussion since there will never be a marriage between us."

"Sit down."

Cassie watched him for a long moment before she finally shrugged her shoulders and complied.

"Why?" he asked.

"Why? What do you mean 'why'?"

"I believe the question was simple enough. Why

167

won't there be a marriage between us?"

Cassie heaved a long sigh and leaned back in her chair. "Cameron, we can barely stand one another. Marriage is a serious commitment. The parties involved should at the very least like one another."

"Is that the whole of your objection?"

"Isn't it enough?"

Cameron smiled. "Cassie, we are two mature adults. What need have we for stardust and magic? The facts are simple. I want you in my bed. You need someone to care for you and the children. Why can we not strike a bargain?"

"If all I needed was someone to take care of me, I could have any one of a dozen for a husband."

"You could, but then you'd lose the children."

"Why? Why couldn't I take them with me?"

"Cassie, most men want to start their own families when they marry, not acquire one ready made. Besides, I've grown quite accustomed to having them here. They will stay."

"You are a beast. I hardly know words worthy of you."

Cameron smiled. "Perhaps, but I know words worthy of you."

Cassie came to her feet. "Please —" she held up her hand — "do me the courtesy of keeping them to yourself."

Cameron chuckled as he came around the desk, blocking her path to the door. "I was merely going to tell you how lovely I think you are."

Cassie took a step back, recognizing the hungry look in his eyes. "I don't want to hear this."

"A shame." He grinned as he shook his head. "I was

going to tell you how much I enjoy watching you smile, hearing your laughter, seeing you play with the children, riding a horse, even walking into a room."

"Cameron, stop it."

"Why?" He smiled as he reached out and caressed her cheek. "Does it bother you to know how I feel?" Cassie gasped as he placed his other hand just beneath her breast. "I can feel your heart, Cassie. It tells me more than your words of denial."

She closed her eyes, as if in pain, then leaned her face against his open palm. Her voice was low and sultry. "Cameron, it could never work. Most of the time you hate me."

"Do I?" he breathed huskily.

"Yes. I can see it in your eyes. It's almost as if you want to believe the worst of me."

Cameron couldn't deny her accusation. In some ways, he did think the worst of her, but no more so than he did of any other woman. They were all the same, after all. But this was not the time to speak of womankind and their shortcomings. It was right that he and Cassie should marry. The more he thought of it, the more sensible it seemed. Now, he had to convince her to see things his way.

"Cassie, I'm not a poor man. You'd have to search far to find another who could better care for you."

"I don't want your money."

Cameron could almost believe that. He had offered her an unlimited account, and she had refused to use it. Even after he'd ordered the clothes for her, she would not accept more than what she considered necessary. It was Diana whose closets bulged. He tried another route. "If you marry me, you guarantee permanent guardianship of the children."

Cassie shook her head. "I have them now. Why can't we keep things as they are?"

"Because I want my own."

"But you can have . . ." Her eyes widened as she realized the implication.

"Exactly. If I were to marry, I doubt my wife would want someone who looks like you living with us."

Cassie's eyes clouded with doubt. "I don't know."

He knew he was pushing, but he didn't care. He'd do almost anything to get her in his bed. "Can you deny the passion that exists between us?"

What could she say? They both knew the truth of the matter. "One doesn't build a life on passion."

"It's a start." He grinned. "Kiss me, Cassie."

"No."

"Why? Are you afraid?"

"Yes."

"If I promise you it will be nothing more than a kiss, would you believe me?"

Cassie's eyes lifted to his dark gaze. "Yes," she heard herself say.

Cameron moved to lean against his desk, guiding her to stand between his legs. "Then kiss me, Cassie."

"Cameron, this will accomplish nothing. I have to think. I'll not give an answer on something so important in the heat of passion."

"Kiss me," he insisted.

Cassie sighed, knowing she shouldn't comply, but unable to resist the temptation. He was so handsome, so very masculine, and—when he chose to be—so sweet, she felt her resistance melting. Her fingers reached up to caress the scar that seemed only to add

170

to his allure. Gently, she placed a soft kiss upon it, and Cameron groaned at the tenderness in her touch.

"Cassie," he murmured, wanting to pull away, embarrassed for her to touch his ugliness.

"Shush," she whispered. "Let me touch you first." Slowly, her fingers traveled the planes and hollows of his face. With a feather-light touch, she moved over his eyes, his cheeks, his jaw, to linger at his lips. She closed her eyes, savoring what she felt, then gasped as he suddenly sucked one of her fingers inside his mouth.

Her body trembled. She'd never imagined anything could be so erotic. The tingling shocks created by his moving tongue ran to her toes, and she felt herself leaning closer, unable to halt a steadily mounting desire. Her breathing grew rapid, her mind dizzy, her body hot and yielding as she pressed against him. The sensual touch of his tongue on her finger was almost more than she could bear. How did he come to know these things? How many women had there been for him to grow so expert at the art of seduction? Cassie didn't want to think about it. She didn't want to know of the others.

Cameron's heart pounded as she gently extricated her finger. He watched her raise her mouth to his. Idly, he wondered if he'd survive the ecstasy of this moment. He had waited so long, wanted her so badly.

Gently, she cupped his face in her hands. Her lips touched his in a feather-light caress. Her tongue slid intoxicatingly over his mouth, urging his lips to part.

Her gently erotic coaxing inflamed him, and it was only with superhuman effort that he allowed her to keep the initiative. Reluctantly, he kept his arms at his sides. His body ached to pull her hard against him and take her mouth with all the savage need that longed to find release.

As he parted his lips and allowed her tongue to slide sensuously inside his mouth, he shivered with a desire that was growing dangerously out of control. Never had a kiss held such promise. Never had he experienced such pleasure. Gently, his hands reached out and moved her closer, cradling her hips to his rising desire.

He heard her moan as she recognized his need and nearly exploded as he felt her rub deliberately against him. It was torture. It was agony. It was the sweetest pleasure he'd ever known.

"It's good, Cassie. It's so good," he murmured against her mouth.

She threaded her fingers through his hair, delighting in the feel of the crisp dark strands as she plunged her tongue deep into the delicious warmth of his mouth. He was right. It was good. Idly, she wondered if it always felt like this, or was it love that made the difference? Love! Good God, no! She didn't love him. Yes, she had told him she loved him in the heat of passion, but it wasn't true. It wasn't!

She pulled away, unable to meet his gaze. Her cheeks flushed as she tried to deny what her heart knew to be true. What in heaven's name was she going to do? She loved a man who felt nothing but contempt and lust for her. Oh God, how had this happened?

Cameron's mouth moved to nuzzle her neck and throat. "It's right for us, Cassie," he murmured against her silky flesh. "You can't deny it."

Cassie wanted to cry. She closed her eyes with the torment. She couldn't deny it. She only wished to God she could. She could not reveal her true feelings. He must never know that she loved him.

"Will you marry me?" he asked softly.

She had to swallow hard before she could speak. "You must let me think on it, Cameron."

He smiled as he looked into her misty eyes. "Think on it then, but in the meantime, why don't we . . . ?"

Cassie laughed, despite the realization of what he had in mind. "You said a kiss."

He appeared to be considering her statement. "Mmm, I did, didn't I?"

"Are you about to go back on your word, Mr. Chandler? Not a promising sign in a man who has just proposed, wouldn't you agree?"

"Me?" he asked, in elaborate mock surprise. "Go back on my word? My dear Miss Devon, I never say anything I don't mean. And I never, under any circumstances, go back on my word."

Cassie fought hard to contain her laughter. "I haven't spoken to you in almost a week. Do not presume I've forgiven you for your outrageous actions simply because we've . . ."

"Darling, I'd not dare to presume anything where you're concerned."

"Why did you do it?"

"Do what?" he asked, pretending he'd forgotten.

Cassie lifted her brow and glared.

"Oh, that," he replied.

"Yes, that."

Cameron shrugged. "I could see Tom was about to get ideas where you were concerned. And since he's my best friend —" he paused dramatically, then grinned — "I felt a need to protect him."

Cassie laughed at the teasing light in his eyes and poked his chest with her finger. "You beast! So you thought to give the ultimate sacrifice?"

"What are friends for?" he said as he pulled her more closely into his embrace.

Chapter Thirteen

Cassie gave a soft, husky laugh. Happy tears misted her eyes as the baby's first shrill cry filled the room. It never failed. She could not assist at a birthing without a certain mystical pleasure filling her soul. Cynics might say what they wished, but it took a divine power, mightier than just mere sexual coupling, to bring about the sweet miracle of life.

The child was placed in his grandmother's capable hands while Cassie saw to the care of his mother. The baby had been unusually large. That in itself would have posed no problem, but the mother was exceptionally small. For this particular woman, any birth would have been dangerous. Beads of sweat broke out across Cassie's lip and forehead. The new mother was horribly torn and obviously in serious trouble. Cassie could only pray that her stitching and cold compresses, combined with strong herbal teas, would stanch the flow of blood. For her patient's benefit, she kept a bright smile on her face, but her heart was heavy with fear and sorry. She knew there was a good chance the mother would die.

Why hadn't this woman been told about birth control? Surely someone in a town this size had to be knowledgeable on the subject. This was not Margaret Saxton's first difficult delivery. The last child born had nearly killed her. If this birthing didn't finish her, the next one certainly would. Why hadn't Dr. Reilly, or Mr. Sutton, the town chemist, suggested a pessary? No doubt the poor woman had never heard of female protection. Cassie groaned to herself as she disposed of the afterbirth and worked feverishly to stanch the flow of blood. Why was childbirth and the act of love that preceded it shrouded in such mystery? The very taboos on the subject were what caused this terrible suffering, along with thousands of needless deaths.

Cassie finished the stitching and folded clean, thick padding to absorb the flow of blood, all the while praying her efforts were not in vain. Still, she managed a genuine smile as she heard the newborn loudly protesting his grandmother's gentle ministrations.

Hours later, Cassie's neck ached with stiffness. She was exhausted from her vigil. It had been a long night. She looked up and smiled as the door slowly opened to admit a pretty little blond girl of no more than six. Shyly, the child offered Cassie a steaming cup of tea. As she sipped at the strong brew, Cassie continued to observe the sleeping woman. The sun was just now making a hesitant show as it inched its way above the horizon, forcing the dark sky to flee before its power. Birds chirped outside the cabin window, and the comfortable domestic sounds of early morning could be heard from the kitchen. Putting her cup aside for a moment, Cassie again examined her patient. Thank God, the bleeding appeared to have lessened. She breathed a sigh of relief, then noticed Mrs. Saxton was finally awake.

"Is the baby . . . ?" the woman asked weakly.

Cassie smiled. "The baby is fine. Mrs. Wells came in to wet nurse him while you slept."

"Thank you. I don't know what I would have done . . ."

Cassie nodded. "You can thank me by listening to my advice. You lost a great deal of blood. When you are stronger, I want to talk to you about preventing future pregnancies."

Even in her weakened state, Mrs. Saxton blushed to the roots of her soft brown hair.

"I know, I know." Cassie gave a dismissive wave of her long slim fingers. "Ladies aren't supposed to discuss such things. But hear me well, Mrs. Saxton, if you don't do something, you are going to die."

Margaret Saxton grew as pale as milk, and Cassie felt a pang of guilt at the abrupt way in which she'd spoken. Still, she refused to soften the warning. There was no other way. She had to scare the woman into listening.

"Do you want your children to grow up without you? Do you honestly believe your six-year-old capable of tending to her brothers and sisters?"

Helpless tears formed in Mrs. Saxton's dark eyes as she shook her head.

"Four children should be enough to satisfy any man," Cassie pressed on.

"My Tom doesn't want any more, but . . ."

"I know. You think there is nothing you can do,

barring abstinence. Am I right?"

"A man has his needs, and I won't have him turning to another."

Cassie smiled. "He won't turn to anyone else, Mrs. Saxton. And there won't be any more babies. After you're healed, we'll talk again."

"Where the hell have you been?"

Even through the haze of exhaustion that enveloped her, Cassie felt her back stiffen with instant anger at his tone. She hadn't slept, but for an hour or so, in nearly two days. She was hot and uncomfortable. She was also drenched to the skin from a sudden evening storm which had caught her midway between Cameron's and the Saxtons'. She wanted nothing more than a refreshing bath and a night of undisturbed sleep. She certainly didn't need this beast's abuse. Slowly, she hung her wet summer wrap on a peg in the hall and pushed her sodden hair from her face. Her lips thinned to a hard line, and her eyes shot daggers as she turned to face him. "Still another of your cordial greetings?" she asked in low, cutting tones. And when her remark brought no answer, she snapped, "I fail to see that it is any of your concern how I spend my time."

Cameron stiffened at her words. His hands were clenched at his side as he fought the urge to strangle her. He had spent the entire night, and the greater part of the day, pacing his study floor, alternately worrying and raging as he imagined her in Tom Billings's arms. He could see her lips covered with the man's mouth, her soft body being touched. He could hear her delicious cries of pleasure. Cameron shuddered at the picture. It was only thanks to extraordinary self-control that he hadn't already gone to the Billings' and killed his one-time friend with his bare hands. And now, after all he'd suffered, to be the butt of her sarcasm was almost more than he could take.

"I asked you a question, woman," he growled. "You'd do well to answer me."

"Would I?" Cassie laughed mirthlessly. "I fail to see what you can do if I refuse."

"Have you something to hide, then?" He eyed her suspiciously. "Is that why you refuse to tell me?" A muscle twitched in his clenched jaw, and the scar that ran down his cheek grew white against his tanned skin. Had Cassie been less tired at that moment, she would have realized the danger of goading him on while he was in such a state.

"Cameron darlin'," she returned snidely, "my life is an open book. I've nothing to hide."

Ignoring her obvious reference to Rosemary, he gave an evil laugh. "Don't you? Why then, didn't you tell me the truth from the start? Why didn't you tell me who you really are?"

"So you've finally gotten around to asking, have you? Well, you're too late. I wouldn't tell you now if you begged."

"When you get to know me better, madam, you'll know I never beg."

"What a shame. Then you'll never know, will you?"

Cassie tried to pass him, but he moved to block her path. "Get out of my way!" she ordered.

179

Laughing cruelly, he threw her own words back at her. "I fail to see what you can do if I refuse."

Cassie gritted her teeth. "Can't you? Then perhaps I should tell you. Suppose I knock you down and step over you?"

For the first time in more than a day, Cameron laughed with real humor. The idea was ludicrous, to be sure, since he stood a good head taller and outweighed her by a hundred pounds or more. "I'd like to see you try."

It was the last straw. Cassie was so angry she was actually shaking. Suddenly, she gave him a mighty shove and grunted with satisfaction to see his heel catch on a loose corner of the carpet. He took a stumbling step backward.

Without hesitation, Cassie took full advantage of her chance to escape. She was halfway up the stairs before Cameron managed to regain his balance.

Bellowing her name, he was hot on her trail. Cassie barely made it to her room ahead of him, jumping out of his grasp just as she slammed her door. In the next instant, he had smashed it into the wall. "Get out!" she ordered fearlessly as she faced him and stood her ground.

Cameron's eyes narrowed dangerously as he ignored her demand. "Madam, this is my house and I'll enter any room I please."

"The house might be yours, but this is my room and I don't want you here!"

"A shame," he said, grinning arrogantly as he stalked her across the room. "Where were you?"

"That's none of your damn business. Are you going

180

to get out?"

"What do you think?"

"Then, I'll leave," she sneered as she dashed for the balcony doors.

It was raining harder than ever, but Cassie didn't care. In a blind rage, she didn't care where she went or how she got there. All she knew was she had to get away from this beast. She would die happy if she never saw him again.

Cassie nearly flew down the stairs to the garden, but barely made it three feet into the darkness before she was tackled from behind and brought down with a short, startled cry. In an instant, he had her rolled onto her back and held helpless beneath him on the sodden grass. Her flailing hands were quickly secured in his and held over her head.

Cassie couldn't take any more. She was too tired to fight him. Tears came to her eyes, mingling with the raindrops that splattered onto her cheeks.

As streaks of lightning illuminated the darkness, Cameron studied her beautiful face. He had to have her. She was like an addictive drug. It no longer mattered if she had been with another. She was in his blood, and he could no longer control his desire. "I don't care," he murmured against her mouth. "It's too late for me."

Cassie dismissed his words, not understanding them, not caring about anything except the touch of his lips on hers. Her tiredness evaporated, as if it had never been. She was instantly filled with energy and all the passion she had for so long kept at bay. All she knew, all she could think of was the sweet taste of his mouth and the rapture his weight brought as he moved against her body.

She was fighting again, only this time she wasn't struggling against him, but straining to bring him closer. Her mouth opened hungrily as she twisted her head, answering the pressure of his lips. Their eager tongues met and moved together, rediscovering the special delights found nowhere but in each other.

In his desperate need to have her again, Cameron never thought to take her inside, where it was cool and dry. Both were oblivious to the storm that raged around them, so caught up were they in a frenzy of touch and taste. Indeed, the pouring rain only served to deepen Cameron's pleasure, making her mouth more luscious, her satiny skin more sensuous. He growled deeply, losing himself in the wonder of her.

Cassie, too, was caught up in a fevered excitement that matched his own. She ached to hold him, and when he finally released her hands, she clasped his broad shoulders and pressed him tightly to her. But it wasn't enough. She was possessed with a need to touch, a need so intense it blotted out all but this man and this moment. She had wanted him for too long to stop now.

Edging her hands between their bodies, she made him groan with pleasure as she rubbed the hard bulge that pressed upon her thigh.

The sensation of warm rain and his warmer hands moving on her breasts, brought Cassie an excitement that bordered on delirium. She offered no protest as he tore wildly at her clothes in a desperate effort to feel her naked beneath.

She moaned as the heat of his mouth seared the cool wet flesh of her naked breasts. She tore madly at his shirt, needing to feel his skin. But the rain had plastered it to his back, and she cried out in frustration. "Take it off," she begged.

Within seconds he was as naked as she.

She moaned again as he covered her wet body with his and coaxed her warm, willing thighs apart. "Cameron, please," she breathed, achingly seductive. "Now."

Cameron had suffered too long, had waited forever. He couldn't fight the demands of his body and her soft urgings. "Yes, yes, my love. Now!" he gasped. He entered her with a sudden, deep thrust, groaning with delight as her velvety softness closed around him.

She clutched at his neck, his shoulders, his back, trying to drive him deeper within her. Desperately, she wound her legs around his waist as her hips rose to meet his movements, crying out wildly at the pleasure that burst to life throughout her body.

"God, oh God," she marveled aloud. She wanted to tell him how wonderful it was, but all that came from her throat were low, guttural sounds of raw pleasure. The sensations she reveled in were close to pain. It was too much. He had to bring her release.

"Come with me," he whispered hoarsely as his thrusts grew stronger and more rapid. "Now, Cassie. Let it go now!" Lights flickered behind her closed eyes as she felt him shudder and fill her with warmth. An instant later, the aching pressure that had racked her body exploded into ecstasy. She would have screamed had his mouth not been there to cover hers.

She lay in a daze. She heard Cameron curse, but her mind would make little sense of it. "Come on," his voice urged, as if in a dream. "We've got to get inside before we freeze to death."

Freeze? Was he serious? Cassie had never felt so warm and so comfortable in her entire life. She gave a long sigh and tried to turn to her side. She was fine where she was. God, but she was tired. She couldn't move a step if it meant her life.

Cameron groaned as he lifted her into his arms. "Damn, my legs are still shaking," he said as Cassie felt him stumble toward the stairs.

Ignoring his rantings and occasional grunts, she snuggled her face into the warmth of his neck. He smelled so good. Lord, if she could always be this close so she could breathe . . .

Someone was rubbing something warm all over her. Cassie tried to push away the massaging hand, but it was too much of an effort. "Cameron," she mumbled. "I'm too tired."

"I know, darling," came a low voice filled with laughter from far away. "I'm almost finished. Then you can sleep."

Sighing contentedly as her head rested at last upon the soft feather pillow, Cassie was asleep before the bed dipped with Cameron's weight.

"I don't believe you." Cassie refused to open her eyes, but snuggled her face deeper into his shoulder and neck. She could feel her cheeks grow warm with embarrassment.

184

"Well, you do," he insisted.

"I do not." She could hear the laughter in his voice. "And you aren't much of a gentleman if you persist in saying so."

Cameron laughed and snuggled her close to his naked body. "Have I ever given you reason to believe me a gentleman?"

Cassie pinched his side. "Not as far as I can remember."

"Ow!" Cameron captured her hand lest she continue to protest her innocence in such a painful way. Suddenly, he swung himself up so that he half leaned over her. "Then take my word for it, you snore."

Cassie opened her eyes to his happy grin. God, but he was beautiful when he smiled. Cassie felt her pulse quicken with the knowledge that she was naked and in his bed. She tried to hide her growing excitement. "You sir, are a rotter."

"Am I?" he chuckled as he stared down into her sleepy eyes, growing cloudier with the stirrings of passion. Suddenly, the sight of a small ear amid a tangle of red curls couldn't be resisted. His teeth took her lobe and played with the soft flesh until chills danced down her back. "Your English is showing," he murmured into her neck. "What exactly does a rotter do?"

"Look it up."

"And leave this bed?" He laughed again. "Not on your life."

It was some time before Cassie could breathe again with any degree of normalcy. Her head rested against his shoulder. His heart was still beating furiously.

185

Cassie placed her opened palm over his chest. "I'm no sure this is good for either of us."

"No?" He smiled as he looked down his nose at her "Why not?"

"Well, for one thing, it makes me awfully tired," she yawned and stretched her lithe young body, graceful as a tawny tigress.

"And for another?" he prompted with a smile.

"And for another, it makes your heart pound like you're running for your life."

"Is that bad?"

"I don't know, but if your heart was weak, I'm positive it couldn't take the strain."

"I think I'll take my chances." He laughed as he rar his hand familiarly down the length of her side and over her hip.

"Where were you, Cassie?"

Cassie could hear the sudden tightness in his voice and felt his body stiffen. She didn't want to lose this new-found closeness to another argument. The idea irked, but she knew he didn't trust her. What she didn't know was why. What had happened in his past to convince him of the infidelity of all women? Cassie was tempted to ask about it, but held her tongue. What they needed was time. Time to wash away the past. Time for trust to grow. Cassie pushed aside the slight hurt, and trying to keep the moment light, teased. "That couldn't be begging I hear in your voice, could it?"

"Cassie!" came a warning growl as his hand tightened on her hip.

Cassie giggled. "I left you a note. Don't you sit at

186

your desk anymore?"

Cameron didn't bother to tell her there was no way he could concentrate on business while she was gone, and therefore, no need to sit at his desk. "I didn't see it. Where were you?"

"I was called to the Saxtons'. Margaret delivered a baby boy yesterday."

"What took so long?"

"There were complications. She almost didn't make it."

With a sigh, he pressed his face into her tousled hair and breathed in her sweet scent.

"Why wasn't Doc Reilly called?"

"He was."

"Drunk again?"

Cassie nodded. "Why were you so upset?" she asked. "You should have asked Diana. She knew where I was."

Cameron was instantly filled with rage. So the bitch had known all along and had purposely kept him in the dark. She had to have known how worried he was. Why, he could barely keep up his end of the conversation during dinner last night. But did she tell him? Cameron stiffened as he remembered. Jesus, she had! She had said Cassie was out on one of her missions, as she liked to call them. But the way she had said it, combined with her teasing laughter and knowing look, had left him with the clear and obviously intended impression that she was covering for her friend. God, but he hated the bitch. It was all he could do to keep a civil tongue in his mouth when in her presence.

With Diana out of reach, he vented his anger on

Cassie. "Damn it Cassie, I won't have my wife gallivanting over the countryside. Do you realize what could have happened to you?"

For as long as she could remember, Cassie had come and gone as she pleased. She was a schoolgirl the last time anyone had told her what she might or might not do. She didn't realize it was his anger at Diana that had caused him to speak so harshly. She didn't think at all, but reacted with instant annoyance to his bossy tone. She sat up abruptly, her tumbled auburn curls cascading in beautiful disarray over her shoulders and down her back. Unmindful of her nakedness, she faced him with a sneer. "You won't have! Who the hell are you? And what do you mean your wife? I haven't said I'd marry you."

"You slept with me last night," he accused. "Do you make it a habit of sleeping with just anyone?"

Cassie's shoulders stiffened, giving him a fine view of deliciously full, swaying breasts. Her cheeks grew pink, but it wasn't embarrassment that set her face ablaze. She was filled with rage at his accusing tone. Through clenched teeth, she hissed at him, "You alone know the answer to that question, Mr. Chandler."

"Do I?" he asked, his anger growing in equal measure to hers.

"Are you so inexperienced as not to know a virgin when you take one?"

"Oh, I know a virgin all right." Cameron cursed, unable to stop the words and know the destruction he was sure to cause. "But I can't claim to know what she does on her nightly jaunts around the countryside."

Cassie gasped and came instantly to her feet. Uncaring that she left him naked, she tore the sheet from the bed and wrapped it around herself. "You, sir, are a foul-mouthed, evil-minded man. Take my advice and stick to virgins. You can be sure of yourself then."

"Not sure of myself," he bellowed as she walked out the balcony doors, toward her own room. "Sure of them!" Suddenly, that wasn't enough. She wasn't going to leave him with an arrogant toss of that long, fiery hair as if she'd had the last word. Cameron jumped to his feet and mindless of his undressed state, ran to the balcony and yelled after her, "And thank you for the advice. I think I will."

Chapter Fourteen

Their sharp, angry voices were followed by an unnerving quiet as everyone within hearing distance suddenly stood stock still and held his breath. An instant later came the echoing sounds of two doors slamming simultaneously.

Even as far away as the kitchen, servants sighed and rolled their eyes heavenward. They were at it again. And there wasn't one among the household staff who could believe that one tiny lady could so often rile a worldly wise man like Mr. Chandler.

If the two upstairs thought their lives private, they hadn't reckoned with the dozen or so servants who unobtrusively saw and heard everything. Cameron would have been enraged had he witnessed the knowing glances and smiles exchanged below at this moment.

"Lordy, but those two are having a time of it," Annie remarked as she placed a cast-iron skillet on the wood burning stove. "What I can't figure out is why it's so hard for some folks to see what's starin' them in the face."

Stevens chuckled as he put his arms around his wife, delighting in her abundantly lush form. His black face nuzzled into her warm brown neck as he murmured, "Maybe someone should tell him. The man hasn't got the sense the good Lord gave him."

Annie shook her head. "Maybe some fool won't mind cuttin' his stay on earth a bit short. But I knows when to mind my business."

Stevens sighed with disgust. "White folks always look for trouble where there isn't any." He grinned as he slid his hands up her soft body and dropped the mannered speech of Chandler's butler. "Now dis po' nigger boy, he knows dat der ain't no sense in fightin' a woman. Best to give her what she wants and git it over wit, I say."

Annie slapped at his fingers as they moved to caress her huge breasts. "You'd best take your hands off me, old man, and stop that sugarin' talk. It ain't goin' to get you nowhere."

Stevens laughed as he felt her nipple respond to his thumb's caress. "Why don't we show him what it should be like?"

"Ha," Annie laughed humorlessly. "If'n he don't know, wit' all dem women sashayin' der skinny behinds through dem bedroom doors . . ." She shrugged.

"Oh, he knows how to bed them all right. What I'm thinking is he's scared of the lady. He just don't know what to do with her after he finishes."

"And you could show him?"

"Damn right!"

Annie grinned. "Old man, you don't know half of

191

what you're talkin' about."

Stevens chuckled as he moved his narrow hips against her rounded backside. "You were spunky as all hell when you first came here. I got you a purrin', didn't I?"

Annie sighed as she remembered the day she had come, chained like an animal, to the Chandler home. "You'd best watch her. She's nothing but trouble," her owner had told Chandler. Thank God, Bennett had considered his pocketbook above his anger, or she would have long ago met her maker.

She had run from the Bennetts' place every chance she got. She had run until it wasn't worth the trouble it took to track her down. Only it wasn't spunk that had caused her to run. No, it had been fear of Rowlins and what the white overseer could do to a body. It didn't matter that once she was caught she suffered all the more. Annie only knew she had to try to get away.

From the age of nine, Annie had known what it was to share the bed of a white man. She had never thought to judge the men that used her then, or since. Like most slaves, she simply considered it another chore expected of the women, even those who were uglier than sin. It seemed most men didn't care who warmed their bed. With the lights out, she guessed, one body was much like another.

No, that wasn't why she ran. It was Rowlins who scared all hell out of her. He had done unspeakable things to her. Things she couldn't think about, even now, years later, without breaking out in a cold sweat. Things she thought she could never tell another human being. Not until she met Stevens. He had understood her horror. With endless patience, he had banished her fears until she felt whole again. His kindness and gentle ways had slowly penetrated her icy contempt until she could once again enjoy the touch of a man without cringing.

Annie banished the gruesome thoughts from her mind and laughed as she wiggled her behind against her husband's arousal. "You talk up a good story, but I ain't seen nuttin' else up lately."

Stevens laughed as he gave her one last hug while rolling his hips suggestively against her still-firm bottom. "Tonight, woman."

"Good evening, Cassie," Cameron said. The automatic spark of delight that lit his eyes was instantly replaced with an icy expression as he tried to exit the drawing room at the exact same moment she was trying to enter.

Cassie squelched a soft gasp and closed her eyes against the delicious sensation that filled her as their bodies fleetingly touched. Defiantly, she stood her ground and refused to give way. She would not give this brute the satisfaction of thinking his touch affected her in the least. She would show him just how little she cared. She wasn't afraid of him, or anything he might do. And she didn't have to answer to him, no matter his views on the subject. Her chin lifted in further defiance. If he thought he gave her even a moment's pause, he was sadly mistaken.

Despite her sworn denials, Cassie did, in fact, spend an inordinate amount of time thinking of the man. Indeed, she had fumed most of the day over treatment that she perceived as exceedingly unfair. What right did he have to accuse her so unjustly? How could he have imagined that she'd been doing anything except caring for her patients? What had she ever done to cause him to believe so poorly of her? All right, all right, she conceded, she had lied to him once. Worse than that, she had lived the lie. But she'd deceived him only because of extraordinary circumstances. Circumstances he had never bothered to ask her about. Well, maybe he had asked, she admitted. But when, in a fit of anger, she hadn't answered, he hadn't bothered to ask again.

Cassie sighed. She didn't care anymore. This whole matter was too complicated for her to cope with. One minute, he wanted to marry her, and the next, judging by the look in his eyes, he hated her with a fierceness matched only by his passion. Cassie's jaw tightened with determination. Well, he'd simply have to find someone else for his whipping boy. She was finished taking his abuse.

"Good evening," Cassie answered lightly as she squeezed by.

After dinner, Cassie sat in the drawing room, trying to ignore his disgusting display. She knew what the beast was about—at least she thought she did, or hoped she did. With a snap of her head, she flung her hair behind her shoulder. She didn't care a whit. Let him make a fool of himself. What he did, or didn't do, bothered her not in the least.

Grinding her teeth together, she watched with growing revulsion as he gushed attention on Diana. How could he make such delicious love to her only this

194

morning and now act as if he didn't know she was in the room? Well, that was just like him, wasn't it? The man obviously had two distinct personalities and she was better off done with him. Cassie sighed heavily. Why, then, was she so unhappy? She should be thrilled, shouldn't she? She should be relieved and laughing for joy that he was paying attention to another. Then, why did she feel like crying?

Dinner had been torture, but this was worse. She couldn't stand to be in his loathsome presence one more minute. She'd plead a headache and go to her room. No doubt the beast would never realize she'd gone.

She started to rise just as Stevens announced the arrival of a guest. "Mr. Billings, sir," said the butler.

Cassie breathed a sigh of relief. At last, someone to talk to. Someone to keep her mind from the happenings across the room.

Tom Billings moved into the room and headed straight for Cassie, offering no more than a curt nod and stilted greeting to his host and one-time friend. They had had words, these two. Words that had come dangerously close to a fist fight, and the resulting hard feelings had seriously damaged their friendship. Tom's eyes widened with surprise at Cassie's more than enthusiastic greeting. For a moment, he thought she was going to throw herself into his arms.

Tom bent and kissed her hand, his voice a low, intimate caress. "I hope you don't mind my calling, Cassie. I was in the neighborhood and thought I'd stop by."

Cassie glanced toward a suddenly stiff Cameron, then smiled at her very welcome guest. "Tom, you know you're always welcome here. Please sit down and talk to me. Would you care for a glass of sherry?"

"Sherry sounds fine," Tom remarked as he made himself comfortable at her side. Did he detect a trace of sadness in her smile? A hint of moisture in her beautiful eyes? He must have imagined it, for upon closer inspection, her eyes were clear and her smile as delightfully sweet as ever. God, what he wouldn't give to convince her to marry him. But every time he brought the subject up, she neatly managed to steer the conversation in another direction. He had to have this remarkable woman. Cameron hadn't fooled him with his arrogant claim. This lady was very much available, and he only prayed she would soon allow him the honor.

Cameron sneered silently at Tom's acceptance of the sherry. Well, at least his former friend had graduated from tea. His eyes narrowed as he watched the pair in cozy, animated conversation. How quickly the bastard made himself at home, he thought. The fact that Tom had, over the years, spent more time in Cameron's house than his own, completely slipped his mind. Uppermost in his thoughts was the easy familiarity with which they seemed to enjoy each other's company. Damn, but why couldn't Cassie smile like that when she was with him?

Cameron had lost all rationality. The unthinkable had happened. No matter how he had tried to prevent it, he had fallen in love. The worst of it was that he was incapable of recognizing what had happened to him. Tonight, he had childishly tried to show her his disfavor. In the process, he had perhaps suffered more than she, for he wanted nothing more than to rid himself of the pushy Diana and hold Cassie in his arms. Now, he found himself looking on helplessly as the woman he adored showered another with her warm attentions. Anger turned to pain and pain became impotent rage.

He cursed under his breath, unable to control himself. Diana's sickly sweet words became an echoing whine as his ears, body, and mind strained toward the other end of the room and Cassie's low laughter.

His tortured body throbbed with the sound of that laughter. What the hell did she find so funny? Why couldn't he bring that sound from her? But he could. A slow smile curved his lips as he remembered. He most certainly could.

Suddenly, the low hum of their conversation ceased, and Cameron was startled to see the hem of Cassie's skirt disappear beyond the doors to the terrace. Where the hell did she think she was going? Without thinking, he made to follow, only to find his arm held fast and Diana's voice prattling senselessly near his ear. For the life of him, he couldn't understand what she was babbling about. All he could think of was what was going on outside. Was Tom kissing her? Surely, he wouldn't dare, not without permission. *That never stopped you, Chandler,* came a mocking voice from the recesses of his mind. Cameron was suddenly on his feet. Christ, he'd kill the bastard!

"What's going on between you two?" Tom asked as he drew her into the shadows of the terrace.

"Who?"

"Cassie, I saw the way you looked at him tonight.

197

Does he know?"

Cassie's response was a self-deprecating laugh. Know what? That she loved him? Good God, that was all she needed. Cassie shuddered to think what he would do with that knowledge. Suddenly, she sighed. All she longed for was peace. Her emotions were strung to the limit. She wanted to cry, to laugh, to scream, but most of all she wanted to run away. She couldn't stand this tension any longer. She had to do something, something that would release her from Cameron's hold.

"Marry me, Tom," she said impulsively.

Tom felt the world tilt crazily as overwhelming joy filled his being. For a long moment, he was barely able to breathe as he took her in his arms and cradled her close. God, but he loved her as he'd never loved another. What a life they could have together. "Do you love me?" he asked, suddenly wary of his unexpected good fortune.

She hesitated, and Tom sighed wistfully as the truth slowly dawned on him. She didn't love him. For just a minute, he didn't care. It didn't matter. He loved her enough for the both of them. But he knew it did matter. She loved another, and although he knew she'd remain forever faithful once the vows were taken, he couldn't bear to take second place in her heart.

"I don't stand a chance, do I?"

Cassie hesitated. How she wished that he did. He was so kind, so steady. She wanted to love him, but she already loved another. "I'm sorry, Tom," she whispered as their mouths came together in what both knew was a farewell kiss.

Cameron was on the terrace before he realized he

had moved, never hearing Diana's startled exclamation as he wrenched his arm free of her. Where were they? His eyes scanned the darkness. He couldn't see a thing.

Something moved within the shadows of the terrace. And something snapped in Cameron's brain as he saw Tom Billings place his lips to Cassie's.

"No!" he shouted, lunging forward in a rage to tear Tom from her side. What happened next was so sudden, Cassie wouldn't remember it all until much later.

Shocked by Cameron's intrusion, Tom turned to him with matching fury. Cameron was glaring at Cassie. It was obvious he was about to heap abuse upon her. "Don't say it. Don't even think it," Tom warned.

But Cameron was too overwhelmed by his own sense of loss to heed the clear threat. His mouth curled into a sneer. "You . . ." he began. Whatever he was about to say was abruptly cut off by flashing lights behind his eyes. And in the next instant he was sprawled upon the terrace floor.

Suddenly, Cassie was kneeling beside his prone figure, murmuring soft words as she lifted his head into her lap and moved gentle fingers over his face.

Tom grunted as he rubbed his knuckles. "I warned you, damn it."

Cameron looked up at him with a glazed expression. "Jesus, I don't know . . ."

Tom had never seen a man look more dumbfounded. Suddenly, all his anger dissolved. He almost felt sorry for the fool. Almost, but not quite. A quick glance at Cassie's face confirmed what he had only before guessed at. What he wouldn't give to see love like that shine in her eyes for him. Tom rubbed his bruised hand again, feeling a small measure of satisfaction. Then, he grinned and asked Cameron, "Don't you know?" A moment later, he was gone.

After making sure Cameron had suffered no serious injury, Cassie dropped his head to the floor, ignoring his low moan of discomfort as it hit the hard stones for the second time. She came to her feet. "I hope you're satisfied. No doubt brute force is your forte, but I wonder if you know how little is actually accomplished by it."

"Me!" Cameron choked as he came to his feet and rubbed his tender jaw. "Madam, it appears you've failed to notice that it was I, not your lover, who took the blow."

Cassie ignored his reasonable statement and continued in exasperation, "He's not my lover. He's your friend. How could you have treated him so shabbily?"

Feeling a horrendous wave of guilt at the treatment he had bestowed upon a man who was once closer to him than a brother, Cameron struck out at the woman he believed responsible. "He was my friend, before you came."

"He's still your friend, you idiot! Although I can't imagine why."

"You were in his arms. Deny that, if you will. Would a friend do that?"

"Not that it's any of your business, but Mr. Billings and I were speaking of marriage before your unseemly interruption."

"And your answer?"

"Is none of your business."

"I think it is."

"I think it's not."

As Cassie made to dash past him, Cameron caught her wrist and snapped her back, flinging her up against his chest. His breath was a warm caress as he forced her against the railing and pressed his hips suggestively to hers. "Your answer?"

Cassie fought against the helpless, melting sensation in the pit of her stomach. Damn, but she hated his arrogance. He was so sure, so sure she had refused Tom's proposal, not the other way around. She couldn't allow him to come out the victor. Not after what he'd done. Not after the way he'd treated her.

Cassie glared up at the man who held her. "Do you want me to tell you I've declined his offer? Well, I'm sorry, I can't. I asked him to marry me."

Cameron gasped with shock. He was stunned, almost as if someone had dealt him a blow in the gut. Stupid goddamned fool, he told himself. You've lost her. You've treated her abominably and you've lost her. He wanted to beg her to reconsider. He wanted to show her, to remind her what it was like between them, but he'd disgraced himself enough for one night. Abruptly, he released her, moved aside and stared out into the black night. His voice was flat, devoid of any emotion. "My congratulations, madam."

Cassie was aghast at what she had done. Revenge was not half so sweet when you watched someone you love suffer, and Cameron made no effort to hide his suffering. Cassie groaned. No matter how she wanted to strike back, she couldn't permit the lie to stand. "He refused me, Cameron."

"Why?" Cameron turned eyes wide with wonder to

face her. He couldn't take it in. He knew Tom was in love with her. Why on earth would the man refuse her offer?

"Because he knows I don't love him."

Cameron reached out to her, but before he had a chance to touch her, Cassie was gone.

202

Chapter Fifteen

Cassie's nervous fingers smoothed a stray lock of dark red hair behind her ear and tucked it into her bonnet. It wasn't the cool night air that raised gooseflesh on her arms and along her back. She was terrified. She couldn't remember a time when she had been more frightened, and she found herself clenching her jaw just to stop her teeth from chattering.

Taking a long, steadying breath, she sat in silence atop the buggy and prayed her mare was too tired to respond to the excited whinnying of the other horses that galloped by. All around her men shouted loudly, calling out threats and curses as they searched the underbrush for the escaped slave. God, what ever possessed her to take such a chance? Why hadn't she gone to Cameron with Sunshine's request? Why hadn't she dumped the problem in his lap?

Cassie sighed heavily. She knew why she had taken it upon herself to rescue Sunshine's husband, and it had nothing to do with the fact that she and Cameron had somehow established a new if strained relationship. The barely controlled sexual tension between them was gone now, replaced by a new courtesy and kindness that hinted at feelings so deep, Cassie dared not ponder them.

Cameron was a fair man, but nonetheless a slave owner. She knew he would return James to his rightful owner, just as he would expect any man to do the same with his property. But Cassie didn't believe one man could own another, no matter his color. And if Cameron were to tell her to mind her own business, as she knew he would, she would have been forced to disobey him. And that would only have led to more trouble.

Was it her imagination? Were the sounds of the chase growing faint? Were these men as tired and uncomfortable, in the endless, drizzling black night, as she? Were they giving up their search? Cassie sighed with disappointment as another voice called out. Of course they weren't giving up. They would never stop searching until they found the man.

Cassie gave a soft gasp as a sudden thought occurred. She shouldn't have panicked earlier and pulled off the road at the sound of approaching horses. Were she to be found hiding in the brush, it would only confirm her guilt. Quickly, she snapped at the reins held loosely in her hands and guided the buggy back to the muddy road. "Stay quiet," she warned the man concealed under the seat. "No matter what you hear, don't make a sound and stay where you are."

As she expected, she was brought to a stop within minutes. "Where might you be goin', ma'am?" came a voice from out of the night.

Cassie pretended surprise at the sound and allowed her voice to quiver with a trace of the real fear she felt. "Who . . . who is it? Who's out there?"

A lone rider came from out of the concealing brush, his horse blocking her path. His voice was harsh and thick with suspicion. "I'm Roberts from the Spencer place. What are you doing out this time of night?"

"Oh, Mr. Roberts." Cassie sighed with pretended relief. "It's Cassandra Devon, Mr. Chandler's niece. I was called to help out down the road a piece. One of the Saxton children was ailing."

Seth Roberts's slow toothy grin was lost in the black night. He had often seen Chandler's niece a comin' and a goin' while he watched from a respectful distance. Since he caught his first glimpse, he had tried to figure out a way to strike up a conversation. Once, when passing her in town, he had tipped his hat and received a dazzling smile. The smile had warmed him for nearly a week. Twice, upon spotting her buggy ahead, he had gone miles out of his way just so he could circle back and pass her on the road.

She sure was a looker, this one. But he wasn't nothin' to hide in a closet. Maybe he didn't have to fight them off with a stick, but he had his share of women. Knew how to service them real good, too. The only trouble was this one was a cut above the usual. Maybe she wasn't one of them rich, uppity bitches. Christ, he hated them most of all. Not one of them treated him like he was worth spit. But she still came from money. He could tell just by the way she walked. She might have to depend on her uncle's charity, but Roberts knew a girl like her didn't marry no white trash. Shit, but he hated that expression, and who the

205

hell cared about marriage anyway? He only wanted a little fun. Even the highest-class bitch was known to enjoy herself in the sack now and again.

It wasn't like she was a prim and proper lady who wouldn't dirty her hands. From the talk hereabouts, he knew she was doin' a mighty fine job healin' his neighbors. She took a splinter out of old Charlie's ass just last week, didn't she? Why, she even worked on an occasional nigger, if all the talk could be believed. Besides, she had a couple of kids, didn't she? No, she wasn't no innocent, else she wouldn't be out this time of night in the first place.

Most important, she talked to him like he was a real person. Roberts felt a warmth in his belly and his crotch began to swell uncomfortably. She did seem awfully glad to see him. Maybe she was hungerin' for a man and didn't feel right about comin' right out with it. You couldn't always tell with her kind. Well, he wasn't one to refuse a female a good time. He'd take odds she never had it the ways he knew. He might not have what it took in his purse, but he had it where it counted — in his pants.

"You shouldn't be out alone on a night like this, ma'am. It's pure foolishness." Roberts automatically tipped his hat and gave a silent groan as rain water soaked his suddenly exposed collar. "The men are huntin' down an escaped slave. A real troublemaker. Why, if the lazy bastard — beggin' your pardon, ma'am — got hold of a lady like you, there's no tellin' what might happen."

"You're probably right, Mr. Roberts. The next time I'm needed, I'll take one of the servants along."

God, but he liked the way she called him "mister."

He couldn't remember anyone calling him "mister" before. Roberts grinned. "Servants" she called them instead of "slaves." The lady sure spoke pretty. And that wasn't the only pretty thing he'd noticed about her. It was a shame it was dark. He wouldn't have minded a good, close look at her right now. She wasn't skinny and sickly lookin' like most of the ladies he'd seen. No, she had the biggest pair of . . . Maybe he could manage more than a look if he could get closer. She didn't know it yet, but what she needed was a man to keep her safe from that no-account nigger.

Roberts grinned slyly. "Mr. Chandler'd have my head if I let anything happen to his niece. I'll bet he don't know you're out alone."

I'll bet you're right, Cassie said to herself. Damn! This was just what she needed. Of all the men to run into, why did she have to find one so worried for her welfare?

"Mr. Chandler knows where I've gone," she returned, praying he'd believe the lie. "I'm not ten minutes from home. I'm sure I'll be safe." Cassie snapped the reins and smiled stiffly, thankful that the darkness concealed her trembling hands. "But I do thank you for your concern, Mr. Roberts."

"There's no way I can let you drive home alone, ma'am," Roberts insisted as he stopped the horse with a strong, steady hand at the animal's mouth. "I'll travel along with you, just to make sure."

Cassie's heart sank as she watched the man slide from his saddle and leap uninvited aboard the buggy. He was tying the reins to the buggy seat before she had a chance to object. "I wouldn't want to put you to any trouble."

"No trouble."

"Mr. Roberts, really," Cassie snapped, a bit annoyed at his highhanded manner. "There is no need."

"I wouldn't want to tell a lady she was wrong, ma'am, but I'm afraid there is a need."

Cassie shook her head. She'd wasted enough time talking to this fool. If he insisted on joining her, she'd just have to allow it. From his obstinate, overbearing manner, she suspected that nothing short of a gun pointed at his mid-section would change his mind. Cassie barely breathed as the buggy jolted forward and then slid over the rutted, mud-slicked road. Please God, she prayed, thinking of James squeezed into the tiny space beneath the seat, keep him quiet. Don't let him sneeze, or cough, or groan at the jostling he's getting.

"I seen you ridin' out from Chandler's place a few times," Roberts offered.

"Have you?" At the sudden thickness in his voice, Cassie shot him a quick glance and felt chills race down her back. Good God, even in this light she could see the gleam of lust in his eyes.

"Yeah. I wanted to talk to you, but . . ."

From the corner of her eye, Cassie could see him lick his lips. She forced herself to remain calm. It wouldn't do to show this man fear. Suddenly, she had no doubt he was the type to take advantage of it.

Straining to keep her voice level, she said pleasantly, "If you wanted to speak to me, Mr. Roberts, you should have come to the house. I'm sure my uncle would have performed the introductions."

Roberts laughed. He could just imagine the high and mighty Chandler introducing his niece to the likes of him. "Not likely," he responded.

She had to keep him talking. There was no telling what the man might do if left to dwell on his undoubtedly lecherous thoughts. "You don't think so? Why on earth not?"

"Miss Cassandra," he said with a grin. "You don't mind none if I call you by your Christian name?"

"Considering the circumstances, I think it quite proper," she returned with a shrug. What circumstances? Good God, what was she rattling on about? If she was going to talk, she'd best make sense.

But he was preoccupied with his own train of thought. "I'm just an overseer. I don't even own a slave."

"Oh, I see your meaning. You believe my uncle would think you not good enough to come calling."

Roberts could only stare in shock, his mouth hanging open, his mind suddenly empty of evil intent. "Do you mean . . . ?"

Cassie breathed a sigh of relief as the Chandler mansion suddenly came into view. "I mean, my uncle may be rich, but I am not. The size of a man's purse is far from important in a relationship, don't you agree?"

"Yes ma'am," Roberts answered dazedly.

Cassie stopped the buggy before the darkened barn. Her feeling of safety suddenly vanished as she realized all were asleep at this hour. If she should find the need to call out, no one would hear her. She snapped the reins again. It would be wiser to stop at the house.

Suddenly, the reins were torn from her hands. "I'll see to the horses, ma'am."

Roberts jumped to the ground, walked quickly around the buggy, and raised his arms to help Cassie down. She hesitated only an instant. "Thank you so much, Mr. Roberts," she murmured stiffly, then almost panicked as Roberts slid her body down the length of his.

Roberts laughed. He had seen the hesitation. She was good, but she wasn't good enough. The bitch was handing him a pile of bullshit, just to get rid of him. He knew a brush-off when he saw one. Did she think he'd be happy with a simple thank you? He had more in mind than a few pretty words. "Is that the best you can do?"

"Excuse me?" Cassie asked feebly, feeling her dread mount. Why had she hesitated to touch him? He had believed everything she told him up to that point.

"Ain't no sense in tryin' to act stupid, girl. You and I both know what I want. Just like we know you'll never let me set foot in that big white house."

"I'm afraid I don't . . ."

"Maybe you don't, honey, but tonight you sure as hell will."

Cassie groaned in pain as his mouth slashed over hers. His brutal kiss successfully muffled the cry for help that had been about to burst forth. Cassie shuddered with disgust as his tongue plunged deep inside her open mouth. She had never felt so violated, so horrified, so filled with disgust. Her heart pounded with a terror she had never before known. This couldn't be happening to her. Surely someone would come in time. Surely someone would hear.

Perhaps, she thought wildly, she could talk him out of raping her. But the moment her mouth was free of his, his hand took its place lest she give in again to the urge to scream. "Easy or rough? How do you want it?"

He was dragging her inside the barn when he suddenly went limp, and, with his arms still around her, fell to the ground. Cassie groaned. Lights danced before her eyes as she fell with him and struck her head on something sharp.

The next thing she knew, strong arms were tugging at her, trying to make her get up. "Miss Cassie, Miss Cassie!" someone was saying, "we got to get outta here. Hurry!"

Cassie opened her eyes with a dreamy expression and smiled as she saw Sunshine's shadowy form bending over her. Suddenly, from somewhere behind her, she heard, "You dumb nigger! You hit a white man. Do you know what they'll do to you for that?"

Cassie was instantly wide awake, and turned just as Roberts lunged from the floor of the barn. His arm reached out and grasped James' legs. The force of the attack flung the two of them into the first stall.

Cassie shivered with disgust as the sounds of flesh pounding on flesh filled the barn. She grabbed a shovel, but couldn't think what to do with it. She wanted to help James, but she knew she'd only be in the way if she entered the stall. In the dark, she'd never be able to tell who was who. Sunshine was cowering in fear, hiding behind her mistress, while Cassie could only jump up and down, wielding the shovel uselessly.

Finally, it grew quiet, and Cassie's heart skipped a beat as a man staggered through the opening. Not until she heard Sunshine's cry of happiness did Cassie relax and drop the shovel. She watched as the young woman flung herself into her man's arms.

Then suddenly, Cassie stumbled back as Sunshine was flung from James' protective arms, landing hard

211

up against her. A roar filled the silent barn as a dark form came flying out of the stall. Swiftly, James ducked the oncoming Roberts, then turned to shove the hurtling figure along. Obviously unable to stop his headlong course, Roberts landed with a thud in a bale of hay. Cassie looked on in wide-eyed wonder, waiting for him to jump up and lunge again. But he remained still. In the sudden hush, all that could be heard was a tiny squeak of surprise and a short gasping breath. Then, Roberts's head fell forward, and his body slumped . . . but did not, surprisingly, fall to the ground.

James and the two women stood staring at him, transfixed with dread, waiting for him to recover and attack again. But nothing happened. Finally, Cassie made her way to the wall of the barn where a lantern and matches were kept. With shaking fingers she lit the lamp and held it up to Roberts's limp form. What she saw in the flickering light made her gag with horror and revulsion.

There, sticking grotesquely out of Roberts's back, were the bloody prongs of a pitchfork.

Cassie gave up trying to pronounce his real, African name. James would have to do. It wasn't important. Her biggest problem right now was what to do with him now that she had him.

Cassie watched the young couple and smiled. It was a rare moment when they were not touching. "How long were you married before the slavers came?"

"Two days."

"You mean you're newlyweds?"

The couple shrugged in unison, never having heard the expression.

"What are we goin' to do, Miss Cassie? We can't stay here."

"I know," Cassie replied as she began to pace. "I have to think."

"But he can't stay here. What if one of the other girls sees him?"

"I know, I know," Cassie repeated as she twisted her fingers into the skirt of her dress. "Let me think. I'll figure out something."

Her heart almost stopped as a knock sounded at her door.

Cameron tossed and turned throughout the night, wide awake with worry. Cassie had obviously left on some errand of mercy and had again forgotten to tell him her whereabouts. Damn, but this had to stop. He had to make her understand the necessity of taking someone with her. He couldn't live with this constant fear for her well-being.

He had jumped from his bed and pulled on his trousers at the sound of her buggy. And then waited for what seemed an eternity before he finally heard her enter the house. He shook his head with disgust. Knowing Cassie, she had taken care of her horse rather than waken one of the stable boys. When was she going to feel comfortable with servants?

Cameron heard her move up the stairs, and was about to open his bedroom door when the sounds of whispered voices suddenly froze his hand on the knob. For one instant, a rage so intense as to blot out rational thought overcame him. She was bringing a man to her room!

At first, he couldn't think what to do. He wanted to charge out and confront her on the spot, but knew his control was nonexistent. There wasn't a doubt in his mind that he would kill, first the man and then her. Jesus Christ! How had she become so important to him? Why should a dalliance on her part send him into such blinding rage?

He leaned against the door and took deep, calming breaths. He had to get control over himself lest tragedy result.

He could hear them talking. Christ, why didn't they have the sense to lower their voices? Didn't they realize how sounds carried in the sleeping house?

Cameron couldn't stand it anymore. He was going to her room and, if his behavior was not exactly that of a sane man, Cassie and her lover would just have to bear the consequences.

He could hear movement behind the closed door and felt his temper begin to rise again. After a few whispered, harried words, Cassie opened the door.

Her hair was somewhat disheveled, but she was fully dressed, in the same clothes she had worn that evening. Well, at least she hadn't come directly from her bed. Cameron didn't know what he might have done if he had found her in a state of undress.

When Cameron looked at her more closely, he gasped, forgetting the angry accusation he was about to lay at her feet. Her forehead was bruised, and there was dried blood on her cheek. Her dress was caked with mud, and the rain had plastered what remained of her torn bodice to her full, lush figure. Shocked and upset, he didn't mince words. "What the hell happened to you?" he snapped.

Cassie faced her inquisitor with a blank expression. In her concern for Sunshine and her husband, she had forgotten her bruise and couldn't, for the life of her, understand why this man should be standing on her doorstep at four in the morning, asking such an odd question. "Who, me? Why?"

"Look at yourself! Dammit, Cassie . . ." His voice was beginning to rise, and Cassie quickly pulled him into her room lest he waken the entire household.

"Keep your voice down. You'll have the babies up . . ."

"I don't give a good goddamn who wakes up. Where the hell were you?"

Cassie tried the same lie she had given Roberts. "One of the Saxton children was ailing."

"And you went there alone in the middle of the night? Didn't I tell you . . ."

"I don't remember your issuing an order," she snapped defensively.

"Whether I did or not, you know my feelings on the subject? What happened?"

"When?"

Cameron was fast losing his patience. "Look in the mirror," he ordered as he dragged her to the mirror over the dry sink.

Cassie gasped when she saw the condition of her face. Cameron gave her a hard shake. Tell me!"

"I . . . I fell."

Cameron breathed a sigh of disgust and shoved her away. In truth, he didn't trust his hands not to slide around her throat. It was obvious she had had a fall,

215

but that wasn't all that had happened tonight. With an outward appearance of calm, he sauntered across the room and seated himself determinedly in an armchair before the cold hearth. "I'm not leaving here until you tell me."

It was then that he noticed Sunshine, standing with her back pressed up against the wall as if the house might fall without her support. As her eyes darted wildly between him and her mistress, Cameron found his anger mounting. The girl was terrified. That much was obvious. Now, what the hell would have scared her so? What was she hiding? Was she in on it? Did she know of Cassie's lover? Was she frightened at having taken part in this sordid mess? Is that why she was up at this hour? But if Cassie brought her lover here, why would Sunshine have remained? Cameron's gut twisted as a thought come to torment. Surely she wouldn't . . . Not with an audience.

"You won't be needed any more, Sunshine," he said. "You may retire."

Sunshine sent her mistress an imploring look.

"It's all right," Cassie assured her. "I'll call you when I need you."

"She won't be needing you. Get out."

But after months of separation, Sunshine couldn't tear herself from the man hiding beneath Cassie's bed. Her eyes moved wildly between the bed and her mistress as she inched toward the door.

A simpleton would have realized someone was under the bed. Cameron cursed and came instantly to his feet. "Stay where you are," he ordered Sunshine. Then, he turned toward the bed. "You, under the bed. You have till I count to ten to come out. After that,

I'm going to shoot."

James, of course, had no way of knowing Cameron was unarmed. And Cassie could not tell him, lest she admit to his presence. Maybe, just maybe, she could bluff her way out of this. If only James would keep his senses about him and remain quiet.

"Cameron, you have no . . ."

"One."

Cassie groaned silently as James moved out from under the bed.

Cameron felt his knees weaken with relief. He sank to the chair again. This man was obviously not her lover, but what was he doing under her bed? He turned to Cassie with an incredulous expression. "What the hell is going on? Who is he?"

Sunshine was sobbing as she clung to her terrified husband, while Cassie stood by, nervously twisting her dress. "Cameron," she began, "please don't take him back."

"Who is he?"

"Cameron, please," she begged. "They'll kill him. He didn't mean for it to happen. He was only protecting me."

Cameron ran his fingers through his hair in frustration. His relief at finding Cassie innocent of his wild imaginings was now replaced by new suspicions that were causing his anger to rise again to a dangerous level. "Who the hell is he, dammit!"

"This is James, Sunshine's husband. They were brought here on the same ship, but separated at the auction." When this information brought forth no reaction, Cassie dared to repeat, "Cameron, I swear it was an accident." And then, thoughtlessly, she added,

217

"He didn't mean to kill him."

"What the hell are you talking about? Kill who?"

Cassie groaned. Too late, she clamped her mouth shut. Why had she said anything? He hadn't known, and if she'd had the sense to hold her tongue, he might never have known. Roberts's body was hidden far beneath the hay. No one would find it for days. She could have somehow disposed of it without anyone's being the wiser. Cassie's shoulders slumped. All her efforts were for naught. What a fool she had been to speak without thinking first.

"If you know what's good for you, you'll tell me. Right now!" These last two words were bellowed across the room. Cassie jumped at the sudden sound and quickly answered, instinctively knowing that any hesitation at all would bring him flying out of his chair.

"Roberts. But he didn't mean it."

Cameron took a deep calming breath. "Woman, kindly stop repeating yourself and tell me who Roberts is and what happened tonight."

"Roberts is . . . was the overseer at Spencer's place. He attacked me."

Cameron's eyes grew hard and his mouth thinned into a grim, forbidding line. He was shaking with rage. That any man would dare to touch her was unthinkable. He was amazed at the calmness of his voice as he asked, "Where?"

"Outside the barn."

"He was waiting for you?" A vein throbbed at his temple.

Cassie trembled. She'd never seen him like this. He looked like he was about to commit murder, and she wasn't sure she wouldn't be his first victim. "No. He

218

was accompanying me home. He said I needed protection."

Cameron shook his head in confusion. "You were with him tonight?"

"No. Well, yes, for a little while. He was searching for James."

"Apparently, James is an escaped slave. Am I right?" Cassie nodded.

"Are you telling me James jumped aboard your buggy on the way home from the Saxtons' and killed this Roberts?" Cameron shot the man a look that promised death. He'd kill the man for daring to involve her in his problem.

"Not exactly."

Cameron turned to face her. "No? Suppose you tell me exactly where you found him, then."

"Down by the river."

"What the hell were you doing there?"

Cassie shivered as she waited for him to explode. She spoke so low he could hardly hear her. "Picking him up."

"What?" he roared as he jumped to his feet.

"I went there to pick him up."

"By yourself?" He couldn't believe it. This woman didn't have the sense she was born with. How could anyone be that stupid? He began to pace.

"Well, I thought . . . What with everyone knowing I'm often called out . . ." Cassie shook her head. "I thought I'd be safe enough."

"Oh, my God," Cameron groaned as he ran his fingers through his hair, then loosed a string of curses even Cassie had never heard before. Fighting for control, he took a deep breath, then turned to address her. "Sit down and stop that damn fidgeting."

Cassie moved quickly to the edge of her bed. When she had finally complied with his order, he said, "I think you'd best start at the beginning."

Obediently, Cassie told him the whole story. When she was finished, Cameron breathed a long sigh, nodded, then came to his feet and spoke dispassionately to the young couple. "Come with me."

Cassie jumped up. "Wait! I told you it wasn't his fault. You can't take him back."

Cameron turned and looked down at her distraught expression, still too enraged to ease her worries. "Go to bed."

"Cameron, please. I'll do anything, anything! Let them go."

In truth, he had no intention of turning the runaway in, for many a slave had passed through his hands heading north to freedom. But Cameron was nothing if not shrewd. Her promise of "anything" was enough to turn his thoughts in other, more agreeable directions. It wouldn't hurt to let her believe the worst. Not if it finally got him what he wanted more than anything else.

He gave Cassie a meaningful look. He didn't have to say a word. She knew from his sudden, blatantly sexual expression, exactly what he wanted.

Feigning ignorance, Cassie sighed. "All right, all right. I promise I'll never go out alone again. Night or day, I'll take someone with me."

Cameron chuckled at her ploy. "Not good enough." He took James by the arm.

"No!"

Cameron raised a quizzical brow, daring her to deny

these two their freedom.

Cassie almost choked on the words, her face aflame, knowing that others were listening. "I'll share your bed."

Cameron smiled and shook his head.

"I'll marry you, damn it! Are you satisfied?"

Chapter Sixteen

Cassie paced her bedroom floor for hours. After Cameron left, she had bathed and changed into a light cotton gown. There was no sense dressing for bed. Sleep was out of the question until she knew the outcome of this horrid night.

The breakfast hour had come and gone and still she had heard nothing. Where had he gone? Where had he taken them? Had he found Roberts's body and disposed of it? Cassie shivered at the gruesome thought. Oh God, why didn't he come back and tell her?

Roberts's horse! Had Cameron remembered? Was it still tied to her buggy? Cassie dashed from her room and almost flew down the stairs. If anyone saw the horse, how would she explain?

Panic stricken, she hitched up her skirts and ran for the barn, uncaring that her ankles and calves were exposed to the stares of the yard workers. Reaching the huge building at last, she sighed with relief. Her buggy stood, as usual, in the leanto at the side of the barn. Roberts's horse was nowhere in sight.

Slowly, almost against her will, she entered the barn. Her eyes were wide with fear as she moved past the stalls, ignoring the snickering welcome of the beautiful animals within, inching toward the huge bale of hay against the back wall. Her blue eyes darted wildly about, nervously seeking that which she dreaded most to find. Was he still here? She shivered with disgust. Had Cameron thought to remove the body?

Cassie knew it had been placed deep within the pile of hay. Hadn't she, in a frenzied state of terror, assisted in hiding the corpse? And yet, she couldn't prevent a tentative toe from reaching out and dislodging a few wisps from the edge. She had to know. She couldn't stand the endless hours of waiting in this debilitating state of fear.

Cassie moved her foot again, trembling, her guilty imagination running wild, almost expecting the bloodied corpse to come lunging out at her.

"I'm afraid he couldn't jump out at you, even if he were still there."

Cassie spun about, gasping with shock. So filled with guilt was she, it took a full minute for her to realize that it was Cameron, and not the constable, who had spoken.

"Is he . . . ?"

"Dead? Most assuredly."

Cassie shook her head.

"Gone? I've taken care of it."

Cassie sighed with relief and had to catch at one of the barn's supporting beams, for her shaking knees were in danger of collapsing beneath her.

"I expect that you'll never again place yourself in circumstances such as these." And when Cassie did no more than stare at her feet, he insisted, "I'll have your

223

word on it, Cassie."

"Cameron, this was an accident."

"And if the man hadn't met his maker, what then?" His mouth thinned in anger. "Were you prepared for the consequences of assisting an escaped slave? Do you know what could have happened to you were you found out?"

This was too much. Not only had she been made to suffer endless hours of agony, but now it appeared he thought a good tongue lashing in order. Cassie's chin lifted and she held up her hand as if to halt any further lambasting. "I'm not about to involve myself again. You need not worry on that account. Where are they?"

"Safe."

"Cameron!"

"The less you know the better."

Cassie almost laughed at the ridiculous statement. "Do you think I might tell someone?"

Cameron was exhausted and more than a bit annoyed that she had shown such disregard for her own safety. Still, he managed to bite back the angry words that threatened. He sighed as he ran his fingers through his hair. "Cassie, am I to be forever bombarded by your constant chatter?"

His attitude enraged her. How dare he keep her in the dark? Didn't he realize she was desperate to know what had happened after he left her last night? Didn't he imagine the extent of her suffering? Her lips thinned and her dark blue eyes narrowed as she suddenly, and belligerently, reached out and grabbed his shirt front. Despite his irritation, Cameron almost laughed, for the raging Cassie stood almost a head

224

shorter than the man she was threatening. "Constant chatter, is it?" she demanded angrily.

Cameron chuckled as he gazed down at her irate expression. "If you want this to work, you'll have to find something to stand on."

Further incensed by his sudden, joking manner, she yanked even harder at his shirt. "Tell me, you wretch."

"That's better." Cameron grinned as he placed his hands about her waist and lifted her to eye level.

"Cameron!" she warned.

"But this is better still." Effortlessly, he flung her over his shoulder.

Cassie gasped at the sudden movement, and it took her a moment before she could find her voice. "Put me down this instant!" she demanded, and, when he chose to ignore her, she punched his back. To her chagrin, she received a none too gentle slap on the bottom in return. "Ow! You beast!"

Cameron was chuckling as he moved through the yard, oblivious to the startled looks of his men. Cassie could not claim the same enjoyment. She was mortified, knowing the servants would have a field day with this episode.

By the time he dumped her upon the bed, she was absolutely livid. In an instant, she was up and charging at his laughing form. Cameron grunted as her head butted against his chest and knocked him back into the dry sink. The mirror above the sink and the pitcher perched upon it crashed to the floor, but Cameron took no notice. All his attention was focused on warding off yet another attack. Swiftly, he captured her wildly swinging arms and held them securely at her back. "You're going to hurt yourself," he warned as he inched her struggling form back to the bed.

"I'm going to hurt you first," she snarled between clenched teeth as she fought to free herself.

"Cassie, calm down, dammit!"

"Ow!" he yelled as the heel of her boot met his shin. Together, they toppled upon the bed, which, under the force of the impact, went crashing to the floor.

Cameron shook with laughter as he held her pinned beneath him. "Instead of fighting me, I would have thought you'd be readying yourself for our wedding."

"Our wedding? Ha!" She laughed sarcastically. "Do you seriously believe I'd marry a brute such as you?"

"You gave your word on it." He smiled smugly.

"I take it back."

"Too late. I've witnesses."

"Do you?" Cassie snorted with disgust. Suddenly, a cunning look entered her eyes. "Produce them if you dare," she said triumphantly.

Cameron laughed. "Cassie, I've told you they were safe. Why isn't that enough?"

"Cameron, please. You can't be so cruel."

Cameron sighed and shook his head in defeat. "I can see you'll never let me rest until I tell you. They're aboard my ship, heading for New York. Are you satisfied?"

Cassie breathed a sigh of relief. "Thank God."

"Now, about our wedding. When do you want to get married?"

"I don't."

Cameron smiled. "Let me rephrase that. How long will it take for you to be ready?"

226

"Five years," she grunted. "Get off me."

Cameron chuckled. Seemingly perfectly content in his present position, he remained where he was. "Let's try again. I know how anxious you are. How does tomorrow sound? Would that be soon enough?"

"Tomorrow!" Cassie stared at him aghast.

Cameron shrugged. "Of course, if you insist, I'm sure Reverend Collins could be persuaded to perform the nuptials this afternoon."

"Cameron, wait a minute."

"That's about as long as I care to wait."

"There's no need to rush, is there?"

"I think it's better to get this settled, don't you?" His mouth twitched with humor. "Why, if we wait any longer, there's no telling who you might ask to marry you. And since I'm perfectly willing to make the sacrifice . . ."

"Cameron, be serious. I don't have anything to wear. It will take weeks . . ."

"Umm, I suppose that does pose a problem. Although I can't imagine why, since you'll have little use for clothing of any kind within an hour or so of the ceremony."

"Cameron!"

His dark eyes narrowed with reproach. "I seem to remember seeing Ellie doing laundry in the only gown that would have been suitable." Abruptly, he shrugged away the annoying memory of how she'd carelessly disposed of his gifts. "Perhaps you and I should pay a visit to Mrs. Hays. She should be able to come up with something, say by tomorrow or the day after."

* * *

227

Cassie trembled before the full-length mirror that now occupied a corner of her room. Meghan swirled behind her in a dizzying cloud of pink gauze and ruffles. "Meghan, you'd best stop that twirling. Your father won't be pleased if you fall and rip your gown."

Meghan stopped her spinning, only to start jumping up and down with enthusiasm. Cassie only wished she felt half as eager to get on with this day's activities. She shivered with apprehension. How could she possibly feel so cold in this heat? The sun blazed down upon the big white house, and she knew that the good-sized crowd gathered in the downstairs drawing room must be sweltering. Still, she shivered.

From her room above, she could hear the subdued murmur of voices as the wedding guests found their seats. Cassie was amazed at the turnout. She had watched, from the upstairs window, as carriage after carriage rolled up to the wide front steps with scores of gaily clad men and women. She would have thought to see no more than half this showing on barely two days' notice.

Jessie fussed with the veiling and the ruffles at the hem of Cassie's white gown. "You look like a ghost, child," the black woman informed her as she pinched at Cassie's cheeks. "Bite your lips."

Cassie automatically did as she was told, her mind on the enormous step she was about to take.

"That's better," the housekeeper said approvingly. "They's almost ready for you."

Cassie shivered. "I'm not going to make it. I'm going to trip and fall down the stairs. I'll make a fool of myself."

Meghan giggled with delight, her childish imagination seeing Cassie turning cartwheels, head over heels, down the stairs.

"You'll do no such thing." Jessie shook her head. "Why, the very idea."

As if in a trance, Cassie allowed the woman to push her from her room toward the top of the stairs. Quickly, Jessie arranged the train of her gown. Cassie groaned. No, she wasn't going to trip; she was going to faint and then fall and make a fool of herself. Her heart thundered in her breast. She couldn't seem to get a breath deep enough to relieve the lightness in her brain.

As the music began and Meghan began her slow, practiced steps to the floor below, Cassie stiffened, almost paralyzed. All eyes lifted toward the small wedding party. Everyone was waiting for her entrance. God in heaven, what was she doing? Why was she allowing this?

Then, with a gentle nudge from Jessie, Cassie began a slow descent at just the right moment. Her eyes darted wildly about, unconsciously seeking a means of escape. How was she going to get through this? It didn't matter that she loved him. If anything, this sham of a marriage was all the more wrong because of that love. He didn't feel the same, and in all probability, never would. Cassie wasn't sure he cared for her at all, with the obvious exception of her responses to him in his bed. She wanted and needed more than that. She groaned in silent misery, for she hadn't a doubt in her mind that she was letting herself in for a lifetime of

229

anguish.

Cameron stood before the minister and smiled as his small daughter, with flashing, devilish eyes, made her way down the narrow aisle. His gaze moved past Meghan to the petite, red-headed woman who had brought his daughter back to him. Cameron was momentarily stunned. God, but she was a beauty. No simpering miss here, no weak damsel, pale of cheek, overcorseted and gasping for breath. His pride of possession was obvious to all as his gaze tenderly absorbed her radiance, her strength, and the most vivid beauty he had ever known. Delight filled his being. Delight, and something else he dared not name as he watched her slow, almost tentative, steps.

Suddenly, his heart stood still as he noticed her come to a halt. Her huge blue eyes were filled with fright. Cameron knew as surely as he would draw his next breath, she was ready to bolt for the front door. For an instant, he almost felt her despair. What chance had she, after all, pitted against his strength, his power, his wealth? Still, if any could give as good as she got, it was this woman. A smile touched the corners of his mouth, for he could honestly say their fights were almost as intriguing as their lovemaking. Almost, but not quite. He sighed with a mixture of anticipation and dread. No doubt she was certain to give him plenty of both.

Perhaps unconsciously anticipating Cassie's last minute change of heart, Cameron had earlier stationed two of the house servants just outside the drawing room doors. Each held one of the twins. Cameron willed her to look at where they stood, for

230

surely the sight of the babies would remind this stubborn woman of what she risked losing should her steps falter.

When she failed to look in the babies' direction, he cursed to himself. Damn! She was going to bolt. Cameron cared not at all that he would find himself the object of ridicule: he only knew he wanted this woman with a desperate longing that knew no bounds. And if he didn't do something and do it fast, it would be too late to stop her.

Cameron cleared his throat, deliberately bringing her attention from the silent, suddenly uneasy crowd to him. Still, she did not move. Instinctively, he knew no tender looks of longing would work now. What she needed was a healthy dose of anger.

His eyes narrowed and his brow lifted tauntingly as he silently dared her to flee. His gaze accused her of cowardice. He soundlessly laughed at her fears. Suddenly, he was biting the inside of his mouth lest he smile with relief as he watched her back stiffen with grim determination. He knew he had nothing to fear. She would come to him, this spirited lady, and in doing so, would fill his life with a happiness he hadn't dared believe possible.

Cassie's lips thinned with anger. So, he thought to laugh at her, did he? No tender looks, no gentle smiles of encouragement from this man. He wanted a wife merely to warm his bed. An evil smile teased her lips. What a shame, then, to have chosen her, for she was no sweet, pliable thing. Filled with quiet determination, she began to move toward him, while her blue eyes promised it wouldn't be long before he'd curse the day he'd asked her to marry him.

Diana watched from among the guests. Her eyes were hard with hatred. The two sneaking sons of bitches were going to pay for this. He had teased her into believing she had a chance, all the while hiding his lust for the bitch. They had been carrying on right beneath her nose, and she'd never even suspected it.

Cassie, the sniveling little bitch, had managed to capture the most intriguing man Diana had ever known. The man Diana had wanted right from the first, and Cassie was going to pay for that.

Diana's eyes narrowed with evil promise. If they thought a piece of paper was going to save them from their just reward, they'd best think again, for she had plans, delicious plans for the two of them.

If Reverend Collins realized the animosity of the bride toward her groom, he gave no notice at first. In truth, the gentle, charitable man attributed her tight-lipped, hesitant answers for nervousness. Yes, he had seen many such as she. He smiled at the obvious state of her nerves and smiled again as he was forced to repeat the vows for her. It wasn't until he asked for the joining of their hands that his gray eyes widened with shock. For when she finally obeyed his request, Cassie extended her hand toward her groom with such force as to appear that she was delivering a punch to his mid-section.

Cassie smiled for the first time in two days at Cameron's sudden expulsion of breath as her knuckles struck his waist. But Cameron was undaunted by her unsubtle display. Almost casually, he secured her hand in his and after some effort, managed to place a gold band upon her stiff, tightly clenched finger.

Cassie struggled to free her hand and glared at her groom. No one, save the minister, observed her last ditch effort to secure her freedom.

Reverend Collins had never seen the like. Why, at any second, he half expected one to throw the other to the ground and begin their fighting in earnest. Instead of loving glances and tender smiles, they appeared ready to square off and await the timekeeper's announcement of round one.

Cameron was smiling, but his gaze held a clear warning, while the lady fairly snarled her responses.

"Would you two like a moment or so to air this problem?"

Cameron and Cassie answered simultaneously.

"Yes!" she hissed.

"Get on with it!" he snapped.

Reverend Collins shook his head. Merciful heavens, were his eyes playing tricks, or had she actually punched his hand?

A moment later, he joined Cameron in a sigh of relief as he pronounced them man and wife.

Cameron was forcibly holding her to his side as he offered his other hand to the minister. "Thank you, Reverend. You must come to dinner soon. My wife and I insist."

Cassie grunted from the pressure of his arm. Damn the man and his insufferable arrogance. She didn't love him. She couldn't love someone like him!

Cameron whispered to her as he lifted her veil to bestow a husbandly kiss. "Behave yourself, or I'll carry you over my shoulder to my room and give you what

233

you deserve."

Having no doubt that he meant what he said, Cassie gave a slight shrug of acceptance. She had made her feelings known. To continue in this vein would only bring about her embarrassment, not his. No, she'd try a different ploy. A wicked smile touched her lips. The man was going to go stark raving mad by the time she was finished.

"Why, sweetheart," she said roguishly, "I know how eager you are, but surely you can control your baser instincts in front of Reverend Collins." Her smile widened as she heard the minister gasp. She shot Cameron a look of triumph as she turned to the well-wishers gathering around them and graciously accepted their congratulations.

Cameron paled at the thought of what his pretty wife might do next. He needn't have worried, however, for if she seemed cold and aloof toward him, the guests merely attributed her manner to bridal modesty. It was later, in the privacy of their rooms, that the real battle would take place.

Cameron turned to a firm slap upon his back. "If I couldn't have her—" Tom Billings grinned— "I'm glad to see you had the sense not to let her slip through your fingers."

Cameron gave his friend a brotherly hug. "It was touch and go for a time," he admitted. "At the last minute, I thought she might change her mind."

Tom laughed. "She loves you, you know. I hope you give her no reason to regret it."

Cameron felt a sudden surge of untarnished happiness, then quickly thrust it aside. It was pure folly to imagine such tenderness on her part. After all, she was a woman, like any other. And if he was foolish enough to expect more from this one, he'd only be doomed to disappointment.

Cassie hurriedly undressed, carelessly throwing her clothes any which way. She had to move fast. She had to be in bed and at least appear asleep before Cameron came upstairs.

She had tried to talk to him after the last of their guests had left. It had been impossible. An important packet of papers had arrived during the party and had to be seen to before he retired.

Cassie lay alone in the dark, marveling at the strangeness of it all. Who would have thought she'd spend her wedding night by herself? Somewhere at the back of her mind, she sensed a vague feeling of disappointment. She was mistaken, of course. This was what she wanted. How could she be disappointed when things were turning out exactly as she had hoped they would?

She wondered what Cameron would do when he found his bed empty. Surely, he would rant and rave. Tomorrow, he probably wouldn't talk to her. Too bad. She hadn't wanted this marriage. He had coerced her into it. Cassie shuddered to realize he owned her now as surely as he did his horses. Undoubtedly, he was as fond of her as he was of them. Perhaps less, she reasoned, for he had owned his horses longer.

She shrugged as she snuggled her head into her soft pillow. She didn't care what he felt. She didn't care anything about him. All she wanted was to be left in peace.

She should have known that was not to be.

Cameron entered his room and lit the candle on the bedside stand. A weary glance at his empty bed caused him a sigh of disgust as he sat and removed his boots. He would have been surprised to see her here. He had purposely remained downstairs, giving her more than enough·time to ready herself for the wedding night, all the while knowing in his heart there wouldn't be one.

No doubt she was snug in her bed, feigning sleep, while he was supposed to act the gentleman and leave her bed. Goddammit! He raged with sudden fury. This was his house. She was his wife. He flung his coat to the chair, his anger growing with every passing moment. He didn't need this aggravation. He was tired. He didn't feel up to doing battle, but he'd take no further nonsense from the woman. 'Twas best she learned from the start who was master here.

Cameron walked the short distance to her room and entered on bare feet. Cassie almost screamed with shock as strong arms suddenly reached beneath her and lifted her from the bed. It took no more than an instant for her to know who held her. Her heart began to thunder against her breast. She was stiff and unyielding as he held her to his chest. "Cameron!" she protested weakly. "Cameron, we have to talk."

"Not tonight," he murmured tightly as he returned to his room holding her securely in his arms.

"Put me down. It's *about* tonight that we need to

236

talk."

"Shut up."

Suddenly, she was flying through the air, landing with a hard bounce upon his bed. Her eyes were wide with fear at his quiet, cold rage. Perhaps she had gone too far. Yes, she should have talked to him first. She should have told him her intentions.

Cameron stood at the side of the bed, his gaze never leaving her own as he slowly finished undressing. "You needn't look so terrified. You've seen me naked before."

"No!" she. choked, barely above a whisper.

"Yes!" he insisted as he reached for the neck of her nightdress and ripped it clear to the hem. A moment later, he wrested her arms from the torn garment and threw it to the floor.

Cameron bit back the groan of pleasure that rose in his throat as he covered her naked body with his. She was so warm, her scent and feel so lusciously inviting, he wondered if he had the strength to do what he must.

"Cameron, don't do this. I don't want this," she gasped, every muscle stiffening against the burning heat his touch inflicted. She wedged her hands between their bodies and pushed. A moment later, her hands were captured within his one and brought above her head.

"That is all too obvious, madam," Cameron grunted as he fought to hold her legs down with his weight. "Still, there is the matter of duty, is there not? And since it's something that must be done, why not enjoy it?

"No, my darling wife"—he smiled with no little sarcasm as he felt her go stiffer and watched her squeeze her eyes shut—"How does it go? Close your eyes and think of England? But not tonight. You'll open your eyes. You'll know all that I do." A slow grin curved his harsh mouth as his voice dropped ominously. "And you'll remember this night for as long as you live."

Outraged at his insolent words, she snarled, "Why you arrogant bas . . ."

Her words were instantly muffled as his warm lips covered her mouth. The kiss went on and on. Cassie fought for control, but despite a valiant effort she felt her resistance waver. She grew dizzy, filled with his taste and scent. How had he managed to acquire such power over her? She didn't want this. She couldn't permit someone else to have such power over her. She groaned as his tongue sought entrance to her mouth and groaned again as she helplessly allowed it. She wanted to cry out that she was no match against his strength and determination, no match against his lust—not when hers could grow instantly as strong.

Her eyes were glazed, her lips swollen, moist and red, when he released her mouth. She was gasping for breath, her chest rising and falling with her rapid breathing. "I won't share your bed. You forced me into this marriage," she insisted, her voice more a whine than a whisper.

"Perhaps, but now that you are married, you might make the best of it."

"I can't breathe. You're too heavy."

Cameron smiled. "You never complained before."

"Oh God, but I hate your arrogance, your conceit, your sarcasm. I hate you."

Cameron gave a cruel laugh. "And you hate this, don't you?" he asked as his free hand found one breast and gently rolled the sensitive tip between his fingers. His mouth was on hers again, his tongue delving deep into the warmth of her, greedily taking of her moistness, breathing her haunting scent. He felt her grow soft and pliable beneath him and laughed at her inability to resist his touch.

Cassie knew well enough the cause of his merriment. "You're disgusting," she snarled the moment their lips parted.

His dark eyes taunted. His grin widened. "Perhaps, but do you hate it?"

"I hate it!" She groaned as if in pain, fighting the growing ache that demanded he give her more.

Cameron chuckled at the obvious lie. His mouth teased hers, brushing it with a feather light touch, creating a fever only his lips could ease. He teased until she could think of nothing but his kiss, and then he broke it, beginning a new torment as his hot, wet mouth traveled to her breast. Slowly, expertly, he teased the soft flesh, avoiding the most sensitive tip, until her body trembled and she nearly bit her lip through rather than beg him to take her in his mouth. Her back arched unconsciously as she offered herself to him, while low, urgent sounds came from her throat.

Then, lights flashed behind her closed eyes and blinding joy filled her being as his lips found her nipple at last and suckled with hungry pleasure. He was driving her out of her mind.

She moaned, aching with need as he increased the delicious torment, moving his left hand from her breast to her belly, and then down to the juncture of her thighs where it lingered searingly. Her legs parted. She gave a silent curse. But it was too late. She couldn't stop. She wanted him as badly as he wanted her.

He released her hands then, and mad for the touch of him, she ran her hands over his shoulders and neck, pressing his mouth closer to her burning flesh. His body shuddered as his fingers brushed the liquid heat between her thighs. She was moist and ready. Oh God, how was he going to find the strength?

Suddenly, his fingers thrust deep inside her. "Do you hate this?" he asked, taking her breath away as he explored the velvety recesses. She couldn't speak, simply arched her hips against his hot, probing fingers.

"Do you hate this?" he repeated as his thrusting hand raised her to fever pitch. "Do you want me to touch you there?"

"Yes, oh God, yes."

"Will you share my bed every night?"

Lord, why did he feel it necessary to talk? Her body was so filled with sensation, she couldn't string the words together for an answer. She groaned, she gasped, but no words would come.

"Will you?"

"Yes. Cameron, please," she moaned as her hips strained toward his next delicious thrust.

Gasping for breath he raised himself up on his hands and knees. His body trembled as if possessed of fever. She was so soft, so eager, so ready for his taking. His body screamed with agony as he pulled away to reach over and snuff out the candle. He couldn't bear to look at the anguished need in her eyes; her thick, curling hair spread out upon the pillow; her naked, lush form — not if he hoped to retain his sanity.

"Go to sleep," he said abruptly. He heard her soft gasp of surprise. "What?"

"Go to sleep," he repeated, his voice devoid of all emotion.

Stiff with shock, she lay silently beside him. What had happened? Why had he stopped? Her cheeks flamed as she remembered her wild reaction to his touch, her clinging arms, the eager lifting of her hips. How could he have turned from her? How could he have been so unaffected by her response?

But he hadn't been unaffected. She had felt the proof of his desire hard against her belly. She had seen it, even as he undressed before her.

Then why? Why had he stopped? What more did he want that she wasn't willing to give? What had she done wrong? Suddenly, she gave a soft gasp. *Nothing! You did nothing wrong,* she told herself, *except try to refuse him. And for that, you were punished. He showed you how easy it was to take you at his will. It matters not that he wants you. Again, he's proving himself the master — even in his lust for you.*

She cringed as she curled up on her side and moved as close to the edge of the bed as she dared. She was mortified. The man wanted to rob her of all her pride. He wanted her to beg! If he thought she would turn to him and ask . . . She gave a small shudder; she'd die before she'd beg. Damn the man and his insufferable arrogance. It didn't matter how badly her body craved his touch. She'd never . . . never go to him.

A tiny sound like a sob came unexpectedly to her lips, and warm hands instantly pulled her gently into a comforting embrace. She was stiff as he gathered her into his arms.

"Go to sleep, Cassie," he breathed into her hair, sick at heart for what he had done. Why had it seemed so important? He knew what her response would be. What had he proven? Why had he insisted on showing her his power over her body? His body ached for her, but he knew now that he didn't want her to bend to his will. He wanted her to come to him. He wanted her to desire him as much as he did her.

He stifled a groan as he rubbed his face in her hair. God, was there any help for them? How were they to survive if neither could overcome such fierce pride?

The words stuck in his throat, but he finally managed to say, "Cassie, I'm sorry. That was uncalled for."

She sighed. She was tired, so tired. Her emotions couldn't take much more. She loved this man. Half of the time she wondered why. He was everything she despised. Arrogant, mean-tempered, willful, and, worst of all, the owner of slaves. Yet, there was no help for it. She loved him. Good Lord, was she out of her mind?

Cassie answered his gentle coaxing and turned toward him. With a mournful sigh, she buried her face in the warmth of his neck. Why couldn't he always treat her so tenderly? Why couldn't she do the same?

He could feel the warmth of her tears against his

242

skin, and his chest constricted in pain. Gently he rubbed his hand over her back. "Do you think there's a chance for us? Could we begin again?"

Without a moment's hesitation, she nodded eagerly.

"Will you share my bed, if I promise to do no more than hold you?"

"Would you do that?" Cassie moved her head from the hollow of his neck. "Would you promise?" She was amazed. She couldn't believe her ears. He had wanted to marry her only to satisfy his carnal desires, and now he was willingly putting aside his lust! What was this man about?

Cameron's tender smile flashed in the near dark room. "I would."

"Why?"

"We've just decided to begin again, haven't we?"

Cassie nodded.

"We'll wait, then," he soothed. "We'll wait until you're ready."

Cassie's eyes were wide with confusion as she stared into his tender gaze. She couldn't fathom his reasoning. Why would he do this? Why wouldn't he insist on his conjugal rights?

Cameron offered no explanation. He didn't understand it himself, and he prayed she'd question him no further. A gentle smile curved his lips. "Since we're beginning again, shall I introduce myself?"

Cassie giggled at his teasing. "I think you might skip that formality."

"Cassie?"

"What?"

He had to ask, had to clear the air if they were ever

243

to have a chance. He had to know the reasons for what she had done before he could begin to trust her. "Why did you lie? Why didn't you tell me from the first who you were?"

Slowly, she told him the whole story, and, listening to the gentle sound of her voice in the dark, Cameron believed her. When she had done, he pulled her even closer to his warmth. Sighing contentedly, she snuggled against him and was soon asleep.

Cameron lay awake for a long time, listening to the gentle, deep sounds of her breathing, fighting to control the aching need to make her truly his. A wry smile twisted his lips, for no matter his blustering comments and sworn vows to the contrary, he hadn't a doubt who was master here.

244

Chapter Seventeen

Cassie gave a low moan of discomfort, rolled on to her stomach, and pulled the pillow over her head. She had forgotten to draw the drapes last night and the summer sun was glaring into her eyes.

As she stretched sleepily, her arm and leg suddenly brushed against something unexpected. She gasped. She wasn't alone.

Slowly, she turned to her side and raised her head. Her eyes grew wide with surprise to find Cameron beside her. Realization finally dawned and she bit back a low chuckle at her foolishness. How could she have forgotten falling asleep at his side? A wry grin touched her lips. Willing or not, she was his wife and had best get used to the idea of sharing his bed. It seemed that the man would insist upon at least that much.

She shifted to lean upon her elbow and take in the magnificent sight before her. Slowly, and hesitantly, she allowed her inquisitive gaze to move over his sleeping form. Timid inquiry soon turned to lusty enjoyment, and a tender, almost wistful smile curved her lips. God, but he was beautiful. She knew men weren't supposed to be thought of in those terms, but there was simply no other word for it.

His bronzed chest was wide, generously covered with dark hair, and even in sleep looked rock hard. Cassie felt a slight tremor as the sight beckoned her touch, and she had to force her hand to remain at her side. She shook her head, refusing the temptation. Instinctively, she knew that the enticement of warm, hard flesh would prove devastating to her senses. Should she succumb and allow herself to touch him, she knew all too well what would follow.

Her gaze traveled downward. During the night, he had pushed down the sheet and Cassie's cheeks pinkened as she took in the long length of him. One leg was uncovered, and the sheet rode low on his hip, dangerously close to exposing that which Cassie yearned, yet feared, to gaze upon. Obviously, more sheet was needed here.

Gently, she lifted the covering and brought it up to his chest. Cameron mumbled incoherently and shifted in his sleep. Suddenly, the sheet was past his waist again, even lower than before.

Cassie gulped, for it barely, just barely, hid him from her suddenly hungry gaze. Her heart thundered. Her mouth grew suddenly dry. She licked her lips, swallowed, and shivered with a burning need to see even more.

Without thinking, she reached her hand out, then stopped in midair, only to return to her burning cheeks. She couldn't move the sheet without touching him, and if she touched him, she'd never stop. No, not yet, she reasoned. They had to grow to know each other. If this coming together were to have any great meaning, they needed time. No matter the agony each might suffer, she knew her decision to be right.

Involved as she was in watching her husband, Cassie had forgotten that she, too, was nude, and the sheet was bunched up at her waist. Cameron's heart hammered against his chest, but he forced his body to give no sign of his wakeful state. Between slitted eyes, he watched as she moved her hand, hovered above him, then pulled back again. He almost groaned his disappointment aloud. He couldn't remember a time when he had so wanted a woman. Please God, soon, he silently prayed.

He felt her moving away, slowly inching her body to the edge of the bed. Cameron knew full well his promise to wait until she was ready before consummating the marriage. Still, that promise did not preclude all intimacy between them. And there was little likelihood of its going any further if she crept from his bed every morning upon awakening.

With a loud growl, he leaped up and lunged upon her startled form. Cassie shrieked with surprise and landed on her back, with him above her.

"Good morning, my love," he said with a grin.

Cassie blinked, astonished at his sudden move. "You don't wake up like that every morning, do you?"

"Only when I'm happy."

Cassie gave a low sultry laugh, and at the sound, Cameron felt an ache begin deep within him. "Perhaps, then, I should take pains to ensure your unhappiness, thereby adding years to my life."

His tender look left Cassie suddenly uncaring that her breasts were naked against his warm chest.

"It's a beautiful morning, is it not?" he asked.

Cassie smiled, knowing he had no firsthand knowledge of the weather save for the cheerful chirping of a bluebird near their window and the warm sunshine that streamed into the room. "Is it? Have you been outside already?"

He smiled at her teasing. "We don't need to be outdoors. It's beautiful enough in here."

Cassie blushed prettily, gave a throaty laugh, and eyed him suspiciously. "One wonders if there are not ulterior motives behind your suddenly glib tongue."

Cameron grinned. "Madam, I apologize if I've been remiss on that score." And at Cassie's smile, he continued. "It's time, then, to put things to rights, don't you think?"

Cassie giggled. "If you're asking my permission to bestow compliments, you may do so at your leisure."

"Might I?" He chuckled softly as his gaze dropped to her naked beauty. "I shall, but right now there are other matters I'd propose at my leisure."

"Cameron!" She gasped at his head suddenly dipped and his tongue slid over the tip of one exposed breast. She tried to raise the sheet, but found it locked in place between their bodies. "You promised," she reminded, her voice a bit more breathless than she would have liked.

Cameron laughed at her obvious and instant response to his touch. "You need not fear, madam wife. I wish only to sample this tempting morsel, no more."

"I think it might be wise, in the future, to wear my nightdress."

Cameron raised himself up. Unashamed of his nakedness, he knelt above her and held her hips securely between hard thighs. Distractedly, he began to caress and knead her satiny flesh, thumb and forefinger seeking her darkened nipple and twirling the sensitive tip until it grew rigid under his touch. "Would you deny me this pleasure, Cassie?"

Cassie had to force aside the fog of desire that threatened to engulf her. "Cameron, what good will it bring? How else are we to resist temptation?"

"But we need not resist. We need but to wait until you are ready. For myself, I find no virtue in forgoing all the pleasures of married life. Do you agree?"

Cassie may have been inclined to agree with what she suddenly considered brilliant logic, but the simple truth was she found herself unable to string two words together. Her eyes glazed over with desire and she sighed with the pure pleasure of his touch.

"I want your promise that if you should feel the need to touch me again, you will not hesitate to do just that."

It took a moment for his words to register, and Cassie's eyes opened wide with shock when they did. "You were watching me?"

"I was."

"But I thought . . ."

"You thought I was sleeping."

Cassie's face glowed fiery red with mortification. "I . . . I didn't . . ."

"But you wanted to," he said matter-of-factly. "You need not fear, Cassie. As now, nothing will happen. Not till you say it is time."

"It's not fair, you know." Cassie gave a breathless laugh as she pulled her horse to a stop along the

249

deserted beach. "There's no way I can win. You"—she shot him an accusing look—"wouldn't even allow me a head start."

Cameron smiled as he dismounted and helped her from her horse. "I remember promising a thing or two, just yesterday. Was a head start one of them?"

Cassie snorted at his teasing, then gasped as he slid her body provocatively down the length of his own until her feet touched the ground. "While you, on the other hand," he continued, "did promise to love and obey."

The pulse in her throat throbbed at the mention of her promise to love. Her cheeks colored with emotion. She lowered her eyes and prayed he'd not read the truth in her expression. Would she ever be able to tell him she already did love him? Would she ever trust him enough? Firmly, she set aside her desire to confess, then shot him a teasing look of disbelief. She took a step back and grinned. "Obey? You? Not likely."

His slow, wicked grin caused a lump to form in her throat. It became an effort for her to simply breathe as his fingers refused to relinquish their hold and moved with erotic teasing along the curve of her waist and hips. Her heart pounded against her ribs and a sudden wave of dizziness forced her to lean against him for support. God, he was so appealing. Vaguely, she wondered how she had managed to get through the intimacies shared that morning without succumbing. How was she to manage tomorrow? How long could she hold out against his allure?

Cameron grinned at her defiant words and her response to his touch which negated those words. "I have ways of ensuring your obedience, you know," he

250

taunted, only half-teasing.

"No doubt, but where's the challenge in that?" Cassie asked, growing more breathless with his every skillful movement.

"Life offers challenge enough, don't you agree?" he asked as his fingers slid from her waist to gently caress the tempting fullness of her breasts. He smiled with confidence as he heard her moan. "It doesn't hurt to assure oneself of an agreeable outcome."

Cassie sighed with relief as he allowed her to break his hold and step away. She couldn't count the number of times she had blushed this morning alone, and she didn't feel disposed to give him yet another display of reddened cheeks. She turned toward the water, welcoming the gentle offshore breeze against her flushed skin as still another wave of embarrassment overwhelmed her. Cassie had never imagined the marriage bed to be so blatantly intimate. She smiled and shook her head. What had she thought? In her inexperience, had she truly imagined a husband and wife to come together — partially clothed and under the cover of darkness — only to part after a quick coupling, never to speak of it?

Obviously, she couldn't have been more mistaken, for barely a moment passed that Cameron didn't tease in reference to their intimacy, no matter that the marriage had not been consummated.

Idly, she wondered if other couples laughed as freely on this subject. She wondered, too, of other husbands. Did they, also, strut about their bed-chambers, gloriously naked and seemingly indifferent to that fact? Cassie felt her cheeks grow warm again as she remembered his lack of modesty. Would it always be thus?

And if so, would she ever get used to it?

Cameron unsaddled the horses while Cassie spread a large, colorful quilt over the fine white sand beneath the shade of a huge tree. After placing a heavy picnic basket at one corner of the quilt, she stood and watched the huge, white-capped waves roll in from the ocean, then crash, and with sudden gentleness lap at the shoreline. Suddenly, strong warm arms slid familiarly around her waist.

Cassie sighed with contentment as she leaned back against him. "What are you thinking?" he asked as he rested his chin upon her head.

"I love the ocean," she began after some hesitation. She glanced up at him and smiled, then returned her gaze to the endlessly moving water. "When I was a little girl, my father had a summer home high above the beach. I used to fall asleep listening to the waves crash against the rocks below." She sighed again. "I think I never slept better."

"Sounds very nice, but that isn't what brought the color to your cheeks. What were you thinking?"

Cassie shrugged, reluctant to share her private thoughts.

"Tell me," he insisted as he lowered his head and brushed his mouth against her neck. "How can I ever come to know you unless you share your innermost thoughts?"

Cassie knew the truth of his words, yet found herself suddenly shy about complying. This was a new experience, this sharing of private thoughts. It was easy enough to say she wanted them to grow to know each other, but hard, in fact, to achieve that end. She stared straight ahead as she forced out the words, "I was wondering if all those who marry experience this particular degree of intimacy."

Cameron chuckled as he guided her to the quilt. Still holding her hand, he sat with his back against a tree, positioning her between his outstretched legs. "Are you suggesting we overindulge?"

Cassie shrugged again. "How can I say? I've no idea as to what's normal."

Cameron sighed as he breathed in the sweet scent of her hair. "I think there is no norm. If the two people involved are agreeable, all things are possible and probable."

"Do you believe others behave as . . . as . . . ?"

"Scandalously?" he asked with a decidedly lecherous grin. "I've no doubt."

"Oh dear," she groaned. "I was afraid of that. Now I'll be thinking the most embarrassing thoughts whenever . . ."

Cameron laughed. "You'd best curb your errant imaginings since your thoughts are all too often clearly read."

"In truth?" she asked with no little surprise as she turned to face him.

Cameron took the opportunity to open the buttons of her blouse. His fingers slid inside.

Cassie was not so accustomed to his intimate touches that she gave his caress no notice, and when he reached further inside to stroke her nipple, she couldn't stop the soft gasp that escaped her throat. "Cameron," she choked, her body suddenly stiffening, "someone might see us!"

Cameron smiled. "There is no one here."

"But suppose . . ."

"Madam, we are newly married. Anyone with eyes in their heads can see I cannot resist touching you."

"Can't you?" she asked huskily and leaned closer.

Cameron smiled as he watched her reaction, knowing it wouldn't be long before she tired of the game they played and invited further liberties. He almost chuckled as she closed her eyes with pleasure. He'd give her a week at the outside.

"Do you suppose this is a phenomenon that affects all those newly married?"

"I do," he assured her just before his mouth took her delectable lips.

"I wonder"—Cassie sighed with delight as his mouth left hers to nuzzle the silken skin of her neck—"how long something like this is destined to last."

"Oh"—Cameron shrugged, his mouth and tongue busy with exploring the delightful shape of her ear—"about forty years, I'd expect."

Cassie laughed at the absurdity of the notion.

"Do you doubt it?" he asked, his dark gaze wandering over her softened features.

"Cameron, be serious. Old people don't . . ."

"Don't they?" he interrupted. "Why ever not?"

"Because . . . because . . ." She lifted astonished eyes to his warm gaze. "Do they?"

Cameron laughed with pure enjoyment. "I've no doubt they do."

"Oh dear," she commented in a decidedly saddened tone.

"Have I given you more to think on?"

"I was thinking of all the poor women who profess to hate their duties in the marriage bed. How sad to endure years of suffering."

" 'Profess' is the key word here, I think. No proper lady admits to her lustful nature."

Cassie shot him a wary glance. "And you contend all ladies have them?"

"Them?" He smiled innocently.

Cassie poked his chest at his teasing. "Lustful natures."

"If they are alive and healthy, they do."

"No doubt you have firsthand knowledge on the subject." She eyed him suspiciously.

"Not as much as you suppose, I'd wager."

Cassie gave him a decidedly unladylike snort and tried to pull free of his embrace. "Surely you haven't learned such expertise . . ."

Cameron grinned at her unknowing compliment to his lovemaking. "Cassie, it's less a matter of lessons learned than thoughts put into action."

Cassie lowered her eyes, her lips pursed primly, her cheeks coloring as she remembered that morning's activities. "Decidedly lecherous thoughts, at best."

Cameron laughed. "Lecherous thoughts *are* the best, don't you think?"

Cassie smiled at his teasing. "I think I've taken a most shockingly villainous man for a husband. Do you intend to corrupt me with these evil doings?"

Cameron turned her to face him more fully, lowered her shift and took her exposed breasts into his hands. "I believe I already have."

Cameron lay with his head in her lap and breathed a long, contented sigh.

"Satisfied?" she asked.

He grinned and eyed her with an outrageous leer. Cassie giggled, knowing full well the double meaning he put upon her innocently asked question.

"Full."

"Annie packed enough food for six. I hope she doesn't expect the basket returned empty."

Cameron rolled over and pulled her down beneath him. "Perhaps she assumed we'd need to keep up our strength."

Cassie laughed at his teasing. "Sir, I'm, beginning to believe you are of but one thought and purpose."

Cameron laughed. "Did this notion just occur? The truth of it is, I've been of one thought and purpose since I first laid eyes on you." He sighed as he pulled her closer. "Even believing you to be my niece did not deter me, but merely increased my suffering."

A wicked grin hovered about Cassie's lips. "Did you suffer overmuch, Mr. Chandler, sir? Shall I make it better?"

Cameron eyed her warily. "And how, pray tell, would you accomplish that feat?"

Cassie shrugged. "I've had some experience administering to people's ills. I've been told my potions are no less than miraculous."

"No doubt. But it's not a matter of medicine that's needed in my case, don't you agree?"

Cassie shrugged again. "Who can say?" A good dose of castor oil cures many an ailment."

Cameron chuckled. "Do you believe a trip to the chamber pot a cure-all?"

"If nothing else, it will take your mind from other pressing matters."

"And I, for one, can attest to suffering the most

256

ACCEPT YOUR FREE GIFT AND EXPERIENCE MORE OF THE PASSION AND ADVENTURE YOU LIKE IN A HISTORICAL ROMANCE

Zebra Romances are the finest novels of their kind and are written with the adult woman in mind. All of our books are written by authors who really know how to weave tales of romantic adventure in the historical settings you love.

Because our readers tell us these books sell out very fast in the stores, Zebra has made arrangements for you to receive at home the four newest titles published each month. You'll never miss a title and home delivery is so convenient. With your first shipment we'll even send you a FREE Zebra Historical Romance as our gift just for trying our home subscription service. No obligation.

BIG SAVINGS AND FREE HOME DELIVERY

pressing of matters." Cameron grinned as he moved his hips against her thigh, allowing her to feel the proof of his words.

He glanced up as the sky began to darken and a chill wind came to ruffle Cassie's hair. Sighing, he dropped a quick kiss to her nose, then jumped easily to his feet, offering her his hand. "I hate to cut this afternoon short, but the sky looks nearly as frightening as you in one of your tempers."

Before Cassie had a chance to rise, huge, fat drops of water plopped upon the quilt. She gasped and shivered as the cold rain penetrated the sheerness of her blouse. Quickly, she gathered up the quilt, throwing the remains of the picnic lunch into the basket while Cameron readied his horse. In a matter of seconds, he swung her into his saddle and joined her there.

Holding the reins to Cassie's horse in one hand, his other around her waist, he galloped toward home. Before they'd gained a hundred yards, however, the rain had become a torrential downpour.

A high wind pummeled the rain against them, plastering their clothes to their bodies. Cassie shivered and pressed closer to her husband in a vain effort to find warmth. Unable to see more than a foot ahead, Cameron knew it was foolhardy to go on in such a blinding storm. He had to find shelter, or risk their being injured by broken tree branches flying at them from all directions.

He turned the horses around, but Cassie was too numb with cold to notice. A moment later, he was pulling her shivering form from his horse. Still in his arms, he brought her into an old, ramshackle cabin.

He left her there briefly to go back outside for the picnic basket.

Cassie brushed her soaking hair from her eyes and watched as he pulled the quilt from the basket and held it out to her. "Take off your clothes, Cassie. This will do you no good on top of your wet things."

Cassie did as she was told, and a moment later Cameron wrapped the heavy quilt around her body, naked but for her drawers, stockings and shoes. "Let me start a fire," he muttered, clearly in some distress as he moved away from her. "Damn!" he snapped as he searched his pocket for match and flint. "Everything is wet." He shook his head in disgust while glancing around the uninhabitable hut. "The fireplace is probably useless anyway."

Cameron was soaked to the skin and freezing. Though the hut offered but scant protection from the elements, he should not have been as chilled as he was. Then, glancing up, he suddenly realized he was still being rained upon. There was a large hole in the middle of the roof. The dirt floor was a river of mud and the only dry place seemed to be one small, junk-filled corner.

Quickly, he flung away the pieces of debris from the spot and moved Cassie against the wall. He would have taken her in her arms then, but his soaked through clothing would have only served to chill her once again.

Water ran from his face. He shivered agin.

"Cameron, take off your clothes and get inside this quilt."

Cameron shook his head. He hadn't a doubt as to what would happen if they were to share the blanket.

258

The sight of her wet, bedraggled figure had been, for some reason he could not fathom, powerfully erotic. His self-control was beginning to crumble after a long day of having his senses teased by her closeness. He was dangerously close to his limit and was not sure how much more he could endure. "I'm all right," he assured her through chattering teeth.

She dropped the quilt to the floor. "If you won't use it, then neither will I."

"Cassie!" He groaned as he retrieved the cover and bundled her up again.

"Do it."

He gave her a long look. "You know what will happen if I do?"

She nodded her head, her lips parted, her eyes suddenly filled with promise.

"Here?" he asked in amazement.

"Does it matter where?" Her voice sounded soft and throaty, and Cameron knew the last of his resolve was gone.

"Cassie, I imagined that our first time as man and wife would be in a bit more luxury than this." He looked about in disgust.

"Take off your clothes, Cameron, lest you take sick and there be no first time."

Chapter Eighteen

Their eyes held for long, breathless moments. The only sound in the shack was the continuous droning of rain against the thin walls and the pounding of suddenly racing hearts. Cassie watched as his long, tapered fingers slowly unfastened the buttons of his shirt.

Her mouth grew dry and the pulse in her throat throbbed as she remembered the delight those fingers could bring her. He would take her now. She shivered with anticipation. The time he'd set aside, to wait until she was ready, was now at hand. Had the storm not intervened, Cassie knew that the mounting sexual tension between them might have stretched into weeks of agonized waiting. She was suddenly very grateful to the powers above for putting an end to needless suffering.

Cassie was unaware of the sounds that came from her parted lips as she watched, mesmerized, by his every movement. With his shirt now open, he began very slowly — exquisitely slow — to pull it from his trousers, then shrug it off his broad shoulders.

Cassie's fingers itched to reach out and touch the firm flesh exposed, but somehow she knew the slightest motion on her part would bring to an instant close this seductive discarding of clothes. Until this moment, she had never realized the beauty and grace of his every movement. Everything about him enchanted her, and she waited with breathless anticipation to sample the joys only he could bring her.

Knowing what was to come, her legs grew weak, and she leaned against the wall of the shack for support as his fingers moved to his waist and continued his erotic disrobing. Her eyes rose to meet his dark gaze, and she knew that the slow peeling away of his clothes was deliberately provocative. His eyes issued a silent dare to resist and she knew it was beyond her power to do so.

Her breathing grew labored and she tore her eyes from his. She had to watch. She had to see all she could. She moaned as her gaze returned to his body, for his trousers suddenly fell to his feet, leaving him gloriously naked, but for his boots. Her hungry eyes moved slowly over the length of him, delighting in the sinewy flesh and corded muscles. Fascinated, she followed the thin ribbon of dark hair as it ran from his chest over his flat stomach to widen once again at his passion.

Cassie had seen him standing thus only this morning, but in the dim light of the run-down cabin, his bronzed, nude body drew her from an aching need she felt she'd never survive without his touch.

Her eyes closed, as if the sight was too much to bear. When she opened them again, even his boots were gone.

Her gazed moved slowly up the length of him. She couldn't bear the thought of waiting a moment longer. The blanket fell to her feet and her hands tore at her remaining clothes.

Moments later, she was standing as naked as he, her eyes pleading for him to close the distance between them. But he did not. His breathing was as ragged and labored as hers. Though the tangible evidence of his desire could not be denied, still he waited.

But Cassie was done with waiting. His shameless, delicious striptease had done away with the last of her reserve. She wanted this man as she would never want another. And she wanted him now.

His name was barely past her lips, and she was in his arms. His low cry of delight brought an answering moan from deep within her throat as flesh moved against flesh.

Cameron gasped as her musky female scent, mingled with a trace of jasmine, came to cloud his mind with a need that was growing dangerously out of control. He'd hurt her if he wasn't careful. She was so small, so delicate, he feared what might happen if he allowed his passions full rein. "I want you," he groaned. "Oh God, I want you. After last night and today, I can wait no more."

Cassie's hands slid up his chest and circled his neck, tugging hard to bring his mouth close. "Then don't wait," she cried, her desperation clear. "Oh God, don't, don't, don't." His mouth stopped the flow of her mindless chant with a hunger that washed away every thought but to take what each offered.

The feel of her naked flesh, hot and soft against him, left him desperate with yearning for more. Blood pounded in his ears as her lips parted and his tongue moved deep within. He drank of her taste, breathed of her scent, his senses soaring as this woman, his wife, moaned with pleasure in his arms. In a desperate grip, he held her against him, held her as if both their lives depended on his strength. And he knew, with absolute certainty, he'd never get enough.

His passions were building too fast. He couldn't stop. He was going to take her unprepared. His manhood was hard, pulsating hot, thick with need, probing against the softness of her belly. Jesus, he'd never known such aching desire.

Fighting for control, he slipped his hand between her thighs, shuddering at the warm, moist evidence of her longing.

An instant later he impaled that delectable part of her upon his rigid manhood. Her legs encircled his waist, her head fell back, and a tortured intake of breath came from between her teeth. White hot flames of pleasure licked at every part of her body, searing her, consuming her. She was wild for him. She pressed closer. She couldn't get enough, not until he began to move. And when he did, she screamed softly as all rationality fled.

She writhed against him, her movements abandoned in her hungry demand for yet more of the thrilling sensations.

Inflamed by her unrestrained excitement, he grasped her firm buttocks with one hand and drew her closer while his free hand moved to the juncture of her

263

thighs. Gently, his thumb stroked the sensitive spot there as his body moved with frenzied urgency.

Stop! he told himself suddenly. She's not ready. It's too soon. But she was ready. He could feel her throbbing muscles closing around his engorged male member. His heart soared, knowing he no longer had to hold back. His lips sought out her breast and took her deep into his mouth, biting, suckling, desperate to take all he could as, with almost vicious thrusts, his body sped toward the blinding light of ecstasy.

He stiffened against her for an endless moment of aching bliss, eyes squeezed shut, not sure if it was pain or pleasure that he suffered at that moment. Then, with a broken cry, his body convulsed, as did hers, filled to overflowing with exquisite, mindless rapture.

Cameron choked out her name, his face buried in her softness. She grew limp in his arms, eyes closed, head thrown back, moaning softly.

Utterly spent, Cameron staggered back against the cabin wall. Joined with her still, he kicked the discarded quilt flat upon the dirt floor and lay down, holding her close in his arms. A moment later, he had them wrapped securely in the blanket's warmth, but still another warmth was invading his senses as flesh pressed invitingly against flesh. Cameron was amazed at the desire this woman aroused in him. He hadn't yet recovered his breathing when he knew a longing to take her again.

Her voice was thick, her words almost slurred, as she murmured, "If you ever do that to me again, I promise retaliation."

"What?"

"Take your clothes off like that."

Cameron chuckled as his mouth nuzzled her throat. "Is there another way to disrobe? You'll have to tell me if there is."

"You know what I mean."

"Did you enjoy it?"

Cassie groaned. "Oh God, I think I'll remember it forever."

Cameron smiled into her passion clouded eyes. "I must be losing my touch if you only *think* you'll remember."

Cassie blinked. "Have you done this before?"

Cameron made as if to think on her question. A smile hovered about his lips. But it wasn't until Cassie slapped his shoulder that he laughed and admitted, "No." A moment later his lips slid with aching promise against her cheek, her jaw, her throat. He lifted his head and watched her eyes half close with pleasure. "And I'll never do it again," he said. His eyes glittered with deviltry as his mouth came to cover hers again. "I promise."

It wasn't until much later that either could breathe with any degree of normalcy. Cassie sighed as she snuggled close. "Am I truly frightening when I'm in a temper?"

Cameron's chuckle in the warmth of her neck was somewhat muffled. "Madam, I hesitate to tell you lest you use your newfound power to greater advantage."

Cassie laughed with joy that her temper could affect a man of such power and pride. "You have answered me, sir, by your refusal to do so."

Cameron eyed her warily and with no little humor.

265

"Take that gleam from your eyes, madam. You'll not cow me, for when in a temper, I'm just as ferocious as you."

"Do you think so?"

"I advise you, madam, do not put me to the test."

"But how, then, are we to ever know?"

Cameron laughed. "Simply take my word for it like a docile, dutiful wife."

Cassie growled. "Docile and dutiful, is it? I'm afraid you've chosen the wrong woman if those were the qualities you expected."

Cameron's tender gaze moved over the flushed skin of her cheeks and throat. Pulling back, he saw that the telltale rosy hue suffused every luscious curve beneath him. In a sudden, fresh access of desire, he pressed his hips hard against hers, murmuring as he did so, "I think you have all the qualities, and more, than I ever expected."

"And what, pray tell, might they be?" she asked, somewhat warily.

"Are you fishing for a compliment, madam?"

"Indeed not! I merely wish to understand your meaning."

He smiled as his finger-tips grazed the soft curves beneath him. "Umm," he teased, his brow slightly furrowed as if considering her virtues. "Let's see, your shape is lush and perfect to my way of thinking. Your skin is as soft as silk. And your responses to my touch have grown in strength with each sampling. In truth, it boggles the mind to think what may occur in say a year or so."

Cassie tried to subdue the aching need that came

instantly to life as his fingers slid over her. She wanted to cry, not make love, for it was exactly as she supposed. He spoke only of her body and her reaction to his lovemaking. She had been a fool to expect him to think more of her. Such qualities could be found in any whore walking the streets of London. "I thought as much," she grumbled bitterly as she tried to move from beneath him.

"Have I angered you?" Cameron looked down in some amazement as he held her in place.

"Of course not."

"I have," he countered, clearly puzzled. "What have I done but speak the truth?"

"You, sir, are nothing more than a lusting beast. Let me up!"

"No. You are going to tell me what's wrong."

And, as her chin lifted defiantly, he warned, "Right now, Cassie. I'll not have ridiculous misunderstandings between us."

"So, I'm not only good in bed, but ridiculous as well. Well, at least that's something, isn't it?"

"Damn it, woman! Don't turn and twist everything I say." He hesitated for a second as if thinking on her words. "What do you mean, that's something?"

"Well, at least I'm not just a body to use, am I? I'm ridiculous. How lovely! Now, get off me."

Cameron chuckled. "How in God's name did you get the idea that I think of you as only a body?" And when she didn't answer, he want on, "Talk to me, Cassie. How am I to know unless you say?"

"You just told me, didn't you?" she snapped, more than a little angry. "You were expounding on my best qualities, as I remember."

"Wasn't I?" Cameron asked, completely baffled.

"Indeed. My body suits you well. I'm ever so pleased for you, Mr. Chandler."

"Jesus Christ! That's enough! You are a thickheaded little minx. If you think I'm going to take your temper tantrums in stride, forget it. I've half a mind to turn you over my knee and see the end of this nonsensical conversation. You, madam, are a willful, stubborn brat who has turned my once peaceful existence upside down since the first moment I set my eyes on you."

Cassie's eyes widened and Cameron could have sworn he saw happiness lurking within their blue depths. "Have I?"

"What?"

"Turned your life upside down?"

"Oh God," he groaned, almost in despair, knowing his words would surely put her in a temper and ruin what could have been a most deliciously spent afternoon. "Now what have I said?"

"You said I was . . ."

"I know well enough what I said." Cameron eyed her faint smile with suspicion. "What I don't understand is why those words should bring a smile to your lips?"

Cassie gave a low, throaty laugh as she ran her hands down his chest to linger with growing expertise at the junction of his thighs.

He swore and pulled her hard against him, helpless but to allow her caress. "You're driving me crazy."

Cassie laughed again. The words he'd uttered were certainly far from romantic. But she would not have believed any sudden profession of love on his part. It was his confusion that finally convinced her she meant more to him than he himself yet realized. It wasn't as she had feared. She wasn't simply someone to warm his bed. She almost laughed again, but the warmth of his mouth and the delicious stroking of his hands soon turned her thoughts to other equally pleasurable matters.

Cassie was exhausted. She wanted nothing more than to soak in a long, hot bath and then join her husband in a warm, comfortable bed. Her body ached in places she hadn't known existed. How many times had they made love? She tried to count, but the memories of the afternoon blurred into one magical moment of bliss.

Cameron helped her down from her horse and held her close to his side as they walked up the stairs of the big house. "Are you hungry?"

Cassie smiled and glanced up into his shadowed face. His dark eyes gleamed in the silvery moonlight. "Not for what you're thinking."

Cameron laughed. "How do you know what I'm thinking?"

"That's easy enough. You think of little else."

Cameron's low rumble of laughter brought a smile of pleasure to her lips. "Since you're so adept at reading my mind, tell me, what do I want right now?"

"You want a bath, supper, and bed."

"Do I? In that order?"

Cassie giggled. "All right, a bath, bed and supper."

"You're growing closer."

"And you're growing positively depraved. What will the servants think? First, we're gone all day and then we spend all evening in bed?"

Cameron opened the door and ushered her inside. Without warning, he pulled her into his arms, careless of who might see them. "Do you care?"

"Of course I care," she insisted and then gave him an impish grin. "No, I don't."

His low, victorious laughter brought a lightness to her heart. "I was hoping you'd say that," Cameron said as he swung her into his arms and started up the staircase. Suddenly, he stopped and leaned against the wall. "Have you gained weight since this afternoon?"

Cassie glared at him. "More likely I've lost a stone or more, with all that exercise forced upon me."

Cameron grinned. "I don't remember your being forced. As a matter of fact, you seemed a more than willing participant."

"Wasn't I forced?" Cassie smiled, feigning confusion. "Oh dear, perhaps I wasn't, after all."

Cameron looked down at her, his expression filled with doubt. "One can only hope you'll always be so agreeable to my every suggestion."

Cassie gave a careless shrug, while a devilish grin hovered around her lips. "One can always hope, I suppose."

"Get undressed," Cameron said as he deposited her at their bedroom door. "I'll ask Jessie to prepare a bath."

Cassie was humming happily as she tossed aside her wrinkled, still damp clothing and slid into a satin robe.

270

She was eagerly anticipating her bath when she turned at the sound of the bedroom door. Cameron, his face gone sickly gray, was leaning against the closed door. "What is it? Is it the babies?" She made to rush past him.

"No." He caught her against him and held her close. His arms like steel, his embrace almost desperate.

"What then? Oh God, not Meghan!"

"No, darling," he soothed as he ran his hands familiarly down her back. But there wasn't any desire in his caress, rather the need to find safety and comfort. "Meghan sleeps. All is well."

"Then what? Tell me, Cameron!"

"Fever. Bennett's slaves have come down with it. I can only pray it will not spread. I've seen dozens die in an hour from it."

"My God," Cassie groaned while pressing her forehead to his chest. "I'll have to go."

Cameron's body stiffened at her words. "No!" he nearly bellowed.

Cassie moved from his embrace, almost ready to let him persuade her not to go, for she truly feared this sickness. But his next words only served to stiffen her resolve to put aside those fears.

"I absolutely forbid it. You will not leave Hill Crest. Not even to go into town. I swear, Cassie, if you don't obey me on this, I'll . . ."

Cassie, in an instant temper, gritted her teeth. "You'll what? Tie me up? Well, Mr. Chandler, get the rope. I'm going."

She stormed to the closet they now shared and began pulling out clothing.

271

"Damn you, I said you're not going!" Cameron was instantly at her side. In a flash, he took every garment from her closet. In three strides, he was at the window and the clothes were spread over the lawn below.

"I am," she insisted. "It doesn't matter what you do."

"Cassie, I'm warning you . . ."

"You can save your words, Mr. Chandler. I'm doing what I must. Would you leave those poor souls in the hands of that drunken fool, Reilly?"

"I don't give a damn about them. You're not going!"

"I should have expected as much from a slave owner. You care more for your horses' welfare than you do for any human being!" Though briefly contrite at his look of shock, she pressed on, knowing she'd made the right decision. "You don't own me, Mr. Chandler. I'm not one of your slaves."

Cameron's mirthless grin sent shivers racing down her spine. His words were low, his tone almost tender, but she could see the danger lurking in his eyes. "Ah, but I do, Mrs. Chandler. You are my wife, if you remember. And you will obey me in all things."

Cassie's eyes flashed fire. "If you believe the lack of clothes will ensure my obedience, think again."

Cameron laughed at her bravado. "Won't it?"

"I'll go like this, if I must."

He eyed her for a long moment before he nodded his head. "I believe you would." Suddenly, he stood before her. His hands moved so fast, Cassie had only started to stop him when he was very nearly finished ripping her dressing gown to shreds. It lay at her feet as he stepped back and dared her, "Go like that."

Cassie gasped with shock and lunged for the bed. In

272

an instant, she was beneath the sheet. But she wasn't fast enough. Cameron got an excellent view of her long legs and beautiful bottom. He cursed the sudden ache that filled his belly. Forcing his voice to remain calm, he desperately tried to cover his weakness. "See that you stay there, or God hold me, I swear I'll tie you in place."

Chapter Nineteen

Cassie neither heard the soft chirping of newly awakened birds, nor realized she breathed the fresh scent of clean, dew-washed grass. She took no pleasure in the warmth of the early morning sunshine upon her cheek. Not today. Today, she noticed and thought of nothing but her destination.

Carefully, she eased her horse off the road, through the thicket of underbrush, heading south toward Bennetts' plantation. She couldn't chance being seen and recognized, for she hadn't a doubt that word would instantly reach her husband's ears and she would be brought back.

Cassie smiled. Dressed as she was in Cameron's oversized shirt, his trousers secured at her waist with rope, the legs raggedly cut off lest she trip over their length, she stood little chance of being recognized as the mistress of Hill Crest. Still, she wasn't about to take any chances.

She was thankful she had remembered his cloak, for it covered much, even if it was too big and swept the ground when she walked. Once she dismounted before

Bennett's huge home, it wouldn't do for questioning eyebrows to be raised at her unusual mode of dress.

Cassie held Midnight's reins while standing before Bennett's plantation. With nothing less than amazement, she watched as Mr. Bennett himself descended the wide steps that led to a veranda which circled the entire first floor. Vaguely, she wondered how such spindly legs could support him. In all her life, she had never seen a man so huge. He was not only tall, but weighed easily as much as three full grown men put together.

Cassie introduced herself and stated her business.

"There's no need for you to bother yourself, missy," Bennett drawled in an accent more common to those living farther south. His fleshy jowls and double chin swung as he shook his bald head. "These niggers here are near spent. It's almost seven years now, about time to replace the lot of them anyways."

Cassie's eyes rounded with surprise. "Indeed? Why would that be?"

" 'Cause they die off, is why." Bennett's look and tone clearly implied he thought her a bit simple.

"Mr. Bennett, you cannot mean they all simply up and die at the same time!"

Bennett nodded and shrugged a massively fat shoulder. "Near enough. I figure the price o' replacin' the lot beats the cost of seein' to their every want year after year. Works out for the best this way."

Cassie digested this information for some moments and miraculously managed to control the urge to fly at the murderous brute. She had heard stories, but had thought them just that. Now, she'd heard the facts and the unthinkable was indeed true. Though physically a

275

good head shorter than Bennett, Cassie somehow managed to look down her nose at this gloating imbecile. Her words to him were laced with disgust. "They die from neglect, is that it?"

"No need for fancy airs, missy. I know you bein' English and all, look at this business a bit differently." He shrugged. "It's a profitable plan though, and well used farther south."

Cassie strove to disguise her horror at this barbaric waste of human life. "I'm sure it is, Mr. Bennett, but you wouldn't mind if I took a moment and looked in on them?"

Bennett shrugged yet again and turned away. "Don't make no never mind to me. Suit yourself."

With more than a little trepidation, Cassie approached the infirmary, which stood amid overgrown foliage and weeds some distance from the main house. From the outside, it was clear the structure was in need of attention. The weather-beaten wood, once whitewashed, was now gray and peeling; the roof was rotted and sagging; and the windows were black with years of accumulated dirt.

But if Cassie thought the exterior a disgrace, nothing could have prepared her for what she found inside. Since no light shone through the dirt-encrusted windows, it appeared as if night had fallen once she closed the door behind her. And the stench! She tugged Cameron's shirt to her nose and mouth as the odor threatened to empty her stomach. Good God, how were these poor souls able to breathe? If this was a sample of their usual living conditions — and doubtless it was — it was no wonder the fever ran rampant throughout this plantation. No one, even slightly ill, could survive in such filth. Cassie shivered with the fear that she, too, might succumb, then pushed aside the terrifying thought, knowing that she had a job that must be done.

The building consisted of but one dirt-floor room shared by men and women alike, with no partitions to separate those more seriously ill. Cassie heard a soft moan almost at her feet and gasped as she realized she had almost stepped upon a woman who was clearly in the last stages of labor. What in God's name was she doing here? Didn't those in charge realize the danger of spreading the illness to a newborn babe?

From the far corner of the room a black woman came toward her. She was horribly thin and stooped with age, her once black hair now completely gray. As she came closer, Cassie wrinkled her nose with disgust, for the woman smelled at least as bad as those lying about. She was covered with a film of dirt which gave a murky gray tone to her black skin, and patches of red, crusted sores were visible inside her elbows and at the base of her neck. This, combined with the fact that lice were clearly making themselves at home in her hair, sent a shiver down Cassie's spine. Vaguely, she wondered how the woman had managed to survive to such an advanced age, when, according to Bennett, all died within seven years or so.

"You shouldn't be here, missus."

Cassie ignored the woman's warning. "What is your name?"

"I'm Black Lizzie. Da massa, him put me in charge."

"Have you any experience in nursing the sick, Lizzie?"

The woman's smile revealed several missing teeth.

"Sho enough do," she stated proudly. "I done had nine little niggers for da massa. And nursed every one of dem thru all kinds of sickness."

Cassie sighed, amazed that any had survived in filth such as this. "I want you to get some help and bring pots of water, clean rags, and vinegar. Ask Mr. Bennett for any blankets he can spare, plus hot soup and quinine. Can you remember that?"

Lizzie responded with a knowing laugh. "Da massa, he ain't gonna bother wit dese niggers. Why you tellin' me to ask for dat? You want ole Lizzie to get in trouble?"

Cassie took as deep a breath as she dared. "I'll ask myself. While I'm gone, I want you to open these windows. The chill of the outside air can't be worse for the sick than this stench."

Cassie returned some time later, her cheeks flushed with anger as she directed a few unwilling servants to carry buckets of cool water, rags, and vinegar into the building. Bennett would part with nothing more. The man simply did not care if these people died or not.

Hours passed before Cassie placed the last wet rag upon still another burning forehead and leaned back upon her heels. Her legs were cramped, her back throbbing with pain from kneeling and bending over the sick. With the sleeve of her shirt, she wiped away the beads of perspiration and surveyed her work. Thanks to the few servants she had commandeered, and Black Lizzie, whom she later found to be the plantation's midwife, the windows had been washed clean, and sunshine now shone brightly throughout the small building. Although their clothing could not be changed, the sick had all been washed and comforted to the best of Cassie's ability. She sighed. It wasn't much, but at least these people needn't die in muck and filth. And she hadn't a doubt that they would indeed die without medicine and food.

Cassie had begged for food, clean clothing, and medicine. Bennett had simply laughed at what he considered a ridiculous request, swearing he'd not waste another cent on his workers' welfare.

There were no blankets to be found, and the countless sick lay side by side on the dirt floor, huddled one against the other for warmth. Most had soiled the rags they wore that passed for clothing, but to have left them naked while their clothing was washed and dried would only have hastened their deaths. As it was, they shivered and moaned with chills and pain. Cassie fought back the tears that threatened. If the vile beast who claimed ownership of these half-starved creatures denied them the care they needed, she could do little more than helplessly watch them die.

Cassie rubbed the ache in her back and sighed at the sound of a galloping horse drawing to a halt near the infirmary. He had come for her. She had no need to look out the window to know her husband waited without, nor did she need to see his face to know his rage. Cassie shrugged. He could rant and rave all he pleased. She had done what she must.

Cameron sat astride his horse, his tall, imposing figure terrifying to all but the woman he had come to retrieve. Slaves scurried out of his sight, peering at him from behind trees and outbuildings, feeling a shiver of dread for the kindly, if foolish, young woman who had come to help them.

Not bothering to dismount, Cameron angrily

watched her leave the house and move a few feet toward him. A nerve twitched in his clenched jaw and his scar seemed to glow almost white against the tanned skin of his cheek.

Without a word spoken between them, Cameron offered his hand. Knowing the horse she was leaving behind would be returned at a later date, Cassie took his hand and allowed him to lift her into his saddle. There was no question of fighting him. Had she offered any resistance, he would simply have carted her off like a piece of baggage.

"Oh God, you smell so good," she said as she snuggled her face into his chest, thankful to breathe a clean, healthy scent at last.

"I wish I could say the same for you, madam," Cameron grunted, yet tightened his arms around her as she made to move away.

Cassie gave him a helpless look, knowing the stench of the sick had penetrated her clothing and hair.

"You needn't bother with feminine wiles, Cassie. I can't remember a time when I've been half so angry. And your sweet glances will not dissuade me from my purpose."

"Will you beat me, then?" she asked, not the least disturbed by that thought.

"Will a beating ensure your future obedience?"

"I'm afraid not."

Cameron stiffened at her cool daring.

"Cameron, I did not wish to disobey you. I had to do what I could for these people. Don't you see?"

"I see you are like others of your sex. Childish, willful, and uncaring of the suffering you cause."

"And what suffering have I caused, but to your male

280

ego?" she snapped, angry at his unfair judgment, sitting suddenly stiff and straight before him.

"You've chanced the spreading of fever, damn it! At least it was contained at Bennett's place. If I were to allow you to return home, God only knows who might next be struck."

Cassie was silent for a moment as she digested his words. She gave a soft groan as she imagined one of the babies or Meghan coming down with fever because of her.

Cameron glanced down at her stricken expression and grunted, "You're a bit late, but I'm happy to see you finally realize the foolishness of your actions."

"Stop!" Cassie cried out suddenly as she struggled free of his hold. A moment later, she was sliding down the horse's side and running.

Cameron gasped in astonishment. Then, seeing her objective, he was instantly off his horse after her.

Cassie took the back lash of the whip quite by accident, moaning as the pain crashed over her shoulder and down her back. But the pain didn't stop her from hearing the bloodcurdling scream that followed only seconds later. And before the man with the whip could strike again at the woman strung helplessly by her wrists to a tree, Cassie was upon him, swinging her fists into his back and kicking his booted ankles like a wildcat. "Stop it," she grunted. "Stop it this instant."

Automatically, the man shrugged her off. Without thinking, indeed without seeing, he raised his hand and delivered a resounding slap that left Cassie all but senseless.

With another moan, she crumpled into a heap at his

feet.

Cameron, still some few feet behind her, watched the scene unfold with nothing less than amazement. Instantly, he fell upon the man, his roar of rage more terrifying than any scream.

His fists beat mercilessly into the startled overseer. Again and again, he struck him, until blood gushed from a broken nose and jagged teeth cut into knuckles, and one man's blood could not be distinguished from the other.

The man, whose name was Rowlins, was known for the pleasure he took in delivering punishment. But his job as Bennett's overseer did not call for matching his strength to another, and it was soon clear that he stood no chance against Cameron's rage.

The man's face was a bloody pulp by the time Cameron's sanity returned. Rowlins was nearly unconscious and either unable, or unwilling, to fight back. "If you ever lay your hands upon my wife again, I'll kill you," Cameron grunted as he released the man's shirt front and let him collapse to his knees.

Upon regaining her senses, Cassie had run to the black girl who was still hanging from the tree branch. Her fingers shook as she untied the rope that held her in place. As the girl fell to the ground, Cassie knelt to examine her injuries.

"Get on the horse," Cameron ordered harshly.

Cassie looked from the moaning girl to her husband's raging form.

"I . . . ."

Before she could finish, she was swept up by his powerful arms and almost slammed into the saddle.

"Don't say a word. Not one word," Cameron warned

282

as he mounted behind her.

They rode in silence for some miles until Cameron reined in before an old cabin.

Cassie glanced at him with questioning eyes as he eased her from the saddle. "The cabin belonged to our last overseer. Since he left, it's stood empty. I've asked Jessie to make it ready for us. We won't be returning to the house until the chance of your coming down with fever passes."

Cassie struggled for breath as his hand pushed her under the water again. She came up choking, her arms swinging and splashing soapy water over the man kneeling at the tub's side. "Damn you!" she sputtered. "Are you trying to drown me?"

Cameron, unconcerned with his wet shirt, chuckled. "The notion is deserving of some merit."

"Leave me be!" Cassie demanded. "I've been bathing myself for some time. I don't need your help."

"You'll have it regardless," Cameron replied ignoring the burning in his raw knuckles as well as another ache that had not eased since he'd first stripped her of her clothes. He dunked her yet again. "I've no wish to share my pillow with the little beasts who have no doubt made themselves at home in your hair."

Cassie gasped as he allowed her head to break free of the water again. She glared at him from between wet strands of red hair. "Were I you, I wouldn't count on sharing a pillow."

Cameron laughed at her threat as he rubbed a soapy cloth over her face. "In the future, you might think twice before acting so impulsively."

"You've got soap in my eyes, you beast!" She slapped wildly at his hands in an effort to fend off his ministrations. But Cameron was not to be dissuaded. His movements were quick and determinedly impersonal as he washed every inch of her. He cursed as the need to touch her with lingering caresses came to assault his senses. But he forced the need aside, straining to hold to his anger. No matter his desires, it would not do to show loving affection. No, the time for severity was at hand. She had to be made to understand she was his wife and would obey him in any and all things.

Water ran in heavy rivulets from Cassie's hair and body as he hauled her roughly from the tub at last and covered her with a thick, absorbent sheet. A moment later, he was tugging at her hair, trying to dry it with another cloth, but Cassie shoved him away. Damn, but she had taken just about all she was going to take from this brute. As he reached for her again, she shoved him harder and watched with nothing less than amazement as his boots slipped on the wet floor and he went flying backward. With a giant splash that nearly emptied the wooden tub, he plopped into the bath, his legs hanging ludicrously over the rim.

For a long moment they were both too stunned to move or speak. Then, Cameron's lips began to twitch with suppressed laughter as he finally found his voice. "I assume you are prepared for the consequences of your actions?"

Cassie laughed at his threat. "What more can you do? I cannot get any wetter." She glanced toward the tub in which he sat. "There's not enough water left, in any case."

"Perhaps not, but there are other forms of punishment."

"Namely?"

"A good thrashing for one."

"I wouldn't, Cameron," she warned evenly, all trace of merriment vanished. "As you've witnessed today, I don't take kindly to that form of treatment."

Cameron grunted as he pulled himself out of the tub. "If ever there was a woman more worthy, I've yet to see her."

"If you touch me, I'll . . ."

Cameron was standing before her now, eyes narrowed with warning. "You'd do nothing but beg me to stop. On that I swear."

Cassie pulled herself up to her full height, head tilted regally, blue eyes blazing fearlessly. "Never!"

This boldly delivered challenge might just have been her undoing except that her abrupt movement caused the sheet to slip exposing her creamy breasts almost to her nipples. Cameron's need to chastise her suddenly dissolved in the face of a greater need. The yearning to touch her rocked his senses, blotting out all anger and reason.

She had never seemed more beautiful, with her wet hair streaming disheveled and wild down her back, her skin pink, glowing and still damp from his scrubbing, her cheeks flushed with emotion.

The anger between them vanished as suddenly as it had come about, replaced by a physical longing both knew to be irresistible. The air of the small cabin fairly crackled with sexual tension. His voice was low and ragged as he gave up any further attempt to hide this ever present need. "Woman, you tempt me greatly." His mouth softened with a trace of a smile. "No doubt

I should turn you over my knee and give you what you so justly deserve."

Cassie's heart raced wildly in response to the passion she saw leap to flame in his dark gaze. Her tongue flicked out to moisten suddenly parched lips. Her voice was breathless and trembling as she asked, "And if you were to turn me over your knee, what is it you would give me?"

"Shall I show you, then?"

Cassie eased the already loosened sheet lower still, allowing it to slide with deliberately seductive purpose to her feet. She stood unashamedly naked before him, more than a little pleased to find this man of great strength suddenly weak in the grip of burning desire. With one small step, she closed the distance between them. Her hands slid up his chest and twined about his neck, tugging ever so gently. "Yes." And as his mouth came down to cover her own, she sighed, "Oh, yes."

Chapter Twenty

Cameron had had no intention of making love to his wife that day, nor any time in the near future for that matter. Indeed, when he'd found her gone that morning his first and only thought had been to strangle her for her disobedience. He had cursed his own foolishness at not staying with her the night before. Had he not been drowning his anger in a bottle, she never could have left the house without his knowledge.

Despite the force of his anger, it didn't last. In its place, came a slow aching dread, unlike any he had ever known. Soon, he was wild with fear. All he could think of was her succumbing to the fever that raged at the Bennett plantation. By the time his sweating horse had covered the fifteen miles between his home and Bennett's, he had been nearly mad with terror for her.

Cameron realized his reaction was extreme but found easy reasons to account for it. It wasn't that he loved the girl, but she was his wife and it was only natural that he should feel this protectiveness. Conveniently, he ignored the fact that he had never felt protective toward his first wife. Also, he reasoned further, the sudden shock of finding Cassie gone against his express orders had caused him to overreact.

Certainly that was all it was. That was all it could be. He could not allow another woman to hurt him again. He wouldn't be able to live through the pain this time. It mattered not that this one seemed so different. She was a woman, wasn't she? And he had never known one to be trusted.

"Cassie," he groaned as his mouth moved from hers to spread warm kisses along the slim column of her throat. His mind swam as he breathed in the scent of her fragrant skin. Again, he murmured her name as his mouth gently touched the red welts that marred her shoulder. It didn't matter that the marks were inadvertently caused. He wanted to kill Rowlins for bringing pain to her. His heart constricted with an unacknowledged emotion as he allowed his gaze to wander over her shoulder to the red lines down her back. "I should go and get something for these bruises."

"No, don't leave me," she whispered, her eyes aglow with tenderness as she resisted his efforts to put her from him. Her lips parted invitingly. "Your touch will do more to heal than any salve."

His mouth was on hers again, a willing captive to the sweet warmth he found within. A low growl escaped his throat as he sought out her taste. His mind spun with need as he reveled in her eager response.

His hands smoothed down her back, relearning every haunting curve and hollow. Every time he touched her was like the first, exciting and new. His hips pressed into her belly; his blood pounded in his brain. And he knew there'd never be a time when he could touch her with anything less than this overwhelming need. She was like air to his lungs, blood to his veins, vital to sustain life.

The day's extreme emotion had left him unable to control the passion that exploded like fire in his brain. His mouth left hers only for a momentary breath, then came again to tease, to explore, to thrill, and finally to possess.

Cassie unexpectedly pulled free of his hungry embrace, leaving him bereft and aching with the need to pull her back. Her brow creased with annoyance as her fingers moved quickly to peel away the fabric that separated their bodies. The shirt, opened at last, was pulled from his trousers and tossed to the floor. Hungrily, her hands moved over his naked chest, palms spread wide as they ran up and down his sides, her thumbs grazing his nipples. She heard his gasp and smiled at the shudder he couldn't control.

"No," she whispered as he began to work the buttons of his pants free. Her eyes were smoky blue as she raised them to his dark, burning gaze. "Let me."

Fighting the overpowering urge to rip away his clothes, he allowed her gentle fumblings, eyes closed, as if in pain, by the time she eased his trousers to the floor. A moment later, he was sitting naked on the bed and she was pulling off his boots.

He thought she'd join him then, but no, she remained kneeling between his legs, content to remain for the moment on the floor. When he offered his hand, she merely shook her head, her eyes gleaming with delight as she contemplated her next move.

With a soft sigh of pleasure she reached out and touched his face. Almost shyly at first, as if she couldn't admit to this wanting, her fingers studied his every feature, moving over his closed eyes, his nose, his strong jaw. For a time, she lingered at his mouth, gasping as his tongue flicked out and teased her finger. She gasped again as he sucked it suddenly into his mouth, causing a wave of dizziness and chills to run the length of her. Pulling reluctantly away at last, her warm hands skimmed the flesh of his chest. Her eyes closed for a moment as she savored the strength of muscles and the erotic mixture of rough hair and smooth skin, until her need to know more of him brought her hands lower, over his stomach and downward.

His heart thudded in his chest as she deliberately avoided the proof of his desire. He fought the urge to capture her hands and bring them to his aching need, but waited patiently as her light touch slid down the length of his legs. His body jerked as her fingers suddenly touched his feet, then slowly reversed their path. Jesus, he wasn't going to be able to take this. The closer her fingers came to the core of his passion, the tighter his muscles strained. He was gasping for every breath by the time her fingers finally touched him there.

He fell back with a tortured sigh, weak and almost insane with the exquisite pleasure she brought to him. He heard her soft, victorious laughter as her mouth joined her hands.

"Cassie," he gasped, his fingers entwined in her hair as her hot, wet mouth took him helplessly along a path toward heaven.

"Did you like that?" she grinned triumphantly as she eased him back on the bed, then knelt poised above him.

"Like what?" he asked innocently as his finger idly teased one swaying breast.

"What I just did?" She smiled confidently.

Cameron couldn't stop the laughter that threatened. "Why? Did you do something in particular?"

"Perhaps I was mistaken and it was pain rather than pleasure you suffered."

He shrugged a shoulder and gave a beautiful imitation of a wistful sigh. "I imagine I can force myself to bear it should you feel the need to do it again."

Cassie straddled his chest, a wicked gleam in her eye. The movement brought her swaying breasts provocatively close to his mouth. "Far be it from me to force you into anything. I just won't do it anymore, that's all."

Cameron groaned. "Witch!" He rolled her beneath him. "I suppose I'm to beg for it now."

"No need to beg. A simple, 'You were brilliant Cassie', will ensure future repeat performances."

"Ah, Cassie," he murmured as his mouth dipped to nuzzle the sweet flesh of her throat, "You were that and more. Much, much more."

It was some time later before Cassie snuggled contentedly against her husband's side, her head resting on his shoulder as her fingers idly threaded through the mat of black hair that covered his chest. "Cameron," she sighed softly.

"Mmm."

"Don't go to sleep. I have to talk to you."

"I'm not sleeping. What?"

"Cameron, we can't allow Bennett to . . ."

"Cassie," he interrupted. "I don't want to hear this. The slaves belong to Bennett. There is nothing anyone

291

can do."

.She lifted herself on her elbow and looked down at him, her eyes wide with amazement. "You can't mean to let him continue on? He told me he replaces them every seven years or so. Do you realize he's murdering these people with his lack of care?"

Cameron's lips tightened with helpless frustration. "It doesn't matter, Cassie. By law, they belong to him. He can do anything he pleases."

"And you'll do nothing about it?"

Cameron sat up and turned his back as he reached for his pants. "What the hell do you want me to do?"

"Buy them. Buy them all."

He turned to look at her. "Jesus! Do you know what you're saying?"

"You said you weren't poor."

"I don't think I've ever met a woman like you. Instead of clothes and jewelry, you want slaves."

"I don't want slaves, Cameron. I want them free." Her eyes dropped as she played idly with the folds of the sheet. "You can't imagine what I've seen today. He treats them worse than animals." Her cheeks colored with shame for their plight. "He has them believing they're less than human. They've lost their pride. Why they even refer to themselves as niggers!"

Cameron shot her a sympathetic look of understanding. "Even if I had enough money to buy the lot, Bennett would only replace them with more. Then what?"

Cassie knelt on the bed, too caught up with her notion to realize the state of her undress. "Then, we could steal them," she stated quite happily.

Cameron laughed. "Could we? Just like that, eh? Is

this my sweet English miss speaking, the one who goes to church every Sunday?" He stood up. "In case you haven't heard, stealing another man's property is frowned upon in these parts. If I listened to you, I'd soon be swinging from a rope."

"Are you afraid?"

Cameron shoved his legs into his wet pants. "Madam, at least I've some sense. With each day that passes I am further convinced that you are totally lacking in that quality. Indeed, I'm beginning to believe you've need of a keeper."

"I find your remarks not in the least amusing," she snapped as she, too, rose from the bed, her gaze searching out the small cabin. "Where are my clothes?"

Cameron laughed as he slid his arms into a still damp shirt. "You have none."

"Well, what am I supposed to wear?" she asked, clutching the sheet to her breasts as she spied the now unwearable clothes he had torn from her body.

"You've shown me once you're not to be trusted. You can stay just as you are until it's time to return to the house."

"You're not serious?

"I am."

"Cameron, be reasonable. I'm not going back to Bennett's place. There is nothing more I can do without medicine and . . ." She let the sentence die as the seed of a thought took root.

"Exactly!" Cameron snorted in triumph. "I knew you'd eventually get another hare-brained idea. No! You will not go back. No! You will not bring supplies. No! You will not nurse them." He was yelling now. "Do you hear me? I absolutely forbid it!"

Cassie sighed. "Cameron, you cannot know what it's like. A man wouldn't let his horse suffer so. They have no blankets, no food. They lie on dirt floors, in filthy rags. At least their last hours could be made more comfortable."

"Not by you."

"Then who? There is no one else."

"If it will ease your mind"—Cameron sighed—"I'll send a wagon filled to overflowing with supplies. Will that suffice?"

Cassie shrugged unhappily. "It will have to, won't it?"

Cassie paced the small cabin, dressed in her chemise and drawers, the only concession Cameron would allow toward modesty. Cameron sat pretending interest in a book. In reality, he barely knew the name of the novel he held, never mind the story, for he rarely took his eyes off her. His gaze constantly sought out the hint of darkened nipples beneath the sheerness of her chemise. His fingers ached to run up the silky length of her long legs. And when she turned in her pacing and offered him a clear view of her creamy slender back and tight derriere, he almost gave up all pretense at reading. The last two weeks had done nothing to diminish his desire for her. Unbelievably, the more he took her to bed, the more he wanted to. Cameron couldn't believe the obsession she held for him. Never in his life had he craved the touch of a woman only minutes after making love to her.

Suddenly, she stopped directly before his chair and tapped her bare foot impatiently on the floor.

Cameron looked up, his expression one of pure innocence. "Yes?"

"How can you sit there and read hour after hour?"

Cameron shrugged and lied shamelessly. "The book holds my interest."

Cassie pointed at the pile on the floor near the bed. "Well, none of those do the same for me."

Cameron grinned. "Perhaps your attention span is a bit shorter than mine."

Cassie shot him a look of disgust. "Perhaps mine would lengthen if I, too, took an occasional walk. How much longer am I going to be held prisoner here?"

"You are not being held prisoner. You may leave any time you please."

"Like this?" she asked as she grabbed her chemise and held it away from her body for his inspection. "No doubt the servants would have a good laugh to see me parading dressed like this across your front lawn. It's been two weeks, Cameron. For God's sake!"

Cameron, not unsympathetic to her enforced quarantine, finally relented. He was fairly certain that if she were going to come down with fever the signs would be apparent by now. "Tomorrow. If you continue to feel well, we'll go back tomorrow."

"Really?" She nearly shouted with joy and almost knocked the chair over as she jumped upon his lap. "Oh God, I can't wait." The slightest squirming of her bottom against his lap brought to her awareness what was uppermost in his thoughts. Cassie giggled. "I think I'd like to read this book."

"Why?"

"I'd like to see for myself what could bring you to this state." She wiggled again, letting him know exactly of what she spoke.

"I think you know well enough what brings me to this state."

Her arms circled his neck as she asked, "Do you think we should do something about it? I wouldn't like to see you in pain, after all."

Cameron grinned. "What do you suppose we should do?"

Cassie shrugged. "I imagine we'll find some method to cure this ailment. We've got until tomorrow to work on it."

Cameron laughed. "Woman, you have astounding faith in my stamina. Till tomorrow, you say?"

Cassie shivered. "Is that so terribly long?" Her lips nuzzled his neck.

Suddenly, Cameron pulled back. His eyes were wide with alarm as his hand went to her forehead. "You're hot!"

Cassie gave a weak smile. "It's nothing. I feel fine." She shivered again. "I'm excited, that's all. I can't wait to go back."

"Goddammit! You're sick! Don't try to lie to me, Cassie. You're burning up!"

"I'm not!" She shivered yet again. "I never get sick. You just want to be proven right."

Cameron mumbled an angry curse as he came to his feet still holding her in his arms. "Thickheaded brat. What the hell am I going to do with you?"

"I can think of one thing." Cassie giggled while snuggling close in his embrace.

Cameron's voice shook with fear as he put her into the bed and covered her. Almost desperately, he held her hands in his. "Stop playing games, Cassie. You're

296

ill. You'll need to conserve your strength."

Cassie watched his face, noticing the terror in his eyes and the sudden gray beneath his tan. Her smile was tender as she sought to bring assurance. "There's no need to worry, Cameron. I'll be fine. I promise. All you need do is remember what I told you."

Cameron groaned in a sudden panic. Thank God, he had written her instructions down. Right now, he couldn't remember his own name. It had happened just as he feared it would. Damn it! Why had she put herself in such danger?

"I think you should give me my first dose of quinine now. Remember, lots of liquids too. If I push off the covers, just pull them up again. And no matter how I complain and fight you, keep the fever down with wet cloths." Cassie gave him another long, searching look. "You look terrified. Are you afraid of catching it?"

Cameron shook his head, unable to speak for the lump that had suddenly settled in his throat. Refusing to think, he mindlessly prepared the medicine and smiled as he watched her grimace at the taste.

"Well, at least you can find something to smile about. Your color is better too. I thought you were going to faint for a minute there." Cassie sighed as she snuggled her suddenly aching limbs deep into the feather mattress. "I feel a little tired. I think I'll sleep for a while."

Cameron sat at her side in a daze and watched as she fell almost instantly sleep. How could she have so calmly instructed him as to what to do? Didn't she realize she was sick and about to get a lot sicker? Wasn't she at all afraid?

As the afternoon turned to evening and the dusk to

night, Cameron grew almost beside himself with worry. Cassie moaned almost constantly, shivering helplessly beneath the heaviest quilt while sweat caused her hair to curl into wet ringlets and her skin to shine in the candlelight. What the hell was he going to do? He couldn't take care of her himself. How could she leave this in his hands?

Occasionally, she awoke, asking only for water, then immediately fell back into a restless sleep. Twice during the night she asked to use the commode. And Cameron knew the seriousness of this illness when she didn't care that his aid was needed.

He never slept throughout the first night. Indeed, he rarely looked away from her, fearful that without his intense concentration she would somehow slip into death.

On the second night she began to hallucinate. There were moments when she thought herself a child again, when she complained of a particular hardship she was forced to endure, or food she was made to eat. Cameron understood only part of her ravings, for the mumbled words came between moans and sighs, while sentences were often left unfinished.

In the chair at her side, he was alternately dozing and cursing his inability to remain alert, when he heard her first clear sentence in almost two days. "Don't tell him. He's mean."

Cameron came instantly awake. Gently, he replaced the moist cloth upon her burning forehead.

"You don't hate him."

Cameron smiled. She spoke so clearly, he could almost imagine her well again. "Hush, darling," he whispered as he sat at her side and cuddled her into his arms. "Rest. You'll soon be well."

"He thinks he owns me. Don't tell him."

"Don't tell him what?" he asked automatically.

Cassie suddenly opened her eyes, but it wasn't Cassie who spoke. And it wasn't simply the childish voice that sent chills down his spine. Her whole countenance had suddenly become immature. If he hadn't known better, he would have sworn she was a child of no more than seven or eight.

"I'm not supposed to tell." Her blue eyes flashed wickedly as her lips curved into a smile. "It's a secret."

Cameron's mouth hung open with surprise. He couldn't speak. He almost wanted to flee. For one insane moment he imagined that she was possessed. Angrily, he pushed aside the absurd notion. She was ill, desperately so. If she acted oddly, 'twas only the feverish ramblings that any might suffer.

Cassie gave an impish, childlike smile. "She loves you, you know."

"Who?" Cameron croaked.

"She's going to be very, very angry. Mummy says I should never tell secrets."

Cameron was about to ask who she was when he suddenly clamped his mouth shut. Jesus, God! What was he doing? He was actually conversing with her, only he knew it wasn't Cassie he was talking to, at least not the Cassie he had come to know. Chills ran up his spine. He had never experienced anything so eerie, but then again, he had never seen anyone so dangerously ill.

Cassie's breathing grew labored and she cried out and fought him when he covered her entire body with a cool, wet sheet. "No!" she cried as she tried to push away the cloth. "It hurts."

"Be still, Cassie, and stop fighting me," Cameron insisted.

"So sick, so sick," she moaned breathlessly. "I can't . . ."

"Oh no, you don't," Cameron grunted as he took her arms in his hands and gave her a mighty shake. Her illness forgotten for the moment, anger replaced concern and he addressed her harshly. "You're going to make it all right. I'll be damned if you're going to die on me now!"

Cassie stopped her mutterings. Her eyes blinked open, and, for the first time since the beginning of her illness, she seemed rational. "I really do hate you, you know," she mumbled weakly as she finally slipped into a deep, restful sleep.

Cameron almost shouted with glee, for he suddenly knew she would make it; her anger alone would see to that. He gave a soft laugh, and, holding her in his arms, he lay down at her side and slept.

Chapter Twenty-one

Cameron muttered in irritation as his shoulder was jostled. He rolled away from the intrusive touch, wanting nothing more than to sleep.

"A fine nurse you turned out to be," came a low, husky grumble. "I can't wake you, and I'm dying of thirst." Cassie struggled into a sitting position and with some effort swung her legs over the side of the bed. God, when had she ever felt so weak? " 'Tis a wonder indeed, I managed to survive such lack of care."

Cameron smiled as he listened to her self-pitying mutterings. When he felt her start to rise, he gently tugged her back to his side. "Where do you think you're going?" With his eyes still closed, he reached out and felt her cool forehead. He smiled again. "I can't decide whether I prefer you sick or well. Certainly, you are equally as bothersome."

He yawned and stretched comfortably. "Do you want some water?"

"No," she snapped sarcastically. "I only asked because I had nothing else to say."

"All right, all right," he chuckled. "Nag, nag, nag."

Cassie watched as he walked to the water pitcher and poured her a glass. Damn the man. What on earth did he find so cheering this early in the morning? Cassie swallowed the water in quick, thirsty gulps while Cameron stood watching her.

"Don't you think you should drink more slowly?"

Cassie glanced up at his smiling face. Although she no longer felt feverish, she was still far from feeling her old self. Her body ached as though she had taken a beating and her head throbbed dully. All in all, she felt terrible, and now, his grinning countenance was suddenly more than she could take. She scowled and asked nastily, "Is there a particular reason for this disgusting show of happiness?"

Cameron laughed at the face she made. "I'd say we've reason enough to smile. You're well, aren't you?"

"Three cheers," she snapped sarcastically as she handed back the glass. She couldn't help but notice his lack of clothing since he stood at the side of the bed and her eyes were almost level with his naked hips. "Would you mind wearing some clothes?"

"Why? Who's here to see?"

"Me!"

Cameron laughed at her blushing cheeks as he sat at her side. "What a contradictory female you are. There are times you nearly rip the clothes from my body, and now, the sight of my nakedness brings you to blush."

Cassie ignored his reasonable statement, unwilling at the moment to give in to his logic. She stirred uncomfortably.

"Have you the need for the chamber pot?"

"I do, but I've also the need for some privacy."

Cameron nodded. "I see you are much improved.

302

You didn't mind my assistance while sick."

Cassie gasped and turned beet red as she pictured the embarrassing intimacy. Her tortured eyes lifted to his merry gaze.

"You needn't feel any shame. I may not have your qualifications, but I do know the workings of the human body."

Cassie lowered her gaze to her lap. "Go away."

"Cassie," he whispered as he snuggled her close in his embrace. "Have you forgotten you are my wife? I would not have objected if our roles were reversed."

"Can we talk of something else?"

"If I bring you the chamber pot, do you think you could manage on your own?"

"Yes."

"In truth?"

"Yes, pleeease!" She pushed at his chest, wishing herself anywhere but here.

Cameron slid the pot close to the bed, got himself dressed and then was gone, all in a matter of minutes.

Cassie was just pulling the sheet back into place when he reentered the cabin. "Jessie left tea and bread. Are you hungry?"

"Are you feeling better?" Cameron asked as he took away the dishes, leaving her to sip at her cup of tea.

Cassie nodded, feeling more like herself. She had napped after breakfast and again after lunch. Following that, Cameron had insisted on bathing her. Now her stomach was full again and her headache had disappeared. She leaned back against the pillows and sipped at her tea with a contented sigh. "Was I very ill?"

Cameron smiled warmly. "You must have been. You told me you loved me."

As Cassie began to choke, Cameron rushed to her side and slapped at her back.

"Good God, I was sicker than I thought!" she gasped once his pounding had stopped.

Cameron laughed at her denial. "I wonder?"

Cassie shot him a wary look. "What do you mean, you wonder? You don't honestly think I . . . I . . ."

"Think you love me?" He smiled at her confusion. "The idea is not beyond comprehension, is it?"

"No, but . . ."

"Well?"

"Cameron—" She bit her lip, her cheeks rosy. Suddenly unable to face him, she lowered his eyes. "You mustn't believe the ramblings of . . ."

Cameron gave a slow, lazy smile, his eyes gleaming with delight. "You know you really must learn how to lie. Now that I know you, it's a wonder you ever fooled me."

They stared at one another for a long moment before she finally shrugged. Her voice held a touch of defiance as she reluctantly admitted, "All right, so I do love you."

Cameron laughed at her grumpy, almost threatening expression. "You needn't sound so annoyed at the idea. Do you find something wrong with a husband and wife loving each other?"

Cassie's head snapped up. Her blue eyes searched his face for any sign of teasing. "What?" she squeaked.

Cameron shrugged. "Didn't you hear me? I said there's nothing wrong with a husband and wife loving each other."

"Really?" she asked, her eyes growing huge as comprehension dawned.

"Really," he answered, his tone tender, the love he had finally admitted to obvious in his gaze.

Cassie suddenly found her eyes blurred with tears. "Even with my foul moods in the morning?"

Cameron chuckled softly. "Foul moods and all."

"Jessie must have run herself ragged," Cassie mused as she fingered the freshly laundered sheets. "What with taking care of the house and the extra work of seeing to our needs . . ."

"Jessie?" Cameron interrupted with a grin, as he tucked her beneath the clean sheet and leaned close, "What about me? I'm ready to collapse."

Cassie laughed softly. She eyed his opened shirt, her eyes wandering over the dark hair of his chest. Sighing comfortably as she snuggled into still another of his crisp shirts, she said, "You look all right to me."

"Just all right?" Cameron teased.

"Now it comes." She sighed wearily. "I suppose I'll be expected to bombard you with compliments, simply because . . ." She hesitated.

"Because you love me," he finished for her. "Do you find it so hard to say?"

"Not at all," she insisted, and then grinned at the sudden silence that followed. "Do you?"

Cameron laughed. "Shall we say it together, then?"

Cassie giggled at the nonsensical turn of their conversation.

"On the count of three?" he coaxed.

Cassie smiled.

"One, two, three."

"I love you." Cassie laughed and then lunged at him, knocking his very willing form down upon the bed. "You beast, you cheated. You didn't say a word."

Cameron was laughing as she tried to shake his shoulders in retaliation. "I know. I wanted to hear you say it. I figured if I was busy talking, I might miss something."

Cassie giggled as she leaned comfortably against his prone figure. "So?"

"So, I guess it's my turn, right?"

Cassie nodded.

Cassie chuckled as he rolled over and held her beneath him. "Cassie, you really are adorable. It's a wonder you didn't have scores of suitors beating down the door."

"Who said I didn't?" A sudden, wicked gleam shone in her eye.

"Did you?"

Cassie shrugged. "I had my share, I suppose."

"Don't tell me, I don't want to hear it."

"Why? Are you jealous?"

"You're goddamned right, I'm jealous."

"I wonder why?" she asked with a sly smile.

Cameron chuckled, wise to her scheming. "Because I love you, of course."

"Do you, Cameron?"

"Is it so hard for you to believe?"

"When you asked"—Cassie grinned—"actually you never asked, did you? You informed me we should marry, I asked you why. You said you wanted me for your bed."

"I do."

"Why didn't you tell me you loved me then?"

"Because I didn't know it then. I only knew I wanted you." Cameron watched her for a long moment. His eyes were dark as he bent his head and brushed his mouth gently over hers.

"When did you know?"

Cameron shrugged. "I've known for some time, but admitted it to myself only when I realized you were sick." He groaned as he remembered his panic. "I was terrified I was going to lose you. At one point, I couldn't even talk for fear of disgracing myself with tears."

Cassie smiled tenderly. "I told you I was going to be all right."

Cameron smiled at her simple logic. "Too bad I didn't have your faith. I would have saved myself more than a little worry.

"I'll always want you, Cassie. I'll always love you." His mouth covered her lips with a gentle, rapturous kiss, as if sealing his pledge.

Abruptly, he pulled himself away. "You'd better get under those covers. You're going to need all the rest you can get."

Cassie smiled. "Why?"

"I'll show you, after you're well."

"Show me now," Cassie insisted softly. Her arms went around his neck, tugging gently to draw him back.

"Cassie," Cameron said, "I don't think we should." He stifled a groan as her hand came between them to brush against his swelling desire. "Cassie, stop it. I'm not going to be able to . . ."

307

Those were the last rational words either spoke for some time.

"Tell me," Cassie whispered as she stroked his cheek with gentle fingers. "How did this happen?"

"Cassie," Cameron muttered, shaking his head as he took her hand and kissed her palm.

"Was it so horrible?" she asked sympathetically.

"No." He shook his head again. "It's simply unimportant."

Cassie smiled. "If it's truly unimportant, tell me."

Cameron sighed. "It happened years ago. I fought a duel."

"Really?" she asked, her blue eyes suddenly bright with excitement. She rolled over on top of him, her elbow near his ear, her hand supporting her head as a mass of red curls cascaded over the two of them. "An honest to goodness duel? Where you fighting over a lady's honor, like a knight in olden times?"

Cameron smiled. "Nothing that fascinating, or romantic, I'm afraid." His eyes grew icy with remembered pain. "The lady involved had no honor. She was my wife."

Cassie gasped, her eyes wide with shock. "You can't mean . . ."

"Oh, but I do," he answered grimly. "I had been away for a time on business. I returned earlier than expected and found my wife entertaining a gentleman in my bed."

"Good God!"

He shrugged, as if the incident were of little consequence. "Needless to say, the men in this vicinity need

308

no longer worry over their wives' virtue, at least not from that one."

Cassie whispered very softly, almost afraid of his answer, "What happened to your wife? Did you kill her too?"

Cameron grinned. "Nothing quite that drastic, I'm afraid, although the thought did occur. She died at sea. She was running away with still another lover."

"Oh God, how terrible! How can you pretend this to be unimportant?"

"I'm not pretending, Cassie. It happened long ago and it is unimportant. My only regret is this damn ugly scar."

"Ugly?" Cassie laughed as her finger traced the jagged line. "Is that what you think?"

"Well?"

Cassie's low, husky laughter and gently spoken words brought a smile back to his eyes. "Don't you realize how attractive you are?"

Cameron laughed. "It's true what they say then, about love being blind."

"Not at all." Cassie shook her head, and, with a devilish grin, continued. "I felt no love the first time I saw you and yet I said to myself, 'Blimey, what a looker!' "

Cameron chuckled tenderly. "Did you? And the scar? It made no difference?"

"Of course, it made a difference. It makes you look ever so dangerous." She eyed him clinically. "I imagine you've caused many a heart to flutter."

"Do you?" He grinned happily, his eyes lighting with pleasure. His hand slid down her back and cupped her bottom. "How dangerous, would you say?"

"Dangerous enough." She eyed him with clear warning. "Were I you, I wouldn't let the knowledge go to my head."

Cameron laughed as he rolled over and cuddled her beneath him. "Oh Cassie, I thank God every day that you're not my niece, in truth."

"And if I were?"

His mouth hovered over her smiling lips. "If you were, I'm afraid my soul would be damned to hell, for I see no way to resist you."

Chapter Twenty-two

Diana gave a most unladylike curse as she spied the empty yard. Then, momentarily forgetting her usually delicate steps, she made her way toward the barn in long angry strides. To say the least, she was not in the best of moods. Actually, her temper had been dangerously close to exploding for days now, and she was nearly worn out from the effort it took to keep herself under control.

Lately, everything seemed to have gone wrong. Not only had that bitch survived the fever, but the loving couple were downright disgusting in the attentions they publicly bestowed upon each other. Diana shivered with revulsion. If she were forced to stand one more night of their tender looks and sweet smiles, she'd throw up. What the hell was the matter with Cameron that he'd become so besotted? Jesus, she thought the man smarter than that.

Her anger was slowly rising. Where the hell was her horse? She had told that idiot Stevens to make sure one was ready. Diana looked at her beautiful new watch pinned to yet another riding habit. Here it was fifteen minutes after the hour and not only was there no horse, but the barn appeared to be empty as well.

She cursed again. When she became mistress of Hill Crest — and she plotted daily toward that end — she would see to this deplorable lack of discipline. God, she had never seen a more lazy group of people in her life. What they needed was a taste of the lash, and she, unlike that stupid Cassie, was not averse to doing what she considered her duty.

She tapped her foot impatiently as her gaze searched out the shadowy barn for a sign of life. A moment later, her attention was drawn to the back room. Someone was laughing. She moved toward the sound.

Joshua was sitting on a low stool, nearly recovered from his accident except for a lingering weakness on his left side. Once he was able, he had exercised every day according to Cassie's instructions, and although it was taking longer than he would have hoped, he was almost his old self again. Were it not for Cassie's quick thinking and nimble fingers, Joshua had no doubt he would have left this world minutes after the horse had laid him low. Due to this fact, and much to Cassie's embarrassment, Joshua considered the new mistress of Hill Crest to be on a par with the angels. When health permitted, he followed her everywhere, seeing to her needs before she had a chance to ask.

At the moment, he was spinning some long, humorous tale while three of the stable boys were busy working on tackle. Diana stood at the tackle room doorway in a rage. How dare they simply ignore her orders?

"Didn't Stevens tell you I wanted to ride this morning? Why isn't my horse ready?"

The three boys jumped to attention at the sound of her voice. The youngest and smallest moved away from the bench at which he worked. "Sorry, ma'am. I didn't know what time."

Diana knew she hadn't told Stevens a particular time, mentioning only she'd like to ride sometime this morning. Still, she reasoned, it made little difference. Her horse should have been waiting for her use upon a moment's notice.

"See to it immediately."

"Yas'um."

With narrowed eyes, Diana watched the youngster walk toward her with the intention of saddling her horse. Without warning, her riding crop suddenly swung out and sliced across the boy's face, leaving an open wound from his forehead to the corner of his mouth. The boy staggered under the impact of the unexpected blow. Those in the room gasped their surprise. Their shock turned to burning hatred as they took in her obvious pleasure at striking the boy.

Just as she raised her hand again, the boy recovered from his frozen state and dashed by. Much to her displeasure, the crop struck naught but empty air. In her intent to inflict further punishment, Diana's arm came down harder than she would have liked. Even through her many petticoats, she felt the burning sting upon her leg. But for the slightest flicker of pain in her eyes, and the almost imperceptible pinching of her lips, none would have guessed of her distress. Still, all knew, for they had seen the lash strike with jarring force. The two boys expertly hid the satisfaction they felt behind blank expressions. But Joshua, having long been freed by his one-time owner, felt no need to hide his enjoyment.

"Take that smirk off your face, you ugly, black bastard."

"I's ugly, that's for sure" — Joshua grinned as he came to his feet to tower over the woman — "and black to boot, but I knows da master'd not be happy to see his property abused."

Diana fumed. No doubt the darky was right. Cameron did seem to have a soft spot for his people. 'Twas best, she reasoned, to let the matter rest. Still, it irked to allow this old man the last word. Finally, she sent the three a murderous glance as she turned on her heel. "In the future, I expect my horse ready on time."

Diana rode along the river. The sky was clear and the weather warm. Too warm. Sweat trickled between her breasts and down her sides while once artfully placed tendrils of hair now stuck uncomfortably to her damp face. Belatedly, she realized she should have worn a lighter garment, but shrugged away the notion of returning to the house in order to change. Most of the day would be gone by the time she accomplished that. Besides, she tried to stay out of the house as much as possible. The last thing she wanted to do was discover the loving couple in yet another nauseating embrace.

Drawing to a stop before a large, felled tree, she used it to aid her in dismounting. A moment later, she shrugged out of her close fitting jacket and pulled her shirt free of her skirt. Careless of who might happen by, she opened the buttons of her shirt. Naked beneath the thin material, she exposed her breasts to the warm air. The sweat-soaked material stuck to her sides and back uncomfortably. For a moment she considered

314

taking it off completely, but no. That would be a bit much, even for her.

Diana left the blouse open and sighed with relief as a cooling breeze came off the water and dried her heated skin. A moment later her hat was flung upon her jacket and she felt much better. Damn, but this climate was unbearable. Even in these lightweight clothes—without a stitch of underthings, but for her petticoats—the heat was oppressive. What she wouldn't give for the cool, damp breezes of home. No wonder the darkies moved so slow. Who could do anything else in this heat?

"It's been a time since I've seen a more beautiful sight," came a deep voice some feet away.

Diana gasped. Her hand moved to her blouse and instantly brought the open sides together. He was sitting on his horse, some feet to her right. His dark hair gleamed in the sunlight as he swept off his hat in a courtly bow. White teeth flashed in his sun-tanned face as Diana studied his form. He wasn't handsome. He wasn't even good looking, but he had that air of authority and a certain delicious male confidence that appealed to almost all women.

Diana's heart began to pound at the explicitly sexual look he gave her. A thrill of excitement ran down her back as intriguingly erotic pictures flashed through her mind. It was not unusual for Diana to feel this instant attraction to a stranger. Indeed, she often felt such stirrings. What surprised her this time was the force of her feelings.

She found herself wondering what would it be like to have this man mount her. God, how long had it been since her last time? Too long, she reasoned, for already

315

she could feel herself growing wet.

She lifted her chin and made a pretense of being annoyed. "You should have announced yourself. No gentleman . . ."

Hearty laughter interrupted her supposed put down. "You're mistaken if you think I'm a gentleman."

He dismounted and began a slow, hip-grinding gait toward her. Diana couldn't take her eyes from his already bulging sex. She heard low male laughter, but was helpless to do more than lick her lips.

"Do you mind if I join you for a minute?" he asked, giving her no option as he sat at her side.

He chuckled softly as his gaze lingered on her hand. "You're goin' to wrinkle your blouse doin' that."

Diana glanced at his grinning face and then down at her hand. She didn't fear rape. After all, no one could take what was freely given, and she instinctively knew it wouldn't take much to give it to this one. Damn, but she was tired of acting the prim and proper miss, and it had been so long!

Diana smiled and released the material. She watched as his gaze lingered on her breasts. "Do you live around here, Mr. . . . ?"

He couldn't see much but a strip of creamy white skin from her throat to her waist, but he could remember plenty. Damn, but it had been a long time since he'd had a white woman, and he had no doubt he'd have this one. "Rowlins," he replied as he wet his lips waiting for the material to separate further. He shrugged his head without taking his eyes from her. "I work over at the Bennett place."

Diana shivered in anticipation as his hungry gaze moved over her. Her voice was already thick with longing and quivered when she asked, "Do you see something of interest, Mr. Rowlins?"

Rowlins chuckled and glanced up, his eyes meeting her hungry glance. "Maybe if you didn't work so hard keeping that thing closed, it wouldn't draw such attention."

Diana gave a silky laugh. "No doubt were I to allow my blouse to fall completely open, we would then discuss the weather."

"I don't know." He shrugged as he leaned way back against the fallen tree. When his gaze returned to her blouse, the breeze was lifting the garment just enough for him to see the underside and tip of one breast. Rowlins grinned and stretched out his long legs in a relaxed pose. "Why don't we give it a try and see?"

Diana hesitated. For as many lovers as she'd had, this was something completely new. Perhaps that was what so enthralled. He was completely lacking in finesse. Oddly enough, it didn't detract from his appeal, but added to her excitement.

Rowlins watched as her gaze traveled the length of him, only to return and rest with unexpected greed upon his male member. Jesus, she looked like she was going to jump him. He chuckled softly. That would be a change. It had been a long time since he'd found a willing woman. Vaguely, he wondered if he'd enjoy it half as much without the usual struggles.

"Why don't you make yourself comfortable?" He patted the ground at his side.

Diana shrugged and settled herself next to him.

As she knew it would, her movement caused her blouse to part. She didn't bother with false modesty, but allowed her breasts to swing free. Once she had settled herself at his side, the blouse offered only scant concealment. Diana's heart pounded and lust showed clearly in her eyes. She couldn't believe her excitement. Even with all her experience, she'd never had it like this before. She was a young girl the last time she'd done it outdoors. Since then, she'd grown to appreciate discretion. Over the years, she'd found that a slow build up of passion ended with her as the master, and she liked nothing better than to force her will on some panting, desperate male.

Rowlins didn't hesitate to push away the fabric that blocked his view. His tanned finger lifted one pale breast for his inspection. His thumb grazed the dark nipple until it grew stiff. "You shouldn't worry about coverin' them. You've got beautiful tits."

Diana's body jerked at the disgusting word, but as quickly as it had come, her revulsion disappeared as his finger continued circling her nipple.

Rowlins smiled as she offered no resistance, but gasped at his touch. The pulse in her throat beat wildly. Jesus, she was hot for this and he was equally ready to bury himself between her legs. "Is your skin smooth and white all over?"

Diana gave a strangled laugh. She could hardly think with his fingers pinching so delightfully at her nipple. "Why don't you see for yourself?" Christ, she prayed he wasn't one of these bastards that took it gentle and easy. She couldn't remember a time when she'd been so instantly ready, and she wanted it now—rough, hard, and hot.

"Why don't you show me?" he said with a lustful grin.

Rowlins released her breast and leaned back to

watch as she drew the blouse fully open so that both breasts were exposed to his amorous view. He nodded thoughtfully. "Looks the same."

Jesus, she was ready to cry with all this teasing. His fingers reached out and his nails flicked over the sensitive tips. Diana gasped as shocks of pleasure tightened her belly. She arched her back, almost begging for more. Why didn't he just get on with it? She wanted to lie beneath him, not play games.

Low groans came from deep in her throat as he teased her breasts with painful little pinches. Rowlins laughed, knowing he was driving her crazy and enjoying every minute of it.

"How are your legs?" he murmured. "Are they as white?"

What the hell was this obsession he seemed to have with white skin? She had no way of knowing that this was Rowlins, Bennett's sadistic overseer who was feared by every black woman on that plantation. She didn't know he had taken every one of them, from eight years of age and up. She didn't know of the rapes, the beatings, the horror these women and children had suffered at his cruel hand, and she wouldn't have cared if she did.

She didn't answer him. She couldn't. She was gasping for breath as he pinched her again, harder this time.

"Are they?" he insisted.

Diana pulled her skirts up, eagerly exposing herself to his view. She parted her unclad thighs, her eyes almost begging for his touch.

Rowlins laughed. He couldn't remember a woman ever being so hot for him — except for the town whores,

319

and they didn't count since they were paid for their efforts. Diana moaned as he slid his fingers into her wet heat. Damn, but this had turned into a great afternoon. He'd never expected such a treat on his way to town.

"Take everything off. I want to watch when I put it into you."

"Yes," she gasped. "Yes," she repeated as she frantically tore at her clothes. She couldn't get them off fast enough.

As she tossed aside the garments, she was somewhat taken aback to note that he now seemed to have forgotten her existence. Diana could have named a dozen men who would have sacrificed breathing before they'd have taken their eyes off this treat.

It was disconcerting, to say the least, to undress before a man and have him simply open his pants and begin to fondle himself. But when she saw his huge organ, she sighed with delight. He was so big, so hard. She knew he was going to hurt her, and—she shivered with excitement—she couldn't wait.

When she was naked but for her stockings and shoes, she followed his guidance and straddled his body. He entered her with a hard thrust, and her body stiffened with the shock of burning pain.

Rowlins knew he had hurt her. He grinned as he watched the flicker of pain in her eyes. Suddenly, his mouth took her swaying breast and his teeth bit down hard.

Diana gasped at the sudden assault. She had wanted it rough, but she never imagined anything like this. Pain wracked her body and she cried out. For a moment she thought to fight him. She tried to pull away but he held her in place.

"Bastard!" she grunted as she struggled to free herself.

Rowlins's deep laughter and low words brought her struggles to an instant stop. "Don't tell me it's not good."

"You could have taken it easier, damn it!"

Rowlins laughed again as he rolled over and held her pinned beneath him. "Is that what you want? You want it easy?" He couldn't remember the last time he had been gentle. For a second, he felt tempted, then gave a mental shrug. No woman was worth the effort. She had wanted to play. Too bad if she changed her mind.

Diana gasped. He was moving inside her now, hot and thick, incredibly huge. Slowly, the pain lessened and pleasure began to grow in its stead. She looked into his grinning face with wide, astonished eyes. She couldn't quite believe how much she was beginning to enjoy this. She laughed in return. Damn, if it wasn't the best she'd had in years.

Diana lay naked upon the grass, her arms around her head, her eyes closed. She breathed a long sigh of contentment. The heat of the late afternoon sun felt good on her body. Too good to bother with covering herself. In any case, she was too tired.

"You lookin' to fuck again?"

Diana mentally grimaced with distaste. God, but the man was a brute. Even if he was the best lay she'd had in years, he hadn't an ounce of class in his entire being. Diana raised her knees and allowed them to

321

part so that the sun's rays might soothe the ache between her legs. The heat felt delicious and she felt her body react to the warming sensation. Yes, she admitted silently, she could almost, as he so delicately put it, 'fuck again.' But her body was unaccustomed to such rough handling, and if she were to indulge in **another bout of sexual acrobatics, she'd be lucky if she were able to stand, never mind mount her horse. As it** was, her whole body ached. Jesus, if he had raped her, she certainly couldn't feel any more battered.

Diana opened one eye and examined her nude body. Thank God, she hadn't a man waiting at home. She'd have a time of it explaining these bite marks and bruises. She'd probably have to wear high collars for the next few days.

"No, darling," she sighed at last. "I don't want to fuck again. What I want is to rest. This sun feels wonderful and I'm a bit sore."

"Yeah, well, I ain't got no time to lay around in the altogether." Rowlins stood and dressed. "I got a load of supplies to see to in town."

"Ta, ta," she called as she listened to his saddle creaking under his weight.

"You goin' to be here tomorrow?" he called back.

"I'll be here," she promised. Her eyes still closed, she listened as he moved away, his horse trotting between the thick brush that lined the river. A grin touched her lips. I'll be here all right. Just make sure you are.

Diana had devised a plan. It had come to her as she lay panting with exhaustion after the first time they had come together. Surely, this man was too much for one woman. The Christian thing would be to share him with her best friend. No, she said to herself, giggling softly, no matter how much she wanted him for herself, she wouldn't be selfish about this. A gurgle of laughter escaped her throat. Yes, Cassie would have him. And if she was less than willing, Diana shrugged, who would ever know?

After Rowlins finished with Cassie, there wouldn't be enough left for anyone to recognize. Certainly, no finger would be pointed at Diana. And she would be there, of course, to console the grieving widower.

Oh God, this was sweet. At last, she had a sure way of disposing of the bitch.

Rowlins hated Cameron. Diana smiled as she remembered the overseer's reaction when she mentioned where she was living. Best of all, he hated Cassie, considering her the cause of his pain. Diana licked her lips, savoring the deliciousness of the plan. It would be some time before Rowlins forgot the beating he'd taken, and Diana was not about to let this opportunity slip away. All she had to do was set up the meeting and Rowlins could take it from there.

"Damn," she grunted aloud. She was sorry now she hadn't told Rowlins to stay a bit longer. The sun had worked wonders on her tender skin. She opened her legs wider, welcoming the erotic sensation. Just knowing she would soon rid herself of that simpering Cassie had caused her to grow excited all over again. She shrugged. No matter. She could do the job as well. Certainly she had more than enough practice of late.

"I want you to understand these people belong to me. If any need chastising, I will see to it."

"But, Cameron," Diana protested. She'd known, of

323

course, that the black bastard would eventually come to him complaining of her treatment. Still, she wondered why Cameron should take such offense. She doubted any other owner would have cared. Why was he making such a fuss over a few worthless blacks? She pouted beautifully. "The boy was terribly rude."

Cameron did a masterful job of hiding his disgust with a stiff smile. It was clear she had spent the afternoon with a man. He had asked to see her immediately upon her return, and she'd had no time to dispose of the incriminating evidence. Her clothes were wrinkled, more than they should have been were she riding, yet not nearly enough had she been making love. Apparently, she'd taken them off. But it was the marks on her skin and her swollen lips that gave proof of an afternoon spent in some man's arms.

Idly, Cameron wondered who it had been, knowing there was no one serious in her life. He shrugged away the thought. He really didn't care if she indulged in an afternoon of casual sex. He had long ago realized what she was and it was none of his concern. It was her whining voice that grated on his nerves. He was angry enough that she should dare abuse his servants. He didn't need this helpless female act. He'd had enough of this woman and her play-acting. He sighed as he returned his gaze to his papers, reminding himself that she was his guest, at least for the time being. And it simply wouldn't do to reveal the disgust he felt at watching her fluttering eyelashes and simpering, sweet smiles. Suddenly, he wanted only to rid himself of her presence. His tone was clearly dismissive as he coldly remarked, "In the future, if you have any problems, come to me."

Diana turned on her heel and left Cameron to his papers. What in the world had come over the man? Surely, he couldn't be this upset because she had struck one slave?

On her way to her room, she glanced at herself in the hallway mirror. Her eyes widened as she came to a sudden stop and took in the sight of her swollen lips and the faint bruises at her throat. Had he guessed her afternoon activities? Did he feel a measure of jealousy? That was it, of course! He suspected her of being with another man. That was why he had acted so cool and distant. Diana's warped mind came to the only possible conclusion. He lusted after her. She could see that clearly now.

She giggled with delight as she finally entered her bedroom. In an instant, she flung away her clothing and was lying naked on the bed as she waited for the slaves to bring water for her bath. A knock sounded at her door, and she slid her arms into her robe as she called out, "Enter."

She eyed the young man's bulging muscles as he emptied the last of the buckets into the tub. Eyes downcast, Adam turned to leave.

Diana had been standing near the door, waiting for the rest of the blacks to leave. A teasing smile touched her lips. How considerate of Cameron to leave the heavy work to the young males. Wouldn't she be a fool not to show this one her appreciation? Diana reached out and closed the door.

She was going to initiate this one. She wondered why she'd never thought of it before. What did it matter he was black? He was male, and for the moment, that was enough.

Adam raised wide, inquiring eyes toward the beautiful lady. His heart pounded with surprise and fear as she suddenly allowed her robe to fall from her shoulders. "I need your help, Adam," she remarked huskily as she settled herself in the tub.

She loved this kind of thing. There was nothing to compare with showing a young man exactly how she liked it. Diana directed him to kneel.

Adam did as he was told, for he dared not do otherwise. His fingers shook, for he had never before touched a white woman. For a minute, he wondered if she would feel as soft as his Janey.

Diana leaned back and watched as he hesitantly and very gently began to soap her shoulders and upper chest. She bade him lower the rag, and smiled as the soapy cloth moved over her breasts, then her belly.

Adam was careful to do exactly as he was told, lest some form of punishment be bestowed. He had never been asked to do this before and wasn't sure what was expected of him.

"Now put down the rag, Adam."

Adam looked at her with more than a little confusion.

Diana sighed. "Use only your hands." She showed him how to soap his hands into a lather and use his fingers to massage between her legs. She smiled at his ability to learn so quickly. She turned slightly to her side, raising her leg to give him easier access, then sighed as she played with her own soapy nipples. God, but this felt good. She had wasted months doing this for herself. Why hadn't she thought of using one of the boys before? If she had, she probably wouldn't have been so hot for Rowlins today.

326

Diana shrugged. No matter. Rowlins would do just fine for the time being. Besides sex, she needed him for one very important piece of business. But after she married Cameron, she'd probably stick to the slaves. She couldn't chance Cameron's noticing Rowlins' telltale marks. No, she's have to be careful then, very careful indeed.

Chapter Twenty-three

Cassie smiled as she leaned back against the thick trunk of a huge weeping willow and listened to Amy's hesitant reading.

" 'And Jesus said, *Suffer the little children to come unto me and for . . . for . . .*' "

"Forbid," Cassie offered.

" 'And forbid them not.' "

The young girl beamed with delight at her accomplishment as she glanced from the Bible to her mistress' smiling face.

Cassie laughed aloud. "I can see you are not at all pleased to find yourself capable of reading at last."

A frown of confusion marred the young girl's face.

"I'm teasing, Amy. You have every right to be thrilled. You've worked very hard. I'm proud of you."

"It's too bad others won't look upon your efforts in the same light," came a deep voice from behind the tree as Cameron parted the overhanging leaves and entered the little circle.

The six children seated around Cassie tensed with guilt and looked to their mistress with worried faces.

Learning to read was expressly forbidden. But Cassie's calm demeanor and casual smile gave not a hint of fear at being caught in an unlawful act, and the children soon breathed a sigh of relief.

"Good morning, Mr. Chandler," she remarked easily. "Won't you join us?"

"I've a need to speak with you in private," Cameron said as he moved toward his lady. Making himself comfortable at her side, he turned to the children, "Would you mind if your lessons were cut short today?"

Again, as one, the six looked to their mistress, and, at her nod, they scampered off to play. Each of them was under eight years old, and, in accordance with Cameron's rules, too young as yet to work his fields.

Cameron smiled, his dark gaze taking in the poised young beauty at his side. His heart swelled with pleasure, for despite the fact that the mistress of Hill Crest was new to her position, the children had looked to her before obeying him. Apparently, there was no question in anyone's mind as to who was truly in charge. The whip, which was regularly put to use by his fellow plantation owners, accomplished little compared to her gently spoken suggestions. Cameron knew there wasn't a soul among his people who didn't hold their new mistress in the highest regard.

"It's a beautiful morning, is it not?" Cassie remarked casually.

Cameron shot her a quick look and then idly began to pick at the sparse grass. "Indeed," he agreed. "I, for one, would hate to see a day such as this end in disaster."

Knowing full well what he referred to, Cassie nevertheless pretended ignorance. "Are you expecting some calamity to momentarily befall us?"

"Cassie, you know well enough of what I speak. It is forbidden to teach slaves to read."

"Is it? I've been here so short a time, I confess to some ignorance concerning your laws."

Cameron sighed. "Do you propose to use this ignorance as a defense once caught?"

Cassie giggled. "Will you turn me in, Cameron?"

"Damn it, Cassie! This is not a matter to treat lightly. The crime is most serious."

Cassie looked up into his stern expression, her contrite manner worthy of the stage. "I fear I suffer some grave deficiency of character. First, I entreat you to steal your neighbor's slaves and now I teach your people to read." Cassie had to bite her lip to prevent the laughter that threatened. "No doubt there was a rogue or two among my ancestors. What other explanation is there for my willful and blatant criminal tendencies?"

Cameron tried to glare at her smug expression, but then gave up and looked again at the ground as he tried to suppress a smile. "I wonder how prone you'd be to laughter after spending a night or two in jail?"

Cassie suddenly came to her knees, turned, and plopped herself into his lap. Her fingers played with supposed carelessness at the buttons of his shirt. As one button after another popped open, she slipped her hand inside to tease his flesh. Wide blue eyes looked up to his frown. "Would you report your wife, Cameron?"

"It is not I that you should fear, madam, but others who might be more averse to your disregard of the law."

"It is not against your laws to teach these people

330

about Jesus. Am I right?"

Cameron nodded. "You know that most believe it their Christian duty."

Cassie smiled. "Well then, what harm have I wrought? I have done nothing but teach them to read the Bible, thereby adding to their knowledge of Jesus." Cassie grinned. "Would you fault me for performing my Christian duty?"

"What I'd like to do is turn you over my knee." Cameron found it suddenly impossible to keep his tone steady as she squirmed against him.

"Mmm." Cassie smiled as she nuzzled the tempting tanned skin she had bared. "That sounds interesting. When would you like to perform this ghastly chore?"

Cameron chuckled. "One can only hope the authorities find your explanation half as delightful as I."

"Or better yet, they find me not at all."

Cameron's hand went under Cassie's skirt and snaked up her leg.

"You'll not forbid me this, Cameron?"

He groaned as his fingers discovered warm flesh above her stockings. "Tell me how I might, Cassie, for I find myself unable to forbid you anything."

Cassie smiled.

"Warn them to tell no one," he said huskily, his mind now distracted.

"It is done," she murmured as his hand moved further up her leg.

She chuckled at his frown when he found his proposed path blocked.

"When?" he asked, his disappointment obvious.

"This morning," she answered, a bit too cheerfully for his liking.

Cameron sighed, his hopes dashed that she might already be carrying his child. Finally, he shrugged away his disappointment, knowing there was time aplenty to have a houseful of children. Right now, due to Cassie's teasing strokes, thoughts other than fatherhood occupied his mind, and the idea of waiting the usual two or three days did not sit at all well. Suddenly, a wicked light entered his dark eyes. "I wonder if you would be averse to a bargain of sorts?"

Cassie's brows arched and her head tipped as she awaited his proposal. "Namely?"

"Well"—he shrugged with deliberate carelessness—"since it is time for your monthly flow, I thought you might service me. Likewise, I will return the favor during my monthly time."

Cassie had to suppress the laughter that threatened at his guileless expression. A devilish glint entered her eyes before she bent her head and nodded gravely. "The idea seems reasonable enough. Agreed."

At first, Cameron thought she must have misunderstood. His brows rose with amazement at her easy acceptance. Then, spying the wicked gleam in her eye, his gaze narrowed suspiciously. "In truth?"

Cassie nodded her head, her lips curved in a deliciously innocent smile. "I see no reason to deny oneself this treat simply because the other is unable to partake." She began to giggle, barely able to utter her final pronouncement. "We shall begin as soon as you start your monthly cycle." She shrieked with laughter as she tried to escape his retaliatory tickling. As the merry sound carried across the yard, the servants there smiled gently and nodded in understanding.

* * *

"Meghan"—Cassie groaned as she strained to keep Milly, the cow, from kicking over the half-filled bucket of milk—"how do you expect to learn how to do this if you're playing with the kittens?"

"Look at them, Cassie," Meghan called over her shoulder, from across the width of the barn. "They're so tiny."

Cassie sighed and leaned back away from the cow. A storm was brewing, turning Milly's usually complacent nature to restlessness. Apparently, she was in no mood to continue with this chore, a chore begun, Cassie reminded herself, only because of Meghan's interest.

Cassie pushed her hair from her eyes with the back of her hand and was just about to come to her feet when the mother cat, aware for the first time that someone was handling her young, came charging into the barn. It mattered not at all to Sandy that Milly and Cassie blocked the shortest path to her kittens. With lightning speed, she ran up Cassie's back and jumped atop the already nervous cow.

Milly instantly tried to dislodged the arrogant, unwelcome cat, but Sandy, resisting all efforts to throw her off, held on tightly, digging her sharp claws into the cow's back. Thoroughly disgruntled, Milly mooed loudly and slapped the air with her tail. When this action proved to have no effect, she stepped sideways, hoping to shake herself free by rubbing against the wall of the stall. Cassie, with no time to rise from the milking stool, was suddenly knocked to the floor. An instant later, the bucket of warm milk was kicked into a huge white spray that covered her from head to toe.

Low laughter was heard from the entrance of the

barn as Cassie, hastening to get away from the unhappy cow, caught her heel in the hem of her long skirt. As she stumbled and fell forward, her head butted Milly's side, enraging the cat, who decided she could take no more of these jarring movements. Scratching her displeasure, she dug her claws further into Milly's back just before she jumped free. In hopeful retaliation, Milly kicked out angrily, catching her hoof in Cassie's skirt and ripping the material at the waist.

Cameron cursed. Suddenly at Cassie's side, he dragged her away, tearing her skirt from her bodice in the process.

"And just what do you think you were doing?" her rescuer asked with amusement in his voice.

Dazed and drenched with milk, Cassie could only blink.

Cameron laughed aloud as droplets of warm milk ran from her long, silky lashes, down her cheeks and onto her heaving chest. "I have men who are perfectly capable of performing this task. You need not take this chore upon yourself."

Cameron's laughter instantly restored Cassie's senses. Wrenching angrily free of his arm, she asked haughtily, "Do you mind?"

"Exactly what were you hoping to accomplish?"

Cassie shot the giggling Meghan a stern look. "I was trying to teach this ungrateful wretch how to milk a cow."

"But she was playing with the kittens."

"Apparently, her interest waned when she realized the length of time it takes to fill a bucket."

Cameron took a step back and folded his arms. He

334

grinned with amazement as he studied his usually immaculate wife. He wondered how she managed, even now, to maintain such a regal bearing as she stood before him in the tattered remains of her dress, her hair disheveled, nearly every inch of her covered in milk. He could not imagine a more beautiful sight. Indeed, were it not for the sound of Meghan's laughter reminding him they were not alone, he would have enjoyed showing her just how much the sight of her pleased him. And how he suddenly thirsted for a sampling of the sweet milk that bathed her skin. "Do you know how lovely you are?"

Cassie shot him a look of disgust, believing him to be teasing. "Instead of finding humor in a lady's mishap, a gentleman should offer his assistance."

Cameron chuckled. "Am I now to blame for the clumsiness of a cow?"

"I blame you only for your heartless laughter at my expense."

Cameron shook his head. "And here I was, simply about to relate the arrival of our guests for tea." He allowed Cassie time to grasp this information before he continued, "Now what do you suppose I get for my efforts? Anger and abuse. I ask you, is that fair treatment?"

"Now?" Cassie asked aghast, her hand reaching unconsciously to curb her wild, damp locks. "They're here already?"

Cameron opened his pocket watch and glanced inside. "If I were promised some future reward, I could show them the garden, thereby affording you ten minutes to ready yourself."

Cassie whirled away, ignoring his teasing. This

wasn't the time for seductive games. The Reverend and Mrs. Collins would be wondering where their hosts were hiding. She was running from the barn as she shot over her shoulder, "Twenty minutes."

She was gone before he had a chance to respond, but Cameron smiled, his eyes glowing with love, knowing it didn't matter how long he had to wait. He'd wait forever if need be.

He turned to look tenderly at his daughter. "Do you think you could take Cassie's place as hostess for a short time? I know she would be grateful for your help."

Meghan nearly swooned, so great was her joy as she proudly accompanied her father to greet his guests. She couldn't remember when she had been so happy. Not a trace remained of the sorrow and unhappiness she'd known before Cassie's arrival. And there wasn't anything she wouldn't gladly do for her new mother.

Chapter Twenty-four

Meghan laughed into the wind as she raced her horse along the river's edge. Each day she grew braver as she dared to explore what was, to her, uncharted territory. She knew, of course, that these daily reckless rides were forbidden, but after early mornings spent with Cassie at the infirmary, no one questioned her whereabouts. Rarely was it even noticed that she was gone for hours at a time. In all likelihood, each adult thought she was with the other.

Right now, Cassie would be busy with the babies, while her father was at work, either in his library or at his office in town.

Meghan sighed, knowing that once Mr. Gates, her tutor, arrived, her freedom would be greatly curtailed. Her lessons would, more than likely, stretch well into the noon hour, and since the family spent each afternoon together, she'd find herself with little free time. But that wouldn't be until the fall. For now, she would enjoy the summer, and the freedom it brought, without anyone being the wiser.

Meghan reined her horse to a slow canter as she searched out a private place to swim. Excitement rippled through her slender body. She knew this was the most dangerous thing she had ever done. Father would be furious if he found out. But, at the tender age of eight, Meghan never thought of the consequences of her actions. Her only desire was to sample these cool, forbidden waters beneath the hot rays of the August sun.

It was too open here, she thought. Perhaps farther down river would be better. Meghan was only just becoming conscious of her body. Gone forever was the carefree child who might disrobe without thought as to who might be present.

She smiled as she came across a small pool of gently moving water. In a moment, she was off the horse and stripping herself of her clothes. The water was icy, but Meghan soon became accustomed to it as she sat for a few minutes at the river's edge. Soon, she was wading farther and farther away from the safety of the shore.

Meghan laughed as the cool water streamed gently around her small body. She had never done this before and it felt marvelous. The knowledge of her disobedience, coupled with the sense of danger, only added to her enjoyment.

Meghan was gaining confidence now as she walked farther into the clear water. The water was up to her waist before she dunked herself beneath its surface and tried to swim. She had seen the boys at her father's plantation do this more than a dozen times. It had appeared easy enough, yet every time Meghan tried to copy their movements, she sank with a disappointed sigh to the bottom.

Was there a trick to this swimming business? Was not kicking your legs enough to keep one afloat? Once more she went down, only to resurface with great splashing, ready to try again.

Meghan never noticed that the water no longer came to her waist. Preoccupied with her efforts to swim, she had wandered out farther from shore than she had intended. Now, she was in shoulder deep water as she again went below the surface.

Meghan had also failed to notice that she'd gotten too close to a dam of twigs and branches that lay hidden beneath the water.

Once again, she easily regained her footing, but, to her amazement, found herself unable to break the surface. Something was holding her back. She turned to see her hair caught upon a branch. She struggled. Her arms splashed water above her head in an instinctive effort to grasp at something solid. She pulled until she was completely exhausted. Her head ached, but her hair remained firmly trapped in place. Her lungs burned. She had to get out! She couldn't breathe! Panic set in and she used the last of her energy yanking at her hair. To no avail.

Meghan never realized she was about to die. Her last thought, just before the blackness came, was the certain discovery of her actions when she didn't return for lunch. Her father was going to be very angry.

She never felt the splashing as someone else quickly entered the water. She never knew that strong fingers tore at her hair until the strands broke and she floated free.

Water gushed from her mouth and nose as she was

dragged ashore. Great, choking heaves suddenly wrenched at her insides until all the water, along with her breakfast, lay upon the sand. Dazed from her ordeal, it was some minutes before she blinked her eyes open to find a black face above her, grinning from ear to ear. She moaned as she closed her eyes again, too sick to think or care who her savior might be.

"You oughtn't be swimmin' by your lonesum. Your papa would give you a fair lickin' if'n he found out."

"Well"—Meghan groaned with the effort it took to talk, since her head was pounding and her throat felt like she'd swallowed her father's razor—"I ain't about to tell him."

The black girl grinned as she looked around. "Your clothes is on the other side of the river. You want me to get them?"

Meghan sighed and turned onto her back, forgetting for the moment her newfound modesty. "No," she said, "they'll only get wet when I cross over again."

"What's your name?"

"Meghan. What's yours?"

"Betsy. You come here much?"

"No. It was hot and I thought I could learn to swim."

"I knows. I saw you."

"Can you swim?" It was getting easier to talk now. Her head and throat weren't hurting quite so badly.

"Sho' enough."

Meghan couldn't keep the touch of excitement out of her voice. "If I come back again, will you teach me?"

"I don't get away much. Mr. Rowlins, he watches everythin'."

"I'll come here every day and wait for you."

And so began a friendship that would grow into

adulthood. Meghan and Betsy met often at the river during that summer. It wasn't until the summer was nearly over that each would reap the rewards of having the other for a friend.

"Can I go, too?" Meghan asked as she skipped along the wooden sidewalk, holding Cassie's hand.

"I don't see why not. The party is to be all day. You can come for the afternoon."

Meghan let out a cry of happiness as she danced merrily around a smiling Cassie. "Will I get a new gown, too?"

"Cassie, for pity's sake. Can't you keep that child quiet? Everyone is looking at us."

Cassie looked over Meghan's head to Diana's frowning face and smiled. "She's a child, Diana. There'll be time enough for her to act the lady."

Diana tried to ignore Meghan's antics as the threesome made their way toward Mrs. Hays's shop. Mrs. Billings was giving a gala party in honor of her son who had just arrived home from school in Europe. Diana had every intention of being the belle of the ball, and since money was no object, she was going to wear the most beautiful gown she could find. She smiled a most secretive smile. Just wait until Cameron saw her. This time, he wouldn't be able to resist.

Diana was still laboring under the false impression that Cameron was smitten with her. Having believed so from the time they met, she couldn't at first understand why he had married Cassie. After a while, however, she convinced herself that he had somehow been led to believe that she wasn't available and had chosen Cassie as a last resort. Diana shot Cassie a look of scorn, knowing no one in his right mind would choose this fool over her.

Diana's thoughts went on to happier endings as she watched Meghan run along the sidewalk. The day was near when this sniveling brat would also be disposed of. Damn, but the child was constantly into everything. Rarely did she walk into her room and find it undisturbed. For some reason, her powders, rouges, pencils, and combs seemed a never ending attraction for the obnoxious youngster.

Diana had complained constantly about this invasion of privacy, and although the child had been reprimanded, her unwelcome intrusions still occurred. For the life of her, she couldn't imagine why Cameron insisted the girl remain at home. Smiling confidently, she told herself that it would not be long before Meghan would be sent back to school, where all noisy, dirty children belonged.

Suddenly, Meghan, skipping backward, smacked into a man who had just turned onto the sidewalk from an alley between a group of stores. Cassie gasped as she heard the man utter a vile curse. As he raised his hand to slap the child away, Cassie quickly grabbed her newfound daughter and pulled her clear of the man's swing.

Rowlins eyed the two women and suddenly cowering child. He guessed instantly who Cassie was. The last time he'd seen the bitch—before her husband had knocked him senseless—she'd been no more than a blur of skirts and red hair. But he was sure it was the new mistress of Hill Crest. Diana was too jealous a woman to have willingly chosen such a delectable piece

342

for a companion.

Rowlins frowned as he remembered the pain he had suffered on her account. Unconsciously, he stroked at his newly healed rib. His fingers itched as he silently reaffirmed his promise. This one, and her husband, were going to get more than a taste of the pain he had suffered.

He licked at his lips at the sight of the angry beauty before him. Jesus, but she was something. His smile grew decidedly evil as vivid pictures danced in his mind's eye. He was going to enjoy taking this one. This one would put up a fight. He liked them the best when they fought.

"Afternoon, ladies," he offered as he took his hat from his head.

Cassie nodded curtly. Her eyes reflected the revulsion she felt as she remembered their last encounter. She made to move past him, but Rowlins blocked her path.

Cassie looked up with some surprise. "Excuse me, sir."

Rowlins smiled again and Cassie felt a shiver of disgust run up her spine. "Perhaps I might be of some assistance."

"I think not."

"The town harbors some unsavory characters. I wouldn't want to see any harm come to such pretty ladies." Cassie didn't mistake the lightly veiled threat in his voice. But it wasn't fear that caused her to speak out, for she felt nothing but revulsion for anyone who would so horribly mistreat another human being.

"Mr. Rowlins," Cassie snapped, "there is little chance of harm befalling us." She looked at him

343

meaningfully as she continued, "Most hereabouts are decent folks."

Rowlins's face grew dark at Cassie's obvious insult. Silently he allowed them to pass, while swearing to himself he'd get even with the bitch. The day wasn't far away when he'd have her in his power. Christ, he could feel himself growing hard just thinking about the things he was going to do to her.

The room was cast in shadow. A gentle breeze which occasionally fluttered the drawn curtains at her balcony doors offered a tantalizing reprieve from the worst of the heat. Cassie relaxed in her bath as the scent of jasmine filled the room.

She had sat in her tub until the water had grown cold. Cassie gave a wry smile. At least as cold as anything could possibly get on this hot summer day. She gave a reluctant sigh as she came to her feet. She couldn't stay here all day. Today was the day of the Billings' party and if she dallied any longer, she'd be late.

Cassie stepped from the tub and reached for the absorbent toweling on a nearby table. Her hand froze in midair as a low voice filled the silent room. "Don't."

She turned toward the sound, a soft, teasing smile forming on her lips. "Shall I go to the party like this?"

Cameron smiled as he leaned comfortably against the closed bedroom door. His arms were folded across his wide chest as he watched his wife's eyes sparkle with saucy humor. A sudden breeze fluttered the curtain, allowing afternoon sun to dapple the darkening room and bring a luminous radiance to her skin.

"We could have our own party," he suggested.

Cassie grinned and asked innocently. "All have been invited to the Billings'. Who would come?" She laughed at his raised brow, knowing the double entendre he'd read into her words.

"Right now, I'm only interested in watching one particular woman come." Cameron's gaze moved over the glistening wet sheen which lightly covered his wife's creamy skin. He longed to lick her dry. Still, he deliberately remained where he was.

Cassie shook her head and laughed. Again, she reached for the toweling.

"Cassie." His voice was lower still, filled with meaning.

Again, she stopped all movement as his husky voice constricted her stomach muscles and brought a sudden stirring of desire. She forgot her original plan to hurry. Her heart began to race as his smoldering dark gaze moved over her. Cassie felt no shame, only power as she stood proudly before him, reveling in the knowledge that she could arouse him this way. His eyes traveled the length of her, and Cassie could feel his touch as surely as if he caressed her with his fingers. She closed her eyes, and, despite the heat, shivered with raw need.

He pulled at his jacket and dropped it carelessly upon the floor. His shirt and boots quickly followed.

"Take your hair down," he whispered as he moved toward her.

Cassie willingly did as she was asked, tossing the pins on her dressing table and smiling at her own eagerness.

Cameron caught his breath as the lustrous auburn

345

curls fell to her shoulders, cascading nearly to her waist. The dark, silky tresses against her white skin created a thrilling picture of loveliness. "Do you know how beautiful you are?"

Cassie smiled. "I know you think I am. That's enough."

The pulse in her throat began to throb and her eyes were alight with the passion he so easily aroused. Her hands reached out in welcome, but he only smiled and shook his head, refusing to move closer. "Do you want me?" he asked.

"Yes." She shivered slightly.

"Do you want me to touch you?"

"Yes." She shivered again.

"Where?"

She looked up, her eyes widening slightly with surprise.

He smiled again. "Show me. Show me where."

Cassie's cheeks darkened with his words. What did he want? He'd never asked her things like this before. Always, he had been the one in control. It was always he who taught and guided. Her confusion lasted only seconds. Then, she smiled, the boldness of her intended actions causing her cheeks to color even more. Somehow, she knew the game he wanted to play. Her hair swung free as she tossed it behind her shoulders. "Here," she sighed as she brazenly ran her fingers over her breasts, lifting them for his pleasure. "Touch me here."

"Lie on the bed, Cassie," he whispered, his voice thick as he fought to keep his hands at his side.

She was fully aware of the effect her nakedness was having on him. All she needed to do was lower her eyes to see the proof of it. "Bring me there," she challenged, her eyes daring him to contain his desire once he touched her.

"Not this time." His voice was provocatively deep and low, causing her to tremble with excitement. "Lie on the bed."

Cassie adjusted the pillows so she was half reclining. She smiled as she watched him discard his remaining clothing. Still, he remained standing at her side.

"Show me again. Show me where to touch you."

Cassie ignored his urgings and reached for him instead. Her tongue darted out in anticipation and licked at lips gone suddenly dry. Her eyes grew hungry at the sight of him. He was so beautiful, she couldn't resist the need to caress the hard muscles of his thighs.

Cameron stepped back, out of her reach. "Show me," he insisted.

A flicker of disappointment clouded her eyes, and she sighed as her gaze met his. He would have his way, she knew. Later, she said to herself. Later, she'd make him cry out for her touch. Her back arched, and again she caressed her own breasts. "It's better when you do it," she whispered weakly, and in truth it was. Except for now. Except when his eyes glowed with such delight, such hunger, such rapt attention. Except when her own touch suddenly brought about this devastatingly erotic sensation.

Cameron chuckled, his voice silky smooth. "Show me where else you want me to touch you."

Cassie groaned. "Cameron."

"Show me where else," he insisted.

His eyes were dissolving her will. She had heard tales of being under another's spell, but until this moment hadn't realized it was actually possible. She didn't want to do this. Never had she touched herself like this, as if she were making love to her own body. She wanted his touch, not her own. Still, she could not resist the magnetic power of his gaze. Her hands slid downward from her breasts, over her ribcage and the soft roundness of her belly, coming at last to rest on the sensitive flesh at the junction of her thighs. "Here," she choked. Her eyes widened as she felt a jolt of pure lust fill her being. Her hands became an extention of his body, his eyes. Her heart thundered in her chest. "Touch me here."

"Show me how."

She moaned, her eyes closing with need, helpless but to do as he asked.

"Show me," he said as he moved to the foot of the bed and knelt at her feet. His voice trembled as did his body. "Open your legs and show me."

Cassie's heart was pounding. She could barely hear his softly spoken words above the roar of blood in her ears. She couldn't think. She could only feel.

"Have you done this before?" he asked softly.

Cassie shook her head.

"When you do this again," he replied, all male arrogance, "you'll think of me."

His eyes glowed with pleasure, his heart filled with pride. How had it happened that this woman was his? What had he ever done to deserve such pleasure? She held back nothing. What more could he ask? Her inhibitions vanished as her need grew as powerful as his own. Cameron watched her face and his breath grew ragged as her hand began to move between her legs.

"Does this excite you?" Cassie asked. The harsh sound of his accelerated breathing filled the room and her own voice grew thick and husky in response.

Cameron could only groan.

Cassie's mouth curved in a tauntingly delicious smile. He knelt closer, enthralled as he watched her fondle herself. Only months ago, she would have cringed at the thought, yet now she felt not a flicker of shyness as she lifted her hips in an unconsciously blatant call.

"You like to watch me do this." It wasn't a question, but a statement of fact.

Cameron nodded. "You're so beautiful."

"Now, let me watch you."

"Cassie," he gasped, knowing their roles suddenly reversed as she drew him under her spell.

"Show me," she whispered, her voice breaking as the ache began to build.

Helpless but to obey, his fingers touched his own engorged flesh.

"Would you like me to touch you there?" she asked huskily.

"Jesus," he groaned as his hand began to move. His dark eyes became black as pitch and flames of excitement danced in their depth as she squirmed before him. And the more she moved, the more he found himself helpless but to watch, struggling to breathe.

He hadn't meant for it to go this far. At the beginning, he thought only to tease her, to watch her, to hear her beg for his touch. But she hadn't. Shy at first, she had slowly grown to enjoy these new sensations at her own hand. And the more pleasure she gained, the more delight he took.

Her breathing grew harsher, more labored and uneven as her fingers quickened their movements. She couldn't stop. The ache was growing into pain, a tightness that forced her eyes shut. A moan was torn from her throat. Her hips rose higher.

Cameron shuddered uncontrollably. He was going to die if he didn't take her now. She was driving him out of his mind. He hadn't touched her. Hadn't dared lest he lose all control. He hadn't even kissed her, yet he'd never known such mind shattering excitement.

Oblivious to the fever she had caused in him, Cassie strained, eagerly beckoning the coming delirium. Her excitement increased tenfold, knowing he watched every movement. She was moaning, her face contorted in almost painful pleasure. She trembled, feverishly out of control. She gasped. A guttural groan escaped her throat, and then, at last, a sharp, anguished cry as wave after wave of blinding ecstasy began to roll over her.

As Cameron watched her wild abandonment, madness overcame control. Unable to bear the agony of not touching her a moment longer, he surged into her moist heat.

"I love you," he nearly shouted as he took her desperately into his trembling arms. "I love you," he groaned as he thrust deeply within her softness, reveling in a joy he had never before experienced.

Cassie cried out at the sudden and unexpected dual climax. Lights flashed behind her eyes as pleasure built upon pleasure and her body surged to meet his almost savage thrusts.

"Oh God, Cassie. I love you," he choked as his body stiffened against her and his seed spilled forth. His mouth ravaged hers, taking all she could give, starved for her taste. His eyes squeezed shut against the blinding pleasure, and he trembled, knowing he'd lost his soul to this woman. For endless moments the aching pleasure convulsed his body until he was mindlessly lost in her scent, her feel, her love. He groaned as the aftershocks came to rock their bodies, unsure that he could bear still more pleasure. At last, he sighed and slumped heavily upon her. His face nuzzled into her soft, damp breast.

But it wasn't enough. He hadn't a chance to relax before the need hit him to take her again. Cassie's eyes widened with surprise as he began to move. Cameron smiled. "I waited too long. I need more." God help him, he always would.

Once she was able to think clearly again, Cassie smiled. Her fingers ran lightly over his shoulder, her lips tasted the moist skin of his forehead. "You know, you shouldn't have done that."

Cameron grinned as he slowly, and most reluctantly, lifted his mouth from her breast and forced his eyes to focus on her face. "Me?" he asked innocently. "All I did was ask you a few questions."

Cassie chuckled, her brows rising and lowering saucily. "No doubt to further your education."

Cameron moaned as he remembered her response. "You didn't have to answer them so thoroughly."

"Didn't I?" She grinned ever so wickedly. "Is this the same man who complains of my willful nature? Who constantly reminds me of a wife's role concerning obedience? Are you telling me I'm no longer expected to obey?"

Cameron chuckled. "Wretch. You picked a fine time

to obey me."

"And you, sir, picked a fine time to exhibit these wayward tendencies. We've a party to go to. No doubt Meghan and Diana are waiting downstairs right now."

Cameron shook his head. "I sent them on. We can join the festivities later. I have other things in mind for this afternoon."

Cassie smiled with pleasure as he ran his hand down her back to cup and squeeze her rounded bottom. She could feel him growing hard yet again, and she stirred provocatively against him. "Have you?" She closed her eyes, her voice low and sultry, her senses reveling in the feel of him. "What kind of things?"

"Well, for one, we're both going to use that bath."

"Mmm," Cassie murmured as she snuggled closer. "And then?"

Cameron pulled a comfortable, none too willing Cassie from the bed and guided her toward the tub. "And then, I'm going to show you more of my wayward tendencies."

"Have you more?" Cassie sighed as she sat in the cool water and watched her husband come to kneel between her legs.

"Much more." Cameron's hands slid over her raised knees, following the silken flesh down beneath the water, stopping only when his wandering fingers found their delightful objective.

Cassie sighed with pleasure, her head tilted against the rim of the tub. "One can only wonder at the depth of your knowledge."

Cameron chuckled. "I think it will take years to discover how deep my knowledge runs."

Cassie's fingers glided up his arms and shoulders,

352

then twined behind his neck, tugging ever so gently. Just before his eager mouth descended on hers, she said huskily, "We'd best get to it then, don't you think?"

Chapter Twenty-five

Cassie wiped at her damp forehead and cheeks before she tucked her handkerchief into her ruffled sleeve. Laughing at the children's antics, she called for them to toss the ball again. Accustomed to the more moderate English summers, she often found herself wilting beneath the harsh Maryland sun. Today, due to the stifling humidity, it had been worse than usual. She had been plagued with nausea from the moment she had ventured outside, and the odor that came from the other ladies—stale sweat overlaid with heavy perfume—only added to her discomfort. She wondered why it was commonly believed that a strong enough dose of perfume could take the place of simple soap and water. Finally despairing of finding a clean breath of air, she'd decided to join the children at their game of ball.

Cameron stood upon the veranda and watched his wife, marveling at how she seemed to fit into any situation. She was at home wherever she seemed to find herself—presiding at a formal dinner, or rolling on the floor with the babies; engaging the other ladies in conversation about art and music, or running through waist high meadows with Meghan at her heels.

It had taken some time, but he had finally managed to escape the cigar smoking men in the library. He smiled. Who in his right mind would closet themselves behind closed doors when a vision such as this awaited?

Cassie's cheeks pinkened and she smiled shyly at the smoldering look her husband sent across the huge expanse of lawn. She lifted her arm, about to return his wave, when one of the children, thinking she was awaiting his throw, fired the ball in her direction. She saw the ball an instant before it smacked against the side of her head. Her knees buckled and she crumpled to the ground. Sharp cries of alarm went up from the crowd as her worried husband hurried toward her.

The next thing she knew, she was lying on a bed in a large, airy room, a cool compress pressed to her brow. Her dress was opened, her stays loosened. Her husband was leaning over her, unconsciously muttering low curses while soft, feminine voices murmured in the background. Cassie moaned as he pressed the cloth harder upon the swelling.

Cameron almost jumped at the sound, realizing she had come around at last. His hands trembled, and he found himself dangerously close to disgracing himself with tears of relief. Gaining some control, he related his wife's wellbeing to the group of ladies who stood anxiously by. Once it was clear Cassie had regained consciousness, the room eventually emptied so that she might have some privacy in which to fully recover.

As soon as they were alone, Cameron scooped her

up to sit in his lap. "God in heaven, Cassie, don't ever do that to me again," he groaned as he pulled her tightly to him.

"I'll try not to." She smiled dreamily as she pressed her cheek against his chest, unware for the moment of her present position or the reason for it.

"Are you all right? Dizzy?"

"I'm fine. No, I'm not dizzy, except when you spin me around like that. What happened?"

"The ball caught you on the side of your head. Does it hurt?"

Cassie smiled, already feeling more like herself. "Just a bit tender," she said as she gingerly touched the injured spot.

"Why didn't you watch? What on earth could you have been thinking?"

Cassie chuckled. "To tell you the truth, there's this man I know. He was making eyes at me. I forgot where I was for a minute."

"Ah yes," Cameron said, laughing, "I remember thinking, could this be my brazen wife, blushing with maiden shyness at a simple look?" He examined the bruise again and replaced the cloth.

"Simple look indeed," Cassie responded as she smacked his chest. "I swear, sir, if one of the ladies hereabouts saw that sizzling look, they'd . . ."

"They'd what?" he grinned.

"In all likelihood, one of two things. They'd faint, or, they'd drag you off into the bushes and have their way with you."

Cameron laughed, his arms holding her securely on his lap. "Are you sure?"

Cassie smiled as she nodded. "Very sure."

"And yet, you did neither."

Cassie's eyes flashed with deviltry. "I, on the other hand, am quite used to your lechery and can take it or leave it."

"Can you?" He chuckled as he remembered their escapades earlier that day. "Who, then, was that in my bed this afternoon?"

"Oh that," she said with a dismissive shrug.

"Yes, that."

"Even I have occasional lapses."

"Do you think you're about to have another?" he asked as his hips moved suggestively beneath her, for it was rare indeed when such close contact with his wife did not instill a yearning he was hard put to control.

Cassie consulted the timepiece pinned to her bodice, then primly shook her head. "Sorry, my time for occasional lapses has passed for the day."

"Too bad," Cameron mused as he ran a finger over the soft mounds of flesh exposed by the loosened bodice.

"Why?" she grinned into his suddenly serious expression.

"I was thinking I'd like to take your clothes off and . . ."

"Don't say it!" Cassie snapped, her eyes looking wildly about, realizing for the first time they might not be alone. They were indeed alone at that moment, but who could say for how long? She sat up straighter and pushed herself into a more loosely held embrace. Her voice dropped warningly. "God help us. If someone overheard, I'd never be able to face them again."

Cameron laughed, and spoke directly into her ear. "The idea certainly perks you up, doesn't it?" He grinned at her scowl. "All I was going to say was, I'd like to take your clothes off and run my hands over your body until I feel you quiver and hear you cry out like you did today."

Cassie laughed. "Oh, is that all you were going to say?" She slumped against him. "You are a beast."

"Am I?" He pulled back to look into her laughing eyes, his expression magnificently innocent. "In that case, I suppose I should forgo the use of my hands, don't you think? A beast would more than likely use his mouth."

"If you don't stop this right now . . ."

"I can see the shape of your nipples through your dress. You want me to touch you, don't you?"

"Cameron, stop it!"

"What do you want me to do to them?"

"I'm going to kill you," she said so sweetly and with such a wide smile that Cameron burst out laughing.

"I think I'll lick them until they're hard and aching. Do they throb when I do that?"

"Good God!" Cassie groaned. "Cameron, someone might come in."

Slowly, he pulled the fabric of her dress down and smiled as a beautiful dark nipple was exposed to his view. "Lovely," he murmured as he began to suckle.

Cassie groaned again, feeling her stomach tighten as his mouth pulled at her breast. "Is the door . . . ?"

Cameron lifted his head and grinned. "I'd best see to it."

"Is she all right?" came a voice directly behind them.

"I'm fine, Mrs. Billings," Cassie responded as she quickly covered herself and tried to come to her feet.

Cameron groaned and Cassie giggled. He was in a

358

fix this time. His teasing had brought about an aching arousal. In truth, his words and touch had done much the same to her, but she, at least, showed no embarrassing outward signs. Cassie gave him an "I told you so look" as she heartlessly stood up and made to join her hostess.

Suddenly, his arm grasped her waist and held her securely before him. From over Cassie's head, he smiled and said. "A few more minutes, Mrs. Billings, and I'll give her into your care."

Mrs. Billings smiled with obvious relief. "Of course," she said, nodding. "You can't be too careful. She took a nasty blow." She left the room.

Cassie's shoulders were shaking with mirth as he turned her around to face him. She knew full well why he'd insisted on a few more minutes of his wife's time. And she could barely speak for laughing. "Are you satisfied?"

"Hardly," Cameron said in a tight voice. "It's going to take a minute before I'm presentable."

Cassie waited in silence, a smile lingering at her lips as she redid her laces and buttons. When she was finished, her eyes dropped to the area below his waist. "Shall I check and see if it's all better?" she asked consolingly, as if speaking to one of the babies about a minor injury.

Cameron grumbled. Watching his wife's fingers brush against her flesh as she closed her bodice had done little to ease his ache. "When you get even, you do so with relish. I've never known you to be so heartless."

"Me!" she cried merrily. "What did I do?"

"You don't need to do anything to make me want

you, but when you groan, I can't . . ." He looked heavenward for strength.

At her unfeeling giggle, he suddenly swatted her backside. "Get out of here while you can, woman." With a wicked leer and bubbling laughter, Cassie left him to gain some control.

Hours later Cassie stepped out onto the veranda, hoping the night air might clear her befuddled brain. She held on to the railing as the darkness spun around her. She shook her head, trying to clear away the fuzziness, but the motion only made her dizzier than ever. She shouldn't have taken that last glass of champagne. But the wine had been so deliciously cool, and, until the last glass, had produced no ill effects.

The hour was growing late, but those in attendance seemed in no hurry to leave. She wished Cameron would hurry back. Earlier, he had been called to town. It seemed there was a problem aboard one of his ships that needed his immediate attention. Cassie had wanted to go with him, but he had declined her offer. Promising his business would take him no more than an hour or so, he insisted she remain.

In his absence, Cassie had danced with every man there, but the excitement had gone from the evening with his departure. She sighed with weariness. If he didn't return soon, she would ask Mrs. Billings for the use of her carriage and driver and await him at home.

Suddenly, strong arms came from behind to circle her waist. Cassie sighed with delight. In her present condition, she never realized it wasn't her husband who held her. Michael Grant smiled as he felt the beauty in his arms lean so eagerly against his chest. The idea had at first seemed so bold. Now, he wondered why he hadn't suggested a breath of air earlier? He had wasted half the night dancing, when he could have been much more deliciously occupied.

"What took you so long?" she asked.

Michael's hand slid over her rounded belly and up to cup her soft breast. "You should have told me you were interested."

The whispered sound of his voice wasn't as deep as usual, but Cassie dismissed it as her imagination. It never occurred to her that any other man might be so insolent as to touch her, and when his hand closed over her breast, she covered it with her own. His hand felt strangely smooth, not callused and prickly with hair between each knuckle. Why was that? She looked down, but couldn't get her eyes to focus.

Cassie giggled. "I've drunk too much champagne. Your hand looks different."

"Close your eyes," came the voice behind her. "Don't worry what it looks like, just feel it."

Cassie sighed and leaned her head back into the curve of his shoulder.

In a blur, she could see him standing at her side. Cassie blinked with surprise. How could that be? He was standing behind her; his face was nuzzled into her neck. She could feel his warm breath on her skin. He couldn't be in two places at one time, could he?

Cassie smiled and reached out, only to have her hand grasped in a painful hold. "Cameron," her voice came slurred, "what . . . ?"

She never finished her question as he snatched her away from the other's embrace. She stumbled with the

361

sudden movement, and grabbed at the railing to keep from falling. Almost in slow motion, she turned her head and watched with no little amazement. The whole world seemed to be spinning by. She couldn't understand why Cameron would be hitting a strange man. But he wasn't strange, was he? Hadn't she danced with him earlier? Suddenly, the man took a mighty fist to his jaw that lifted him off his feet and sent him flying over the railing.

Cassie blinked again. Cameron and she were alone. Could she have imagined the whole thing? Had he really knocked someone over the railing? But why?

Cameron was barely out of breath as he turned to his wife. Murder flashed in his eyes and a hateful sneer twisted his mouth. "Whore!" he growled, shaking with the fury that possessed him.

Cassie stared at him, unable to comprehend his accusation. Although not able to understand his words, his attitude was clear enough. And she was suddenly sure that were it not for the effects of the champagne, she would have been furious. "What . . . ?"

Wordlessly, Cameron took her hand and dragged her around the mansion toward their waiting buggy. He picked her up and threw her into the seat. Cassie groaned as she felt the sudden impact.

Cameron couldn't remember a time in his life when he'd been so close to losing control. He knew if he touched her now, he'd never stop. Not, that is, until she was dead at his hands. How had she taken him in? Wasn't he wise, even yet, to the ways of women? How could he have believed her to be different? Jesus, she had stood right in front of him and brazenly allowed that man to paw her. And then, without a shred of shame or guilt, she had smiled and beckoned him closer. God almighty, even Sarah had more class than to expect him to join her and her lover. His mouth twisted with disgust. She had actually seemed surprised that he should have taken exception to her offer. Would he never learn? He had sworn he'd never let down his guard. But he had. He had let himself be duped, taken in by outward appearances, ignoring what he knew to be true of all women. His stomach knotted in pain. Good God, was he destined to live out his life in this continual anguish?

Cassie's mind was slowly shaking off the excess alcohol. She knew he was angry, but she didn't know why. All she had done was allow her husband a few liberties, the same liberties he had taken on numerous other occasions. What in the world was the matter with him?

"Cameron," she started, only to be instantly interrupted.

"Shut up, you lying bitch. Don't say a word. If you do, I swear I'll kill you."

Cassie's mind might have still been somewhat fogged by alcohol, but she recognized now that this was no ordinary rage that gripped Cameron. Her eyes widened with fright. His features might have been cut from stone. Not a trace of gentleness did she find in his face. Wisely, she chose to take his warning to heart. Whatever the problem was, she'd have to wait until her senses completely cleared and he grew calm before they could talk.

Cameron almost threw her to the ground once the buggy stopped before their home. And when she stumbled and fell, he only yanked her to her feet and dragged her inside.

Cameron stared straight ahead. His voice was low with pain, but Cassie didn't recognize it as such. She heard only contempt and fury. "Get out of my sight."

For a moment, she thought to give him an argument, to clear the air between them, but when she saw the way he looked at her, she shivered with dread. The man was surely as close to insane as it was possible to get. Pure hatred glowed in his eyes. And Cassie knew she'd take her life in her hands if she dared to disobey him now.

Dawn was breaking before Cameron staggered into their room. Even from the bed, she could smell the brandy. For a long moment he simply looked at her. Silently, he walked toward the bed, tearing off his clothes until he stood naked before her. "Take it off." He motioned with his head toward her nightdress.

"Cameron, I think we should talk," Cassie said as she sat up. She had lain awake for hours trying to piece together the jumbled events of the evening. Then, when everything suddenly became clear to her, she had gasped in shame.

"Do you?" he smiled without a trace of humor. "Well, I have other things in mind, Mrs. Chandler. I think we've talked too goddamned much as it is."

"Can't you let me explain?"

"Why? So you can lie some more?"

"When have I lied?" she demanded righteously.

Cameron chuckled mirthlessly and shot her a knowing look.

"I've explained about that," she said earnestly. "You understood once I told you my reasons."

"Oh, and I also understand your reasons for what happened last night. And since I was rude enough to interrupt your little tete-a-tete, I thought I'd make up for it now. You don't mind, do you, if I take his place?"

"Cameron, you don't understand."

"Don't I?" He laughed again. "You've forgotten, I think. I've had more than enough experience with women to know they're all the same. Whores, one and all. And you, my sweet little wife, are no different."

He was kneeling on the bed now. "Are you going to take that damned thing off, or shall I?"

There was no way that Cassie was simply going to lie there and allow him to abuse her. She didn't care that her actions might cause her greater harm. He had closed his heart to her words and he wouldn't be all that gentle in any case.

Before giving herself any time to reconsider, she rolled out from under him and was lunging for the door. Even in his drunken condition, Cameron was faster than she would have supposed. Still, he only managed to grasp the back of her gown as she sped out of the room. Cassie heard it tear, but fear drove her on. She had to get away from him, and right now she didn't care if the whole world saw her naked back.

Cameron, too, was totally heedless of his undressed state, ignoring the shrieks of startled servants as he followed her down the stairs.

She would have made it, she reasoned moments later, if only the stupid front door hadn't still been locked. She would have been gone before he had a chance to catch up.

365

Cassie was fumbling with the lock when his arms reached out for her and she was hauled, kicking and punching, up the stairs. But it was like hitting a mountain. Nothing she did mattered. Cameron's mouth was grim, his eyes hard and unfeeling as he climbed the stairs. A moment later, she was flung to the bed.

Cassie lay there for a long moment, trying to catch her breath.

"You enjoyed Grant's touch enough," he finally said, smiling bitterly. "You could always fake some enthusiasm, you know."

"I thought he was you, you beast!" She punched the bed, wishing it was his head.

"I should beat you for that," he spat from between clenched teeth. "Especially when you lie so convincingly."

"It's true. I drank too much. I was standing outside trying to clear my head. He came up behind me. I never saw his face."

"And you simply fell into his arms. How romantic."

"I told you, I thought he was you."

"Shut up! I don't want to hear any more lies."

Again, they stared at each other, each waiting for the other to make the first move.

Cameron forced aside the loving ache that filled him when he looked at her. Her hair framed her face in wild disarray, her breasts rose and fell provocatively with each rapid breath—and his gaze could just make out the hint of shadow between her legs. Sternly, he reminded himself that this woman, no matter how lovely, deserved no gentleness. She deserved abuse at least as harsh as she had given. After a long moment, he shrugged. "Just because I've found you out . . ."

"Found me out, bullshit!" She rolled to her feet and stood angrily before him. She'd taken enough of his false accusations. If he meant to beat her, to rape her, so be it. She wasn't going to go down without a fight. "There's nothing I can do or say that would change your bloody mind, is there? You either trust me or you don't. And you don't," she accused.

Cassie took a long, calming breath before she went on, "Don't confuse me with your first wife, Cameron. You know in your heart what I am, no matter what you think you saw."

Pain twisted his guts and he had to force his hands to his sides lest he smash her lying face. He had to hand it to her, though. She was good at this. She actually wanted him to discount what he'd seen with his own eyes and believe her instead. Amazing! What power did she think she possessed?

And this act of bravery. He honestly didn't know what to make of it. Sarah had at first acted sweetly innocent. She had let him believe he had no call to act the jealous brute. Later, she had shrugged away his accusations, not bothering to worry what he believed. He shook his head. It didn't matter. After all was said and done, she was still a whore, and Cassie, no matter what her attitude, was one as well.

"You're quite right. There is nothing you can say to make me disbelieve my own eyes. I don't trust you." With that, he grabbed his pants, shirt, and boots and walked out the door.

Chapter Twenty-six

Diana laughed with pure joy as she raised her arms high over her head and spun around her bedroom. At last! Damn, it felt like she had waited forever, but the love birds had finally given up that nauseous cooing. To put it more bluntly, they were barely speaking, and when they did, it resembled something closer to snarls.

This definitely called for a celebration. Adam would be up soon with her bath water. Maybe today she'd give him a little treat. If she was fair—and Diana giggled, she wasn't—she'd say the boy deserved that, and more, for his conscientious efforts.

Vaguely, she wondered if he'd chosen to share his newfound knowledge with his friend, Janey. The girl's eyes certainly shone when she spotted the boy. Diana chuckled. And never a thank you for his clever teacher. That was gratitude for you. Idly, she wondered if Janey wouldn't like to join them someday. Perhaps, she shrugged, but that would have to wait until she became mistress here.

A knock sounded at her door, and Diana, in the midst of brushing her long hair into shimmering waves of ebony, called out, "Enter."

She smiled at his reflection in the mirror as he hauled two heavy buckets into the room. His eyes were lowered to the carpet in submissive obedience. Diana liked them best this way. It didn't matter what they wanted, after all. It only mattered that she was satisfied.

Just the sight of his bulging arm muscles was enough to set Diana's heart aflutter. Damn, if he wasn't just about the most beautiful black she had ever seen, and when he grew to full manhood—not that his manhood wasn't full grown, she chuckled—he'd be something else indeed.

Diana walked to the door, closed it, and sat upon the bed as Adam filled the tub. She opened her robe as she waited for him to finish the chore.

Adam groaned at the sound of her husky voice, knowing what was in store. "Come here, Adam. I've a present for you." Diana leaned back on her elbows and spread her knees. Her robe hung open from her pale shoulders, and she glanced appreciatively down at her smooth, naked flesh. "I'm going to show you something Janey is going to love."

Adam wanted to cry. It wasn't that he didn't enjoy this, for there wasn't a sixteen-year-old boy alive who wouldn't love the things she made him do. It was the fear of getting caught. Mr. Chandler would be furious.

Adam wasn't stupid. He knew the people living here were treated fairly. Most, like his own family, were freed only months after they were bought. He was doing some bad things, and Mr. Chandler would probably throw him and his family out if anyone ever told. He wanted to run, to be free of her, but what choice did he have? He couldn't tell. He didn't dare. Not after what he'd already done.

Adam turned to face her at last. His reluctance instantly disappeared as his huge brown eyes took in her position. A charge of lust shot through him. He couldn't help it. He'd do anything she said.

"Do you want to leave, Adam?" Diana smiled knowingly. "Is that why you took so long?"

"No, ma'am."

"Come over here, then. It's time I showed you something new."

Diana prolonged it as long as she dared. First, she told him what he was going to do. Then she painstakingly showed him where his tongue would go. After that, all she had to do was lie back and watch his eyes move over her. She knew he didn't want to do this, but, like most men, he was helpless once a woman's legs were opened to him.

She shivered as his tongue lapped at her, bringing her climax ever nearer. He was a fast learner, careful to pay attention to her every wish. "Play with my nipples, Adam," she instructed and groaned with delight as he did so.

Diana opened her eyes. She liked to watch his black hands on her skin. She liked to feel his touch. She liked everything they did together.

Her stomach was tight, so tight. Damn, she was going to come already. It was too soon. She didn't want it to be over so fast.

Diana cried out as the waves of pleasure came.

As it turned out, her timing was disastrous. If he had not had to search for that paper, he would have passed her door sooner. If she had locked her door when she closed it, it would not have opened under his hand. If she hadn't come so fast, if she had covered her mouth when the final pleasure came, he might not have heard her cry and thought that someone was in pain.

Cameron's mouth twisted with disgust as Diana called out, "Enough, Adam. That was good, but enough."

The boy was kneeling between her spread legs, apparently not at all ill at ease. Even at first glance, it was obvious this was not the first time they had been together. Jesus, if it had been Meghan who opened this door . . . He left the thought unfinished, unwilling to imagine the questions an eight-year-old might ask.

Cameron silently closed the door. In truth, he was not concerned about interrupting the whore's pleasure. What he wouldn't do was embarrass the boy in front of her. And he knew Adam and his family well enough to know his unexpected presence would do just that.

Cameron remembered himself as a boy and smiled, for he had been constantly hard with need. Even when he didn't want to be. Thank God for the Widow Thornton. At least she had banked some of his fires and saved him many an embarrassing moment. But even he, who would have jumped anything willing, was discreet enough to take his pleasures away from home. No, he was sure it wasn't the boy at fault here, for he'd have to be a saint to refuse what was so clearly offered. That she dared to offer it in his house, made him almost crazed with rage.

Cameron walked into his room and slammed the door behind him. He hadn't slept here since the night of the party, but his clothes remained. Idly, he thought about moving them and then rejected the idea. The closets and drawers in the room Cassie once used were too small. If the truth were known, the bed itself was too small. He sighed with disgust. It was she who should move her things. He should have suggested it before. Vaguely, he wondered why he didn't do so right now.

Cassie's head shot up from her needlepoint. Her lips thinned with annoyance. Lately, she was only happy when he was gone from the house. She couldn't take much more of his alternating rage and icy cold moods. But she'd be damned if he was going to cow her. "What's the matter now?"

"Where the hell is that paper I left on the hall table?"

"I put it on your desk."

"I looked on my desk. It's not there."

Cassie grumbled. "If you took care of your things, you wouldn't lose them."

"Don't speak to me like I'm one of the children."

"Then don't act like one of them."

Cassie sighed as she came to her feet. This was getting them nowhere. Since the night of the party, a kind word hadn't passed between them. And Cassie didn't have a clue as to how to set things right. All she knew was she couldn't take the strain much longer.

Silently, she led him back downstairs to his library. She went directly to his desk, and, to his amazement, picked up the paper he'd been searching for from the top of the clutter.

Just as she was about to leave, he caught her wrist in his hand. Startled blue eyes looked inquisitively up to black. She swallowed before she spoke. "Do you want something else?"

Cameron almost groaned at the innocently asked question. For an instant, desire so strong as to rock his senses flared to life in his eyes. Did he want something else? He almost laughed aloud. He wished to God he didn't, but he couldn't look at her without wanting her. No matter what she had done, he wanted her. And the knowledge made him furious. He was out of his mind. That was it. She had driven him crazy and he only just now realized it. Pain replaced the need that had shone so clearly, until he gathered enough strength to subdue even that emotion. His gaze grew flat and cold.

It was time, he thought, to slake his desires with someone else. Many men took mistresses. The idea was not repellent. He needed a woman, and no matter how much his wife aroused him, he wouldn't touch her—not after what he'd seen, not ever again.

"No," he snapped abruptly as he flung her wrist away, with icy contempt. "There's nothing more I want."

Although Cameron's tone was grave, he had to suppress a smile as he looked at the embarrassed, frightened boy who stood before him. "There's no use denying it, Adam. I heard Miss Diana groaning. I thought she might be sick. Without thinking, I opened the door. You know what I found."

Adam closed his eyes, capable only of muttering, "Oh God, oh God."

"What do you think I should do about this?"

Again, "Oh God, oh God."

"Perhaps I should tell your mother."

The "Oh Gods" grew in intensity.

Cameron almost laughed aloud. He could just imagine Annie's fury if she found out. She would surely take a stick to the boy. "I understand the temptation, Adam, but if you were living at another plantation, the owner would have had you killed for touching a white woman. Do you know that? Do you know the law?"

"Oh God, oh God."

"If you don't mind, would you save your prayers for bedtime, or church?"

"What?"

"I said, 'Do you know what you've done?' "

"I'm sorry, sir."

"Sorry you've done it, or sorry you got caught?"

"Both," Adam answered honestly. "I couldn't tell. I couldn't. Not after the first time."

Cameron commiserated with the boy's plight. Of course, he couldn't tell. The bitch had probably threatened him if he did. "If you knew it was wrong, why did you do it?"

"I . . . I couldn't stop. I didn't know at first."

Cameron's eyes widened with disbelief.

"I didn't, I swear. She made me help her in the bath. She showed me things."

"I'll bet she did," Cameron muttered in disgust. "You won't be bringing water to her room again, Adam."

"Yes, sir, but suppose . . ." A flicker of fear clouded the boy's eyes.

"I'll make sure of it."

Adam nodded.

"You can go back to your chores now. We won't speak of this again."

Adam continued to nod as he backed all the way out of the room.

Cameron had a time controlling his laughter. God, he wished he and Cassie were speaking. He was dying to tell someone about this interview.

Diana straightened the already perfect folds in her dress and gave a final pat to her exquisite hairdo. Her heart was pounding with excitement. This was it. This was what she'd been waiting for since she first came.

Her hands shook as she knocked and opened the library door. "You sent for me, Cameron?"

"An hour and a half ago," he muttered with barely veiled contempt as he consulted his timepiece.

"I'm afraid you caught me in my bath." She only wished he had. She giggled and smiled suggestively.

Cameron had had enough of her blatantly seductive ways. She was lucky he was a civilized man, for she deserved worse than what she was going to get. He'd never been one to mince words and he wasn't about to start with this one. He almost snarled as he unleashed the full force of his rancor. "You will be gone from my house upon the morrow, Diana. I only hope to God I never see your face again."

"What?" She blinked as if she couldn't fathom his meaning. This wasn't what he was supposed to say. "What?" She asked once again.

"I think you can hear well enough. Shall I repeat it?"

"Why? Jesus Christ! Why?"

"Without going into details, let's just say I know what's been going on upstairs. Shall we leave it at that?"

"No, damn it. Let's hear it all. I want to know what you're accusing me of."

"I know about you and the boy, Diana."

He couldn't! Oh God no, he couldn't. The boy wouldn't have told and she certainly hadn't. How? How the hell had he found out? Diana groaned. "He . . . he . . ."

"No, he didn't tell me."

"He forced me. I had no choice."

"You lying little bitch! Did you think I'd believe that?"

"It's true. He raped me."

"The boy pleasured you. It was only you who gained satisfaction. Isn't that right?"

"No! That's a lie. It was him. I was afraid to tell. Afraid of what you would do to him. I know you want me. I wouldn't do anything do jeopardize our relationship. I was waiting for you to finish with her."

"What!? What the hell are you talking about? What relationship?"

"I know." Diana waved his amazement aside with fluttering fingers. "You don't have to pretend any more."

"Jesus! How the hell did you ever come to think that? What have I ever done to make you think I wanted you?"

"I could tell by the way you looked at me. You were nice."

"Nice!" He couldn't stop his burst of laughter, so ludicrous was her supposition. "I was nice? And from that, you assumed I wanted you? Are you out of your mind? Or do you sleep with everyone who is nice to you?"

Diana shrugged. "I'm a woman of the world. I knew you wouldn't be satisfied for long with Miss Goody . . ."

"Shut up! You haven't the right to utter her name, never mind make fun of her morals."

"You don't love her. You don't even talk to her."

Cameron breathed a long sigh. "Get out of my house, Diana. You have until morning. You may take all the things you bought, but get out."

"Cameron, I could make you happy," she pleaded. His look of disgust was clear. "I doubt it."

"Give me a chance. I promise . . ."

There were loud sounds in the hall. Someone was moving something.

Cameron shook his head, his scorn oddly mixed with pity.

Diana's shock at being found out turned rapidly to rage as she read this new emotion. How dare he pity her! How dare he lead her on all this time? An idea dawned. Suddenly, she knew why he didn't want her. She had to be right. He preferred boys to women. His rage over the minor incident in the barn was ample proof. If she needed more, there was his anger over Adam. Of course. That was it!

Her smile was sly as she looked at him. "I think I know the problem here. You don't like women much, do you?"

The sounds outside the door were growing louder. Someone grunted. Something banged into the wall.

"Meaning?"

"Meaning, I thought it was me, but it was the boys all along."

Cameron roared at the absurdity of her suggestion.

"Does your ego not permit the thought that I find you not in the least desirable?"

"I've never had a real man refuse me before," she remarked snidely.

"It's obvious to me you've never had a real man, period."

The sounds were just outside the door now.

"Oh!" Diana muttered. Her eyes narrowed with hate and Cameron felt a shiver of foreboding run up his spine. She was going to hit back in some terrible way, but he didn't know how.

Suddenly, her hand reached for the bodice of her dress. She tore at the pink material until she was naked, clear to her waist. Meanwhile, her other hand grabbed at the pins in her hair, scattering them upon the floor as she flung her long hair into wild disarray. But for the lack of bruises, she looked the very picture of a lady who had been unexpectedly assaulted. She turned then, laughing evilly at his astonished expression. Her eyes glittered with triumph as she opened the door.

"Please, no more," she cried, her face crumpling before his startled gaze, her eyes suddenly filled with tears.

And Cameron could only give a helpless groan as Cassie, eyes wide with shock, took in the whole scene.

Chapter Twenty-seven

Cassie stood silently outside the library door, her gaze following the sobbing Diana as she raced up the stairs. Once she was out of sight, Cassie turned to meet her husband's suddenly tortured gaze.

Nonsensically, Cameron felt himself marveling at how gracefully her head moved upon her slender neck.

For a long moment, neither spoke — Cassie because of her surprise, Cameron because there wasn't a damn thing he could say to make her understand.

Suddenly, Cassie remembered the poor man who labored beneath the weight of the heavy filing cabinet. Without a word to her husband, she directed Stevens through the doorway.

Cameron cursed as he recalled asking one of his men to deliver it to his home. Why had it come today of all days? He grimaced with self-disgust. Damn, but life was just full of little twists and turns, wasn't it?

He wanted to laugh; he wished to hell he could. Had it not been so tragic, the situation was really marvelously funny. The woman he hated most of all had just ruined what little chance he and Cassie might have had. And here he stood, like some imbecile, without a word of excuse, watching condemnation turn to pain in his wife's eyes.

Why didn't she rant at him? Why didn't she say something?

But she did say something, after Stevens had positioned the cabinet near his desk. Turning to follow the butler out of the room, her parting words to Cameron shriveled his soul. "Sorry to interrupt."

Cameron had nursed a bottle of brandy most of the afternoon. He was well into his second bottle by the time night had fallen. It hadn't helped. He couldn't seem to get drunk enough to erase the look in her eyes. And God, most of all, he wanted the oblivion that drink would bring. He didn't want to think. He didn't want to remember.

He sat before the cold hearth, a helpless captive as pictures of her flashed through his mind. Cassie, her hair blowing free as she rode her horse. Cassie, glistening wet as she walked unashamedly naked from the river. Cassie, hiding her smile at something Meghan said lest the girl feel she was being made fun of. Cassie, spinning circles with one of the babies held high above her head, laughing at the tiny squeals of joy. Cassie, leaning over him, her gown falling open, her hair a glorious mass of clean, sweet curls brushing his face. Cassie, smiling wickedly, her dark blue eyes growing darker still as she hatched some plan to avenge one of his teasing remarks. Cassie, her soft, full lips parting as she awaited the touch of his mouth. Her low cries, her wild abandonment.

Cameron threw the empty glass into the cold, blackened hearth and came shakily to his feet. Holding his head as if in pain, he willed the pictures away. What was she, to haunt his thoughts? Only a woman, after all. And like any other, easy to replace.

"Liar," came a voice from a dark, tortured recess of his mind. Cameron laughed bitterly at the folly of his denial. Jesus, it never stopped, did it? He had barely known a minute's peace since the train wreck in England. When was it going to stop? "When?" he asked aloud.

The house had been quiet for hours. But the quiet felt ominous tonight. It wasn't just quiet. It was as silent. A shiver of fear ran through him. It was silent as it had been before Cassie had come.

He couldn't go through the loneliness again. Not after having known her. It didn't matter what she was. He simply couldn't bear it if she left.

"Enough!" he said. He couldn't take it anymore. He was going to clear the air between them. He was going to tell her exactly what had happened. And if at first she didn't believe him, well, he would simply make sure she did.

He fairly ran up the steps to their room. Without hesitation, he opened the door and stepped inside. His eyes blinked with surprise. She wasn't asleep. She was sitting in a chair, her gaze drawn to the door. Was she waiting? Did she know he would come?

Suddenly, Cameron felt unreasonable anger. Did she think him so under her spell that he would come and beg for forgiveness? Forgiveness for something he had never done? Something he had never thought to do?

Cameron leaned against the door. He wasn't drunk, but he was damn close. Still, it didn't matter the amount of alcohol he'd consumed. He'd never beg. Never!

The harsh words tumbled from his mouth and, upon hearing them, he found himself no less astonished than she. "Your lying friend is leaving in the morning. If you want to join her, I won't keep you here."

Cassie felt her heart sink. She hadn't expected him to come on his knees begging forgiveness. That wasn't Cameron. But neither had she expected this cold, indifferent arrogance. Where had the man she had grown to love so desperately gone?

Cassie looked up. For the longest moment they simply stared at each other with undeniably hungry eyes. Finally, Cassie realized what she was seeing and almost laughed with glee. His words might be harsh, even cruel, but his eyes gave him away. His eyes were so tender, so wistful, and, for an unguarded moment, so filled with pain and love, she felt tears mist her eyes. That the man loved her could not be denied. Suddenly she knew his actions to be a facade.

"Did you hear what I said?" he demanded.

Cassie rose from her chair and moved toward him. He had come this far. No matter how much he might want to, he'd come no further. "Do you want me to go?" she asked quietly.

His words belied the look in his eyes. "I told you, you could." *It will just about kill me, if you do,* he finished silently as every fiber of his being cried out for her to stay.

"Do you?" She was close now. She could smell the brandy on him. She almost smiled. So it had taken drink to bring him here. Cassie gave a mental shrug. It didn't matter. What mattered was that he had come. Her fingers reached out and touched his cheek.

He didn't answer. He swallowed twice, but no words seemed able to pass the lump in his throat.

"Tell me you want me to go. I'll do as you say," she whispered, her mouth so close he could feel her breath against his jaw.

"I can't," he choked. "Jesus, I can't." He gave an agonized groan as his arms came around her and his lips covered her mouth.

The passion between them flared instantly to life, the force of it so powerful that it rocked him back and he staggered, for a moment, against the door. From somewhere in a mind dazed with desire, came a thought. It wasn't possible to want like this, to need like this, to love like this. But it had happened. Once before, he had thought himself under her spell, but the magic had been as nothing compared to this moment. He felt lost, drowning in helpless need.

His tongue ravaged her mouth, taking her essence deep into his being. She tasted warm, she tasted sweet. And best of all, she tasted of Cassie.

His mouth tore itself free and he gasped for breath, moaning with pleasure as her scent filled his lungs. His heartbeat hammered in his ears as he watched her passion-softened mouth pout with its sudden loss. "More," she whispered, her eyes half closed, her arms around his neck as her body, achingly soft and warm, pressed him harder against the door.

383

Cameron groaned. He didn't know where to kiss her first, touch her first. He wanted all of her and he wanted it all at one time.

He had no will but to take her. He had no life without her in his arms. Had he tried, he couldn't have counted the times they had come together, yet somehow it always felt as if it were for the first time. The taste of her mouth again brought him a shock of pleasure. The roughness of her tongue against his was a thrill anew. His hands moved desperately over her curves. Had she always felt this soft, this lush? Again, came the need of discovery. He knew she should have felt familiar, but it wasn't so.

He tried to slip her gown from her shoulders, but the lack of space between their bodies kept it from falling to the floor. Neither thought of taking only half a step away from each other, which would have made it possible. If the truth be known, neither thought at all, so desperate was their need, so fevered were their senses.

Cassie's nails scratched at his chest as she fought a battle against the buttons of his shirt. Frustrated, she finally gave up and pulled his shirt free of his pants. Her soft moan of pleasure as she ran her hands over his bare chest was music to his ears. She was robbing him of what little sanity he had left. He felt aflame. Hot and thick, his desire pulsed until he thought he'd explode. He had to have her. He had to have her now!

Sweeping her up in his arms, he carried her to the bed. Instantly, unable to be gone for as long as it took to undress, he fell upon her. His only concession to her need was to tear his own clothes open.

Cassie, too hungry for his touch, cared not that he

came to her fully dressed. She needed this proof of his love and it no longer mattered how it was given.

She cried out as he took her then, wanting to scream with the pleasure that filled her body and mind. For an instant, sanity returned. He stopped. His breathing was shallow and rapid. He stared at the woman beneath him. "Did I hurt . . . ?"

"Oh God, no. Oh please, no. Cameron," she groaned, and her words became broken and disjointed, mixed with sighs, overlaid with gasps, interrupted by kisses as he plunged deeper and deeper into a sweetness that could only compare to heaven.

It wasn't until the aftershocks had finally dwindled down to delicious contentment that Cameron realized Cassie was making odd sounds. It took him a long moment to understand that the sounds were not his own strangled cries. He looked into eyes shimmering with tears. Instantly, he pulled back. "You're crying!" he gasped, suddenly horrified. He'd never seen her cry before and the pain that filled his being was not to be borne. He cursed. "I did hurt you! Why didn't you say something?" He'd been so damn wild for her, he hadn't realized she probably hadn't been ready. How the hell could he have lost all control?

Cassie wiped the tears away and laughed. "You didn't hurt me, numbskull. And I wasn't crying. I never cry. I'm happy, that's all."

Cameron rolled to his side. Their bodies still joined, he cradled her in his arms and gave her a quizzical look. "You give a pretty good imitation of crying. As a matter of fact, I've never seen anyone do it quite so well." He looked at her long and hard. "And what's this numbskull business?"

"Slipped out, sorry." She giggled. "I guess I picked it up from Meghan."

"Well," he sighed, "I suppose it's better than some of the things you call me."

Cassie laughed and scratched at her chest. She looked down at her body and chuckled. "Look, I'm wearing buttons of my own."

Cameron smiled, his gaze following her fingers. During their lovemaking, neither had noticed that his shirt had slid between their bodies. The buttons of his shirt had left their mark upon her naked flesh.

"Too bad they aren't real. I'd like to open you up and get inside." His arms closed possessively around her.

"Oh?" She laughed softly. "I think there are much nicer ways of doing that."

"Doing what?"

"Getting inside."

Cameron laughed. "Are you implying naughty things?"

"Me?" Cassie pushed him to his back and straddled his waist. She gave him her most sophisticated look, "Darling, I never imply." Suddenly, she ruined the whole effect with a giggle. "If I'm interested in naughty things, I just do them."

"Do you?" He grinned. "You'll have to go a long way before you convince me of it."

"Oh?" Her eyes widened as she accepted his dare. "I have every intention of convincing you, you know."

"And just how do you plan to go about it?"

For a moment she looked a bit confused and Cameron had to fight back the urge to laugh. "Well, we could always try . . . No, no, that wouldn't work." Her lips twitched as she shot him a sly look.

"What wouldn't work?" he asked, his interest definitely piqued.

"Nothing," she sighed.

"Don't give me that innocent look. What wouldn't work?"

Cassie laughed aloud. "Nothing. Really."

"Cassie," he warned.

Her shoulders were shaking with mirth. "I didn't think of anything yet. I only said that to make you crazy."

Cameron groaned. "You didn't have to go far. I'm already halfway there."

Cassie looked down at him, her index finger tapping at her lip, something she always did when she was thinking. Her eyes narrowed as she studied his form. "I do believe that you're probably the sexiest man I know."

Cameron frowned. "And where the hell did you pick up that word? One can only hope not also from Meghan."

"Sexiest?" Cassie grinned. "I don't know, must have heard it someplace."

"And what do you mean probably?"

She shrugged and gave an elaborate sigh. "Well, I can't be absolutely sure, since I've never had another positioned thusly."

"Take my word for it," he answered, all male arrogance. "You won't find one better."

"Won't, or can't?" Cassie teased.

"Neither."

Cassie let that go. Apparently, he didn't see any great humor in this particular form of teasing. Instead, she asked, "Would you do me a favor?"

"What?"

"Remember that day when you made me touch myself?"

Cameron closed his eyes at the exquisite memory and nodded. "You drove me crazy."

"I want to do that to you. Do you mind?"

He smiled. "I don't think that's too much to ask."

"But you can't touch me in return."

"Cassie, I don't think . . ."

"Until I tell you. Is it a deal?"

"A deal," he whispered as her lips hovered over his mouth. Then, he prayed those wouldn't be the last sane words he'd ever speak. They very nearly were.

Cassie was lying upon his totally relaxed body. Actually, he couldn't imagine himself more relaxed were he dead. Her elbow was propped upon his chest, supporting her head. She was looking, not at his face, but into his hair in which she idly traced patterns.

"Did you do it because you were trying to get even for what you thought I had done?"

God, what kind of a woman was this? He had not asked for forgiveness. From all appearances, she had not expected him to. And yet, she forgave. It didn't matter that she was wrong in her assumptions. Still, she forgave. Did she love him that much? Cameron couldn't fathom it. Surely he had not given her cause. He had not always treated her as she deserved. Suddenly, he felt in awe of the strength of character she possessed. "I did not touch her," he said at last.

Cassie looked down into his eyes for a long moment. And then, she simply nodded.

"Do you believe me?" he asked, his astonishment clear in his voice.

Cassie gave him a soft smile. "I do."

"Do you trust me that much? To disbelieve your own eyes?"

Cassie laughed as she pinched a hair from his chest. "I'm not sure I trust you at all."

"Ow!" Cameron rubbed his injury. "Unless you want me to return the favor, I'd advise you to stop that."

Cassie giggled. "I have no hair on my chest."

Cameron chuckled. "Ah, but you do."

"Where?" She leaned back, supported by her arms and surveyed her smooth chest and swaying breasts.

"Right here." Cameron caught her left breast and held it up for inspection. "You have one hair, right here."

"Yuck! Pull it out. That's disgusting."

"No." He grinned as he turned over and held her beneath him. "I like to swirl it against my tongue."

Cassie grinned. "You really are odd at times."

"Perhaps." He shrugged. "But you are more so."

"How?"

"How?" he repeated. "How can you believe what your eyes tell you is false?"

"You said you didn't touch her. Everything is not always as it appears."

Cameron closed his eyes. He knew she wasn't only speaking of this afternoon, but of a night some two weeks past. "Tell me what happened."

Cassie sighed, a bit unwilling to bring the subject up again, not at all sure the telling would matter in the end. "After you left, I dance with just about everyone there. It was hot. I was drinking champagne. Never having sampled the wine before, except for a sip at our wedding, I didn't realize its potency." She shrugged. "I just seemed to grow happier and happier. Finally, I guess, I had one glass too many and was probably quite drunk, although I didn't know it at the time.

"Anyway, I walked out to the veranda for a breath of air and to clear my head. But the more I shook it, the cloudier everything got. I was dizzy and had to hold on to the railing or fall.

"Suddenly, you were there, whispering something in the moonlight. At least I thought it was you. I leaned back and let you—" she shook her head— "him hold me. Suddenly, you weren't behind me anymore, but standing at my side. I couldn't figure it out.

"Needless to say, I won't be sampling any more champagne."

Cameron laughed. He knew she spoke the truth. Why hadn't he simply looked in her eyes before? The woman couldn't lie worth a damn. He had realized that once before, but had forgotten the fact in his jealous rage. He could see it all now. He could remember her look of confusion. A look he had not before allowed himself to notice. "Not without me, you won't."

Cameron's tongue came to trace her lips. "Wait." She pushed at his shoulders. "It's my turn to listen."

Cameron rolled over on his back. "You're not going to believe this one." He sighed, half afraid of the truth in his words, for as far as he could tell, she had never suspected Diana's true nature. He told her everything, starting as far back as when they were aboard ship. What he had heard and therefore seen upon opening Diana's bedroom door. His interview with Adam, and then, the final confrontation with the lady in question.

Cassie scooted up and leaned her back against the headboard. Her arms circled her legs, her chin rested on her knees as she listened.

When he was finished, there was a long moment of thick silence.

Suddenly, he stiffened at the sound of her voice. "You're right, I don't believe it." He turned to face her, his eyes filled with despair, only to find himself hit smack in the face with a big fluffy pillow. Her laughter was joyous and true as she jumped on him and straddled his waist. The pillow was tossed away and replaced by her mouth. Desperately, she rained kisses over his face, all the while murmuring, "What do you mean, 'I won't believe this one'? You scared me half to death."

Cameron rolled over again, once more holding her beneath him. His eyes glowed with pure joy. Why hadn't he remembered he was never happy, had never been truly happy unless she was in his arms? "Well, she was your friend, wasn't she?"

"And you thought I'd believe her over you? I think I'll hit you again."

Cameron's eyes twinkled with delight. "I'd rather you kissed me instead."

Cassie seemed to be considering. "Well, on second thought," she said, then dissolved into giggles as he proceeded to tickle her.

Suddenly, he found himself on his back. It was apparent his wife gained extraordinary strength from being tickled. "I love you," he said, his voice husky with emotion.

"I know," she gasped, struggling to regain her breath. And then, turning to face him with laughter lighting her eyes, she sighed with pretended weariness. "I guess I love you, too."

Cameron chuckled at her little act, and just before his lips came to claim her mouth, his eyes softened to adoration. "I guess you do."

Chapter Twenty-eight

"Why?"

Diana shrugged as her fingers continued to stroke between her legs, her attitude as nonchalant as if she sat in a drawing room, working on a piece of needlepoint. "I figured they needed some privacy."

Rowlins chuckled. He pinched at a rosy bouncing nipple almost as soon as he settled himself at her side. The bitch lied almost as well as she spread her legs. But he knew her better than that. Something had happened. Maybe she had made one too many advances toward the bastard. He knew she was hot to get into Chandler's pants. Maybe her good friend had found her out and tossed the lady out on her ear.

Rowlins shrugged. It didn't matter. Nothing really mattered except getting even with those two. Nobody hit Rowlins and got away with it. Not even his dear old daddy. Jesus, he could remember the beatings like it was yesterday. But it was he who had given the last licks. The day had come at last, when he was the stronger of the two. And when that stupid old bastard had started at him in one of his drunken rages, Rowlins had put an end to them, and him, for good.

His mouth thinned into a straight, angry line. He'd seen the sly looks the niggers gave him. They were glad he had caught that beating. But he'd made them sorry. Rowlins smiled at the remembered lashings, which had been so richly deserved. He'd made every last one of them sorry they'd ever been born. "Sure you did," he answered, his tone one of clear disbelief. "So you moved into the Billings place?"

Diana nodded and then glanced at him with a look of annoyance. Jesus, she was lying here naked as the day she was born and all he could think to do was talk. What the hell was the matter with him? "Do we have to talk about that now? I've been waiting a long time. I've made this all hot and ready for you." She lifted her hips as she plunged her fingers deep into her body.

Rowlins laughed, knowing better than to think she was doing this for his pleasure. He began to open his shirt, purposely taking his time. "How long have you been waiting?"

Diana shrugged. "About a half hour, I guess."

"And you been doin' that all along?"

She nodded her head again.

"How many times you come?"

"Three, if you count the one while I was riding over here."

Rowlins laughed again. "Christ, nobody ain't safe

394

around you, are they? Not even the back of some poor old nag."

Diana shrugged.

"When we gonna do it?"

"Right now, if you get over here!"

"I was talking about your friends," he said flatly. "We've waited long enough. Nobody's goin' to suspect it was me gettin' even. When we gonna take care of them?"

"Soon," she promised. "Shit!" She suddenly groaned, unable to prolong her pleasure any longer. Her voice was low and gasping as she grated out, "Get over here, hurry!"

Rowlins smiled and slowly opened his pants. Rarely did he bother to completely disrobe. Taking his time, he positioned himself between her legs. He looked down at his flaccid member, surprised to find himself soft even though he'd found her, as usual, sprawled naked on the ground, hot and ready for him. Idly, he supposed it was fun, this little playtime she arranged each afternoon, but it was also a bit boring.

He liked it better when they weren't so damn willin'. He liked it better when they gave him a fight. His mouth watered as he thought of the red-headed bitch who was goin' to spread her legs for him. God, he got hot every time he thought about it.

Hard now with just the thought of what he was going to do to Cassie, he thrust himself into the all too willing woman before him.

He was finished in just a few minutes and Diana groaned with disgust. He might be the best hung stud she'd ever come across, but he had a lot to learn about pleasing a woman.

"You ready yet to tell me the plan?" he asked as he flopped to his back, not giving a damn that he'd left her hanging. Her naked body squirmed discontentedly at his side.

Diana sighed, biting back the curses she was tempted to utter. She'd finished this later, with or without him. It didn't matter. She really didn't need him anyway. Not for this, at least. Soon enough, she reasoned, she'd need him for other things, much more important things.

She slid her arms beneath her head, careless of her naked state as she stretched out and began to talk. "You ever notice the drums?"

Rowlins shot her a look of disgust. "What has that got do with our plans?"

"Just about everything."

"You gonna tell me, or what?" he growled impatiently after a long moment of silence.

Diana gave a secret smile. "What always happens the day after the drums stop?"

Rowlins shrugged, his expression one of confusion mixed with annoyance. "It rains," he answered sarcastically. "How the hell should I know?"

Diana giggled, knowing he hadn't any idea what she was talking about. "After the drums, without fail, a slave has escaped."

396

Rowlins shrugged. "So?"

"So, every time the drums start, Chandler leaves the house. Something always comes up at his office, or on one of his ships. Don't you think that's quite a coincidence?"

"What are you getting at?" he asked, his interest piqued now.

Diana shot him a look. Jesus, but the man was dense. "Don't you think that's a bit odd?"

A puzzled frown wrinkled his brow. "What, that he has work to do?"

"Every time the drums start?" She was really exasperated now. She'd never realized just how stupid this man was.

"Are you sayin' he's one of those . . ."

"The word is 'abolitionists,' darling. Yes, I think he's part of the Underground Railroad."

Rowlins whistled through his teeth as a grin split his lips. "Jesus! Are you sure?"

Diana sighed with disgust. "Of course, I'm not sure. I doubt he'd be going around telling everyone, would you?"

"How we gonna prove it? Nobody'd take our word against his."

"I know that. The trick here is not to bother proving it."

"What the hell are you talking about? We'd get rid of the bastard for sure. And then I could get my hands on . . ."

"Listen to me for a minute, will you? If by some

miracle we managed to follow him, even if we caught him in the act, he'd only say he found the slave and was about to take him in. Like you said, no one would believe us over him."

"So, what do we do?"

Diana smiled, enjoying for the moment the beauty of her plan. "We wait for the drums. Chandler will leave about a half hour after they start. Cassie's going to get a message that someone needs her help, and, being the sweet angel she is, will rush out to offer her aid."

"And we'll get her alone." Rowlins licked his lips with anticipation.

"Right." Diana stretched enticingly, to no avail. The man did not so much as glance at her smooth body. A tiny frown marred her pretty face. What the hell did it take to make this stud pay attention? "After we have a little fun with her, we'll make sure her loving husband finds out where she is."

"Are you out of your mind?" he almost shouted as he sat up. "The bastard will kill us both." He calmed some and shook his head. "No, it's better, I think, to ambush him somewhere."

"And let him miss out on all the fun?" Diana shook her head, her smile so evil it gave even him the shivers. "Shame on you. I didn't know you were so greedy."

"After awhile" — she shrugged — "maybe in a week, maybe more, he'll get a little note with instructions on where to find her. He'll be warned to come alone.

We'll both be armed and waiting for him."

"Jesus!" Rowlins looked down at Diana, his eyes alight with renewed respect.

"After we finish with them, we'll dump the bodies somewhere." She sighed with mock pity. "Everyone will be so upset to think the unfortunate couple ran into a band of cutthroats. They were so much in love, poor darlings." Diana smiled and finished silently, *They'll be doubly surprised to find your body along with theirs.* "Of course, I'll be forced to take up residence in Chandler's home. After all, someone will have to take care of the poor, orphaned babies. And I, as Cassie's best friend, wouldn't think of shirking my duty."

Rowlins fell back and howled with laughter. "Perfect. Just perfect."

Suddenly, he sobered and shot her a questioning look. "Where are we going to take her?"

"First, to your cabin. It's more comfortable there and nobody will bother us if they hear her screams. Later, we'll bring her to a cabin I've found. Don't worry, it's deserted and a perfect place to keep watch. He can't sneak up on us. We'll see him coming for miles."

Diana sighed as delicious pictures of the two of them suffering flashed through her mind. There was a time when she had hoped to get rid of Cassie so she might have the bastard, but after their last encounter, she knew the futility of that notion. She shrugged aside her disappointment. It was his money she wanted, anyway. Diana hadn't a doubt that once she was guardian of those little brats, she'd have to beat the men away from her door.

Idly, she mused that Italians were said to be great lovers. A smile teased her mouth. Maybe a trip to Italy was in order. After all, it wouldn't hurt to see for herself the truth of the rumor.

Diana smiled as she glanced over at Rowlins. He was fondling himself, no doubt thinking much the same thoughts as she, with one important exception. She was smart enough to know he'd be after her when this whole thing was over. He'd want his share of the rewards, of course, no matter what he might say now. And she wasn't about to share Chandler's money with anyone. It was her plan, after all. Diana almost laughed with glee at how surprised he was going to be.

Her eyes softened as she reached out to cover his hand with hers. "Need some help with that?"

"Don't give me one of your shrugs, Cameron," she snapped as she watched him take off his boots and wiggle his toes. "I won't be treated like a fool."

Cameron eyed her with a touch of amusement. "Are you suggesting I've taken up with some woman?"

"Not unless you've a lot more stamina than I think. I expect I keep you pretty much exhausted."

Cameron laughed, knowing the truth of that statement. In the weeks since their reconciliation, a night hadn't passed without their making love. In itself, that was not a problem insofar as stamina was concerned. It was the number of times each night that called for extraordinary strength. He'd have to have been superhuman, in fact, to leave Cassie's bed and see to another woman's wants.

"Where have you been going?"

"Cassie," he sighed as he leaned back in the comfortable armchair, his eyes on the golden liquid swirling in the glass he held. "Sometimes it's best not to know all."

"That's ridiculous! Don't try to group me with these empty-headed women around here." Cassie glared at him. "I won't be put off, Cameron," she warned. "If you've any hope of getting a moment's rest, you'd best tell me and be done with it."

Cameron sighed. "If I tell you, I want your promise we won't speak of it again."

"Given."

"I take it you know the meaning of 'abolitionist?' "

Cassie's eyes widened with surprise. That was the last thing she ever expected him to ask. "I do."

"Well, I imagine you'll feel quite pleased to know your husband isn't the owner of slaves, after all."

"What?" Cassie's eyes widened even further.

"The people who work here are free to come and go as they please." He glanced at her puzzled expression and took her look for disbelief. "If you want proof, we can go into the library. I have books showing the dates they were freed and the amounts of monies paid since, in yearly salaries."

Cassie was dumbfounded. She had thought of him for so long as the owner of slaves. She had loved him for so long, despite her hatred of the practice, it was difficult now to sort out all these revelations.

She took a long swallow of her sherry as her thoughts raced on. "And your disappearances? How do they relate?"

"The Underground Railroad."

"You're part of it!" she almost shouted as a thrill of new respect filled her being.

"Lower your voice."

"Does no one know?"

Cameron gave her a look of reproach. "It's not something one boasts of unless they feel a need to have their necks stretched."

Cassie knew the truth of these words. The abolitionists up north were held in the most villainous regard. No doubt the slave owners hereabouts would not think too long and hard had they a chance to dispose of one of the hated group.

"Does anyone know?"

Cameron shrugged. "Stevens."

"And Annie?"

"No."

There was a long moment of silence between them. Cassie finally sighed, her love for the man showing clearly in her voice. "I hope you realize you've destroyed the last thing I held against you."

"You mean I'm perfect?" Cameron grinned.

"Hardly," Cassie shot him a quelling look. It wouldn't do to inflate his ego more than necessary. The man was much too cocky as it stood. "Still, you've come up a bit in my regard."

"Have I?" Cameron's eyes were warm with laughter as they caressed his lovely wife. "What do you suppose I can expect in that case?"

"What do you want that I haven't already given?"

"Nothing," he said truthfully as he left his chair and joined her on the couch. "Except maybe . . ."

Cassie grinned at his teasing. "What?"

"Massage my feet. They're killing me."

Cassie laughed. "I thought you were riding all day. Riding usually affects another part of the anatomy."

"You are more than welcome to massage that part of me as well, any time you wish. I've got calluses there."

Cassie chuckled at his leering grin. "Lie down and put your feet on my lap. I'll see what I can do to ease this terrible affliction."

Cameron closed his eyes and sighed with delight as she began to rub the ache from his feet. "I knew I'd one day find a reason for taking a wife."

Cassie gave a low, throaty laugh. "You could always ask one of the servants to perform this chore. I doubt that only a wife is capable."

"True. But would they be so gentle while about their work?"

There was a moment of comfortable silence be-

403

tween them before Cassie asked. "Is it dangerous, this work you do?"

Cameron shrugged. "Not really."

"Cameron . . ." Her voice was decidedly sly, with just a touch of what he thought to be pleading.

"Don't say it!" he interrupted. "Don't even think it!" he snapped, his voice filled with warning.

"I was only . . ."

"No! Absolutely not." He pulled his feet from her lap and stood at her side, towering over her with what he hoped was a threatening glare. "I will not have it, do you hear?"

Cassie dissolved into a fit of giggles. "What in the world did you think I was going to ask?"

Cameron eyed her warily. "What were you going to ask?"

"Actually, I wasn't going to ask, but rather suggest that when your feet felt better I might then begin to work on your calluses."

Cameron sat down beside her. He had the grace to look slightly embarrassed at his outburst.

"What did you think?"

"Nothing!" he answered shortly. If she hadn't thought of joining him on his nightly excursions, he wasn't going to be stupid enough to give her the idea.

"You thought I was going to ask to join you."

"I did not," he lied.

"You did," She laughed again, enjoying his reddened cheeks.

"Cassie, this is nothing to laugh about. This is

404

deadly serious business. And I do mean deadly!"

"I know. I haven't forgotten my hand in freeing Sunshine's husband." Cassie shivered as she remembered that night and the terrible fear she had suffered.

"What would you do if you were stopped?"

"I won't be."

"But if you were?"

Cameron shrugged. "I'd simply say I found them."

"Them? Do you often have more than one at a time with you?"

"Sometimes whole families."

"Whole families? That means babies! And babies cry! Damn it, Cameron, don't try to tell me it's not dangerous. Suppose a baby should cry out? Do you suppose the men tracking slaves down would ask questions first?"

"You need not get yourself in an uproar. It doesn't happen often."

"But it does happen."

Cameron sighed and took her stiff form into his arms. "Cassie, I cannot leave half to follow later. Besides, no mother would leave her child. And no man would leave his woman. What is the alternative?"

"A bullet," she said with absolute dread. He felt her shudder.

"Listen to me, darling," he said as he rocked her soothingly. "There are no guarantees in life. I could fall from a horse and die. All that any of us can be sure of is this minute."

Cassie lifted blue eyes misted with unshed tears. The fear of what might lie in store for him was almost unendurable.

"Does it make sense to worry over what might happen? Will you suffer any less?"

Cassie gave a wistful sigh. "Why couldn't you have been that unsavory character I first thought?" She looked down at her fingers knotted in her lap. "I don't want to love you so much. I don't want to live with fear."

Cameron chuckled. "Did you think me an unsavory character at first?"

Cassie smiled. "Your dalliances aboard ship were not with ladies of the finest character. Also, it came as quite a shock that you owned slaves. All in all, it put you in less than an agreeable light."

"Still, you somehow managed to love me?"

"There is no accounting for some people's taste, is there?" She sighed.

Cameron smiled as he hugged her closer. "I love you, Cassie, and would not have you suffer. Shall I shirk what I feel is my duty?"

"Would you? For me?"

"There is nothing I wouldn't do for you."

"I'd not ask it of you." She hesitated. "Not just yet, in any case."

"When, then?"

"If I were to have a baby, Cameron. I'd ask it then, for I'd not wish him to never know his father."

Cameron laughed. "Are you so sure our first will be a boy?"

"Actually, I was counting on it," she said cheerfully as she shook off the last of her fear. "He will be needed, don't you think, to take care of his little sisters? Especially if one of them should come across an unsavory character."

"Like their father?"

"Yes." She smiled as his hand cupped her breast. "Like their father."

She laughed at his low, menacing growl.

"I'll kill the bastard."

Chapter Twenty-nine

But for her eyes, Cassie did an excellent job of hiding her mirth as a juicy red strawberry, covered with cream, flew suddenly across the table and landed in Cameron's hair. The children blinked in surprise, then watched, almost mesmerized, as the dripping fruit slid down, over his ear and onto his shoulder.

Cameron sighed, picked the gooey mess from his shoulder and rubbed as best he could his sticky hair and the stain left on his jacket. "I'm told that in civilized households children are fed and asleep before their parents sit down to eat."

"What a shame. Imagine all the fun they miss."

"Indeed," he remarked drily. "And besides being fun, it's also informative. For instance, one wonders how I could have gone on all these years never realizing babies eat with both their ears and mouths." He nodded pointedly toward Christian who was trying to put a strawberry in his tiny ear.

Cassie's laughter turned to a gasp as Christina suddenly decided to upend her bowl and wear it as a bonnet. As sugary juice ran down the baby's face, Meghan giggled at her father's expression of despair.

Just as Cassie jumped up to clean the mess, Stevens walked into the dining room. "I've a message for you, Mr. Chandler."

By the time Cameron returned to the table, the servants had taken the children upstairs and Cassie was sipping at her after-dinner tea.

"I have to go," he stated hesitantly, for he knew it would be no easy job to leave. He didn't bother with explanations or some transparent lie that he'd been called to his office or ship. Both knew what he was about.

Cassie opened her mouth to say something, but thought better of it as she watched his mouth thin to a hard, determined line.

Silently, she followed him into the library and watched with growing apprehension as he strapped a gun around his waist. Cassie bit her lip. She would not tell him not to go. She was dying to say it, but she was determined not to.

Cameron hesitated a moment before her. He smiled as he read her troubled, fearful expression. "You're a good girl," he remarked, knowing what it cost her not to beg him to stay.

She didn't want to be a good girl. She wanted her man, and she wanted him out of harm's way. Cassie felt as if she might burst, so strong was the need to beg him not to go. It was one thing to talk of his leaving but quite another to actually have it happen. She prayed that this would not be the last time she'd ever see him.

His fingers came to hold her jaw. "I love you, Cassie," he murmured. "And because you're so good"—his eyes twinkled with erotic promise—"I'm going to give you something special when I get back." He kissed her then, a lingering, sweet kiss that tasted of all the promise and love in his gently spoken words.

But it wasn't enough for Cassie. She couldn't stop the desperate need to keep him in her arms. Her lips parted, and she heard him groan as her tongue slipped deep into his mouth. She clung hungrily to him, using her body to convey her unspoken plea that he stay with her.

"I've got to go," he said as he broke away at last. His voice was harsh with need, his eyes aflame with yearning.

Cassie watched in continued silence as the front door closed behind him. Her voice was choked with unshed tears when she finally murmured, "Be careful."

After he left, Cassie paced for what seemed like hours. She should have insisted she go with him. No matter the danger. No matter her fright. Anything

410

was better than this anguished waiting.

She didn't care about his objections. He could rant, he could threaten, he could rage. It mattered not. From now on she was going with him. She'd follow him rather than be left behind. Never again would she spend a night like this.

She threw aside her needlepoint. What was the sense? She could hardly hold onto the needle, never mind make delicate stitches. She glanced at her timepiece again and groaned. Would the hands never move. Would the time never pass?

When a knock sounded at the front door, she nearly flew from her chair. Her heart pounded furiously. She knew it couldn't be Cameron. He wouldn't have knocked, not if he were able to open the door unaided.

Her face was white as she watched Stevens open the door to admit a man, someone she'd never seen before, holding a note. She almost cried with relief as she read the hastily scribbled lines. It wasn't from Cameron. He wasn't hurt. As a wave of dizziness came over her, she clung to the doorway for support. She had to get control of herself. Someone was ill and she was needed. She hadn't the time to faint.

Cassie snapped the reins over the lone horse as she and Joshua hurried down the dirt road to the Stewards' farm. Thank God for this call, she reasoned. She needed something to take her mind from tonight's happenings, both imagined and real. And there was nothing like hard work to provide a distrac-

411

tion.

"Sho' is a warm night," Joshua said while wiping at his forehead with a snowy handkerchief. Usually, it was he who drove when there was a call for her help, but tonight Cassie felt the need to do the job herself.

"It is that, Joshua," she agreed about the almost suffocating heat. "How long do the summers usually last?"

"Well into September, I'd say," he replied.

Cassie sighed. Suddenly, she longed for the cooling breezes of England, where the temperatures never rose to such extremes. There was at least another full month of this heat to look forward to. Well, that wasn't so bad, she supposed. Not if she had Cameron at her side. She almost giggled. Not that he was known to keep her cool.

Cassie smiled as intimate pictures of their time spent together came to flood her mind. She was so preoccupied with these agreeable images she almost didn't see the fallen tree ahead that blocked the road.

It was times such as these that Cassie was thankful she had heeded Cameron's advice. She grinned. Actually, advice was too mild a word. An order was more like it. Joshua was to accompany her each and every time she set forth on one of her missions. Cassie had to admit that she did feel safer traveling these dark roads with a man at her side, although she'd never give Cameron the satisfaction of hearing her say it. Were Joshua not with her tonight, Cassie would have been forced to turn the buggy around

412

and look for another way to reach the Steward farm.

Joshua jumped from the buggy. The tree wasn't as big as he'd first imagined. It wouldn't take no more than a little nudge to clear it off the road. His arms were around the tree's trunk when he thought he saw something glitter in the shadows to his right. He turned his head and narrowed his gaze. He never knew what hit him. He was dead before his body crumpled to the ground.

Cassie heard the gunshot, but never realized Joshua had been hit, for the loud sound had caused the horse to rear up and block her view. For one wild moment, he danced upon his hind legs, pawing at the empty air before him, his eyes suddenly crazed with fear. Cassie watched in helpless fascination, sure he was going to fall back and crush both her and the buggy.

She might have had a chance to escape what lay ahead had she not instinctively moved to control the animal. For surely, despite the obstacle still blocking his path, the horse would have dashed off, taking himself and Cassie on a wild flight over the countryside.

Cassie hadn't a moment to think before two masked riders were upon her. Before she could utter a single word of protest, she was lifted from the buggy's seat and placed in the saddle of one of the riders. Her eyes widened with horror as she suddenly saw Joshua's crumpled form in the moonlight.

Terror clutched at her heart and froze her tongue.

413

Scream! . . . Scream! came a voice at the back of her mind. Someone might be about. Someone might hear. Don't just sit here. Fight them. Don't let them win! But dazed and horror stricken, all she could do was stare at Joshua's body.

She hadn't a chance in any case. Almost instantly, something was pressed over her face. Cassie gasped as sickly sweet air entered her lungs. She choked. She gagged. And each time she did, she inhaled more of the noxious fumes until blackness overtook her.

The unbearable ache was upon her again. She had gone back to sleep, hoping the pain might be gone when she awakened, but it was worse than before. She was so tired. She wanted to give into the need to sleep again, but the pain in her arms was too severe. She tried to move. She couldn't. Something was holding her fast.

Cameron was lying on her arms. How could that be? she wondered. His leg often covered hers in sleep, and there were times she might awaken a bit stiff from the enforced position, but never did he cause her pain such as this.

Someone was giggling nearby. Cassie blinked her eyes open and stared, truly puzzled, at what she saw. It took her a long moment to remember, for the pain, mingled with the effects of the drug, had left her temporarily confused. Her heart began to pound with fear. Someone had killed Joshua, and that same someone had hung her bound hands to the rafters of a small cabin. She was held suspended above the floor, her head thrown back. The first sight to greet her eyes was a dark, roughly hewn ceiling.

How long she had been like this? She didn't know. All she knew was that her shoulders, arms, and wrists held all her body's weight. Her shoulders felt as if they were being pulled from their sockets.

Cassie groaned with the pain, but the agonized appeal fell on deaf ears. She could hear low voices below her, laughing softly. She wasn't alone. A chill of fear crept up her spine, and she shivered, the slight movement making her cry out again. God only knew what they were going to do to her. God only knew why.

"Please," she groaned. The effort of speaking seemed to intensify the pain, yet she had to ask. "Please, help me."

The laughter grew louder and considerably more merry, yet Cassie knew nothing but pain.

She moved her head, and, for the first time, realized she was naked as she felt her long hair brush against her hips. She looked over one shoulder. Nothing but floor. She looked in the opposite direction and almost laughed. This was the most ridiculous dream anyone could ever have. Why would she dream of Diana, lying naked in Mr. Rowlins's arms? Why him?

Wake up, wake up, you fool, she murmured to herself

between dry lips. She closed her eyes and looked again. They were still there.

Suddenly, a foot reached out and nudged her, causing her to sway. Cassie screamed as agony filled her mind to overflowing. Never had anyone felt this pain. Never had there been suffering to equal this.

"Shall we lower her some?" came a man's voice, penetrating the nightmare of burning anguish.

"Why?"

"I can't do much if she hangs up there."

Diana sighed with disinterest. "She won't join us, you know."

"Why don't we see?"

Diana shrugged. "Go ahead."

Cassie closed her eyes as the rope was released and she was lowered to the floor. Her knees buckled and she screamed again as she fell, all her weight once again on her arms. No hand reached out to assist her, and it was only with a tremendous force of will that she managed to find her footing.

She was gasping for breath, her mind reeling with pain and relief, then still more pain. Her hands fell limply before her. Her arms were useless and throbbed as if on fire. In a daze, she looked at her hands. They were blue. Her wrists were cut from the rope and blood had seeped down her arms.

Cassie closed her eyes, willing the pain under control, but the blood was rushing back toward her hands now, bringing a fresh wave of piercing torment.

416

From somewhere in the back of her mind, she realized it was daylight. She looked toward the unwashed window. The sun was shining. How long had she hung there?

"No, that won't do," came the man's voice again. "I can't see, if her hands fall that low." Cassie heard a low chuckle as unseen fingers suddenly began to probe at her most private places. Amazingly, she just stood there. She couldn't find it in herself to care. She didn't care that she stood there naked. She didn't care what he saw, or what he did. All she could think of was the agony in her arms and hands. "And this," the man continued, "is something I particularly want to see."

The rope was pulled again. Cassie's heart pounded with terror. "No!" she cried aloud. *I'll do anything. Don't pull me up again!* Cassie gave an audible sigh of relief to find her hands were held now at waist level.

"That's better, don't you think?"

Diana laughed. "You probably shouldn't have let her feet touch the ground. She'll kick you."

Rowlins grinned into Cassie's dazed expression. "Is that true?"

"What?" Cassie asked, for she hadn't been listening to anything, so immersed was she in her suffering.

"Will you kick me?"

Cassie could only blink at the question. Kick him! Kick him! What in God's name was he talking about? She couldn't think beyond the pain in her arms, and he was asking her if she would kick him?

417

"Come on over here and finish," Diana urged. "She can wait."

That seemed a reasonable enough request to Rowlins. The woman he really wanted was not exactly her old self, and he didn't want her like this. He wanted her with some fight in her. He wanted some fun for a change.

Cassie swayed and took a step for balance. She wished she could sit, but dared not give into the need, for her arms would once again be stretched above her.

She no longer thought this a dream. It was a nightmare, but it was real. Why were they doing this?

Cassie had witnessed Rowlins's cruelty before. In truth, she would have expected no less from the animal, but how could Diana be a part of it? Granted, Cameron had ordered her from his house, and since then, the two women had hardly seen each other, except for one or two accidental meetings in town. Still, Cassie would never have imagined the woman to hate her so much.

She had been such a fool. How had Diana managed to keep her true nature hidden for so long? Cassie had known, of course, the woman's quick temper and lack of patience with the children. But how was it that she'd never guessed that Diana was actually depraved? And depraved was the only word Cassie could think of as she watched the two of them couple with uninhibited glee beneath her astonished

418

gaze.

Although they touched and caressed each other, both seemed to have eyes only for their naked captive. Cassie felt no sense of shame as their eyes raked her body. She felt only pain — and contempt.

Unable to hide her disgust, she turned away, but she couldn't turn off the horrible, animalistic sounds. Her gaze wandered over the room. Now that the pain had diminished to a throbbing ache, her mind seemed to clear and she sought a means of escape.

The door was no more than eight or ten feet away. It didn't appear to be locked. Didn't they fear discovery? Cassie gave a sigh of despair. The door might as well have been barred with a hundred locks, for, tied as she was, there wasn't a chance of her reaching it.

Whose cabin was this? Where was it located? Hadn't anyone heard her screams?

Cassie shivered with revulsion as she spied a rat in a corner, nibbling at what appeared to be the remains of a loaf of molding bread. The windows were closed. The cabin was suffocatingly hot. She felt her stomach lurch. The place smelled of dirt, unwashed bodies, and sex. Sweat ran down her face and burned her eyes. More sweat trickled from under her arms down her sides. She fought back the urge to vomit. It appeared they were finished at last, if all that groaning was any indication.

Prepared, if necessary, to beg for her freedom, Cassie risked a glance at her one-time friend. She was filled with icy horror at the absolute evil which

419

suffused Diana's expression.

"You'll be wanting your turn, I expect." Diana remarked in a self-satisfied tone.

Cassie could only stare, frozen into shivering silence by this replica of Satan.

Rowlins rolled onto his back. His hands beneath his head, he studied Cassie's body at his leisure.

Again, Cassie felt not a tremor of shame. Her eyes grew hard with hate, and a slight smile touched her lips. Cameron would kill him for this. It didn't matter how she suffered at this monster's hands. He was already dead.

Rowlins and Diana both laughed at Cassie's expression. She was easy enough to read. "Do you imagine I'm afraid of the bastard?" Rowlins asked, laughing again.

Cassie's smile was almost pitying as she listened to him laugh at her expense. "Were I you, I'd be thinking of a way to disappear. Although I doubt it will do much good."

Rowlins came to his feet and stood before her. His hand reached out and pinched at her nipple. "Confident of an imminent rescue, no doubt."

Cassie ignored the pain he inflicted. Her head held high, she smiled. "I am."

He laughed again. "Well, I wouldn't hold my breath."

"He'll find me. You can be sure of it," Cassie insisted, and prayed that her words were true.

Rowlins chuckled. "When he does, which of you

shall I kill first?"

Diana was still lying upon the blanket. She was rubbing her hands over her body, apparently gaining much pleasure in this task, for she moaned, while a touch of annoyance showed in her voice. "Bring her over here, for God's sake. Enough of talking."

Rowlins grinned. "I think my friend is right. Would you care to join us, my lady?" he sneered.

"I would not, thank you."

"Perhaps you would rather watch instead."

Cassie's lips curled in disgust. She didn't answer him.

"No? Well, that's good. That's very good indeed. I like my women with a bit of spirit."

Instantly, Cassie picked up on his words. "A pity then, to have chosen me." She smiled almost sweetly. "I'll not fight you."

Rowlins bit his lip. He knew he had made a mistake. He didn't want that hot, sex-crazed whore lying on the blanket, but even more, he didn't want this cold, emotionless bitch standing proudly before him. Jesus, were the nigger girls the only ones who knew how to put up a fight? Certainly he'd found no real satisfaction in taking anyone else.

A gleam of merriment entered his eyes. "Why don't we wait, then? Maybe you'll change your mind later."

Suddenly, he yanked at the rope. A blood curdling scream was torn from Cassie's throat as her arms were snapped up and she was again lifted off the floor.

The last thing she heard before the blessed blackness came was the two below chuckling their pleasure.

Chapter Thirty

Standing in the doorway of her cabin, waiting for her family to finish super so she could get on with the last chore of the night, Betsy heard the cries. Everyone heard them; you'd have to be deaf not to. Maybe he'd kill this one. She'd been screamin' on and off for most of the day now. How much could a body take?

Betsy felt sorry for the girl. But she was also glad it wasn't her.

It was getting dark and Rowlins hadn't come out of the cabin all day. Betsy wondered who it was he had in there. Usually, he wasn't interested in a person after he had his way. This one must be someone special. He was beating her, she could tell. Once or twice she heard the whip hit something and then another scream.

She was dying to see, but there was no way she was going near that place—leastways not till after dark. She smiled a secret smile.

She couldn't remember the last time anyone had been dragged to his cabin. Most always, he did what he had to do on the ground. It didn't bother him none who saw. There weren't nobody here who'd dare stop him anyways. And if it was whipping he had in mind, he usually just threw a rope over a tree branch and did the job—one, two, three.

Betsy glanced at the darkening sky. Soon, she thought. Soon, she'd be able to sneak on over there and see for herself what was going on.

Cassie's mind slipped in and out of reality. Sometimes she even muttered a sound that resembled some sort of grotesque laughter. But that only brought the pain again. She was playing with the children. Christina was crying. She hated the feel of grass and rarely ventured off her blanket, while her brother eyed the velvety green lawn with a hungry gleam. Actually, he tried to eat anything he could lay his hands on. Cassie smiled as, even now, he fought her efforts to relieve him of a mouthful of dirt.

Often enough she had found evidence of his liking for pebbles and dirt upon changing him. Cassie shrugged, hoping she got most of it. She supposed what she had missed wouldn't cause him any great harm, for he had so far survived what she could only call a most unsuitable diet.

Christina was crying. Cassie sighed. Did the child

never stop? What was it she wanted now? But when Cassie looked at the baby, she was laughing. Who, then, was crying?

Cassie felt the sobs in her throat. It was her! Why was she crying? She awakened to uproarious laughter. She never knew—nor would it have mattered if she had—that she had unconsciously relieved herself, and the two who so enjoyed her suffering had seen it. For just an instant she wondered why they were laughing. She had only that instant before her mind registered her agony again. She screamed. She screamed until her throat grew raw, almost as raw as her back. Earlier she had imagined her pain to be unbearable, but it was as nothing compared to this, Long ago, her hands and shoulders had gone numb. No longer was it hanging that brought about this agony. Now, it was the whip, which lashed at her back, her buttocks, her legs. There wasn't a place that didn't hurt. She couldn't think beyond the horror of it. She prayed for death, for that alone would bring relief.

The tail of the whip snapped at her breasts, and Cassie's whole body was jolted with the shock as it tore at her nipple. She screamed again. Even in her agonized state she noticed that the volume of her screams had gotten lower. Her strength was ebbing. Thank God! When he had shoved the broom handle inside her, she had thought that was the end of her. She had blacked out, only to awaken to a cramp that caused a low, guttural groan to be torn from her

425

throat. Soon after, something soft and warm had passed out of her body. Strangely, tears of sorrow came to her eyes. Had she been pregnant?

God, why didn't she die? How much more was she to bear? She didn't even think of rescue. She wanted death. She longed for it. She prayed for it.

They were insane, of course. No one would inflict pain such as this unless they were mad, or in league with the devil.

Actually, Rowlins had not whipped her as bloody and raw as she imagined herself to be. He had laid on the whip carefully, having had much practice in the art. He knew how to inflict the worst pain while rarely cutting the skin. He had no wish to see her die. Not just yet, in any case.

He sighed with disgust. She had passed out again. The next time she awoke, he was going to take her down. He was going to have her then. It no longer mattered that she wouldn't fight. He was tired of waiting.

Betsy crept close to the window and peered inside. She almost gasped aloud at the sight that greeted her. It wasn't a black woman he had in there. She was white! Betsy didn't think he was allowed to do that. But she didn't know for sure. As far as she could tell, he was allowed to do near anything he wanted.

Betsy moved to another window. She wanted to get a look at her face. Suddenly, her eyes widened with

426

surprise. Good Lord Almighty! This was Meghan's mother. The same lady who had saved her from Rowlins's whip! Her man had given him a beating for hitting her by mistake. What would he do if he found out about this?

Diana was growing bored. She never would have thought the bitch so weak. Every time Rowlins hit her she passed out again. And that was accomplishing nothing.

"I think you should cut her down. This isn't much fun for any of us."

Rowlins shrugged and untied the rope, letting Cassie fall unconscious into her own urine and blood.

"Let her sleep until tomorrow," Diana suggested. "I imagine she'll be a bit more cooperative then."

Rowlins nodded his agreement. "Guess it can't hurt none."

"Come over here."

Rowlins shot her a look of disbelief. "Jesus, lady, you're goin' to suck me dry."

Diana chuckled, her eyes lighting with evil pleasure. "Exactly what I had in mind."

It was almost dawn by the time Betsy reached Hill Crest. Her body was covered with sweat. She had run for nearly eight hours. She had gotten lost. She had run in circles for a time, but she hadn't stopped.

427

Not even when the pain in her side threatened to kill her.

Cameron paced the floor of his library waiting for word. His face was a tight mask of apprehension. But for that one time, she had never been gone this long before. He checked his timepiece again. He'd been back since two o'clock. Here it was six in the morning and still no Cassie. He tried to talk himself out of this unnamed fear. But no matter how he reasoned, he couldn't shake it. Nothing was wrong; she'd simply been delayed. If there was a problem, she would have sent Joshua back to tell him. She knew he would worry.

Cameron ran to the front door at the sound of hoofbeats. A lone rider was galloping up his drive. Tom Billings pulled his horse to an abrupt stop only a few feet from the front steps and dismounted in a cloud of dust. "Where the hell is Cassie?"

"What do you mean? What are you doing here?"

"Where is she, man?"

"She's gone out somewhere. I've been waiting for her or Joshua to bring me some word."

"Joshua is dead."

"What? Where?"

"One of my men just got back from town. He took the short cut, you know where the road forks off to the Higgins place?"

Cameron couldn't hear his words. There was a

ringing in his ears. Almost dumbly, he watched his friend's mouth move, but no words registered. "Cassie. Where is she?" He ran down the steps and grabbed Tom's collar, almost cutting off his air.

"Hold on a minute, will you?" Tom broke free. "Your buggy was found along the road. Joshua took a bullet in his head."

Cameron ran back up the stairs and into his library. A moment later, fully armed, he ran past Tom, heading for the barn and his horse.

"She's not there," Tom called out.

Cameron came up short and looked around, his eyes settling finally on the man at his side. "What do you mean she's not there? Where is she?"

"That's what I asked you, remember?"

Cameron looked awful. His scar stood out pure white against his tanned skin. His eyes were wild and red-rimmed with lack of sleep and fear. The strain of the last twenty four hours had deepened every line on his face until he appeared to have aged ten years in one night.

Cameron, Tom, and Stevens had gone for the buggy and Joshua's body. They had searched the area carefully, but could find nothing save the signs of two horses. When they had attempted to follow the trail, it had disappeared at the river.

They had searched that area, and beyond, well into nightfall. After dark, they used lanterns and still found nothing. Cameron couldn't sleep when he returned to Hill Crest. He knew he should, for he'd need every ounce of strength he had with another day of searching ahead. But there was no sense in trying. He couldn't even sit still long enough to doze.

Again, he glanced at the sky. At last, the sun was making a feeble attempt to vanquish the cursed night's blackness. Silently, he begged it to hurry. They needed light and they needed it now!

Tom and the rest of the men would be at Hill Crest soon. Cameron checked his weapons, knowing before he looked they were loaded and ready for use. Still, it was something to do, something to occupy his fingers. Fingers that itched to kill the man responsible for taking his wife, for bringing this torturous fear upon him.

Cameron no longer cared what the man, or men — since there were two sets of prints — had surely done to his wife. At first he'd been wild with the sure knowledge of rape. Now, he only prayed to find her alive. For the first time in years, he prayed, begging the Almighty simply for her life.

Betsy felt a moment's trepidation. It was early morning, barely light, and yet the yard was filled with men on horseback. For a moment, she was afraid to make herself known, but then the memory of what she had seen drove her forward.

She ran toward the house. Unmindful of the danger, she hurried between nervous horses, never hearing the curses of startled men as she passed. Betsy ran right into the house, careless of the dirt she tracked in. Sweat streamed down her face, and she held her hand to the pain in her side.

"Mr. Chandler," she gasped, so breathlessly no one heard.

Cameron was walking out of the library. A group of men surrounded him. He never saw the girl.

Someone shoved her aside. Betsy was flung against the wall and leaned there for a moment trying to regain her breath.

Suddenly, she shouted, "Stop!" All eyes turned on her. There was a moment of total silence. Betsy felt a numbing fear run up her spine. Now that she had their attention, she was too scared to speak.

"Who are you?" came a voice from out of the crowd of men. Betsy looked up, not sure who it was that had spoken. Her big, dark eyes searched out the group of men. "Mr. Chandler?"

"Here," came an answer from one of the tallest.

"Your lady"—she was gasping for breath—"Rowlins has her."

"What?"

"I saw dem through the window. He's got her tied up."

"Take care of her," the man said to someone Betsy couldn't see.

Almost as one the group moved out the door. An instant later the air was filled with the sound of thundering hooves.

It was just dawn. Birds were chirping gaily from their cozy nests as the sun inched its warm rays over the earth. The air was clean and fresh, the grass wet with dew.

Cameron noticed none of this. His mind was set on murder. No one spoke during the short ride to Bennett's plantation. Every man there knew Rowlins was as good as dead.

Cameron brought his horse to a halt about two hundred yards from the cabin, not wishing to make the riders' presence known to anyone who might still be there. "Tom and I will go on alone."

No one asked his reasons, for there was not a man among them who would have cared to have a stranger look upon his loved one in the state Cameron was sure to find Cassie.

Cameron and Tom left their horses with the men and sped on foot over the weeds and overgrown shrubs toward the faded, whitewashed cabin. The plantation was coming awake. A few blacks ventured outside their cabins and stretched. Others were returning from a morning trip to the privy.

Guns drawn, Cameron inched up to the house. A quick, careful glance in the window showed him three naked people, seemingly asleep. It took all his will power not to scream out his rage at the sight of his wife. She was lying where she had fallen, naked and bloodied, her hands bound, her eyes closed. He only prayed she, too, slept.

Rowlins was sprawled upon a blanket. Cuddled at his side was Diana. Blind with rage, Cameron barely managed to keep from smashing through the window with his bare fists.

The door opened silently beneath his hand. Immediately, he checked his wife and sighed with relief to find her chest rising and falling. She lived! He almost cried, his relief was so great. Silently, he dispatched a quick prayer of thanks. On closer inspection, he noticed her breathing was shallow but steady. Her skin felt hot and dry. She was sick. More than anything, he longed to cradle her in his arms, but he dared not. There was a matter of seeing to her safety, and that meant dealing with these villains first.

Tom met Cameron's eyes over Cassie's sleeping form. He nodded his relief at Cameron's half-smile and walked toward the sleeping couple. Cameron threw a rag of a blanket over his wife. She slept on.

Rowlins awoke with a gun barrel pressed hard against his teeth. "Don't move. Not an inch," Tom warned softly.

Diana stirred and stretched sleepily. She opened her eyes at Rowlins's involuntary jump. A smile flickered in her eyes for just a second, before she realized where she was and who it was standing over her.

She gasped. Her first instinct was to roll away and run, but Cameron stood to one side of her and Tom

433

on the other. There would be no escape.

"Wait a minute," she started, her desperation clear. "Don't lose your head. Cassie's all right. We didn't do anything. We found her and brought her here to help her."

Cameron's laugh was sinister. "Did you now? Well, I think you deserve some sort of reward, don't you?"

"No," she answered weakly, so terrified she couldn't stop her teeth from chattering. "It was the neighborly thing to do."

Cameron laughed again, and the sound sent chills down her spine. "Then it's lucky for us we won't be having you two for neighbors much longer."

"What . . . what do you mean?" asked Rowlins in a garbled, terrified voice. Tom's gun was now lodged firmly within the man's mouth.

Cameron looked at him with deadly calm, and Rowlins's stomach turned to ice. For an instant, he thought he might vomit from the fear that coursed through his body. Cameron's lips split in a horrifying grin. "You're dead," he said in low, even tones that betrayed not a trace of his rage.

Rowlins's eyes grew even larger with fear as Cameron slowly took aim. Coldly and purposefully, without another word of warning, he shot off the man's sex.

Tom gasped—knowing a bullet in the man's mouth would have been the more charitable act—as a huge, gaping wound opened between the man's legs and bright red blood gushed upon the floor. Rowlins's scream of horror and despair was chilling even to the man who had done the shooting. But Cameron did not allow himself even a momentary twinge of pity. One glance at his wife was all he needed to remember his almost insane need for revenge.

All eyes turned to the man who writhed upon the floor. Rowlins never thought of the pain. Indeed, the pain had no bearing on this moment. His life's blood was gushing from his body and he barely took notice. All he could think to do was hysterically grab at his dismembered part and desperately try to force it back on while he kept screaming, "No! No!"

Unobserved, Diana had managed to move from the blanket. Naked, she stood over Cassie, a gun pointed at the sleeping's woman's head.

Cassie, so weak from the loss of blood, had hardly stirred at the sound of the gun blast. "I wouldn't be thinking of shooting anyone else if I were you," Diana warned.

Both men turned at the sound of her voice. Icy rage glittered in Cameron's eyes as he saw the gun. "Put the gun down, Diana. You're not going anywhere."

Diana laughed. "You think not? Drop those guns," she said to them both. "Hand me my clothes," she instructed Tom.

Tom bent down and threw the articles to her, but neither man gave up his weapon.

"I said, drop those guns!" She cocked the pistol. There was a heavy sound as Tom's gun hit the floor, but Diana barely had time to take notice as another gunshot blasted the cabin. She looked puzzled for a moment, feeling nothing but an itch at her jaw. Automatically, she reached up to scratch it, then gave a strangled, grotesque scream as her hand came away filled with bone fragments, flesh, and blood.

She had less than a second to realize she'd been shot and the man before her was about to finish the job. She didn't care that she was about to die. She was taking this bitch with her. An evil gleam came into her half-crazed eyes. She'd get her final revenge. She squeezed the trigger. The last thing she heard was the sound of her gun exploding.

Chapter Thirty-one

Someone was making a low, whimpering sound. She wished they would stop. The sound was bringing an unbearable ache to her head. No, she was wrong. There was a chair being scraped across the floor. Yes, there it was again. Someone was moaning. Whispered voices. She tried to open her eyes and see. She couldn't.

PAAAIIN!

It hit her all at once. She gasped as her breath was ripped from her lungs by the sheer force of it. Where did it come from? She couldn't remember. She tried to think, but the effort was too great. Everything hurt, especially her head. Why should that be . . . ?

No, please, she didn't want to come back. The blackness offered her peace. An escape from the pain. A voice was insisting. She knew by the tone even though she couldn't understand the words. *I don't want to. Leave me alone,* she wanted to cry, but her

437

mouth wouldn't move.

She took a shallow, gasping breath as the pain splintered like broken glass into thousands of razor-sharp shards, penetrating every nerve ending. Suddenly, it seemed to gather force, and slithered, like a vicious, poisonous snake, spitting out its burning venom far into the depths of her being. Someone was moving her. Couldn't they stop? Couldn't they leave her alone? A scream was bubbling up. She didn't want to let it out. It always hurt more when she let it out. No more. Please God, no more.

A pinch on her arm? Was it a pinch? Amazing. Through this white-hot blaze of pain she could still feel a pinch. Shadowy images. Darkness. Muffled voices. Floating. She reached eagerly for the void and then sighed with relief when she didn't have to reach anymore.

Cameron watched as the doctor injected the morphine into her arm. Why couldn't he give her more? And if that was too dangerous, why not more often?

God, he had thought to have suffered the agonies of hell when he couldn't find her, but was this any better? She was home. She was safe. But was she going to live? He needed to know she'd make it. Without her, there was no reason to go on.

Dr. Woodward, brought from Baltimore, leaned over his new patient and grunted. His blue eyes smiled at the anxious man standing across from him.

"She's taken some abuse, but she'll be all right."

"Her head?" Cameron asked, his lips set in a bitter, tight line. He hadn't been able to kill the bitch fast enough. She had pulled the trigger just as he had. Thank God the bullet had only grazed Cassie's head.

"She'll have a headache for a while."

"And the blood?" Cameron asked, his face growing gray as he recalled the pool of congealed blood beneath her. Her legs had been covered with it. There was even a dry brown coating of it between her toes. His head had reeled at the sight. He hadn't imagined a body could hold so much blood—lost so much.

Dr. Woodward nodded. "She lost the baby, I'm afraid. But she's young. There wasn't any permanent damage as far as I could tell." He smiled at Cameron's confusion. "There'll be more babies."

Cameron felt his knees give way. He clung to the wooden bedpost lest he fall from the shock of this news. She had been pregnant. Why hadn't she told him?

"How far?" his voice was hoarse with aching emotion. "How far was she?"

The doctor shrugged. "I'd say no more than a month or six weeks."

She hadn't known, came a low soothing voice. *Maybe she'll never have to know.*

"When she wakes up, you can give her a few drops of laudanum in a glass of water. It will help the pain.

439

I've left you some salve for her back." He nodded toward the jar on the dresser. "She'll be fine. Don't worry so."

Cameron thanked the doctor, then turned back to look at his wife. He wanted to laugh, but he dared not even smile lest he give way to the hysteria that threatened. Don't worry. Don't worry. God, he sighed. If only that were possible. The worry and the guilt had nearly driven him mad. Perhaps he had suffered a lapse in sanity. He gave a silent curse. It didn't matter. His first act in the cabin should have been to protect her from further harm. And he had failed to do so. Once she was found, he should have forgotten his need for revenge and just taken her from that place, leaving those responsible in Tom's capable hands. But he had not. No. He had to see to their punishment himself. And by doing so he had added to the suffering of this woman who meant more to him than his life.

Cameron sat on the edge of the bed, his head in his hands as he replayed the terror of that morning.

He had killed the bitch, yes, but not before her last-ditch effort at revenge. For a long moment, he had thought Cassie was dead. He had seen her body jump from the bullet's impact. He had watched as the blood gushed from the wound. Mindless with terror, he could only stand there and stare. It was Tom who ran to Cassie. Tom, who tore at his own shirt and pressed the makeshift bandage to her head. Tom, who had nodded to his friend that Cassie still breathed. And Tom, who had gone into Baltimore to find the best doctor available.

It was all Cameron could do to get Cassie home. She was as light as a feather in his arms, but his arms were weak and trembling. He had taken his time, of course. He knew she couldn't take being jostled along with the injuries so far sustained. It felt as though hours had passed before he managed to get her into her bed. And now, all he could do was wait. Perhaps this was the worst. No perhaps about it. This was the worst.

He remembered his terror when she had been struck with fever. It was as nothing compared to the emotion that grabbed now at his guts and tore until he nearly cried out from the pain. He had cared for her then, but now he knew what it was to truly love.

Jessie brought up a tray. Cameron shook his head when she gestured to the food. He didn't want to eat. He couldn't have swallowed a bite if he tried.

"I expect it will make a difference to her" — Jessie shrugged — "if you die." Her tone implied that she personally didn't care one way or the other.

Cameron managed a thin smile at her sarcasm. "I doubt a missed meal or two will cause my demise."

"A meal or two? Do you remember when you ate last?"

Cameron shook his head. "Go away. I'll eat when I'm hungry."

"I'll leave the tray."

Cameron nodded. She could leave any damn thing

she wanted. Nothing would matter until Cassie woke up.

There was light and sound just beyond the soothing circle of sleep. She struggled to bring herself into the light. But it didn't seem to matter how hard she tried. The outside world remained in shadow, refusing to come into focus. It was too much effort, she decided. She was too tired. It was better to sleep. But the thirst! Dear God, when had she ever known such thirst? Her tongue was stuck to the roof of her mouth. It felt swollen, almost like a foreign object. It threatened to choke her. "Water," she cried aloud. And the thunder that crashed in her brain at the sound made her want to scream. But she held back. No, she wouldn't scream. As before, it would only make it worse.

Her head rose from the pillow with the pressure of a gentle hand. Something cool was pressed to her lips. Water dribbled down her chin. She gulped down a mouthful and then another. She swirled some of the water through her parched mouth, then moistened her cracked lips. Oh, heaven! What blessed relief. She sighed as she slid back—deep, deep—into the warm cocoon of soothing sleep.

It was three days later before Cassie opened her eyes. Vaguely, she remembered pain. Had it been only a dream? No, there was a dull throbbing in her head and soreness in her body. She had suffered pain, but at the moment she could not remember how or why.

Her eyes searched out the room beyond the four-poster bed. It was a big room. The walls were papered in rich brown and gold stripes. The furniture was heavy and dark, but the fabric that covered the French doors and bed was light and airy. Sunshine filled the room and a cool breeze fluttered the draperies. She snuggled deeper into the comfort of the huge, soft bed. It was a comfortable room. A man's room, she thought. Shadowy and cool, it was conducive to sleep and rest.

It took a bit of an effort, but she managed finally to turn her head toward the soft, snoring sound. There was a man sitting in a chair pulled close to the bed. He was asleep. His dark, bearded chin rested upon his chest as he breathed deeply.

Cassie smiled. He looked as tired as she felt. She must have made a sound for he came instantly awake.

His eyes blinked with surprise. He appeared amazed to find her watching him. "How do you feel?" he asked.

Cassie smiled into his warm, dark eyes. "Shall I report you for sleeping on duty?"

Cameron chuckled. He felt like laughing aloud, or crying. He wasn't sure which. He felt like grabbing her up and swinging her around the room. She was

443

all right. She was finally all right. His voice shook with emotion. "And get me fired?"

"I'm thirsty."

Instantly, a glass was brought to her lips. "Not too much. It might make you sick."

"My head hurts." Cassie lifted a shaky, weak hand to her head and felt the bandage. "Was there an accident?" she asked, puzzled.

Cameron only stared at her. She didn't remember. Should he tell her? Should he remind her of the torture she had suffered? He wasn't sure what to do. His dark eyes studied her more closely. She seemed different somehow. The change was barely perceptible, but there was a change. Suddenly, he found himself afraid, but the sensation had hardly registered when her next words hit him with the force of a blow to his gut. And he knew the truth of his unnamed fear. "Are you my doctor?" she asked.

Cassie smiled as he swept her from the bed and settled her upon the cushioned armchair near the small fire. "I'm sorry to be such a bother."

Cameron turned back to the bed and ripped the sheets and covers free of the mattress. He did it so that he wouldn't give in to the almost overpowering need to take her in his arms and do more than settle her in a chair. Jessie would be along in a few minutes to make the bed up fresh. It wouldn't hurt to give the woman a helping hand, he reasoned, especially if in doing so it saved him from making a serious mistake. "You're no bother," he assured Cassie.

"I'm sure you must have other, more important things to do than to wait on me."

Cameron shook his head. There was nothing more important than her. How much longer would he be forced to wait until she knew that?

"Are you a gentleman of leisure, then?"

Cameron smiled as he settled himself opposite her and handed her a cup of steaming tea. "Many would argue the point."

Cassie looked momentarily confused.

"Of calling me a gentlemen," he offered.

Cassie gave a low laugh, which seemed to make him shift uncomfortably in his chair. She could feel her cheeks growing pink as his warm gaze followed her every movement. "I think you haven't much of an opinion of yourself."

Cameron shrugged. "I know well enough my failings."

"Do you? I wish I could say the same." She tried to smile, but the constant fear that haunted her days and nights turned the smile into a pitiful caricature of its former beauty. "Do I have many?"

"Failings?" He smiled, his eyes filled with an unnamed emotion. "Hundreds." And at her look of disappointment, he added, "You'll remember soon."

"Why won't you tell me?" She almost cried with frustration, for she had asked him this a dozen or more times over the last two weeks. Thus far, he had

445

refused to yield to her pleas.

"You need to remember at your own pace. It would do no good to tell you," he insisted.

Cassie sighed with disgust as she sipped at her tea. "Did the doctor tell you when?"

Cameron shook his head. "He doesn't know."

"But I will remember? He did tell you that?" Her voice was threaded with panic.

Cameron nodded. "He said you'll remember when you're ready."

Cassie sighed again and gave a small nod of her head, knowing the uselessness of pressing him. Still, it was driving her mad, this not knowing. When she'd first awakened he had told her his name. Since then, nothing. Deep down, she knew she'd not be able to stand it much longer, for not remembering somehow made the lingering shadows even more frightening. "Was it so horrible, what happened?"

Cameron shrugged. "It is over. Soon it will be remembered and then forgotten forever." His voice deepened meaningfully as though he were making a pledge. "Nothing like it will ever happen again."

Cassie shivered as his tone sent chills of fear along her spine. Quickly—for it seemed as if the dark horrors that hovered constantly just out of reach were ready to pounce upon her consciousness—she forced her mind to other matters. She wasn't ready. Suddenly, she found herself gasping for breath as sweat broke out along her upper lip. That she wasn't ready was an undeniable fact. She might profess her need to know, but when hints of the truth had begun to take shape, she had run, like a coward, from the overwhelming fear of it.

Cameron didn't miss the sudden glazing of her eyes, nor her rapid, strained breathing. "You remembered something."

Cassie swallowed, willing her sudden terror under control. "No. I started to, but . . ." She lifted terrified eyes to his anxious expression. "I was afraid."

Cameron reached for her hand. Gently, he held it within the warmth of his. "I promise you, you have nothing to be afraid of. Not anymore."

Cassie smiled beneath his reassuring gaze and, believing his words, breathed a sigh of contentment. From beneath lowered lids, she studied his strong, handsome face. Why did he seem so familiar? She couldn't remember ever seeing him before. And yet, the notion persisted that she had known him before and known him well.

Cassie might not have remembered what had brought her to this state, but she did know one thing. They were not mere acquaintances as he professed. His touch was too gentle, his gaze too lingering. They had been more than just friends, she suspected. Much more than that.

The idea intrigued her. "Did I love you once?" she asked abruptly.

Cameron sputtered a mouthful of tea into his lap, and his cheeks colored as he went about the business of cleaning up the mess. "Why do you ask?"

447

Cassie shrugged. "They way you look at me. I don't think men look at women like that unless . . ." She shrugged, leaving the sentence unfinished.

Cameron grinned. "Unless?"

"Unless they were lovers," she finished bravely. Her cheeks were blazing now, but she would not take her eyes from his amused gaze.

"But you don't remember being my lover." It was less a question than a statement.

Cassie shook her head sadly. "No."

Jessie came in then with an armful of freshly laundered linens. The two women smiled at each other, but no words were exchanged. "Have you told the servants not to speak to me?" she asked softly.

Cameron shook his head. "They are aware of the problem."

"Was I kind to them?"

Cameron chuckled. "It was only I who took the brunt of your anger."

"Was I often angry?"

Cameron smiled, his eyes softening with remembered pleasure. "No."

Jessie was soon finished. Cassie began to tremble when other servants entered and started filling a huge tub with hot water.

From her first conscious moment, Cassie knew Cameron had personally been seeing to her care. She hadn't thought to question his actions, for it had seemed as natural as breathing when each day he had fed her and seen to her comfort. When he had bathed her, she had never lain naked to his view. Only small areas of her body were uncovered as necessary. As his hands had gone about the chore, his eyes had shown not a flicker of emotion. His touch had been as impersonal as a doctor's.

But now she was about to have her first real bath in two weeks, and Cassie wondered if Cameron planned on assisting. A warmth began in the pit of her belly and spread into her chest. She was embarrassed to feel her nipples growing hard with something like anticipation. Would she ask for privacy? Did she truly want any?

They were alone again. The room was suddenly silent but for the crackling of the fire and the sudden effort on her part to breathe.

"Your bath awaits," Cameron offered when it seemed clear Cassie had no intention of moving. "Would you rather I carry you? Do you feel too weak?"

"No," Cassie breathed, her voice shaking slightly. "I can manage."

Cameron stood, but made no move to leave the room. Cassie's eyes widened a bit. "Will you not leave?"

Gently, he reached for her hand, bringing her slowly to her feet. He guided her shaking form toward the tub. "It's best, I think, to remain." *Best for who?* his mind screamed. *Best to find your guts ripped apart watching her, touching her, knowing nothing can come of it?*

449

"But I can manage," she almost pleaded, suddenly fearful of the soon-to-be-shared intimacy. This was not going to be just a sponge bath like the others. As far as she knew, she had never stood naked before him or any man, and although she found herself trusting him, the notion was hard to adjust to.

"Indulge me on this, Cassie. I'd not leave you alone to find you've slid beneath the surface." He smiled into her eyes. "All my efforts would then be for naught."

"Send Jessie back."

Cameron shook his head and smiled as he pulled her nightdress over her head, reading her sudden shyness correctly. "I've seen you before; you need not feel discomfort."

"Were we that close?"

"We were."

Cassie sighed and allowed him to do as he would. She was too weak as yet to fight this, in any case. Gently, he lifted her into his arms and placed her in the soothing waters of the bath.

As he knelt at her side, his eyes showed not a flicker of the torment that racked his body. Seemingly indifferent to her nakedness, he soaped a small cloth into a lather.

"I wonder if I'll be happy about this when I remember all?" she asked, her mouth turning down in a childish sulk.

Cameron chuckled at her tone. It was clear she wasn't happy right now. But Cameron couldn't find it within himself to deny his eyes or his hands the pleasure of touching her. He went on, though he knew it could come to nothing but pain, for he wouldn't take her again until she was stronger, until she remembered, or at least until he was sure she once again returned his feelings.

Gently, he soaped her back. He smiled with relief to see that the marks were almost gone. A few more applications of salve should banish the remaining soreness.

His heart hammered in his chest as the cloth moved over her shoulders and down her arms. His fingers shook, and he prayed she wouldn't notice her effect on him. He had to remain in control. He had to remember the doctor's advice. Don't rush her. Let her remember on her own.

Cassie leaned back and closed her eyes as the cloth dipped to cleanse her breasts. She bit at her lip, forcing back a moan of pleasure. What would he do if he knew she wanted his touch? Her cheeks flamed at the wanton thought, while a shadowy picture formed at the back of her mind. She remembered a man's mouth touching her there. She couldn't see his face. Was he the man? Cassie bit back her groan of frustration. She strained to bring the picture closer and watched in silent despair as it evaporated before her eyes.

She stiffened as he lowered his hand to her midriff and belly. Her heart pounded. Her legs closed tightly, fearful of the hand that moved lower.

Why couldn't she relax? Why did his touch bring searing delight and an aching warmth to her insides?

He seemed so at ease touching her body. Why couldn't she feel the same? Had this happened before? Did he know her body? Was it as familiar to him as it was to her? Cassie smiled. But her own body wasn't familiar to her. When she looked in a mirror, a stranger stared back. What had happened? Why couldn't she remember?

He was lifting her from the tub. Slowly, he released her legs and allowed her to stand, holding her gently against him. Her wet body instantly soaked his clothes, but he was beyond caring. He was shaking. She knew from his low groan that he was fighting a losing battle to keep his distance. His voice was muffled, aching with some unknown need as he held her still in his arms. "Just for a minute. Just let me hold you for a minute."

Cassie sighed and leaned comfortably into his body, greedily absorbing his strength. God, when would this helplessness be over? She was so tired of being weak. So tired of not being able to remember.

For a moment, Cameron thought that he might die of the need that racked his body. Finally gaining some control, he sighed, wrapped her in a towel and laid her upon the freshly made bed. She was lying on her stomach as he spread the thick, soothing ointment over her back. This time, he had not kept her modestly covered as before.

She was deliciously naked to his view, and

452

Cameron cursed the need that never, for a moment, left his mind and body. He almost groaned aloud with the force of it. His hands moved over her back, her buttocks, her legs; each movement, every gentle caress bringing his pain ever closer to the breaking point. How was he to go on, knowing they had once shared an intimacy so delightful, so breathtaking as to seem unreal in remembrance? And knowing, too, that she remembered none of it.

His body trembled, starved with desire for her, and he thanked God that she didn't face him. If she knew, if she saw his arousal, would she be frightened? Would she cower in fear? Would she feel shame? Or would she answer the silent urging in his eyes with a gentle, knowing smile?

There was no need to apply the salve to her inner thighs, yet Cameron seemed unable to stop his hands from moving toward the beckoning heat. Both he and she gave a soft gasp as unerring, questing fingers probed deliciously in new, uncharted areas.

A low groan unknowingly escaped his throat as his senses reveled in the softness of her flesh. Cassie raised herself upon her elbows and looked over her shoulder. Their eyes held as his hand continued to move higher. She knew she should tell him to stop, but offered no objection as new, enticing feelings suffused her body.

How was it possible that she allowed this man such liberties? No matter that they might have once been close. In truth, she knew him but two weeks. Was she of loose morals? Would the touch of any man make her heart flutter so erratically? Would another's tender glance bring warmth to her cheeks? Cassie had no answers. She couldn't understand the need she had for him to go on, yet recognized the craving to be as strong as any she might have known. It was all new, yet somehow vaguely familiar. She shivered as his fingers came closer still to the joining of her thighs. Her eyes closed and her breathing grew shallow and light. She felt only his fingers, knew only his touch. All she could think about was wanting more.

"Are you cold?"

She shook her head, able only to moan into her pillow. She neither beckoned him on, nor told him to stop. She seemed incapable of doing more than reaching for her next breath as she waited, breathlessly waited.

Chapter Thirty-two

She was running along the seashore. Her home wasn't far away. If she craned her neck she could almost see it, high above the cliffs, set back safely from the edge. She had been laughing as she ran. But now her heart was pounding with fear. This had happened before. She knew it would, but she couldn't stop it.

And then it came, just as she had imagined. Its huge, flapping wings beat at the air around her. She breathed in the musty, heated scent and shivered. It was the scent of death. Its black wings blocked out the warmth of the sun and chilled her to the marrow of her bones. It circled above. Cassie tried to outrun it, but it was no use. It was always there, ready to snatch at her. It watched as she tried to hide, its lidless, piercing black eyes seeing all. There was no escape. Suddenly, it was reaching for her, its talons sharp as they ripped into her shoulder and back.

She couldn't let it take her. She couldn't bear to

know what would happen if it did. She looked around, desperate to find help. A man was running toward her. In a few minutes he would be at her side, but she knew it was too late. She didn't have a few minutes. She didn't have any time at all. She screamed as the bird lifted her easily into the air. She screamed again as its huge beak pecked hungrily at her neck.

She reached out an arm to the man below, whom she now recognized as Cameron. Her eyes pleaded silently, begging for help, only to find herself whisked off into the sky. She felt his despair. She knew she faced death.

She screamed again as all but the suffocating blackness of Death's feathers faded from view.

Cameron's heart pounded in his throat. Naked, and stumbling from sleep, he lunged into her room. She had been screaming again, no doubt dreaming the same dream. Soothingly, his warm hands reached for her, only to find her bed empty. She was gone!

Cameron bit back a harsh curse, his heartbeat accelerating in fear. He turned to search out the room and found her almost instantly. In her sleep she had walked again, this time into a wall. Unable to go further, she had simply stood in place while her dreams took her toward horrors her conscious mind refused to accept.

"Cassie," he soothed gently as he took her into his arms. "Cassie, you were dreaming again." God, if only she'd talk about it. Maybe then it would lessen in strength. Maybe together they could win out against this fear.

"I know," she breathed shakily as she leaned her cheek into his warm chest, awakened instantly at his touch. "I know it's a dream. I always know it's a dream, even as I dream it. And still, I can't stop the terror." She shuddered uncontrollably.

"Darling," she heard him mutter comfortingly as he pressed his lips to the top of her head. After a long moment she felt him sigh. "You'd better get back to bed."

"Come with me," she whispered in the darkness, her cheeks aflame with her brazenness, even as her body trembled still with the effects of the dream. It didn't matter that they were virtual strangers. She needed to be held and she needed this man to do it.

He had hardly touched her since that day almost three weeks ago when he'd insisted on helping her bathe. Since then, it was almost as if he were afraid to be alone with her, for his visits had grown short, his conversation brisk, his manner formal and cool.

Cassie couldn't forget what had happened after the bath. His gentle caresses had scorched her flesh, the heat of his hands searing until the core of her being threatened to burst into flame. But suddenly, he had pulled away. After a muttered excuse he was gone, leaving her bereft, her body trembling, aching for an elusive something she somehow knew they had once shared. "I'm afraid," she said now.

Cameron groaned. He wasn't going to live through

457

this. Inch by inch, he was dying. And the pain couldn't be greater if she'd plunged a knife into his belly. "Cassie," he murmured, his hesitation clear.

"Please," she cried desperately as her hold tightened around his neck.

A low growl rumbled deep within his chest as he brought her into his arms. A moment later, she was on the bed, still pressed against him. He couldn't seem to loosen his arms. His mind told him to release her, but his body refused to obey the command.

Finally, he managed to let her go long enough to light a candle on the bedside table. "To ward off the demons." He grinned at her questioning glance.

Gently, he eased her stiff body back up against his. His hand ran down her back and up again. Over and over, he caressed her until the heat of his fingers penetrated her thin nightdress.

At last, he could feel her body relax against him. "Better?"

"Umm," she sighed. "Did we ever live on a beach?"

"No."

"Did I, as a child? Did I ever tell you?"

"Yes, you mentioned a summer place once." He looked at her questioningly. "Why?"

"It's in the dream. I'm always on the beach. I keep trying, but I can't make any sense out of the rest of it."

Cameron smiled. Finally, she was telling him about the dream. His heart filled with joy. It was a beginning. She'd be able to combat the horror of it once it was discussed. "Don't try," he soothed, "Dreams don't always make sense. It's enough to talk about it. The doctor says the dreams will probably stop then."

A moment of silence passed. He stirred uncomfortably. His body was beginning to respond to her closeness, to her warmth. "I think I should go."

"No, Cameron, don't leave. I need to talk to you."

"Can't it wait until tomorrow?" His voice was almost pleading.

"I don't know if I could ask this tomorrow."

He remained at her side with a reluctant sigh.

She breathed deeply and snuggled closer. Cassie wasn't ignorant of his naked state. The soft light of the candle confirmed what she had only at first suspected. That knowledge, combined with his warm scent, kindled an excitment within her that washed away the last remnants of the dream. It took a long moment before she braved the question, and when she did, she spoke into the curve of his arm. "Do I love you?"

Cameron smiled, his gaze falling upon her wild curls. "I don't know, do you?"

Cassie heard the smile in his voice and answered unashamedly, almost without thought "Yes, I think I do. What I meant was, did I love you before?"

"What?" his whole body grew stiff as he lifted himself to his elbow and turned her onto her back. For a long moment, he stared down into her face.

"What did you say?"

"I said, did I love you?"

A look of annoyance flickered in his eyes. "Before that."

A smile curved her lips. "Oh, you mean the part about my loving you now?"

Cameron nodded, his whole body throbbing with the same aching need that had haunted him for weeks. He found himself holding his breath as he awaited her answer. "Do you?"

Soft laughter bubbled up as she replied, "How could I possibly not? You've been so wonderful, so kind, so patient."

"Oh," he answered, his disappointement obvious as he lay at her side again. "It's gratitude you feel."

Cassie pulled instantly out of his arms, came quickly to her knees and faced him. Her tone was affectionately chiding. "Numbskull! If it was gratitude, I'd say I was grateful. I know when I'm in love."

Cameron fought back joyous laughter. His heart thundered wildly in his chest. Unconcerned about his naked state, he calmly stretched out before her, his arms folded under his head. He wanted to jump for joy, yet he remained leisurely in place. She had called him "numbskull" again, a word she had picked up from Meghan, a Meghan she had no knowledge of. Something was happening. This was the third time in a week she had said something she could only have known from their time together. "Are you in love?" he asked.

"Yes!"

"So you love me." He sighed, straining to keep the wild happiness he felt from showing. He did not succeed, for his eyes fairly glowed with his elation. "What do you propose to do about it?"

Cassie chuckled as she snuggled beside him again. "I take it the idea does not repulse you."

"I guess you could say that."

"In that case, I was thinking . . ." She deliberately hesitated.

"What?"

"Well, I was wondering, if it wouldn't be too much trouble, do you think you could . . . you could maybe . . ."

"Out with it, damn it!" he growled as he rolled over and pulled her into his arms.

Cassie laughed. "Stay here tonight and maybe every night and . . ."

"And . . . ?" he prompted.

"And make love to me?"

"Oh, my God." He groaned as he closed his eyes against the pain.

Cassie giggled, well aware of his suffering. "Well, if it's too much to ask . . ."

"Shut up," he murmured, just before his lips covered hers. Neither thought the remark unusual, for to both their ears it sounded as if he said, "I love you."

He had waited so long. Week after endless week

461

until more than a month had passed. And still he waited. Her health had returned, but not her memory. And now, at last, he waited no more.

His mind swam with the pure joy of being able to touch her again. To feel her lips beneath his, soft and warm, filled with eagerness, was almost more than he could bear. To taste her sweetness, to breathe her scent filled his mind with madness. He wasn't going to be able to control this need.

There were no gentle tastings here. No teasing of the senses, no light, taunting caresses.

Cassie groaned as his tongue filled her mouth, thick and hot, greedily taking what he could, leaving behind his own, intoxicating taste. But it wasn't enough. It could never be enough. His tongue returned to fill her again and again, until her body pressed eagerly against his, unconsciously urging him for more.

Impatient hands tore her gown away. Cameron growled fiercely as he ran his hands over her body, searing her flesh, branding her with his mark forever.

He was above her, his body trembling as he fought for control. Her legs parted at the pressure of his thighs. It was too much. He had waited too long. He entered her in a swirl of blinding light and breathless ecstasy. He fought for control, but it was no use. His body couldn't stop. "I can't," he choked. "I'm sorry, Cassie." He groaned as his body shuddered convulsively and his seed burst into her warmth.

Moments later, he lifted his head from his wife's

462

neck and stared in amazement at her amused expression. He had been prepared for disappointement, perhaps even annoyance, but laughter? Would this woman never cease to amaze him?

"A bit anxious, weren't we?" she asked impishly.

His attempted smile was more like a grimace. The pleasure of holding her, filling her was, even now, too great to bear. "That never happened to me before," he said in lieu of an apology.

Cassie giggled at his sheepish expression. "Of course, I have only your word for that."

Cameron grinned. "For a lady who can't remember, you seem mighty confident that greater things are to come."

"Some things you just know." She shrugged.

"And you know it's better than that?"

She shrugged again. "I can't say positively, and since I can't remember very clearly, I wouldn't be averse to a lesson or two."

"Oh, you wouldn't?" Cameron grinned at her innocent appearing expression.

Cassie's eyes twinkled with delight. "Indeed not. Actually, I was thinking you might suggest something."

He was leaning on his elbows above her, his dark gaze greedily absorbing the beauty of her face. His finger was idly tracing the line of her brow when she asked, "Would you?"

Cameron laughed. "Of course." He made as if to think. "Well, let's see. First, I'd suggest—and this is only a suggestion, mind you . . ."

Cassie nodded in a desperate play at being serious.

"First, I could touch your lips."

"With what?"

Cameron's eyes glittered. "Mmm, a leading question, if I've ever heard one. Let's start out with my finger. Would that be all right?"

Cassie nodded. "And then?"

"And then, maybe my mouth."

"Hmm, this is beginning to sound good. What happens next?"

Cameron laughed. "Taking your mouth into consideration, I would probably continue touching it for a very long time."

"With your lips?"

Cameron nodded, his eyes alight with humor.

"And then?"

"Well, maybe I'd follow the line of your jaw to your ear. Does that sound good?"

Cassie nodded. "Very good."

"And after I tasted you there, I'd move down your neck."

Cassie swallowed.

"And then I'd lick and kiss your breasts. Probably suckle them too."

Cassie gulped. Her voice was slightly breathless and definitely uneven when she said, "That sounds interesting."

"Oh, it is. Some people say it's very erotic as well as interesting."

"I guess I could believe that." She could hardly breathe as she listened to his seductive commentary and watched the glowing promise in his eyes. "What would you do next?"

"Next, I'd kiss and touch every inch of you."

"Every inch?" she asked, her breathing growing more shallow and labored. "You wouldn't leave any part out?"

"I wouldn't leave any part out."

"I think I like the sound of that."

"I think you'd like the feel of it better." He gave her a knowing grin. "Shall I begin?"

"Tell me one thing first. Do you do this to all your ladies?"

He shook his head. "Only the ones I love."

Cassie nodded as she digested this information. "Have you loved many?"

Cameron smiled, his dark gaze tender. "I've only loved one."

Cassie grinned, her heart beating wildly with happiness. "Does the lady to whom you're doing this, do anything in particular?"

Cameron smiled. "Anything she wants."

"Perhaps some needlepoint?" Cassie giggled.

"Needlepoint's fine. He grinned arrogantly. "If she could keep her mind on it."

"Maybe plan the next day's menu?"

"That too. Although I'd hate to taste the results."

"You think she'd have a hard time concentrating, is that it?"

Cameron gave a low, wicked laugh. "Why don't we try it and you tell me." He brought his fingers to her mouth. Gently, just grazing the skin, he traced the curve of her lips until they parted on a sigh. His finger grew bolder then, touching the sensitive flesh just inside. "Do you like it so far?"

Cassie closed her eyes and gave an almost imperceptible nod.

"Pay attention now. I'm going to ask questions later. This is the next step."

Cassie's laughter was cut short by the gentle pressure of his mouth. Tenderly he touched his lips to hers. Cassie's laughter turned instantly to a moan of delight. His mouth was warm, his lips firm, his scent clean. Her head was spinning by the time he pulled away.

"Oh," Cassie breathed. "I like that very much."

"Good. Because I intend to do it for a while yet." He kissed her again, this time with slightly more purpose, and when Cassie's lips parted under the pressure of his mouth, he deepened the kiss to a hungry assault. His tongue, gentle at first, tantalized the flesh inside her lips. And Cassie thought she might float away if his body wasn't holding her down. Suddenly, that wasn't enough. His tongue drove deep into her mouth. Again and again, his mouth changed position so that he might discover every inch, drink in all her taste, breathe in all her scent.

As his tongue began the slow, erotic simulation of what he'd soon do to her body, Cassie groaned.

Though his mouth remained on hers, tingling sensations drifted over the length of her.

"You do that very well." She gasped as he tore his mouth from her at last. "Have you practiced this often?"

Cameron wasn't about to be led down this dangerous path. He smiled as his mouth hovered just above her lips, and answered with her own words. "Some things you just know." He needn't have bothered, for Cassie forgot her question the moment his mouth was joined to hers again.

She moaned. "The first and second steps are awfully good."

"Do you think so?" He chuckled softly. "Hold on, here comes the next one."

For a long time no further words were spoken. The only sounds to be heard were soft murmurings and sighs of pleasure as his mouth continued on its designated path.

It was all deliciously familiar, yet excitingly new. Had he done these things to her before? Had she always loved it this much?

She groaned as he slid further down her body. He hadn't shaved since that morning and the stubble of his beard increased her delight as his jaw and cheek rubbed lovingly against her breast.

True to his word, his tongue, hot and moist, licked hungrily at her flesh, driving her wild with its sizzling heat until she arched her back, silently begging him to take her into his mouth. But Cameron

avoided the darkened tips of her breasts as he redis-
covered the satiny texture and flavor of her creamy
flesh.

She was whimpering soft, wordless sounds as she
gently coaxed his head toward her nipples. He had to
take her in his mouth. She'd die if he didn't do it
soon.

Cassie gave a low, aching sound of rapture as his
mouth suddenly covered the sensitive tip. Flames
seared at her body as he sucked her deep into the
scorching heat of his mouth. It threatened to boil her
blood, incinerate her entire being as his teeth nipped
and his tongue soothed.

A rumbling groan came from deep within his chest
as her taste and scent suffused his senses. He was
drowning, even as his mouth devoured her.

Cassie sighed, unable to believe the magic of this
moment. She wasn't disappointed as he slid further
down her body. Her breasts might ache for more, but
the rest of her body hungered too. Anxiously, she
awaited the next assault, delighting in the feel of his
body brushing against hers.

His mouth nibbled and kissed her midriff and her
belly, until she thought she'd go mad. She wanted
more. She had to have more.

He slid lower still, and her breath caught in her
throat as his mouth moved over the junction of her
thighs, pausing for only a second as his tongue
dipped into her moistness and then down her legs.

Cassie was dazed with sensation. He had brought

her from a rational human being to a crazed, over-heated, pleasure-seeking creature.

Suddenly, she was flipped to her stomach. He was kissing the bottom of her feet. Cassie cried out as the pleasure grew almost to pain. She grabbed at the bedclothes as he moved up her leg. She'd never realized before how sensitive the back of her knees could be.

He nipped at her thighs, her hips, her buttocks, and then laved all with his tongue. Slowly, his mouth moved up her back. She was dying. She couldn't take any more of this ecstasy.

She groaned as he nuzzled her shoulders and neck. She wanted to tell him to stop, but she couldn't force the words between each gasping breath.

He turned her gently to her back, and then he began again. His mouth was on hers, stealing her breath, replacing it with his own, drinking of her taste, absorbing her essence. She was floating. It was more than she could have imagined, more than she dared hope.

His lips were suddenly and abruptly gone from her mouth. Cassie blinked her surprise and then cried out, "No!" as he parted her thighs and the heat of his mouth joined to her woman's core.

"Yes, I need to taste you, to breathe you," he murmured, his mouth once again against her burning flesh as his tongue took what it would, leaving behind the most erotic sensations a body could know. "I've waited so long, so endlessly long."

She was delirious. Out of her mind. There were no words to describe the delight. Her body was aching, striving toward an unknown objective. He gripped her hips and held her against his mouth. The ache became a soft cramp, then grew stronger, then stronger again. Her body felt as if it would break, split apart, fly off into the universe, lost forever among the galaxy of stars.

"I can't," she murmured as she fought away the coming pleasure, for the exquisite ache held a promise so powerful it threatened her very life. She tried to pull away, but his hands only tightened. "You're killing me." With a growl, his tongue took her woman's taste deep into his being.

"Then you'll die of pleasure," he murmured, but she never heard. It was too late. She couldn't pull back, she couldn't breathe, and she couldn't live through this ecstasy. Her hips strained against his mouth, no longer needing to be held in place. Wild for more, she opened to his hungry kisses, greedy for every movement of his tongue in order to live.

Wave after wave after wave. Blinding lights. Thundering blood. Demonic pleasure. Incoherent sounds. Convulsive trembling. A gasping cry. And finally, a low, breathless sigh.

He entered her then, adding tenfold to her pleasure with a hard, smooth thrust. Cameron closed his eyes against the wonder of the feelings that suffused his body. Her contractions of pleasure continued, gripping him tightly within the delicious warmth of her.

"I can feel you throbbing against me." He shuddered as he strove for control. His voice was husky, raw with need when he asked, "Do you know how that feels?"

Cassie smiled, her hips pushing hungrily against his. "Will you tell me?"

Cameron shook his head. "It's better, I think, to show you."

"Show me later," she said as she turned them so that she lay on top of him.

Cameron looked at her with some surprise.

"You said the lady could do anything she wants, remember?"

"Not now, Cassie, I can't."

"Yes, now," she returned boldly. "I want to touch you, too. I want to feel the pleasure."

"Oh God," he groaned as she began to imitate his every action. Her tongue licked, her mouth sucked, her body squirmed, flesh against flesh, until he thought he'd die with the pleasure of it.

His breathing grew ragged as her mouth moved down the length of his body. Harsh sounds escaped his throat as her tongue and lips followed the thin line of hair below his flat stomach. His moans of pleasure urged her on. Lower and lower.

His body jerked as she took him deep into her mouth. "Cassie," he cried. "Stop," he moaned, but his hands cupped her head, pulling her closer, belying his words. "Too much, oh God, it's too much," he said between gasping breaths.

Suddenly, he reached down and slid her body up. A moment later she was straddling his waist and he was filling her to the hilt.

Cassie's head was flung back and she swayed drunkenly.

He rolled her beneath him again, and, in control once more, thrust himself deeper and deeper into her moist warmth. "Are you thinking of your wifely duties now?"

Cassie mumbled incoherent words.

"Are you?" he insisted as he strengthened each thrust.

Cassie tore at his back, strained against his hips, cried out her need. Her eyes were squeezed shut, her every breath an effort as the torture came and grew in agonizing leaps until she was mindless but for one thought. She had to find release. "Cameron, Cameron, please," she whimpered.

"Don't fight it. Let it come. Let it take us both."

"Yes, yes, yes," she babbled mindlessly, until the pleasure came again, this time stronger than before, wilder than before. Her cry of triumphant release was muffled by his lips as tears of joy misted her eyes.

Cassie's heart was filled with warmth. She knew she had brazenly coaxed him into sharing her bed. But she'd somehow known they had once had a relationship. She couldn't have felt so comfortable, so at ease with him if he were truly a stranger. Her spirits soared and she giggled softly. She had made love with her own husband. "You are a beast."

Cameron chuckled, his eyes closed with contentment. "You'll turn my head with such compliments."

"Why didn't you tell me I was your wife?"

"Do you . . . ?"

"Remember?" Cassie interrupted as she glanced up and then snuggled her face against his damp chest. She settled herself more comfortably upon him. "No, you called me your wife when you were in the middle of . . ." She shrugged as she heard his deep chuckle. "You know."

Cameron laughed heartily. "It's called making love."

Cassie slapped his chest. "I know what it's called." She leaned on her elbows and looked down into his eyes as she struggled to keep a straight face. "Were you always this bad?"

"Am I bad?" He grinned, seemingly delighted with her opinion of him.

"Horrid," she answered emphatically. Something flickered in her eyes. Obviously thinking of something else, she moved to straddle him, unwittingly giving him a luscious view of swaying breasts, tiny waist and smooth hip. "You know, when you grin like that, you remind me of someone." She hesitated for a long moment before the picture of a little girl came clearly to her mind. "I must be mistaken." Suddenly, her eyes widened with something like shock. "Do we

473

have any children?"

"Together?"

Cassie gave him a dry, impatient look. "No, apart."

"I have a child."

"Do you?" She blinked, clearly amazed.

"Don't look so surprised. It's been known to happen."

"But she's not mine," she said almost sadly.

"You know it's a girl? Do you remember her name?"

Cassie shook her head. "When I close my eyes, I can see her face. She looks exactly like you." She shot Cameron a questioning look.

Cameron nodded. "I was married before. My wife died."

Cassie gave a nod of her own. Unthinkingly, she commented, "I know, she was running away . . ." She stared at him, her mouth open with surprise that the words should come so easily. "With her lover?" she asked, as if she wasn't sure she remembered correctly. Suddenly, her finger tip touched his cheek and ran the length of his scar. Her intent gaze locked with his dark eyes, and she watched as pure happiness filled their depths. She asked with something like awe, "Was she out of her mind to leave someone like you?"

Cameron grinned as he pulled her down and hugged her tightly against him. Ignoring her question, he laughed. "Oh Cassie, it's coming back. It's starting."

"I know," she whispered and shivered with apprehension. "I think I'm afraid."

"Don't be," he soothed as he brushed her hair back from her face. Just before his lips claimed her mouth, he murmured, "They're only memories. I'm here. I'll always be here."

"Cameron, she's not going to bother me. I want to see her. As a matter of fact, I can't wait to see her." Cassie slammed the brush down and turned to face him. They had been arguing most of the morning. His back was to her as he shaved. She could tell by his rigid stance that she wasn't making any headway.

She walked over to him and wrapped her arms around his middle. "I'm not sick. I just can't remember," she said softly. "Are you afraid I'll hurt her?"

"Thickheaded wretch," he said as he turned and took her in his arms. "There's not a possibility of that. You couldn't hurt anyone. You don't have it in you."

"Then, why?" Cassie fairly ached to see the one face she could remember. Why wouldn't he allow the girl to come home?

He smiled. "Because I wanted to surprise you with a trip. I wanted to take you somewhere and keep you all to myself for just a bit longer."

Cassie's eyes widened with surprise. A radiant smile curved her lips. "When did you come up with that?"

"Last night."

She laughed. "Last night?"

He nodded, his eyes alight with deviltry. "I thought, since you're shown me how much better you are, we could chance a short honeymoon."

"We've never had one?"

He shook his head and rubbed his soapy cheek against hers. "An oversight I'm about to correct."

But Cassie had better ideas than rubbing cheeks. She turned her head and slid her tongue along the contours of his mouth. "When we get back, then? Will you let her come home?"

Cameron gasped and then gave a deep, satisfying groan as her tongue quickly took advantage of his parted lips. "Umm," he promised, in the affirmative, but it was already too late, for both had forgotten the question.

Chapter Thirty-three

"I wish you were less obstinate. How am I to know what or how much to pack if you won't tell me where we're going?"

"Pack enough for a few weeks." He eyed her frilly nightdresses spread neatly across the bed. With a careless toss, he flung them behind him to land in a pile of fluff and lace ruffles upon a chair. "You'll have no need of these."

Cassie gave a soft laugh at the determined glint in his eyes. "No?" she asked, in supposed innocence. "Will I find the nights unusually warm?"

"You might say that." His eyes twinkled merrily.

"Are we bound for the tropics, then?"

"Darling, I'd venture to say you'd find the nights warm were we bound for the North Pole."

Cassie arched a delicate brow at his obvious boasting, then gave a deliberately weary sigh. "Cameron, one of these days we're going to have to discuss your sad lack of confidence." With that, she threw a pillow at his head.

Cameron chuckled as he dodged the pillow. Cassie yelped as he grabbed her around the waist, spun her to face him and flung her upon the bed. Before she had a chance to initiate a means of escape, his body covered hers. "Are you implying I merely boast of my abilities? Shall I prove the truth of it?"

Her body bucked as she tried to dislodge him. "If you expect me to finish packing in time, I wouldn't start anything," she warned, her eyes alight with humor.

Cameron's eyes darkened with pleasure, for her movements, though unintentional, were most definitely arousing. Actually, almost anything the woman did aroused him. He couldn't remember a time when he didn't need to touch her, to kiss her, to love her. "How long do we have?"

Cassie giggled, recognizing the signs. She knew full well her effect on him. "You just told me an hour. Have you already forgotten?"

"It's hard to remember anything when you move like that," he answered honestly. His hand was snaking under her skirt. She felt the strings to her drawers come undone. "You won't be needing these, either. Don't pack any."

"Cameron, we haven't time," she insisted lamely as he pulled the drawers down her legs. "I have to finish."

"We've time enough for this. I expect it to take only a moment."

Cassie laughed. She couldn't stop a shiver of excitement from racing through her as his fingers moved enticingly up her thigh. "Really?" she asked, her voice quavering slightly. "That sure of yourself, are you?"

"Watch."

Cassie groaned as his fingers slid unerringly into the warmth of her body. "Cameron, stop it," she said in a choked voice, even as her legs parted to accept him and her hips arched into his thrusts. She couldn't stop her trembling response. A moment later she didn't think to try. His tongue stroked her mouth as his fingers continued their magic. Her cry was absorbed into his mouth. Her climax was sudden, powerful, mind-shattering, and almost instantaneous.

Cameron smiled. When she once again managed some control over her breathing, his eyes showed clearly his delight.

Cassie sighed, pretending outrage. "Now my hair is a mess, my skirt is wrinkled, and I doubt I have the strength to finish packing. I hope you're satisfied."

"The question is, I think, are you satisfied?"

Cassie snorted. "If you think I'm so mad as to further inflate your ego, think again. You're arrogant enough, thank you."

Cameron smiled, all male confidence, as he rolled off her and allowed her to struggle to her feet. Her knees trembled beneath her weight. Cameron's sharp eye didn't miss the slight quiver. "You already have."

Cassie shot him a warning look. "You can take that satisfied smirk off your face, right now."

"Am I smirking?" he asked, pretending great surprise.

"Beast!" she growled. "Get out of here, so I can finish."

Cameron gave her a hungry look and smiled. "If I promise I won't touch you again, can I watch?" he asked, much too sweetly innocent.

"Would you promise that?" Her eyes widened in disbelief.

"No." Cassie couldn't control her laughter as he came from the bed and moved toward her with a most purposeful gleam in his eye. She shivered with excitement. God, but she loved it when he looked at her like that.

"I just thought I'd ask," he said as his arm snaked around her tiny waist and he pulled her up against him.

It was another two hours before the bags were packed and they left the house.

Standing in the bow of the *Baltimore Lady,* Cassie held onto the railing. She smiled with sheer delight as the onrushing wind dislodged the pins from her fiery hair and swirled the loosened mane in wild disarray about her face and shoulders. A fine spray of ocean water covered her hair and skin with a sparkling, diamondlike mist.

480

"You'll be soaked to the skin if you stand here much longer."

Cassie grinned as she tilted her head toward her husband. Shooting him a knowing look, she taunted, "And it would cause you much distress to find my clothes plastered against me."

"On the contrary, madam. It would cause me much delight. I worry only of the chill you might take."

"Neither of us would worry of chills if you put your arms around me, sir." She smiled in gentle invitation.

Cameron instantly complied, and, for a long moment, they silently watched the ship cut through the dark waters. Then, breathing into the side of her neck, he remarked softly, "I do believe that was the first time you ever asked me to touch you."

"Was it?" she asked as she turned astonished eyes toward his teasing expression. At his nod, her gaze turned playful, "In that case, I'd best watch myself more carefully in the future."

"It wouldn't do to let me think you're interested, is that it?"

Cassie smiled as she turned in his embrace. "It wouldn't do at all. Ladies aren't supposed to like this sort of thing."

"So I've heard." Cameron sighed. "One wonders what it would take to get a certain lady to admit to the truth of it."

"No doubt you've heard the proverb, 'Actions speak louder than words'?"

"Indeed, and I readily agree. Still, there are moments when a man needs to know he's wanted for himself, rather than merely in response."

"And you think you're not?" Cassie's laughter was silky soft and filled with mystery.

"Have you ever tried to seduce me?"

"Have I ever needed to?"

"Don't change the subject."

Cassie giggled. Her mouth reached up and brushed against his jaw. "Shall I seduce you, sir?"

Cameron shrugged, feigning disinterest. "You might try if you wish."

Cassie's eyes gleamed as she accepted the dare. "But you don't suppose I can manage it?"

"I couldn't say, since I'm unacquainted with your capabilities."

"I wouldn't boast of my capabilities, as do some." She eyed him knowingly. "Still, I expect I can manage this chore."

"Can you?" he asked, trying for an innocent tone, but unable to keep the eagerness from his voice. "One wonders how you might go about it."

Cameron's back was to his crew as he held her close against him. Both were aware that even in the growing dusk they were in clear sight of anyone strolling the deck. Still, Cassie knew no one could see her daring movement as she brought her hand between their bodies. Boldly, she caressed his growing desire.

Cameron's eyes widened with surprise. Quickly, he

covered the emotion, pretending only slight interest. "Is that your plan?"

"It's part of it."

"And you expect *that* to work?" he asked in supposed disbelief.

Cassie chuckled, wise to his scheming ways. "Among other things."

"Namely?"

"Shall I show you here?"

"Show me in our cabin. Tell me here."

Cassie shrugged. "A certain man I know has taught me, well, a number of interesting things."

"Is this man special to you?"

"Mmm, yes. Very special indeed."

"What exactly is it you feel toward this man?" Cameron insisted, always in need of her declarations of love.

"Well," she mused, "that's not an easy question to answer."

"Give it a try."

"I love him," she said huskily as she gently stroked back the lock of hair that had fallen across his forehead. "That's a fact. But he is surely the thickest man I know."

Cameron grinned, his eyes alight with pleasure. "And you know so many?"

Cassie ignored his taunt. "And besides being thick, he can be so infuriating."

"Indeed?"

"Oh yes. You see, once he puts his mind to

something, nothing can persuade him otherwise. And when the urge comes upon him . . . Oh Lord, I swoon at the thought"—she raised her hand to her brow theatrically—"he doesn't care if he rips away my clothes. Why, he's ruined at least a dozen night-dresses alone. As a matter of fact he once . . ." Cassie gasped as she watched a picture slowly unfold in her mind's eye. "Cameron, did you tear my whole ward-robe?"

Cameron chuckled. "I'm afraid I did."

"And did I return the favor?"

Cameron pulled her closer, his delight evident. "You see, you do remember. Each day you remember more."

Cassie was silent for a moment. Finally, she breathed a long sigh and looked up at him. "Where was I?"

"You were telling me about this man you love and the interesting things he's taught you."

"Oh yes, and they were that."

"Still, you've yet to tell me what they might be."

"Well, for one thing, I know how to give a proper kiss."

"A *proper* kiss?" he asked, clearly unimpressed.

Cassie shook her head. "I mean to kiss properly."

Cameron smiled as he nodded. "I see. And how does one go about that."

"It's easier to show you than to say."

"It's better, I think, to wait until dark before we sample this new knowledge. I wouldn't want to find myself fighting off my entire crew."

Cassie laughed and tried to pull out of his embrace. "Just finish telling me," he insisted, his arms refusing to relinquish their hold.

"Well, after you were kissed quite thoroughly . . ."

"Would you use your tongue?" he interrupted.

"Oh, indeed."

"Go on."

"Well, after that, I would run my mouth down your body."

"All the way down?"

Cassie nodded.

"How far down?" His voice was taking on a definitely husky quality.

She laughed. "Oh, all the way. Probably to your toes."

"Would you stop anywhere along the way? Anywhere in particular?"

"I would."

"Where do you think?"

"I think about here," she remarked as she returned her hand to the junction of his thighs.

"And then what would you do?"

"I'd kiss you again."

"Would you?" He moved his hips only a fraction of an inch into her caress lest his crew surmise their deliciously wicked conversation. "There?"

"Would you like that, do you think?" She grinned knowingly.

Cameron closed his eyes and groaned.

"Now, do you believe I'm capable of seduction?"

Cameron's body shuddered. "I'd believe you capable of anything."

"Sails ho," came the distant voice of the lookout from high atop the main mast, interrupting their conversation.

A voice at the helm called out for direction.

"Starboard, sir, four hundred yards," came the lookout's reply. "And coming fast."

Cassie did not at first take much notice of the sudden activity around them. Other ships had often been sighted during the week they had already spent sailing down the eastern seaboard. She had no notion that this particular ship was any different from the dozen or so others they had encountered. Not, that is, until Cameron called the lookout to identify the oncoming vessel. It wasn't the answer that chilled her heart, but the look in Cameron's eyes. "It flies no flag, sir."

Cameron cursed and instantly ordered the crew to run up all sails. "There could be trouble. Get below," he said as he instantly left her side.

Cassie watched in some amazement as the seamen ran unerringly to their posts. Barefoot, they scrambled up the masts. With perfect balance, they walked along the yard. Suddenly, one loud crack after another sounded in the tension filled air as the huge white canvases were unfurled. Once secured, the sails catapulted the ship forward with such sudden ferocity as to nearly topple Cassie over the railing. Orders were called, lines were tightened, the boom rolled smoothly to port, and the ship turned into the wind.

During the past week, the shoreline had often been in sight. Today, however, the *Lady* had ventured farther out to sea than usual. Cassie's gaze now searched out the horizon as fear trickled down her spine. How far out were they? Could they make port before . . . before what? Why was she so afraid? Why did the crew seem so obviously nervous?

Was it a pirate ship that followed? Were they in real danger? Did that danger extend to the possibility of their losing their lives?

Cassie couldn't stand the suspense. Anything was better than the course her imagination was taking. It didn't matter that Cameron now stood at the helm barking out orders. She didn't care that he had just told her to go below. She had to know what might lie ahead.

Darting out of the path of running crewmen, skirting dangling lines and neatly coiled rigging, she finally managed to reach him. "What is it? Why is everyone hurrying so?"

Cameron shot her a startled glance. His surprise at finding her standing at his side soon turned to annoyance. "Didn't I tell you to get below? Suppose they should fire upon us?"

"Do you think they will? Are they pirates?"

"They fly no flags, Cassie," he said, letting that fact speak for itself. Suddenly, he thundered, "Goddammit! O'Malley, secure that rigging on number two

487

mast!"

Turning to Cassie again and noticing the fear in her white face, he lowered his voice and strove for a more soothing tone. "I want you to go below, Cassie. There's a good chance we can outrun them; we're not but a few miles from shore. But if they should fire upon us, I don't want you hurt by flying debris."

"What about you?"

He brushed aside her concern. "I'll be all right."

"I'm staying!" Cassie raised her hand, forestalling any objection. "If the ship takes a direct hit, I might be trapped below. If I'm going to die, I want it to be here with you."

Cassie said the words with a calmness she didn't feel. Still, no matter her fear, it would be more terrifying to go below and await her final end there. She knew she was right when Cameron didn't fight her decision. Suddenly, his failure to argue with her filled her with real panic. Like a child, she wanted to jump into his arms and beg him to hold her safe until the danger passed. But Cassie wasn't a child, and the last thing Cameron needed was a hysterical woman on his hands. She took a deep breath and fought for control. If she wanted safety, she'd best let the man be about his business.

No one aboard cared a whit that their running appeared an act of cowardice. To remain and try to fight would have been suicidal. The *Baltimore Lady* was a merchant ship. No cannon marred its smooth, clean lines. The few arms aboard were short range handguns.

No one had to tell Cassie that their flight was fraught with danger. Under normal conditions, it would have been an act of madness to run full speed into the approaching night. But now, they had no alternative. They had to run, or risk capture, for no one harbored any doubts that the oncoming ship was anything less than what it seemed.

An hour later it was dark at last, and Cassie drew a long breath of relief. The moon and stars were blotted out by thick clouds. As she stood at the railing and peered out over the ocean, she could see nothing but black water. If the ship following them couldn't be seen, she reasoned, neither could they. Lights and fires had long been extinguished, and Cassie smiled, knowing they were protected by a veil of darkness. Surely, they would make it to safety.

A man's voice rang out as he tripped over something and fell with an audible thud to the deck. The sound seemed unnaturally loud in the imposed quiet.

Cameron whispered to his first mate, "Mason, tell that idiot to shut the hell up! How long has he worked on ship not to know sound carries over the water? Pass the word to the rest. I want silent running. Anyone making unnecessary noise will personally answer to me."

Cassie sat in the ship's stern and leaned against the railing. She smiled. Not more than ten feet separated her from Cameron, yet she couldn't see a thing. Hour after hour passed as the ship continued to cut

489

through the black water. All was silent except for the eerie creaking of the lines and the swish of the ship's wake.

As the ship took the swells, its gentle swaying motion gradually lulled Cassie into a light sleep.

She huddled deeper into herself as the wind began to howl. Great gusts snapped at the sails, jarring the ship forward and causing the mast to groan under the sudden impact. A heavy drop of rain splashed on her forehead and ran down her face. A storm was fast approaching. Cassie only prayed they'd make it to shore before they were blown off course.

She gave a low, mournful sigh as moments later the rain came down in earnest. It took no more than a blink of an eye before she was soaked to her skin. For a second, she thought to go below and search out a covering, then discarded the notion. She owned nothing that would protect her from this kind of rain, and she knew she would only grow wet again once she returned to the deck. In any case, she doubted her ability to find the stairs or the cabin doorway in the dark.

When she heard the sound of wood being split asunder, she at first put the noise to the raging elements. An instant later, she knew the truth of it as her body began a helpless slide across the deck. Her startled cry was lost in the thunderous crash and low groan that followed as a gaping hole was torn in the hull. Thick wooden beams, some wider than the span of a man's two hands, were crushed like paper against the massive boulder that stood in the ship's path, treacherously concealed by the black, turbulent night.

Cassie was flung, as if weightless, across the smooth, wet planking and through the widely spaced railing posts that separated the poop from the main deck fifteen feet below. Instinctively, she caught one of the thick posts, and clung to it, swaying dangerously above the black emptiness.

For a heartbeat, there was total stillness, then sudden yelling and the running of many feet. Cassie didn't have to be told that the ship was lost. Nothing could take that kind of punishment and remain afloat.

She hung there for endless moments as Cameron went about the immediate business of seeing to his ship. Her heart stood still when she heard him give the order to abandon ship.

She gave a low cry. For a second, she thought he might have forgotten her. Were they going to leave her behind? Her arms were beginning to ache. Her hold tightened in a desperate grip as her wet fingers threatened to slide away. She couldn't stay like this much longer. She had to get help.

Through the noise of wind and thunder, Cameron heard the soft cry and searched through the blackness for its owner. "Where the hell are you?" he bellowed over the wild storm.

"Here, here! I'm over here," came her response.

Cameron moved toward the sound. Inadvertently,

his boot hit against the post she held and smashed into her fingers. She cried out as the pain raced up her arm. Without thinking, her fingers let go. Now she hung by one arm, and her swinging weight wrenched at her shoulder. "Cameron," she gasped, "down here. I'm hanging over the railing."

A vague, shadowy picture flashed through her mind, and, for a brief moment, her agonizing position seemed somehow familiar. Why should that be? she wondered. A moment later, she forgot the thought, her attention once again on the need to maintain her precarious hold.

Cameron cursed as his fingers groped toward the sound of her voice. At last, his hand touched upon her wrist and clung to it. Quickly, he pulled her up and over the railing. She was in his arms. Their mutual sighs of relief were lost in the roar of the storm and the now hysterical voices below them.

Flashes of lightning lit up the sky and Cassie stared through the teeming rain in wide-eyed amazement as crew members ran wildly over the deck, shoving and bumping into one another in a frantic dash for safety.

The longboat was ordered lowered. "Let's go," Cameron said sharply as he nearly dragged her down the steps to the main deck. They were perhaps twenty feet from where the men were exiting the ship when the terrifying boom of a cannon was heard at close range. A whistling sound was coming toward them. Closer. Closer. Cameron pulled her back and flung her to the deck near their cabin door. He covered her body with his.

Upon impact, the night was rent with agonized screams, screams so horrifying they nearly muffled the vicious sounds of nature. Flying pieces of wood became deadly missiles.

Cameron's body jumped as he took two small, razor-sharp fragments in his back. Ignoring the pain, he came to his feet and bellowed above the raging storm. "Cut it loose. Cut it loose!"

Cassie never noticed the shoreline was within sight. Her mouth hung open with shock. She couldn't believe her ears. He was telling the men to leave, while dozens of others, including herself and this madman, were left helpless on deck.

Perhaps he had cracked under the strain. Whatever his reasoning, she couldn't allow him to condemn her and the rest of the crew to certain death. She had to do something. "No!" Cassie cried as she scrambled to her feet, intent on reaching the now slack lines. Rain slashed into her mouth as she called out, "There's more. Don't leave us!"

Chapter Thirty-four

There was no time to explain, not a second to waste. Clamping his hand over her mouth and muffling her hysterical pleas, Cameron dragged her back from flinging herself over the side. He was muttering a round of curses as he shoved her toward their cabin.

Cassie tensed at the sudden, high pitched whine of another cannonball coming at the ship. This one missed its objective by no more than ten feet. She gasped as it splashed into the sea and raised a shower of water colder than the rain.

"Bastards," Cameron muttered as still another broadside was fired. He dragged her trembling form into his cabin. Cassie watched in silent amazement as he stripped off his jacket and shirt. An oilcloth bag was snatched from his trunk and filled with a blanket, his discarded clothes, two knives, and a handful of beef jerky. Without a word, his hands fumbled beneath her skirt, and her petticoat joined the grow-

494

ing assortment of articles in the bag. Cassie was too shocked by his actions to offer the slightest objection. Her head was spinning. What in God's name did he think he was doing?

Her mouth opened at last, ready to bombard him with accusations, when he grabbed her hand and dragged her out of the cabin. A moment later, they were running along the deck, skirting the debris and gaping holes left by cannon fire. They stopped only when they reached the bow of the ship. For a moment, his eyes scanned the waters below. Apparently finding what he was looking for, he nodded and suddenly jumped.

Cassie screamed as she felt herself plunging through the darkness. Since her hand was still in his, she was dragged headlong into the sea. Black water closed over her head, filling her mouth and nose. She railed at him, choking and gasping for breath as her head broke the water's surface, "You maniac! You could have told me you were going to jump." Angrily, she pulled against his grip. "Let go of my hand!"

But Cameron had other things on his mind. He didn't even hear her words, or recognize her anger. Another cannonball burst free of its cylinder and slammed into his ship. Chunks of jagged wood filled the sky. One heavy piece, rising higher than the others, hung in the air for a moment, then crashed back to the churning waters with a loud splash. Its sharp edge dealt a mighty blow to the side of Cassie's head.

She moaned at the jarring impact, but the sound was involuntary. She never heard it, nor did she realize she slid beneath the water.

Cameron grabbed at the large piece of floating wood he had spied from the deck. He turned to pull Cassie closer. Amazement shadowed his eyes when he found her hanging limp, her head beneath the water. Panic grabbed at his guts as he quickly pulled her up. His mouth hovered close to her own, and he sighed with relief as he felt her soft breath against his face.

Cameron lifted her higher still, so that the upper portion of her body now lay across the wide planking. He plopped the oilskin bag at her side. Then, holding tightly to both her and the planking, his strong legs began to kick, moving them closer to the shore.

Cameron estimated they were no more than half a mile away. There was no doubt in his mind he'd make it. What caused him a moment's panic was the blood. The side of Cassie's head was covered with it. Somehow, she had sustained a wound. Guilt assailed his being, and he loosed a wild string of curses mingled with desperate prayers.

If she died, it would be his fault. Why had he insisted they take this voyage? Why was it so necessary to have her to himself? Surely, they could have found another way to be alone together. If he hadn't been such a selfish fool, Cassie wouldn't now be unconscious, perhaps, God forbid, dying.

The water was filled with other men holding to floating chunks of wood. Those in the longboat were taking some of the injured from the sea. But Cameron was loathe to call out for help lest he further endanger those who might come to his aid. The longboat was just out of range of the cannon, while he, as yet, was not.

The tide was pushing him farther down shore than he had expected. It didn't matter. Once they were ashore and he'd assured himself of Cassie's welfare, they'd surely find one another.

But Cameron hadn't counted on the lust for blood of the men who attacked his ship. They didn't hesitate when the order came to lower their boats.

Cameron looked behind him and gave a sad groan of loss as his abandoned ship was set aflame. In the light from the flaming vessel three small craft could be seen bobbing in the water. The pirates were searching out helpless prey. Shots were fired, cries heard. Cameron grunted as he pushed harder. He had to get Cassie away. The bastards were shooting at the floundering men for the simple pleasure of killing. Soon, the water would be filled with the scent of blood, and that, of course, would bring the sharks.

Cameron held back the scream that threatened as something huge and heavy brushed past his leg and jarred his body. He stopped all movement. He held his breath. His heart thudded with the coming horror. His eyes closed, his body tensed. He waited for the excruciating pain he would feel when the huge jaws clamped down on the lower half of his body. And when this one finished his bloody assault, the others would come and make quick use of Cassie. But amazingly, the eating machine moved on, showing no interest in Cameron's temporarily paralyzed form, the scent of blood drawing him instead toward the injured men some distance away.

It took some minutes before Cameron realized he was still alive. Finally, he set out again, this time making less aggressive strokes, and allowing the tide to bring him closer to shore.

Cassie moaned as he half dragged, half carried her up the narrow stretch of sand and into the woods. He looked down at her semi-conscious figure. Her head bled still. There was a deep cut just above her ear. She moaned again as he tore a piece of her skirt and pressed the soft pad to her cut.

Cameron had to get her help. He hated to leave her alone, but the longboat had been beached some distance down the shore. He had to get the clean water and medicine he knew were in the boat.

He cursed as he searched through the oilskin bag. Why hadn't he thought to bring medicine, or something at least for the pain that she would feel when she awakened? He emptied the bag's contents on the ground and nodded with some satisfaction. Almost everything was dry. He pulled his shirt from the jumbled clothing. Quickly, he stripped away her soaked dress and underthings. Gently, he covered her with his shirt, then wrapped her in the blanket.

He slid the two knives into the waistband of his trousers. His legs shook with fatigue and his body was awash with fear at leaving her alone as he moved out of the woods and began the long walk down the beach. If luck was with him, he'd find his men and be back with what he needed in less than half an hour.

Moments later, the voices of two men could be heard as they walked along the shore not far from where Cassie lay. "I tell you I heard a woman."

"We're wasting our time. Somebody's goin' to see the fire. We gotta get out of here."

"We got a while yet."

"Maybe it was only a cabin boy."

"I know the sound of a woman, stupid. The bitch is probably hiding in the woods."

"Right. She swam by herself through the sharks."

Cassie moaned again.

"Did you hear that?"

"I didn't hear nothin'."

"I tell you I heard a moan. She's in there."

"Jesus, I never seen a hornier bastard in my life . . ." Danny cursed as his partner pushed him forward and he tripped over Cassie's still form lying just inside the cover of woods.

"What did I tell you?" Jack announced triumphantly.

Danny chuckled lasciviously. "I've got to hand it to you, Jack. She's a soft one, she is."

"Wanna take her back to the ship?"

"Yeah, but not till we're done."

A man knelt on each side of her. Jack pulled away her covering. When he spied her clad only in a shirt, he grinned. "Looks like she was waitin' for us."

Danny's eyes bulged, and a thick tongue slipped out to lick his lips at the sight of Cassie bare legs. He agreed with a short nod. "That it does."

"Jesus! Will you look at that," Jack exclaimed as he pushed the shirt up to her shoulders.

"Will we toss for first turn?"

"No fuckin' way. I heard her. I'm first."

"I found her," Danny almost whined.

Jack was already fumbling with the ties on his trousers. Murder gleamed in his hard eyes. It didn't matter to him that Danny had been his friend for the last two years. They had lived together, eaten together, and traveled most of the Atlantic side by side. When in port they had whored together. Still, he wouldn't have hesitated to slice his friend's throat if need be. "I'm first."

Danny shrugged. The woman was a beauty to be sure, but he knew Jack all too well. Nobody was worth dyin' for. He, too, was working his already stiff member into a ready state. "Just hurry it up, then. I ain't goin' to be able to wait too long."

Cassie moaned. God, the pain was there again. Her head was pounding. The ache was unbearable. Was she in the cabin still? Would Cameron never come for her? But he had come, a soft voice reminded her. Cassie smiled as the memory returned.

Yes, he had come. He had taken her away. He had held her secure in a warm cocoon of love.

Cassie wanted to laugh aloud. She had loved him before, and now, she had grown to love him for a second time. And all the while, he patiently waited. God, was there a man to compare?

She opened her eyes and blinked, unable to believe the sight that greeted her. The total blackness of the night had given way to a murky gray as the storm moved on. She was able to see the man facing her quite clearly. His skin was pockmarked. A mustache drooped over his lips and ran down the sides of his mouth. Water ran over his face. It dripped down his stringy, shoulder-length hair and onto her belly. He was kneeling between her open legs. Her body was naked to his view. She shivered with disgust. She was wet and cold. Why was she lying naked in a drizzling rain? This couldn't be happening. Of course it wasn't happening. It couldn't be true. She was dreaming, that was it! In a moment she'd awaken and find herself warm and cozy with Cameron at her side.

Suddenly, harsh fingers grabbed at her thighs, pulling them farther apart. Cassie knew this was no dream. It was a living nightmare! "No!" she screamed as Danny grabbed her flailing arms and held her to the wet sand.

He chuckled, and, in an effort to stop her cries, covered her mouth with his. Cassie gagged as his tongue pushed its way deep inside. The stench of his breath and the brutal assault of her mouth brought bile to rise threateningly. She tried to force it back, but only gagged again. It was no use. She couldn't stop the sickening lurch of her stomach. It erupted and gushed from her throat, hot and bitter, into his mouth.

Danny released her hands. He choked and spat upon the ground. Enraged at her involuntary reaction, he delivered a stunning blow to her jaw. "Bitch!"

But the blow did little toward rendering her senseless. In truth, she barely felt the punch, so intent was she in fighting off her attackers. She'd never allow this. They'd have to kill her before she'd lie still and allow her body to be abused.

The moment he freed her hands, her nails raked the length of Danny's face while her legs kicked wildly at the man kneeling before her. Danny cursed again and delivered yet another jolting blow.

Jack's leering grin showed two missing front teeth as he leaned over her. "Hold her still," he grunted as she tried again to kick him away. Those were the last words Jack would speak before meeting his maker. Something hit his chest with a breathtaking jolt. For a second, he thought she might have succeeded in freeing herself. Befuddled, he stared stupidly at his chest, expecting to see her foot or knee pressing against him. But that couldn't be. His hands held her legs. How then, had she kicked him? Jack's eyes widened with surprise as he finally noticed the handle of a knife protruding from his chest. For just an instant, he wondered how it had gotten there. He only had that instant before the blackness closed over him. He never knew his body slumped forward.

The sight had barely registered in Danny's brain when a hand grabbed at his head, holding it still for just the fraction of a moment it took for his throat to be sliced.

Cassie screamed again as a shower of blood squirted over her breasts. Her empty stomach heaved with disgust as the warm liquid pumped over her. She shivered with revulsion as its sickly sweet scent penetrated her senses.

She didn't realize she'd been rescued. She only knew that her captors had loosened their hold. She scrambled to her feet and started to run as Cameron pushed the two bodies aside. She didn't think of where she was going. She didn't care that she was covered only in a shirt. She had to get away.

Cameron cursed as he saw her dash into the dense foliage. "Cassie," he called. "Cassie, damn it, stop!"

Cassie stopped at the sound of his voice. With a cry, she turned and was instantly enclosed within the warmth of his arms.

Silently, he thanked God that he had returned in time. Although sobbing with fright, she seemed otherwise unhurt. With a soothing word, he left her briefly to retrieve the supplies he had brought from the boat. Gently, he stripped away the blood soaked shirt, then cleansed the stains on her skin. He rewrapped her in the blanket, grabbed his bag, took her in his arms, and moved farther into the woods.

On a rise above the beach, he sat beneath the protection of a huge oak and held her until her sobs lessened and she slept.

An hour passed before she stirred. When he glanced at her face, he noticed her eyes were wide with astonishment. She seemed momentarily befuddled. "What are we doing here?"

"Oh, God," he groaned as he pulled her tightly against him. "You didn't forget everything again?"

Cassie blinked and then smiled into his worried face. "No. I remember it all now."

"Everything?"

Cassie nodded and sighed as she pressed her cheek to his chest. For a long moment, she listened to the steady beat of his heart, gaining strength before she spoke of the horror. Her gaze was soft and filled with hurt when she lifted her face to his. "Why did she do it?"

"Diana?"

Cassie nodded.

"She was evil, Cassie. Some people are just that. There is no other reason for the things they do.

"How's your head?"

Cassie raised her hand and realized he had bandaged her head as she slept. "It hurts, but it's all right." She looked around. From atop the rise, she could see the now calm ocean below. "Where are we, do you think?"

"Oh, I'd guess somewhere along the Carolina coast."

"Which one?"

"Probably South." He tucked the blanket more snugly about her.

"Aren't you going to sleep with me?" she asked.

Cameron shook his head, suddenly fearful of her rejection should he touch her. How would she react after what she had suffered? "I'd better keep watch."

The moon hung low and full in the sky. Cassie's gaze swept the waters below, and she saw that they were empty.

She opened the blanket and smiled invitingly. "The ship is gone. Share the blanket with me."

Cassie awoke to the sound of birds chirping as they flew merrily from branch to branch overhead. She turned her head slightly and watched the sun's brilliant light peeping over the shimmering horizon. All the uncomfortable dampness of the previous night was gone. The air smelled clean and fresh. Its warmth was a soothing caress against her skin.

Her head nestled on Cameron's shoulder. His arm held her loosely against his naked body. Their clothing hung on a tree branch. Judging by the warm breeze, it wouldn't be long before everything was completely dry.

Cassie sighed and gave a small shiver as the events of the night came to assault her. God, how close they had come to losing each other. She shivered again and forced the unpleasant thoughts from her mind.

Suddenly exhilarated with just being alive, she wanted to jump up and dance for joy. She wanted to laugh, she wanted to cry. Life was so sweet. Her hold around his middle tightened. She never wanted to let him go.

Barely an inch separated her lips from his chest, and Cassie could not resist kissing the warm, tempting flesh.

It was heaven to be able to touch him like this. His body was hard and yet soft, smooth and yet rough. She'd never get enough of touching him, of kissing him. She gave a silent prayer of thanks for this blessing. Her mouth moved over smooth skin. The hairs on his chest were delightfully rough against her face. Hungrily, lustily, her tongue followed the line of hair as it thinned out over his belly.

"I hate to stop the momentum, but you started in the wrong place."

Cassie shot him a look of surprise, noticing for the first time that he was awake. She came to her knees, momentarily flustered at being caught in this wanton act, uncaring that her position invited a leering look of appreciation from her husband. "Did I?" She chuckled as she recognized the hungry look in his eyes. "You'll have to forgive me, I'm afraid. I haven't the expertise as some."

Cameron smiled, thanking God again for this woman and the love they shared. "Oh, it isn't expertise I yearn for. Indeed, you appear most competent." He sighed in an effort to show only minimum interest, but his clearly aroused body betrayed him.

Cassie laughed and pushed away the hand that had unerringly slid between her legs. "What are you complaining about, then?"

"Not complaining, simply reminding. On ship, you said that when you seduced me you'd first kiss me quite thoroughly. After that, you'd run your mouth down my body."

"Oh, yes. I remember now. I did say that, didn't I?" She bit at her bottom lip, pretending to think on the matter. "And I suppose I am seducing you."

"You did and you are," he confirmed in all seriousness. "Why did you start so low?"

Cassie grinned. "When I awoke, my lips were already there."

He was having a hard time suppressing a smile. "Is that the whole of it?"

Cassie nodded.

"So, if you were to awaken and find your lips lower still, you would have begun there?"

She eyed him warily. "What exactly are you getting at?"

Cameron grinned helplessly. "Just filing away information for future reference."

Cassie shook her head, despairing over the workings of his mind. "Even half-asleep your mind holds the most evil tendencies."

Cameron chuckled as he grabbed at her waist and made to pull her over him.

Cassie refused his embrace, pushing his arms back

to his sides. "I can't seduce you if you show no resistance."

"Must I show resistance?"

"Well, not resistance exactly, but you mustn't be so eager if you want me to do this right."

His finger grazed the tip of a swaying breast. "It's not an easy thing you ask. Especially dressed as you are."

"Then, close your eyes and pretend I'm dressed. Stay perfectly still," she warned, "so I can be about this chore. Can you do that?"

"I'll try," he returned obediently, while a devilish smile threatened his somber expression.

And he did try, for all of two minutes.

FIERY ROMANCE
From Zebra Books

SATIN SECRET (2116, $3.95)
by Emma Merritt

After young Marta Carolina had been attacked by pirates, shipwrecked, and beset by Indians, she was convinced the New World brought nothing but tragedy . . . until William Dare rescued her. The rugged American made her feel warm, protected, secure—and hungry for a fulfillment she could not name!

CAPTIVE SURRENDER (1986, $3.95)
by Michalann Perry

Gentle Fawn should have been celebrating her newfound joy as a bride, but when both her husband and father were killed in battle, the young Indian maiden vowed revenge. She charged into the fray—yet once she caught sight of the piercing blue gaze of her enemy, she knew that she could never kill him. The handsome white man stirred a longing deep within her soul . . . and a passion she'd never experienced before.

PASSION'S JOY (2205, $3.95)
by Jennifer Horsman

Dressed as a young boy, stunning Joy Claret refused to think what would happen were she to get caught at what she was really doing: leading slaves to liberty on the Underground Railroad. Then the roughly masculine Ram Barrington stood in her path and the blue-eyed girl couldn't help but panic. Before she could fight him, she was locked in an embrace that could end only with her surrender to PASSION'S JOY.

TEXAS TRIUMPH (2009, $3.95)
by Victoria Thompson

Nothing is more important to the determined Rachel McKinsey than the Circle M—and if it meant marrying her foreman to scare off rustlers, she would do it. Yet the gorgeous rancher felt a secret thrill that the towering Cole Elliot was to be her man—and despite her plan that they be business partners, all she truly desired was a glorious consummation of their vows.

PASSION'S PARADISE (1618, $3.75)
by Sonya T. Pelton

When she is kidnapped by the cruel, captivating Captain Ty, fair-haired Angel Sherwood fears not for her life, but for her honor! Yet she can't help but be warmed by his manly touch, and secretly longs for PASSION'S PARADISE.

Available wherever paperbacks are sold, or order direct from the Publisher. Send cover price plus 50¢ per copy for mailing and handling to Zebra Books, Dept. 2427, 475 Park Avenue South, New York, N.Y. 10016. Residents of New York, New Jersey and Pennsylvania must include sales tax. DO NOT SEND CASH.